William Benemann

Male-Male Intimacy in Early America
Beyond Romantic Friendships

D1606370

Pre-publication
REVIEWS,
COMMENTARIES,
EVALUATIONS . . .

"William Benemann has written a sweeping history of male homosexual relationships in early America, during an era when there was not even a name for such intimate bonds. There are two challenges faced by this work. First, the sources merely whisper of such relationships, and so it was a Herculean task to synthesize hundreds of primary and secondary sources to uncover the hidden transcripts of these men's lives and loves. Second, homosexual identity was socially constructed in the late nineteenth century, and so many scholars have assumed that a quest for earlier identities was futile.

Benemann takes to this task with gusto, undaunted by the challenge. His archivist eye is watchful for even the slimmest evidence of male intimacy and sexual relations with other men, but he is admirably careful not to project twenty-first-century gay sensibilities onto eighteenth-century historical figures. The book's major strength is its scope. From the metropolises of Europe to isolated settlements on the North American colonial frontier and early American cities of Philadelphia, Boston, and Washington, DC, Benemann maps the social geography of homosocial worlds where men found sexual partners and lovers in other men. In addition to its geographic scope, this book illuminates male intimacy in early American literature, religion, politics, medicine, and the military. Benemann has not only dared to speak of this 'unspeakable' love in every aspect of early American society, he has revealed quite a remarkable history."

Steve Estes, PhD
Assistant Professor,
History Department,
Sonoma State University

More pre-publication
REVIEWS, COMMENTARIES, EVALUATIONS . . .

"In the 1970s Michel Foucault drew a sharp distinction between homosexual acts and the modern concept of homosexual persons. While this distinction has been immensely useful, it has nonetheless proved too airtight. William Benemann's *Male-Male Intimacy in Early America* is part of an exciting new wave of scholarship that demonstrates the existence of both identities and communities that are clear precursors to the ones we would now call 'gay.'

This book is a treasure trove of historical information, and also a showcase for acute interpretation. Benemann demonstrates that the archive of life in early America is teeming with descriptions of intimate relationships between men. The results of his extensive research amply demonstrate that male-male intimacy in the period was far more complex, and ran deeper, than we have been either willing or able to see. Every chapter contains archival riches: excerpts from letters, commonplace books, period journals, novels, and biographies combine to form a fascinating picture of how men who loved other men expressed that love.

William Benemann's *Male-Male Intimacy in Early America* is an invaluable contribution to the history of sexuality in America, not only because it radically improves our understanding of intimate bonds between men in this period, but also because the study of those bonds has implications for how we understand both homosexuality and heterosexuality—then and now."

Christopher Nealon, PhD
Associate Professor,
Department of English,
University of California, Berkeley

"Historian and archivist William Benemann, editor of *A Year of Mud and Gold: San Francisco in Letters and Diaries, 1849-1850*, revisits the provocative territory of the emotional/social/sexual worlds in early American male-male relationships. Departing from the work of other historians, Benemann often questions, amplifies, or reconsiders their conclusions. The author is careful to define his terms, for example using "male intimacy" to connote the fluidity of psychological and physical closeness, as he focuses on men's lives from colonial times to the early antebellum period. Wary of projecting a twenty-first-century analysis onto complex and often unknowable relationships, Benemann uses the terms 'romantic friendship' to describe close affectionate relationships between two men who were social equals, 'romantic mentorships' when the two men are of differing ages or socioeconomic status, and 'erotic employment' when one serves as the employee of the other. This meticulously researched, arduously argued, and remarkably detailed exploration is a welcome addition to the literature. Benemann's pioneering effort offsets the dearth of historical information on our gay male forbears."

Jim Van Buskirk, MLIS,
Program Manager,
James C. Hormel
Gay & Lesbian Center
San Francisco Public Library

Male-Male Intimacy in Early America

in Early America

Beyond Romantic Friendships

Male-Male Intimacy in Early America
Beyond Romantic Friendships

William Benemann

HPP

Harrington Park Press®
An Imprint of The Haworth Press, Inc.
New York • London • Oxford

For more information on this book or to order, visit
http://www.haworthpress.com/store/product.asp?sku=5479

or call 1-800-HAWORTH (800-429-6784) in the United States and Canada
or (607) 722-5857 outside the United States and Canada

or contact orders@HaworthPress.com

Published by

Harrington Park Press®, an imprint of The Haworth Press, Inc., 10 Alice Street, Binghamton, NY 13904-1580.

Cover design by Lora Wiggins.

Quotations from "The Virtuous Curriculum: Schoolboys and American Culture," PhD dissertation, University of Pennsylvania. © 1991 Cynthia M. Koch. Used with permission.

Quotations from E. Anthony Rotundo, "Romantic Friendship: Male Intimacy and Middle-Class Youth in the Northern United States, 1800-1900," *Journal of Social History,* 23(1):1-25. © 1989 *Journal of Social History.* Used with permission.

Quotations from Richard Godbeer, "The Cry of Sodom: Discourse, Intercourse, and Desire in Colonial New England," *William and Mary Quarterly.* Third Series, 52(2):259-286. © 1995 Omohundro Institute of Early American History and Culture. Used with permission.

Permission has also been granted by the following institutions or organizations to quote from archival materials in their collections: The H. Furlong Baldwin Library of the Maryland Historical Society, Baltimore, Maryland; The Historical Society of Pennsylvania, Philadelphia, Pennsylvania; The Huntington Library, San Marino, California; The Library of Virginia, Richmond, Virginia; The Missouri Historical Society, St. Louis, Missouri; The New-York Historical Society, New York City, New York.

Library of Congress Cataloging-in-Publication Data

Benemann, William, 1949-
    Male-male intimacy in early America : beyond romantic friendships / William Benemann.
        p. cm.
    Includes bibliographical references and index.
    ISBN-13: 978-1-56023-344-2 (hard : alk. paper)
    ISBN-10: 1-56023-344-3 (hard : alk. paper)
    ISBN-13: 978-1-56023-345-9 (soft : alk. paper)
    ISBN-10: 1-56023-345-1 (soft : alk. paper)
    1. Homosexuality, Male—United States—History. 2. Male friendship—United States—History. I. Title.

HQ76.3.U(United States).x
306.76'62'0973—dc22

2005014632

For Kevin

Éist, a stór, tá ceol ar an ngaoth
Is casfar le chéile sinn roimh dhul faoi don ghrian . . .

ABOUT THE AUTHOR

William Benemann is Archivist for the School of Law at the University of California, Berkeley, and Adjunct Curator for lesbian, gay, bisexual, and transgender materials for The Bancroft Library at Berkeley. His book *A Year of Mud and Gold: San Francisco in Letters and Diaries, 1849-1850* received *Library Journal*'s highest recommendation for academic and public libraries. Mr. Benemann has been a contributor to the biographical compilation *Gay & Lesbian Literature,* as well as a book reviewer for the *Journal of the History of Sexuality.* He is the founder and current curator of the Gay Bears Collection in The University Archives at Berkeley, an archival collection focusing on the history of sexual minorities at the University of California.

CONTENTS

Preface

In spite of the ideology which would have us believe that women's sexuality is an enigma, it is in reality men's bodies, men's sexuality which is the true "dark continent" of this society.

Rosalind Coward

There were no gay men in America in the eighteenth century.

The statement is obviously false, and yet it is extremely difficult to prove the contrary. If we take one step forward we trip over the stumbling block of semantics. (Gay? Sodomite? Bugger? Homosexual? Queer?) If we push on anyway we hit what appears at first to be a stone wall of evidentiary silence. (Where are the love letters? The diaries? The public documents?) Break through that wall, and we need to come up with an interpretation of the existing evidence that can thread its way between the twin land mines of homophobia on the right and political correctness on the left. Little wonder then that historians of sexuality have shied away from the exploration of this troublesome aspect of early American history.[1] They have found it more attractive to concentrate on Europe, where the topic is better documented and the findings are less ambiguous.

What do we mean when we talk about homosexuality in eighteenth-century America? The word "homosexual" itself was not coined until the late nineteenth century, and it is admittedly difficult to conceptualize Americans *being* something without having a word for it. In the period under discussion the words most commonly used for the concept were "sodomite" (from a misunderstanding of the sin of the people of Sodom) or "bugger" (a reference to an eleventh-century Bulgarian sect which professed the Manichaean heresy and refused to engage in procreative activities). Both terms referred to participants in male-male sexual activity (along with a host of other meanings), but neither carried the modern sense of sexual orientation. It would have been meaningless in the eighteenth century to talk about a "latent sodomite" or a "bugger orientation." Action was ev-

MALE-MALE INTIMACY IN EARLY AMERICA

erything. But that is not to say that men who felt a strong sexual and emotional attraction to other men were unaware that those feelings set them apart from the majority of Americans, or that they did not know that there were others just like them, fellows who shared their minority status.

Even if it were possible to fix on an acceptable definition of homosexuality when speaking of eighteenth-century America, the historian is still faced with a gaping void when it comes to documentation. Homosexuality has been labeled the *crimen inter Christianos non nominandum,* the sin not to be named among Christians, the unspeakable crime against nature, the love that dare not speak its name. Woven into Western society's attitude toward homosexuality is the imperative of silence. Men (and, to a much lesser extent, women) were condemned and executed for committing an act their accusers would not specify, for fear that even uttering the word would create scandal. Throughout the American colonial period and well into the early years of the Republic the penalty for sodomy was death, so it is not surprising that men who sought other men as sexual partners did not advertise their activities, and left behind little evidence which might be used against them in a court of law. But evidence—however obscured—*does* exist. The problem arises with interpretation.

If we open a letter written by a young woman and read, "Often too he shared my pillow—or I his, and how sweet to sleep with him, to hold his beloved form in my embrace, to have his arms about my neck, to imprint upon his face sweet kisses," we can reasonably assume that she and the man in question shared a sexual relationship. There is no justifiable grounds for changing that assumption when we learn that the words were actually written by Albert Dodd, a Yale undergraduate in the 1830s, describing his relationship with a fellow student, Anthony Hall.[2] There is no valid reason to assert that passionate language in a letter between a man and woman implies a sexual attraction, while exactly the same language exchanged between two men is "just the way male friends wrote about one another back then." Yet this type of willful disbelief in the prevalence of historical homosexuality, and refusal to accept passionate male-male discourse as anything other than a literary convention, is all too common.[3]

I will give one example of the genre, not because it is outstandingly egregious, but because the book in question is an otherwise-excellent biography of an eighteenth-century American who plays a minor role in the current study. A recent biography of John Laurens, son of the president of the Continental Congress Henry Laurens, is quite frank about the young man's passionate attachment to men and his clearly secondary interest in women.

> In his relationships with other men, particularly with his closest friend, Alexander Hamilton, [Laurens] illustrated how the man of feeling constructed sentimental attachments that tended to restrict women to the marginal role of spectators exhorting their men to virtuous accomplishments in the public realm. . . . [H]e continually centered his life around homosocial attachments to other men.[4]

Laurens impregnated and then married the daughter of a family friend, but then abandoned her in England (eight months pregnant) when hostilities broke out in the colonies. He never saw his wife again, and never saw his daughter. "The wife and child left behind in England," his biographer notes, "seemingly occupied little space in John's thoughts."[5] When Martha Laurens belatedly learned that John was in France on a diplomatic mission she traveled with their child to meet him, but by the time she arrived he had already returned to America.

While indifferent to the fate of his wife and daughter, Laurens formed a passionate "romantic friendship" with Alexander Hamilton. In his letters to Laurens, Hamilton was frank in expressing his devotion. The biographer quotes a few of the less steamy passages from the extant correspondence held by the Library of Congress (some of which is now unreadable because it was censored by John C. Hamilton, an early editor of the manuscripts). "I wish, my Dear Laurens . . . to convince you that I love you."[6] (The ellipsis inserted by the biographer refers to the omitted words "by action rather than words"—perhaps a troubling concept.)[7] "You should not have taken advantage of my sensibility to steal into my affections without my consent."[8] Hamilton assured Laurens that Hamilton's marriage to the plain but rich Elizabeth Schuyler would have no effect at all on their continued intimacy. He wrote bawdy passages referring to, among other things, the size of his penis and signed off his letters with an affectionate, "Adieu my Dear."[9] The biographer concedes that the Laurens-Hamilton letters "appear to contain homosexual overtones" if the passages are "taken out of context," but he dismisses the language as merely an epistolary convention. "Their relationship was platonic," he pronounces with assurance, "a bond formed by their devotion to the Revolution and mutual ambition for fame."[10]

I would agree strongly that it is important to place these passionate declarations in context. Certainly not all professions of male-male devotion were declarations of sexual attraction—no more in the eighteenth century than in the twenty-first. But placed in context the ardor shared by Laurens and Hamilton achieves weight and significance. The Laurens biography includes ample evidence that he was cold toward women and emotionally drawn to men, and that Hamilton—whatever his later relations with women—at this stage of his life was much more devoted to his "friend" than to his fiancée. The biographer admits that there was something odd and inexplicable about Laurens's recklessness in battle:

> Yet for all the similarities with other gentlemen officers—the emphasis on status, the importance of honor, the passion for fame—something about John was different, even unsettling. . . . His continual risk-taking involved more than an outward combat against British tyranny; he also engaged in personal combat against an inner self he had rejected, the irresolute man who lacked self-control.[11]

The biographer is at a loss to explain Laurens's recklessness (which eventually led to his death), attributing it to an attempt to atone for unnamed "prior sins."[12] The biographer categorically rejects any suggestion of sexual attraction between the two men—but then is puzzled to explain their behavior.

Much of the evidence suggests two men passionately in love and perhaps sexually involved with each other who could not imagine a future in which they could continue to enjoy such intimacy. Why must a reader then assume that in their private correspondence these two men were merely participating in a nonsexual literary convention? If their discourse was common for the era and the language signified nothing more than the self-fashioning of two men of sensibility, why did Hamilton's literary editor irretrievably obliterate parts of his letters to Laurens and write in the margin of one, "I must not publish the whole of this"?[13] There is no irrefutable proof that Laurens and Hamilton were lovers, but there is sufficient circumstantial evidence to render indefensible any unqualified pronouncement that they were not.

The pervasive reluctance to concede even *latent* desire between two men sets up serious obstacles to our understanding of the place of sexuality in American history. Until recently historians have been hampered by three intellectual barriers: a misconception about the prevalence of same-sex eroticism, a reluctance to abandon restrictive labels such as "homosexuality" and "heterosexuality," and an inability to move beyond negative preconceptions about "the gay lifestyle" toward a more nuanced understanding of human sexual behavior. Much of the current discussion of nineteenth-century "romantic friendships" therefore has been based on circular logic. Historians begin with the assumption that homosexual activity is rare, aberrant behavior. They then demonstrate that passionate attachments between American male friends were extremely common—so common that they label them "normal." But these normal, common attachments cannot be assumed to include at times actual homosexual activity. Why? Because homosexual activity is rare, aberrant behavior.

Missing from this logical loop is any detailed knowledge of the sexual practices of Americans during the early years of the Republic, and in the absence of any reliable information there is, I would argue, no justification for a priori statements about the prevalence of same-sex relations. The best we can do with the information currently available is to assume that human sexual response has not changed so very much in the past 250 years (which is precisely the assumption we are *already* making when we interpret the discourse of heterosexual desire). In 1948 Alfred Kinsey wrote that "at least 37 per cent of the male population has some homosexual experience between the beginning of adolescence and old age," and that "4 per cent of the white males are exclusively homosexual throughout their lives, after the onset of adolescence."[14] If we apply Kinsey's figure of 4 percent to the 1790 United States Census (taking into account the fact that people of color were not recorded by age or gender), we need to assume that 32,292 white adult males with a homosexual orientation were living in the United States in 1790.[15]

Who were these men? How did they meet one another? Where did they seek information about male-male sexuality? What were their options in life? These are the questions explored by the current study. There is no need to tie ourselves into ontological knots by focusing on the essentialist/constructionist debate, or by trying to identify the exact moment in American history when a "homosexual identity" was first formulated. If we begin the discussion with the assumption that there *were* men in the late eighteenth and early nineteenth centuries who were emotionally and erotically drawn to other men, it is a large enough task to recover their *exterior* lives, and perhaps by reconstructing the milieu in which these men moved we may be able to create a platform on which to begin the investigation of their thoughts and feelings. Yet defining that milieu will not be easy. In this study I will attempt to investigate what Christopher Nealon has aptly termed "the mystery of the vast but elusive presence of homosexuals in America."[16] These 32,292 homosexually inclined men were, I contend, hiding in plain sight.

In discussing the bonds that developed between American men in the eighteenth century I will attempt as much as possible to reconstruct what is known about their sexual conduct, but the surviving evidence that has been uncovered to date is so slim that in many instances I will be able only to speculate. Although it would be unwise to assume that a deep and abiding affection between two men necessarily implied a sexual relationship, it would be equally wrong to assume that such a relationship *never* included a sexual component. Nor should it be assumed that the fact of a man's having married and had children is conclusive proof that he was not attracted to other men. That is certainly not the case in the twenty-first century, and it should not be presumed for the eighteenth. Although sources such as court records and popular newspapers can be extremely explicit in their description of male-male sexual encounters, private correspondence during this period is usually less frankly sexual (with a few notable exceptions). In interpreting ambiguous language there is always the danger of "presentism"—the attribution of a modern gay sensibility to men who knew neither Freud nor Stonewall. But the reader should keep in mind that presentism can go both ways, and we should not insist that men in the past *must* have shared the same sexual "comfort zone" as the majority of American males today. We need only look to the extensive literature of prison sexuality to understand how fluid the concept of a sexual comfort zone can become; acts that a man with a heterosexual orientation once viewed with horror and disgust may be avidly pursued in the absence of a female referent.

I join my voice to those who have begun to question some of the theories of Michel Foucault concerning the formation of a homosexual identity.[17] I do *not* believe that a homosexual orientation was nonexistent until it was socially constructed during the late nineteenth century. From my reading of sources from the colonial, Revolutionary, and post-Revolutionary period, I am convinced that there were men who were homosexual and who—without the help of physicians, clerics, legislators, or sociologists—regarded themselves as different from their comrades, a difference based solely on their sexual response. I also believe that there were de facto gay communities. Some of these communities were congruent with specific geographic places. Others were real but floating, linked to a profession rather than a physical place. Still others had their existence only on a subconscious level but were nonetheless a powerful impetus to bring men together. I believe that men-loving men in the early years of this country were aware of the concept we now label as "queer space," and that they took active steps to separate themselves from the heterosexual majority in order to join their brothers in an underground community based on a shared sexual response.

In this exploration we will be entering a territory so barren of familiar landmarks that we must create our own language in order to describe what we see. As much as possible I will avoid the use of the word "gay," which carries with it too much modern political and social baggage. I will use the word "homosexual" sparingly, in recognition of the fact that the word had not yet been coined at the time these men were living. I will instead borrow one term and create two others.

I will use the term "romantic friendship" to describe a close affectionate relationship between two men who were social equals. The term has been used extensively in scholarship focusing on the effusive writings of young male couples during the mid-nineteenth century, usually with the implied understanding that the relationship was not sexual (despite the steamy rhetoric of the surviving correspondence). I will use the term with the explicit contention that a romantic friendship might indeed have included a sexual component, since I have come to believe that eighteenth-century Americans did not draw borders around sexual behavior with quite the clarity and severity of their Victorian successors. A fluidity to male intimacy admitted a wide repertoire of physical expression, and those expressions ebbed and flowed with time and circumstance.

Romantic friendships usually arose between men of similar age and social class. The relationships were passionate but in most cases fleeting, not because the men were unable or unwilling to make a lasting commitment, but because they could not envision a future in which they could ever consider themselves to be a recognized couple. America included only one city that could begin to rival the size and social complexity of Berlin, Paris, or London. Only Philadelphia was large enough to provide men-loving men with the anonymity of numbers. In rural areas among the lower classes it might be possible for two men to live their lives together working the same farm or pursuing the same craft, but in more urban areas, especially among the socially prominent (whose stories are the ones most likely to be preserved in surviving documents), heterosexual marriage was the only acceptable goal. Men entered into romantic friendships with the understanding that one—and probably both—of the partners would eventually marry and establish a traditional family. Though many tried to maintain an emotional connection with their partner, the demands of their new roles as husband and father rarely allowed for continued intimacy. This arc from passionate devotion to wistful nostalgia is documented again and again whenever long runs of male-male letters have been preserved.

In contrast to romantic friendship I will coin the term "romantic mentorship" to describe a close affectionate relationship between two men with a substantial age gap, though sometimes between men of similar age but of differing socioeconomic status. Again, I will assume that a sexual relationship was possible. Men in these types of relationships drew on the models of classical Greece and Rome, which had been presented to them as schoolboys. Here was a way they could think about themselves, taking their cue from the *Phaedrus* rather than the King James Bible. Whether the sexuality was explicit or sublimated, there was an undeniable erotic component to these relationships. The connection usually faded when the younger partner entered into a heterosexual marriage.

I will also explore a third type of relationship, which I will call "erotic employment." These relationships involved two men of very unequal social status, with one man (usually significantly younger) serving as the employee of the other. As an employee—secretary, valet, paid companion—the younger member performed specific duties for which he was paid a salary, but he also served a sexual function. The relationships could also include an emotional component, and there was frequently some level of respect and even affection between the men, but at base the arrangement was economic, and it would cease whenever the wages ceased.

These terms should be viewed as a convenient way of classifying certain male-male relationships, but it should be stressed that these relationships were not static over time, nor did both partners necessarily view the same relationship in the same way. As we shall see, the dynamics of male relationships changed and evolved with altered circumstances, and lovers frequently became good friends. In some cases the two men viewed their relationship very differently at the same time: one considering it to be a romantic mentorship, the other seeing it as merely erotic employment.

Much of the discussion in this book will focus on largely unexplored territories of late eighteenth- and early nineteenth-century American male-male relations, on the complex web of profound affection and sexual attraction, on the place where *agape* flows into *eros*. Basic to the discussion is an understanding that sexual orientation should not be viewed as two rooms, one labeled "straight" and one labeled "gay," with a door between them which may open enticingly (or ominously) for some people. One of the pitfalls of this particular visualization is the assumption that once a person passes through the door from straight to gay, the door slams shut and no return is possible. This bifurcated view of humanity is frequently seized upon by gay hagiographers who will claim as their own anyone who ever expressed erotic attraction to another person of the same gender. One need only search the Internet for the profusion of lists of Great Gays to see the result of this type of affectional reductionism. The other side of the coin is biographers who insist that unless irrefutable proof of actual genital contact to the point of orgasm can be found, their subject must be considered a bedrock heterosexual. Implicit in both these views is the assumption that a person must be one or the other. A more useful model is the one presented by Alfred Kinsey in 1948. Kinsey described sexual orientation as a continuum, a scale from one to six with one being entirely heterosexual and six being entirely homosexual.[18] Most human beings fall somewhere between the two extremes of the scale.

I have chosen the term "male intimacy" because it can imply both a psychological and a physical closeness. By the term I do not mean mere good-hearted comradeship, but rather an intense affectional bonding which necessarily includes sexual attraction, whether the two men acknowledge it or not. In the twenty-first century American men have a well-developed sense of the boundaries that separate them from other men. From boyhood onward we receive unmistakable signals about what types of approach and response are appropriate between males. Like the buried electrical cables that serve as invisible fences to keep livestock from straying, culturally imposed alarms keep us at the proper emotional (and physical) distance from one another. Although he may have difficulty articulating exactly where the ambiguous border area lies, every American male knows instinctively when he has crossed into it. Our eighteenth-century forefathers had a similar sixth sense, and it is that crossed border of intimacy that will be the focus of the current study.

This book will focus primarily on the lives of men-loving men from the colonial period to the opening years of the antebellum period. The intimate lives of women are beyond the scope of this study, and it certainly should not be inferred that the pressures and options which molded the lives of American homosexual men during the country's early years necessarily reflect the lived experiences of lesbians. Feminist scholars are only now beginning to investigate that very different story.

The current study should be viewed as an exploratory sketch, a rough map of largely unknown territory. As Rosalind Coward has asserted, male sexuality is the "dark continent" of American history. Much remains to be explored, but there is ample evidence of a thriving and complex culture waiting to be discovered.

Acknowledgments

This study was aided enormously by the skill, knowledge, and professionalism of the staffs of a wide range of archives. In my travels in pursuit of gay men in early America I was fortunate to be able to call upon the services of the following collections: in Washington, DC, the Library of Congress Manuscript Reading Room, the National Library of Medicine History of Medicine Division, and the Society of the Cincinnati Archives; in Philadelphia, the Historical Society of Pennsylvania, the Library Company of Philadelphia, and the Philadelphia City Archives; at West Point, the United States Military Academy Archives; in St. Louis, the Missouri Historical Society; in San Marino, California, the Huntington Library; in San Francisco, the University of California, San Francisco Medical Archives; in Berkeley, the University of California Bancroft Library and the Robbins Collection of Religious and Civil Law at the Boalt Hall Law Library. In addition, I was provided with photocopies or microfilms of archival materials by the National Archives, the New Jersey Historical Society, the New-York Historical Society, the Rutgers University Libraries, the Beinecke Library of Yale University, the Harvard University Archives, and the Oneida County Historical Society. To all the individuals who opened their collections to me, I owe a large debt of thanks.

My travels were supported by a generous research grant from the Librarians Association of the University of California, and while my original topic—developing ways of uncovering hidden archival material on gay and lesbian lives—was rendered largely superfluous by a simple addition of "gaydar" to standard archival searching skills, I trust with the appearance of this book they will agree that their funds were well spent.

This text went through many wildly different metamorphoses before reaching its current form as I responded to a succession of readers, most of whom were more frank than kind. It is a better book for their frankness. Of those readers I would like especially to acknowledge Richard Holway, whose comments were always courteous as well as cogent, and whose good humor and enthusiasm for the project saw me through more revisions than any author cares to face.

I thank my employer, the University of California School of Law at Berkeley, for allowing me the flexibility of scheduling in my "day job" that allowed me to pursue my passion. It is difficult to imagine a more humane and nurturing work environment.

A number of scholars of gay history and culture provided support and encouragement over the years I worked on this research project. As acknowledged in my notes, Lawrence Cohen and Massimiliano Carocci provided insight and language skills. Les Wright was particularly helpful in guiding me through a critical phase of the publication process. His sage advice was very much appreciated.

Katherine Beals served as Lamaze coach for this rather strenuous and prolonged birth, and supplied the e-mail equivalent of milk and cookies as we struggled with our respective manuscripts. She has revealed to me a whole new dimension to the concept of family.

Finally and always, I thank my partner Kevin Jewell, who for over two decades has been my working week and my Sunday rest.

Chapter 1

The Freedom of the Frontier

Marvilous it may be to see and consider how some kind of wickednes did grow & breake forth here, in a land wher the same was so much witnesed against, and so narrowly looked unto, & severly punished when it was knowne . . . even sodomie and bugerie (things fearfull to name) have broak forth in this land, oftener then once.

William Bradford, *Of Plymouth Colony* (1642)

Mr. Gallatin assured me the other Day that the Grecian Vice was common among the Indians as well as among the back Woodsmen.

Augustus John Foster (1806)

The casual observation of Secretary of the Treasury Albert Gallatin, jotted down in Augustus John Foster's commonplace book, provides a key to understanding an important aspect of early American history: settlement patterns encouraged the proliferation of male-male sexuality.[1] The margins of American society—the ever-receding frontier to the west and the open seas to the east—provided the opportunity for extensive male-male sexual activity. Among those taking part in this activity were men who engaged in male-male contact solely because few female partners were available, as well as men who had fled their home towns specifically in hopes of finding a place where they could act upon their attraction to other men. The distinction between the two is important only if we insist on a binary model of sexual orientation. If we accept a more fluid view of human sexuality, we can understand both the openness to same-sex activity *and* the sincere eagerness with which most men looked forward to the "civilizing" effect of the arrival of women. It is likely that most men who engaged in male-male sexuality were neither driven to it by uncontrollable frustration nor fleeing from any possible sexual contact with

1

a woman. Male-male sexuality was simply one of the many adjustments necessary for living on the margins of a new world.

Even in the Puritan colonies, where extended families rather than large numbers of unmarried males had emigrated, the scarcity of suitable marriage partners led to sexual experimentation among the men. "But it may be demanded," Governor William Bradford sputtered in 1642, "how came it to pass that so many wicked persons and profane people should so quickly come over into this land and mix themselves amongst us? Seeing it was religious men that began the work and they came for religion's sake?"[2] Bradford speculated that these wicked persons had been sent over by family members "under hope that they would be made better" by the rigors of life in a religious colony, or perhaps that shocked families had sent their black sheep out of England "that they might be eased of such burdens, and they kept from shame at home, that would necessarily follow their dissolute courses."[3] Bradford drew clear distinctions between "us" and "them," unable to imagine that sincere members of his own colony might be capable of engaging in "things fearful to name."

Among the common folk of the Puritan colonies, however, there was a sense that the New World was a new world, one with special dispensations. It was not possible to replicate exactly European community life, nor was such a replication necessarily desirable in all cases. Europe was viewed as hopelessly corrupt, while America was pristine with possibilities. Few colonists were eager to import all of the social controls they had sailed so far to escape. Leaders such as William Bradford often shook with paroxysms of righteous indignation about sexual improprieties simply because their fellow colonists *did not*. Richard Godbeer has written of the indulgent attitude of the New Englanders:

> Whereas ministers perceived sodomy as one of many acts, sexual and nonsexual, that expressed human depravity, some lay persons apparently recognized a special inclination toward sodomitical behavior in certain individuals. The extant sources reveal a few occasions on which New Englanders, sensing that official discourse was of limited use in making intelligible their actual experiences and observations, created what seemed to them more appropriate categories and frameworks of meaning. This informal and inchoate discourse did not go so far as to invoke a "homosexual" identity as such, but it does seem to have

posited an ongoing erotic predilection that transcended the acts themselves. Villagers and townspeople were, moreover, seldom willing to invoke official sanctions against sodomy, despite theological and legal denunciations. Whatever their leaders' expectations, they viewed and treated sodomy on their own terms.[4]

The idea of America as the land of the new sexual dispensation was strengthened by what the colonists observed (or thought they observed) about the sex lives of the Indians who occupied the country before them. Although at first aghast at the red man's apparent lack of modesty about private matters, the colonists eventually came to appreciate the sexual restraint exhibited by the tribes they encountered. White women taken captive by Indians fully expected to be ravished, and were puzzled when their honor remained intact. The Indians' restraint in these instances was to a large extent motivated by a strong incest taboo. White settlers were captured in order to secure new members for a dwindling tribe; raping a member of one's own clan would have been a grave transgression. The religious practices of many Indian tribes also included a strict code of warrior continence. "The Indians will not cohabit with women while they are out at war;" wrote trader James Adair in 1775, "they religiously abstain from every kind of intercourse even with their own wives, for the space of three days and nights before they go to war, and so after they return home, because they are to sanctify themselves."[5]

Perhaps making a guilty comparison with lax European sexual mores, the amazed colonists began to ascribe an even wider chastity to the Indians (at least to the men). The sophists of the Enlightenment found in the native North American a convenient prototype of Natural Man, and praised (among other virtues) his freedom from the tyranny of sexual desire. It was mostly a spun fantasy: men who had never been beyond the coast of Normandy projected their philosophical theories onto the unspoiled Native American, fashioning a paragon from a few snippets of second-hand anthropology. Diderot, for example, claimed that *"le goût anti-physique des Américains"* was a result of the enforced celibacy of Indian men who needed to range far afield on hunting expeditions.[6] (Apparently the Frenchman saw in the all-male hunts no opportunity for sexual release.)

From the seventeenth century to the eighteenth, European and colonial perceptions of American Indian sexuality underwent a slow inversion. Indian men were at first assumed to be lust-crazed beasts, lurking in the forest, aching to ravish vulnerable white women. With familiarity came a grudging admiration and an acknowledgment that Indians were not so prone as white men to making unwanted sexual advances to colonial maidens. As the power balance shifted and the Europeans took control of the new land, the Indian warrior's manhood increasingly came into question. What had at first been seen as laudable restraint was in time taken as evidence of a weak libido. Benjamin Rush assured his readers that it was "universally acknowledged that the venereal propensities among Indians are in a very feeble state," and he attributed the condition to the strain on their groins caused by long horseback rides.[7] In an 1801 dissertation James Tongue argued that Indians could not possibly have been the origin of venereal disease, since everyone knew that they rarely engaged in sexual intercourse.[8] "A proof of some feebleness in their frame, still more striking," wrote Englishman William Robertson, "is the insensibility of the Americans to the charms of beauty, and the power of love. That passion which was destined to perpetuate life . . . is the most ardent in the human breast. . . . But the Americans are, in an amazing degree, strangers to the force of this first instinct of nature."[9] Frenchman Corneille de Pauw wrote that among American Indians the women were very masculine looking, but that the men "had no beards, their bodies hairless, like those of eunuques; that they were almost insensible to the passion of love; had milk, or a kind of milky liquid, in their breasts . . . ," and they lacked pubic hair entirely.[10] Comte de Buffon insisted, "In the [American] savage, the organs of generation are small and feeble. He has no hair, no beard, no ardour for the female."[11] The American Indian male had in the course of a century gone from brutish ravisher to listless hermaphrodite. What was going on here?

First we need to understand how Europeans projected their own fears and insecurities onto the people they encountered in the New World. Already primed with the ancient legends of Amazonian warriors, the first explorers brought back tales of women who were so libidinous that their husbands were not man enough to satisfy them. In the opening years of the sixteenth century Amerigo Vespucci issued a warning (or a challenge?) to any man who dreamed of sailing to the Indies.

For their women, being very lustful, cause the private parts of their husbands to swell up to such a huge size that they appear deformed and disgusting; and this is accomplished by a certain device of theirs, the biting of certain poisonous animals. And in consequence of this many lose their organs which break through lack of attention, and they remain eunuchs.[12]

By 1801 when St. John de Crèvecoeur published *Journey into Northern Pennsylvania and the State of New York,* the lure of sexual tourism remained strong, but the locus of anxiety had shifted. Crèvecoeur's description of an Iroquois council includes a passage that closely fits the queer theorists' concept of the "homoerotic gaze"— the objectification of the male body by a male observer. Here the Native American retains his exotic sensuality, but the fear of emasculation by poisonous women has been replaced by a different source of performance anxiety: the European knows he can never measure up to the Indians' primordial virility.

Their blankets of beaverskin fell off their shoulders, revealing their mighty chests and muscular arms on which in their youth various animal and insect figures had been tattooed. At such a scene a painter could have drawn bodies that were perfect in proportion, limbs controlled by muscles lightly covered with a kind of swelling that was unknown to the whites, and which among the Indians attests to vigor, strength, and health: heads and faces of a special type, the like of which one sees only in the depths of the New World's forests.[13]

Crèvecoeur's body-builder Iroquois had no more relation to reality than Vespucci's grossly engorged penises, but it was the Indian-as-symbol which engaged the white man's imagination. It is important to note that Crèvecoeur's paean to Indian masculinity and James Tongue's assertion that Indians are nonsexual were published in the same year. They represent the split in the American psyche where Indian sexuality was concerned. As a conquered race, Indian men were pathetic and impotent. Or noble vestiges of a virile civilization. Or savages too passive to prevail against the vigorous thrust of European manhood. Or prelapsarian Adams, immune to the enticements of lusty, dusky Eves.

These self-canceling contradictions were finally reconciled in a philosophy that neatly blended nostalgia with genocide. The Indian in his "natural" state was indeed worthy of respect, and even envy. His life was at one with the elements, simple and pure. If his passions were few, so were his needs. But unfortunately the Indian's primitive virtues condemned him eternally to an inchoate state of unfulfilled potential, and therefore justified his destruction. His freedoms were in actuality fetters holding him (and the land) back from the glorious march of human progress. Wrote Samuel Williams in 1793:

> We need not hesitate to pronounce that these disadvantages far exceeded any advantages that could attend it; and operated with a certain and fatal tendency, to continue man in a state of infancy, weakness, and the greatest imperfection. The freedom to which it led, was its greatest blessing; but the independence of which the savage was so fond, was never designed for man: And it is only in the improvement of civil society, that the human race can find the greatest increase of their numbers, knowledge, safety and happiness.[14]

Independence, it was said, is not the natural state of man. The improvement of civil society, an increase of numbers, the safety, happiness, and stability of nuclear families permanently settled in large interconnected communities—this was progress. And it was progress that could take place only in a world of strictly regulated sexual outlets, a world based on marriage, procreation, and domesticity in which the free-ranging, sexually continent Indian had no place. The Indian's perceived disinclination to engage in sexual intercourse was an affront to the forces of civilization, and it provided justification for both the expropriation of his land the destruction of his lifestyle. Through a rhetorical sleight-of-hand, then, Natural Man was convicted of a crime against nature. Conveniently, just as the idea of the Indian as "unmanly" came into prominence, observers of tribal life began to record that the gender confusion was even more shocking than anyone had ever imagined.

On December 22, 1804, explorer William Clark wrote in his journal at the Mandan Villages, "a number of Squars women & men Dressed in Squars Clothes Came with Corn to Sell to the men for little things."[15] He later told editor Nicholas Biddle,

> Among Minitarees if a boy shows any symptoms of effeminacy
> or girlish inclinations he is put among the girls, dressed in their
> way, brought up with them, & sometimes married to men. They
> submit as women to all the duties of a wife. I have seen them—
> the French call them Birdashes.[16]

The phenomenon Clark is describing is the berdache tradition, a word
derived from the Persian *bardaj* through the Arabic *bardag,* which as
early as the sixteenth century was borrowed by Romance languages
to denote a passive partner in male-male sexual intercourse.[17] The
term was introduced to the North American continent by French trap-
pers who observed male-male sexuality among the Indians they encountered. Berdaches or "Two-Spirits" came to the role in a variety of
ways: some were reared by their parents to take on the role of the opposite sex, while others voluntarily adopted the status upon reaching
puberty, or after a trauma or a vision quest. Clark reports that the
berdaches he encountered were men who dressed as women, but
transvestism was not universally observed. Among the Pima and the
Comanche, the berdaches imitated the speech and behavior of women
but were required to dress as men. Cheyenne berdaches of all ages re-
portedly dressed as old men, while among the Navajo, Paiute, and
Shoshone, cross-dressing was practiced only if it was the man's personal choice. In some instances gendered clothing was regulated only
under certain circumstances. The Navajo required berdaches to dress
as men if they married, whether their spouse was male or female. The
Miami required male clothing for berdaches only when they went to
war. Berdaches were usually biologically male, though they could
also be women who took on the gender role of men.[18]

Berdaches usually performed the chores of whichever gender's
clothing they adopted, but it was not unknown for a berdache man to
both cook with the women and hunt with the men. Their intermediate
gender status was believed to give them special powers; Teton parents
asked the berdaches to bestow secret names upon their children, and
among many California Indian tribes the berdaches were responsible
for burial and mourning rituals. Among the Illinois tribe no major decision was made without first consulting a berdache. When a man became a berdache he usually assumed the female role in sexual relations with other men, and it was this connection with homosexuality
which drew the ire and disdain of non-Indian observers.[19]

The negative reaction to this indigenous American practice has a long and varied history. Alvar Núñez Cabeza de Vaca, who explored Florida between 1528 and 1533, later wrote, "During the time that I was thus among these people I saw a devilish thing, and it is that I saw one man married to another, and these are impotent, effeminate men [*amariconados*] and they go about dressed as women, and do women's tasks."[20] The major objection of European observers seems to have been the institutionalized nature of the berdache tradition, with its explicit rejection of the male role. Occasional or situational male-male sexual contact was understandable (particularly if it was mutual and entailed no invasion of the male body), but for a man to embrace the feminine role in insertive sex was simply beyond comprehension. Their horror at the idea of male-receptive sexuality blinded most observers to the mystical or religious functions of the berdache. So scandalized were many of the early writers that they slipped into Latin to describe the aberrant behavior.

While somewhat reluctant to use the term "homosexual" to describe the berdaches, modern anthropologists and ethno-historians agree that male-male sexuality was a common feature of berdache life, and that this sexual activity played a major role in the disappearance of the tradition. In most precontact tribes, the berdache assumed a privileged status and was held in high esteem. He was considered to be holy and mysterious, revered—even feared—as a shaman or a seer (though the roles of shaman and berdache were not necessarily linked). Gradually throughout the nineteenth century the berdaches' prestige fell until they became objects of ridicule and a source of embarrassment. Nancy Lurie's interviews explain why: "Most informants felt that the berdache was at one time a highly honored and respected person, but that the Winnebago had become ashamed of the custom because the white people thought it was amusing or evil."[21] Perhaps the most famous berdache was a Zuni named We'wha, whose 1886 visit to President Grover Cleveland in the White House was documented by Will Roscoe.[22]

The white male response to the American Indian—as reality and as symbol—was complex and contradictory. The need to defend the New World against the slurs of European chauvinists forced American writers to become linguistic contortionists where Indian life was concerned. The newcomers, in defending their right to expropriate Native American territory, needed to portray Indians as infantile and

backward, half-civilized creatures who were unwilling or even incapable of exploiting the country's resources to the fullest extent. The
accent needed to fall unambiguously on "savage" not "noble." Yet it
was the noble savage who demonstrated the patriots' contention that
America was not a backward land where everything was smaller,
poorer, and less well developed than its Old World counterpart, as
some eighteenth-century writers had suggested. The American colonists weighed the Indian as Natural Man against the degenerate European courtier, and in the same way that American trees were taller,
American horses were swifter, American fruit was tastier and American birds sang in the springtime with a sweeter note, the Native
American was obviously more of a man than any snuff-sniffing European fop could ever hope to be. Yet the Indian needed to be subjugated,
so the colonists took the two stereotypes—Vespucci's monstrously
endowed savage and Buffon's puny, hairless hermaphrodite—and
fashioned an imago which fell exactly in the middle: the Indian did
indeed have an impressive penis, but he was disinclined to use it. This
convenient construction resolved the cognitive dissonance over Indian masculinity and allowed the settlers to proceed with the destruction of Indian culture. Yet confusion remained in the hearts of many
white American men. If the Indian was infantile, he was also boyishly
free, and along with disdain, the usurpers felt a deep pang of envy. To
many American men the free-ranging Indian represented an attractive
alternative to the forced conformity of colonial society.

From a few plantations clinging precariously to the edge of the Atlantic, colonial society grew into a complex agrarian culture, yet the
patterns of obligations and opportunities for young men remained unusually static. To a curious extent, gender roles in American culture
retained the peculiar imprint of the early plantation years. The settlements bordering on the Chesapeake Bay, for example, were strikingly
different from their sister colonies to the north. The Plymouth, New
Haven, and Massachusetts Bay colonies were established primarily
by multigenerational families, and as a consequence they were able to
develop a view of society based on the philosophy of Sir Robert
Filmer. The household to a New Englander was an integral part of the
structure of government, a subunit which replicated governmental
functions on a miniature scale. Just as the king was the head of the nation, the husband/father was the head of the family, a position which

carried with it implicit privileges and obligations as well as unquestioned authority. Any opposition to the power of the husband/father was, in effect, an act of treason against the whole government.

Along the shores of the Chesapeake, however, a very different philosophy prevailed. In Virginia the early immigrants included large numbers of unmarried indentured male servants, and throughout much of the initial phase of colonization, men outnumbered women four to one. Indeed, Virginia had the most lopsided gender ratio of any colony in British North America.[23] Unable to re-create the small patriarchal units envisioned by Filmer, Virginians adopted a more open, fluid view of human society. Following the philosophy of John Locke, they saw external government and family structure as distinctive entities.[24] Idiosyncratic responses to the gender ratio imbalance were viewed as an inescapable part of Southern life.

Yet deviance had its limits. Given the small number of available women in the Virginia colonies, it is perhaps not surprising that authorities feared that unmarried men might seek an alternate means of sexual release, and they moved quickly to condemn it. The first anti-homosexual statute in America was promulgated by the leaders of Jamestown Colony and published in London in 1612 in the volume *For the Colony in Virginea Britannia, Lavves Diuine, Morall, and Martiall, &c.* The law stated, "No man shal commit the horrible, and detestable sins of Sodomie vpon pain of death; & he or she that can be lawfully conuict of Adultery shall be punished with death."[25] It is interesting to note that the statute gives equal weight to the crimes of sodomy and adultery, and that while women are specifically noted as partners in adultery, they are excluded from the discussion of sodomy. This may be in part a result of the writers' ignorance of the existence of lesbianism, and in part a reflection of English legal tradition which required proof of penetration and emission of semen for a sodomy conviction (biologically impossible where two women were concerned). After 1619, Henry VIII's Buggery Statute of 1533 was considered to be in effect in the Virginia colony, but there were few sodomy prosecutions under the statute. Capital crimes required the corroboration of two eye witnesses, a stipulation difficult to fulfill for any private sexual transgression.

By the eighteenth century the gender imbalance in Virginia had improved somewhat, but women remained in the minority, primarily because so many died in childbirth. The unhealthful climate resulted in a high mortality rate in general, and when a Virginian died his or her surviving spouse quickly remarried. It was not unusual for a colonist to have two or three spouses during his or her lifetime. Families inevitably became a jumble of children from current and previous marriages, and frequently included children adopted by a later step-parent when both the biological parents had died, as well as formal or informal guardian/ward relationships. Sir Robert Filmer's neat interlocking pattern of government and household could not be discerned in the patchwork crazy quilt of Chesapeake family relations.

Because of the gender imbalance in Virginia during the early period, men were forced to (or were free to) develop alternative household structures. It was so common for two unmarried men to join together to live and work on the same piece of land that the relationship was given a name: each man was the other's "mate." The relationship between mates was so strongly regarded that it could endure even after one of the men took a wife. Only when *both* men married did a type of social mitosis occur, two new households being created where previously there was only one.[26]

Although male-male sexuality was emphatically prohibited by law there is some evidence that Virginians were willing to look the other way, tempering regulation with reality. When in 1630 a court sentenced a man named Hugh Davis "to be soundly whipped, before an assembly of Negroes and others for abusing himself to the dishonor of God and shame of Christians, by defiling his body in lying with a negro" it is the interracial aspect of the sex act which seems to cause the greater consternation, not the homosexuality.[27] Indeed, so vague is the condemnation of the sex itself that historians are divided about whether this was an act of sodomy or simply fornication with a woman.[28] That the punishment is to be delivered before "an assembly of Negroes and others" may be read as an attempt to warn other black women not to engage in interracial sex with white men like Davis, but that assumes a greater degree of freedom of choice for black women than was a reality at the time. Restricting the audience primary to blacks may have been part of the general pattern of withholding information about sodomy from tender members of the (white) community, or it may merely have been an attempt to humiliate Davis further by punishing him in front of his "inferiors." Certainly it was the convention of the court to use the term "negro woman" when referring to a black female; its absence here is a strong indication that Davis's partner was a man.[29]

Because of the Virginian's reluctance to pry into the household arrangements of his or her neighbors, two white men could live together quietly without interference. The problem with these male-male households, as far as the colonial government was concerned, was that so many laws vested privileges or responsibilities only in the head of the family. In a traditional marriage the identity of the "head" was clear, but where two men formed a household there was the possibility of legal ambiguity. Consequently in 1644 the House of Burgesses passed a law specifying who should be "master of the family" in the case where two men "make a joynt crop."[30] This act may be considered America's first domestic partnership ordinance, since it not only provided legal recognition that a relationship existed between the two men but also specifically designated that that relationship constituted a "family."

Two mates who engaged in a "joynt crop" relationship were usually living in isolation from their immediate neighbors and even from their slaves or servants, and if they engaged in intimate behavior the details were easily concealed.[31] The two men tended to be social equals, with an equal investment in maintaining their privacy. More difficult to keep from gossipers was sexual contact between males of different social classes, though neighbors were likely to ignore unconfirmed rumors as long as the sex was performed privately and no overt force was involved. As Colin L. Talley has written,

> A master and servant having sex in the middle of the night posed little threat to the production of corn or tobacco the next day. That a dominant male would seduce an adolescent behind the barn did not prevent the planting of seeds, the care of animals, or the harvesting of crops; nor did it threaten the sexual division of labor.

American colonists were able to look the other way because of an implicit understanding that such behavior was unavoidable—and temporary.

> This particular same-sex erotic behavioral pattern did not actually threaten the institution of marriage because it was rarely ex-

clusively homosexual, and the vast majority of same-sex erotic behavior never reached the attention of the courts much less the written record.[32]

Though early Virginia law provided for an alternative household structure, and prevailing custom allowed for a certain amount of nontraditional sexual activity, the acquisition of a spouse and the establishment of a nuclear family were essential to any definition of social success. Pressure ultimately to conform to society's expectations was every bit as strong along the shores of the Chesapeake as it was in Massachusetts Bay. Unmarried adults of both sexes—but especially males—were "almost in the class of suspected criminals."[33] Contemporary society had little patience for anyone unwilling to participate in the marriage market. One Maryland newspaper in 1798 thundered, "*That* MAN *who resolves to live without* WOMAN, *or that* WOMAN *who resolves to live without* MAN, *are* ENEMIES TO THE COMMUNITY *in which they dwell,* INJURIOUS TO THEMSELVES, DESTRUCTIVE TO THE WORLD, APOSTATES TO NATURE, *and* REBELS AGAINST HEAVEN AND EARTH."[34]

From the earliest colonial times the goal for any ambitious young man was marriage and the establishment of a household. An unmarried woman passed from the control and protection of her father to that of her husband (or, if she failed to marry before her father died, to that of another male relative), but for an unmarried man the situation was more pressing. He could chafe under the authority of his father, or join in a partnership with a male mate to create a separate family. If he did not eventually marry, at some point in his life he would assume the mantle of the "confirmed bachelor"—a role viewed by society with a combination of amusement, scorn, distrust, and pity. As Vincent Bertolini has written, "In his solitary and unmonitorable status as an autonomous adult male, the bachelor represented the transgressive triple threat of masturbation, whoremongering, and the nameless horror—homosexual sex."[35]

A suspicion of "unnatural" inclinations hovered over any man who seemed to be avoiding the altar. The pseudonymous "Old Bachelor" writing in the Richmond (Va.) *Enquirer* during the opening years of the nineteenth century assured his readers that his failure to marry could not be blamed on the two most frequent causes of prolonged bachelorhood:

Hence I am not distinguished by the disgusting and loathsome neglect of my person on the one hand; nor by the elaborate tidiness, formality and precision of my dress and appearance on the other. My rooms are not polluted by the fumes of tobacco and brandy; nor my toilet covered with lotions and patches and powders.[36]

In other words, it was not that marriageable women found his lack of personal cleanliness repulsive, nor that his sexual interests were unspeakably perverse. The *Enquirer*'s "Old Bachelor" (a composite persona created by William Wirt, Dabney Carr, St. George Tucker, and others) was well aware that a man who was financially independent and reasonably presentable and yet *unmarried* ran the risk of raising inevitable questions about his sexual proclivities.

Bachelors in colonial America were penalized, harried, and hemmed in. Colonial Connecticut imposed a fine of one pound for each week a bachelor lived on his own. Maryland imposed special punitive taxes on him. Some local laws required bachelors and spinsters to live within an established household; others permitted a man to live alone only with the expressed permission of the village authorities.[37] To marry was a man's civic obligation, the only course open to a law-abiding citizen.

A man who was uninterested in marriage presented society with an intolerable ambiguity which needed to be resolved. The solution for some men was simply to leave the community. The open sea promised an all-male environment accustomed to frank male-male sexuality. Newly opened territories also provided a setting where nuclear families were few and the expectation of marriage was temporarily suspended. The professions of soldier, sailor, merchant marine, whaler, riverman, trapper, or itinerant trader provided an unmarried man with a context in which to live his life until he either found a wife or accepted the status of confirmed bachelor, and in these female-deficient environments, men were free to turn to one another for sexual release, if they so desired. In 1948 Alfred Kinsey noted that the patterns of this type of sexual behavior had altered little since pioneer days. While most of the men surveyed by Kinsey in remote locales preferred sexual contact with women, they had adopted a very pragmatic approach to male-male sexual relations. "[T]here is a fair amount of sexual contact among the older males in Western rural areas," wrote Kinsey.

It is a type of homosexuality which was probably common among pioneers and outdoor men in general. Today it is found among ranchmen, cattle men, prospectors, lumbermen, and farming groups in general—among groups that are virile, physically active. These are men who have faced the rigors of nature in the wild. They live on realities and on a minimum of theory. Such a background breeds the attitude that sex is sex, irrespective of the nature of the partner with whom the relation is had. Sexual relations are had with women when they are available, or with other males when outdoor routines bring men together into exclusively male groups. . . . Such a group of hard-riding, hard-hitting, assertive males would not tolerate the affectations of some city groups that are involved in the homosexual; but this, as far as they can see, has little to do with the question of having sexual relations with other men.[38]

But escape to the West was not always an option. For those men unable or unwilling to leave their communities, the pressure to marry was virtually irresistible and they were driven to compete for the attention of any woman who might become available. Competition was particularly fierce for the hand of a woman if (through dowry or through inheritance, if a widow) she could bring to the marriage much-needed capital. It was a source of constant rancor to some men that enormous economic power could be vested in an "inferior" and "fickle" being such as a woman. Thwarted and humiliated, many planters developed what Kenneth A. Lockridge has described as "a savage misogyny in which women . . . become the metonymy of the metropolitan enemy responsible for their failure as colonial self-constructors and the symbol of the chaos and effeminacy they feel this failure will entail in themselves."[39]

Fear of being emasculated by the failure to marry well—and fear of the social and economic consequences of that failure—led men to establish among themselves social and emotional bonds which were byzantine in their psychosexual complexity. Lockridge uses as an illustration the commonplace book of a Virginian named Robert Bolling, written from 1760 to 1767. Bolling's notebook is a strange mélange of poetry, misogynist vitriol, and pornographic drawings in which he alternately moons over and excoriates various women who have spurned his advances. These denunciations frequently take the form of warnings to his male friends, warnings which display an obsession with the graphic details of his friends' sex lives. Lockridge reads these passages as "fleeting evidence of male homosocial, and even homosexual desire in Bolling's works."[40] The manuscript notebook includes crude sexual drawings, most of them of figures whose gender is obscured to the point of ambiguity, though some of the sketches are clearly male nudes, including one of a friend with a detumescent penis accompanied by a warning that overexerting himself on his wedding night might lead to his death.

Much of the current scholarship on male-male relations in early America has focused on so-called romantic friendships—intense emotional bonds between two young men—but Bolling's notebook is evidence that frank eroticism at times drew together a small group of male friends. Eighteenth- and nineteenth-century male homosocial friendship groups (as distinct from individual romantic friendships) are now beginning to receive some attention, most recently by Anya Jabour in her essay "Male Friendship and Masculinity in the Early National South."[41] Jabour focuses on a group of ten young Virginians who conducted an extensive correspondence among themselves in a type of epistolary round-robin, with each correspondent pledging his love for the next in the warmest possible terms. Jabour quotes numerous examples of deeply passionate homoerotic language but holds back from asserting that the written words imply actual sexual relations—ready to acknowledge a phenomenal amount of smoke, but unwilling to assume the presence of fire. Her reticence stems from a reluctance to make definitive statements about the past which are unsupported by surviving evidence (particularly when discussing intimate relations), yet it is difficult to imagine how early American male-male sexuality may be detected *except* through interpretation of the written word, however ambiguous that word may be. Heterosexual misconduct is frequently uncovered because of an unplanned pregnancy, but homosexual contact leaves no DNA trail for investigators to follow. Unless and until science develops an equivalent to DNA tracing for nonprocreative sexuality, we must turn to the written documents of the period to understand the details of male-male intimacy, and though proper interpretation of ambiguous language is a challenge, it is one historians must embrace—or leave an entire aspect of American history unexplored.

Given the challenge of understanding at a distance what men such as those in Jabour's group were feeling, perhaps it would be instructive to take as a model modern gay male social relationships, to see if there are any possible correlations in the group dynamics. Since at least the mid-twentieth century, gay men in America have formed social networks in which physical and emotional intimacy is fluid, depending more on libido and proximity than on the heterosexual ideal of a chaste courtship leading to a lifelong monogamous marriage.[42] Friends become lovers, ex-lovers remain friends. Many contemporary gay men surround themselves with a band of trusted comrades, some of whom were at one time their sexual partners. Groups frequently coalesce around one or two long-term couples, though the exact composition of the group changes over time as new people are introduced and others move on. The emotional bonds between individual members vary from marriage-like unions to mere casual friendships, but the group as a whole provides the social support of an extended family. Is it possible that this same pattern of social interaction prevailed in the early years of the American Republic?

Jabour uses as her central figure William Wirt, who served as the nexus of a number of homosocial liaisons within the group of friends, but who formed his closest emotional relationship with Dabney Carr. In the Wirt-Carr correspondence we can see the clear outlines of the type of affectional bond which constitutes the central union of many modern gay circles. William Wirt first met Dabney Carr when the two new lawyers began riding the circuit from courthouse to courthouse in Albemarle County in the early 1790s. They became fast friends, even inventing playful nicknames for each other. Wirt eventually left to take a position in Williamsburg, but he continued his friendship with Carr through visits and warm letters sent back to Charlottesville. In 1802 Wirt wrote to Carr that he looked back on their days traveling together with a "swelling of the heart" which brought as much pain as happiness: "Ah! This is not a pleasant emotion—my heart aches at the association of ideas—gone forever are those pleasures!"[43] Kept apart by their new jobs (and eventually by their respective marriages), the two men sought to preserve their intimacy through letter writing. Wirt assured Carr, "I have preserved every scrip of a pen that I ever received from you—they are among my most valued treasures," and later effused, "Your letters always spread such a sweet glow through my breast as to refuse participation to any other subject. . . . It is most grateful and flattering to me to find this secret intimacy and consciousness which seems to subsist between our hearts and under-standings."[44]

Their secret intimacy did not preclude the desire to take a wife and raise a family, and when Carr announced his engagement he knew he could count on his friend's support. "Yes," Wirt replied with gushing enthusiasm, "at this moment I have the very swelling of the heart which you describe. O! it is a delicious pain. I wish I had hold of your hand—you should be electrified with a vengeance." Wirt's happiness for his friend was sincere, but so was his sense of abandonment:

> Well and so you are married!—married!—quoth I again . . . and I—a buoy loosened from its anchor and drifting along upon the trackless surge. It pains me to look forward to the remainder of *my* life—fearful, gloomy void! . . . How safely, how sweetly are you moored![45]

Within a few months Wirt announced that he too had chosen a wife. This was not a unique sequence of events. Male friendships could continue at the same level of intensity only if both partners "failed" to marry. As soon as one man took a wife the dynamics of the relation-ship inevitably changed, and frequently the remaining partner also married soon thereafter (in some cases even marrying his friend's sis-ter). Some men took their partner's marriage as a signal that it was time for them, too, to move on to the next stage of life, but for other men—and especially in the case of Wirt—this rapid marriage seems primarily an attempt to reestablish the balance and symmetry of the original male-male relationship.

Wirt's marriage (not to Carr's sister, but to the sister of another member of the circle, Francis Walker Gilmer) allowed the two men to continue their intimacy almost unchanged, and indeed the entire group seems to have been able to make the transition from bachelors to married men without breaking off their emotional ties. Unlike the New Englanders studied by E. Anthony Rotundo (who found male intimacy and marriage to be mutually exclusive), the men in Jabour's group continued their close companionship even after the members began to take wives.[46] For reasons not yet fully understood, the Vir-ginians in Wirt's social circle were able to make the transition to the role of husband and father without abandoning the role of dearly cherished friend. Perhaps there were cultural differences between the Yankees' practicality and Southerners' romanticism which elicited differing ideas about the role of male friendship in a man's life—or perhaps Wirt's circle started from a level of much greater intimacy than their New England counterparts.

Achieving the status of "husband" was the next expected step for a young man after establishing himself in a career; there was simply no other socially acceptable option. When Mildred Gilmer Wirt died in 1799 after only five years of marriage, William Wirt married once more, this time to Elizabeth Gamble. Their marriage was by all evidence a very happy one; Margaret Bayard Smith, wife of the publisher of Washington's *National Intelligencer,* considered the Wirts the "beau-ideal" of "domestic habits, style of living, and character."[47] Wirt's and Carr's marriages were successful and brought both men great happiness, and yet there are ample hints that they might have preferred an alternative future, if one had been possible. "I have certainly never loved [a] man as I love you—and never shall," Wirt wrote to Carr. "If I could have lived along side of you all the days of my life, I should have been happier and I am persuaded should have made a better figure both in law and literature."[48] Barred from being spouses for each other, the two men set about creating the next best thing to a marriage: they spent as much time together as possible, and when apart wrote long, loving letters. But letters were not enough. Male friendship may content itself with handshakes and backslaps, but male love yearns to be eternal.

William Wirt and Dabney Carr entered into a type of surrogate parenthood: Carr named one of his sons William, and Wirt in turn named one of his sons Dabney. This was not merely a conventional case of two men acknowledging and honoring a lifelong friendship by naming a son after a dear friend (a common practice during the period). Wirt writes in very specific terms of his desire to use the ritual naming of their sons as a method of propagating their relationship, of extending it into the future through the lives of the next generation. For Wirt the reciprocal exchange of names was an intentional simulation of a married couple's ability to incarnate their love through the creation of children, and to project that love into the future through the lives of succeeding generations. "Our children will learn to know and love each other as their fathers have done before them."[49] William Wirt and Dabney Carr would in a sense *become* William Carr and Dabney Wirt in a type of double-helix intertwining of identities.

Marriage did not dull Wirt's deep longing for Carr. A dozen years after their respective marriages he was still turning to his friend for emotional support. "O! that you were here," he wrote plaintively. "Am I ne'er to see you more?—I long for your hand—I hunger after your face and voice—can you not come down this winter, if not sooner?"[50] The tone of this discourse—the swelling and aching, the holding and hunger—suggests a physical dimension to Wirt and Carr's relationship, but here we enter into the realm of the intimate unknowable. Perhaps any inchoate homosexual feelings were merely sublimated into passionate language. It cannot be assumed that the hand-holding is synecdochic for a sexual embrace. No evidence has yet surfaced to prove that they were sexual partners.

Jabour quotes similar passionate sentiments expressed by other members of the group. Francis Gilmer wrote to William Wirt, "I cannot refuse writing a few lines, out of the abundant love I bear for you," while Wirt wrote to Benjamin Edwards, "I have read, a half o' dozen times, with swimming eyes, your precious letter."[51] This apparent lack of emotional exclusivity would certainly argue that these men as a group were using effusive but (to them) conventional rhetoric to describe their mutual friendships—that is, if we assume a traditional one-man-one-woman heterosexual courtship model. If we use instead the model of contemporary gay male friendship circles, it is entirely possible that these men while in their late teens and early twenties passed through a period of shared emotional and physical intimacy but then (having no option—and perhaps no desire—to live as openly gay men) entered into traditional marriages. This pattern would be consistent with Kinsey's twentieth-century research, which revealed that 10 percent of American males were "more or less exclusively homosexual for at least three years between the ages of 16 and 55."[52] As married men, Wirt's circle attempted to keep their former intimacy alive as best they could through frequent visits and passionate letters, while in no way bemoaning their fate as husbands and fathers.

What is perhaps most striking about Wirt and his circle of friends is how blatantly they enjoyed one another's companionship, even when contemporary Virginians were censorious. As early as 1854 Wirt's biographer felt it necessary to address rumors about the group. Wrote John P. Kennedy,

I do not wish to conceal the fact that at this time of the life of Mr. Wirt, he was not altogether free from the censure of having sometimes yielded to the spells of the tempter, and fallen into some occasional irregularities of conduct. I am aware that this charge has been made in graver form, with some amplitude of detail and circumstances.

Being careful not to be too graphic about the group's activities, Kennedy acknowledges Wirt's youthful indiscretions and he crafts a careful defense.

Such a character we may suppose to be but too susceptible to the influences of good-fellowship, which, in the jollity of youthful association, not unfrequently take the discretion of the votary by surprise, and disarm its sentinels. The fashion of that time increased this peril. An unbounded hospitality amongst the gentlemen of the country, opened every door to the indulgence of convivial habits. The means of enjoyment were not more constantly present than the solicitations to use them. Every dinner-party was a revel; every ordinary visit was a temptation. The gentlemen of the bar, especially, indulged in a license of free living, which habitually approached the confines of excess, and often overstepped them. . . . The too frequent recurrence of these misadventures in that day, have furnished food for much gross calumny in regard to him, and have led to the fabrication of coarse and disgusting charges of vulgar excess, which I am persuaded are utterly groundless.[53]

It may be that Kennedy is talking about nothing more serious than occasional drunkenness, but he employs all the code words which invoked homosexual transgressions during the period: irregularities of conduct, fashion, peril, license, temptation, indulgence, excess, gross, grave, coarse, disgusting, vulgar. He explicitly states that it was the presence of other men which encouraged Wirt to yield to this vice, and he hints at further rumors too disgusting to repeat. Given the social practices of the period, to suggest that a young Virginia gentleman at times drank too much hardly falls within the realm of gross calumny, so it is probable that Kennedy is cloaking graver transgressions.

In later life Wirt credited his evangelical wife for saving him from a life of dissipation and sin. He turned from a youthful Jeffersonian-style deism to become a devout Presbyterian, reading the Bible daily and writing religious essays. He was an early feminist, and praised the saving grace of women's piety as a much-needed moral force for the new Republic.

Complicating any attempt to parse the grammar of male-male intimacy in this place and time is the well-documented pervasiveness of misogyny in American society, misogyny which did not necessarily manifest itself (overtly or even subliminally) as homosexual desire. The expression of a preference for male company cannot therefore be viewed with any certainty as a rejection of heterosexuality. In his earlier study, *On the Sources of Patriarchal Rage: The Commonplace Books of William Byrd and Thomas Jefferson and the Gendering of Power in the Eighteenth Century,* Kenneth A. Lockridge discusses the anti-female writings and transcriptions of two men who do not appear ever to have been significantly drawn to members of their own sex.

Lockridge analyzes the commonplace book kept by Jefferson from the ages of thirteen to nineteen (1756 to 1762), a period when he was mourning the death of his father and chaffing under the domination of his mother, Jane Randolph Jefferson. Among the passages of literature which the young Jefferson copied out are a long series of misogynist diatribes, including an excerpt from Milton's *Paradise Lost* which questions God's wisdom in having created women at all:

> O! why did God
> Creator wise! that Peopl'd highest Heav'n
> With Spirits masculine, create at last
> This Novelty on Earth, this fair Defect
> Of Nature? And not fill the World at once
> With Men, as Angels, without feminine?
> Or find some other Way to generate
> Mankind?[54]

What Milton's Adam is calling for—and what the young Jefferson apparently endorsed strongly enough to want to copy the passage into his commonplace book—is a society composed entirely of men, with the men taking upon themselves the sole important function of women: reproduction. The thought is echoed in a second passage also transcribed by Jefferson, this one from Euripides: "Yea, men should have begotten children from some other source, no female race existing; thus would no evil have fallen on mankind."[55] What is striking about these visions of a womanless world is that they reflected the actuality of life on the geographic margins of early America.

William Byrd provides an even stranger entré into the psychosexual world of colonial life. His *Secret Diary* reveals that he was an abundantly active heterosexual with no suggestion of attraction to other men, but a recent discovery documents that he was at the very least aware of homosexual activity. Byrd added handwritten annotations to his copy of *Le Dictionnaire des arts et des sciences,* creating a "Supplement" of eighty-nine French sexual terms, to which he appended definitions and usage examples written in French and/or Latin. Included are seven terms referring to explicitly homosexual acts, such as: "Acculer, a tergo anum petere, cum puero sodomitiée rem habere." [To have anal sex, to penetrate the anus, to sodomize a boy.] "Arser, membri arrectionem pati. J'ay arsé toute la nuit." [To bugger, to be the passive member in anal intercourse. I was buggered all night long.] "Branler, fortiter futuere. il m'a branlé en cheval hénnissant." [To masturbate (literally to shake or jerk), to fuck robustly. He jerked me like a neighing horse.][56]

Byrd's "Supplement" is only a fragment, breaking off at the beginning of the F's, but it must have been extensive to reach eighty-nine terms in the first six letters of the alphabet. For the purposes of the current study it is interesting for what it reveals about homosexual activity from the point of view of a Virginian who was primarily (perhaps exclusively) heterosexual. Of the seven terms included in the fragment, six refer to homosexual anal intercourse; only one refers to homosexual masturbation and none refers to oral sex. Of the six references to anal intercourse, three refer to sex with a boy and three to sex with another man. No original source for the quotes has been identified, but they are remarkably free of moral censure. "J'ay arsé toute le nuit" is certainly the boast of someone who finds receptive anal intercourse to be an enjoyable activity, free of gender role complications.

Men like Jefferson and Byrd developed their ideas about gender roles first from what they observed of life on their plantations, and then later from what they were taught in school. The lesson was unambiguous: the male sphere is competitive, the female supportive. Schoolboys were taught to value the contributions of men over those of women, and to cherish above all the institution of male-male friendship. The curriculum of most American primary schools in the early years included basic arithmetic, some geography and natural history, and (especially in schools for boys) large doses of the language, history, and literature of Greece and Rome. For a doctoral dissertation titled "The Virtuous Curriculum: Schoolbooks and American Culture, 1785-1830," Cynthia Koch reviewed over 2,000 school reader lessons from the period to demonstrate that their goal was both to provide students with practical knowledge and to inculcate in them certain moral and ethical principles.[57] Though Koch's study focuses primarily on the concept of virtue broadly defined, her examples may also be read for what they say about gender-based interpersonal relations.

Since the curriculum was designed to teach young (mostly Protestant) Americans basic moral and ethical principles, it is perhaps surprising that the Bible played only a minor role. In the schoolreaders reviewed for Koch's study, few included scriptural passages in their compilations of readings, and most of the Bible stories which did appear were presented in "retold" versions, such as Milton's account of the Adam and Eve myth as it appears in *Paradise Lost*. In one of the most popular readers, Noah Webster's *American Selection of Lessons in Reading and Speaking* (which went through at least twenty-five editions between 1785 and 1814), there are no Bible study lessons at all. When Bible stories *were* included in a schoolreader, the Old Testament in particular was interpreted "less than literally—as history, as literature, but invariably not as the word of God."[58]

Instead of quoting orthodox Christian scripture, the school texts turned again and again to the literature and history of Classical times: the fall of Troy, the wanderings of Ulysses, the founding of the Roman republic—these were the stories which were held up as moral exemplars. Some of those narratives, however, presented problematic depictions of love and sexuality and expressed sentiments which were at odds with traditional views of the relations between the sexes. The stories of Achilleus and Patroklos, Damon and Pythias, or Zeus and Ganymede presented male-male passion in very a different light than the Book of Leviticus. The messages being inculcated by the Greek and Roman authors certainly did not promote the virtues of heterosexual coupling. Women are dangerous sirens who lure men from the path of noble virtue. Marriage is a civic duty which should be entered into rationally and cautiously, with the head but not the heart. The only true, enduring, and ennobling love is between two men. Even the greatest of the gods appreciated the sexual allure of young boys. In time this relentless encomium to the joys of male-male love necessarily wove itself into the psyches of many students and became a part of the way they responded in their own personal relationships.

Robert Wirt (son of William Wirt) and J.S. Thompson were West Point cadets who shared a deep emotional bond which was not broken even when Robert was expelled from the Military Academy in disgrace. Thompson wrote, "I have known but one person in whose bosom I found a heart that responded to the feelings of my own, a heart that reciprocated the sentiments of mine, a heart that had 'locked me in its love.'" Upon learning of Wirt's death in 1825 Thompson excused the intensity of his grief by declaring, "Pythias would have bled for his Damon—Harmodius did sigh for the absent Aritogiton."[59]

References to Greek male-male love appeared in strikingly incongruent places. Thomas Jefferson added to his wife's grave marker a passage in Greek which translates: "Nay if even in the house of Hades the dead forget their dead, yet will I even there be mindful of my dear comrade." The quote is from Achilleus's lament over the body of his slain companion, Patroklos. Though Jefferson was familiar with a broad range of the world's literature, a literature rich in the words of men mourning the loss of the women they loved, he returned to a quote he first encountered as a young boy, a quote referring to the eternal love between two men. That in the depths of his grief Jefferson thought of Achilleus's lament says much about the impact of those early images on developing imaginations.

Schoolmasters no doubt obscured the homosexual references in the Classical authors, but adolescent males are notoriously adept at deciphering sexual subtext. For some students the subliminal message about homosocial relations would have no more effect on their emerging sexuality than would memorizing the multiplication tables, but for any student who was beginning to recognize that his romantic interests lay not with girls but with his male comrades, the stories of ancient Greece and Rome could provide a context and a vocabulary with which to think about—though perhaps not fully understand—his sexual desires.

On a subtler and more subjective level, there is the question of how English-speaking students may have been influenced by the concept of gender in Latin grammar. To a young man reared in a binary society with very clear definitions of the male and the female spheres of activity, what was the effect of encountering in Cheever's *A Short Introduction to the Latin Tongue* a passage such as, "The Masculine is more worthy than the Feminine, and the Feminine than the Neuter: but in things that have no life, the neuter is most worthy"?[60] Perhaps the notion of a third gender opened new possibilities of perception for these young American students.

For young men in America the literature of ancient Greece and Rome provided a way to think about—and, more important, to express—their desire for emotional intimacy with another man. Whether or not that desire included a longing for physical intimacy, whether homosexual desire was sublimated or conscious, these stories gave them permission to pursue their feelings in a socially acceptable framework. The near-universal familiarity with these stories among the educated class meant that these men had a common vocabulary, even if the words resonated differently for some men than for others.

As schoolboys became sophisticated men, the stories lingered in their memories but were joined there by a growing awareness of the sexual dimension of passionate male friendships. Men unable to accept the idea of male-male sexuality still clung to the stories, but placed them in a prelapsarian time when two men could merge souls without touching genitals. In the preface to his 1752 translation of *Epistolae ad Atticum,* William Guthrie explains,

> The following Pages evince, there was a Time, when Friendship in the human Breast could rise into a Passion strong as their Love, and sacred as their Religion, but without the Impurities that sometimes debased the one, and the Superstition that always polluted the other.[61]

Unlike the heroes of ancient Greece and Rome, Guthrie lamented, two men devoted to each other in the enlightened eighteenth century needed to wrestle with the possibility of impurity, debasement, and pollution.

It was not only that the schoolreaders painted a romantic picture of male-male love, but they also presented a discouraging portrait of heterosexuality. When Koch in her survey of early American school texts focused on stories of heterosexual courtship and marriage, she discovered a litany of sorrows. Sixty-eight percent of the heterosexual love stories depicted unrequited love or love ending in tragedy. It was only the love between men which endured.

> Friendship as portrayed in the schoolbooks was often presented as a relationship between men that carried an ardor equal to that of romantic love between men and women. . . . The weight of evidence, in fact, points to stronger emotional ties between friends than between [heterosexual] lovers . . . . it seems from the schoolbooks that the cultural expectations of friendship were more explicit than those for love and marriage. Friendship was portrayed as a mutually rewarding relationship for both parties. Not so with love and marriage, where emotional distress and the inequality of the partnership characterized a relationship that was ambiguously drawn in the popular texts.[62]

From an early age, then, American men were taught to value a male-only world, one filled with bosom friends. In struggling to understand his own sexuality, it was not necessary for a man to understand the concept of sexual orientation, or to renounce women or—especially—to declare his amatory preference. America presented a myriad of places where men could avoid the imposition of the matrimonial straitjacket while taking advantage of new options for sexual conduct. As we shall see, a man need only move to the margins to find a world of personal freedom, heroic friendships, and unencumbered sensuality.

Chapter 2

Warme Brüder, Mouches, and Mollies

Since half of Paris was so inclined, none of the innkeepers was unaware of the practice, and all were on their guard concerning such activities.

Abbé de Boisrenard, 1724

Damn'd Fashion! Imported from Italy admidst a Train of other unnatural Vices. Have we not Sins enough of our own, but we must eke 'em out with those of Foreign Nations, to fill up the Cup of our Abominations, and make us yet more ripe for Divine Vengeance?

Satan's Harvest Home, London, 1749

Throughout the eighteenth century immigrants arrived in America's port cities in ever-increasing numbers. Most of them sailed from Europe, where the rise of science and the decline of religious orthodoxy had brought about unprecedented changes in societal structures. While the American colonies were struggling to carve small villages out of the wilderness, Europe in the eighteenth century experienced the rapid rise of major urban centers with populations large enough to sustain (and to some extent, to *hide*) a homosexual subculture. Recent scholarship has provided documentation of the extent to which gay communities arose in cities such as Berlin, Paris, and London during this period. Few young men arriving in Boston or New York or Savannah would be unaware of the existence of buggers and sodomites in their home country, and an analysis of the homosexual subcultures of Europe can provide some idea of the expectations of immigrants to America.

Berlin in particular experienced a rapid increase in population during the eighteenth century (doubling to more than 100,000 citizens), and as the city grew into the major political and cultural capital of the region, an old expression took on new meaning. *"Stadtluft macht frei"* ("city air makes one free") at one time referred to the custom whereby a serf could win his freedom if he could escape to one of the German *freistädte,* or free cities, and live there for one year and one day. Europe lacked the wide-open frontiers of America, but with the burgeoning of cities there appeared in Europe a new opportunity for escape and rebirth.

In his study of homosocial networking in the eighteenth century, Simon Richter draws a vivid picture of an emerging German cultural milieu in which sexual orientation was a vague, somewhat transient concept. "Almost without exception," Richter writes,

> the male producers of culture in the Age of Goethe were the inhabitants of a virtual, semi-intimate, public/private space of homosocial and homoerotic encounter, imagined or otherwise. Individuals reputed to have liaisons with other men and boys freely mingled with men for whom sodomitical relations were out of the question. Such a milieu might be termed tolerant, and the designation would not be out of keeping with Enlightenment principles. Nonetheless, an unnecessary distinction is implied between those who tolerate and are tolerated. It may be more accurate to speak of a network in which the participants were virtually and potentially linked in friendship according to a Greek model of varying and blurred dimensions.[1]

James D. Steakley has documented that "a fairly continuous homosexual subculture was in place [in Berlin] by the late eighteenth century."[2] He quotes the anonymous writer of *Briefe über die Galanterien von Berlin* (believed to be Johann Friedel) describing a social gathering of men and women he attended during a visit to the capital in 1782. "I noticed from time to time," Friedel writes, "that the fellows embraced with the warmest tenderness, kissed each other, squeezed hands, and said such sweet things to each other as a fop might say to a lady." He is astonished when his host explains that these men are *warme brüder.* "Warm brothers? What's that?—'You don't know anything about that, and already four months in Berlin, that surprises me! . . . Almost no good-looking boy is safe from these gentlemen. As soon as they spot one, they chase after him like a stag in rut.'"[3] The next evening the host obliges Friedel's curiosity by taking him to a boy bordello. "With astonishment," Friedel continues, "I watched the embraces with which the older rams met the younger ones. Neither sweets nor expense was spared to win the lad. There a foursquare Bacchant toasted his Ganymede with full wine glass, there a second one cuddled against his boy with the warmest feeling of delight; here on the other hand a loose lad played with the belt of his Zeus, and there the victor disappeared with his Thracian booty."[4]

This sudden flowering of male-male sexuality in Berlin was to a great extent initiated by the reign of Frederick the Great. Frederick ascended to the throne of Prussia in 1740 and immediately began re-shaping his realm into a reflection of the court at Versailles. In this Frederick was reacting against the ham-fisted anti-intellectualism of his father, King Frederick William. Father and son had long been at odds, particularly since the king was repelled by the young prince's effete Frenchified ways. Steakley refers to Frederick's "manifest homosexuality," and though other writers are more reluctant to apply the label quite so explicitly, it is likely that Frederick William suspected his son's sexual proclivities from an early age. He attempted to separate Frederick from his close friend Hans Hermann von Katte, who was popularly believed to be a sodomite. Unable to bear the humiliations his father constantly heaped on him, Prince Frederick at the age of eighteen decided to flee to Paris with von Katte. The plan was discovered, Frederick was imprisoned in solitary confinement, and von Katte was convicted of treason. The king ordered that von Katte's execution be carried out beneath Frederick's window. The prince is said to have looked down at his friend and waved. "Forgive me, Katte," he called out. "There is nothing to forgive, Prince," the doomed man replied.[5] When the executioner raised his sword to give the fatal blow Frederick fainted and was spared the grisly sight.

Regardless of his orientation, Frederick was expected to marry and produce an heir to the Prussian throne. In 1733 he married Elisabeth Christine, Princess of Braunschweig-Wolfenbüttel, and although the marriage was probably consummated, he made no effort to conceal the fact that he found his wife's presence unbearable. The Stadtpalais in Berlin was remodeled to allow each of them to maintain a separate household. Separate stairways assured that they would not even encounter each other by accident when moving about the palace. Frederick spent most of his time at Rheinsberg Castle or (after 1747) at his beloved Sanssouci in Potsdam, leaving the queen behind in Berlin. He made it clear that the marriage was a mere formality, visiting his wife only once a year, on her birthday. At Rheinsberg and Sanssouci, Frederick surrounded himself with the most handsome and dashingly uniformed Hussars in the kingdom and entertained a long line of intimate male friends. In *The Secret History of the Court of Berlin,* the French diplomat and gossip-monger Count Mirabeau quotes the king speaking to an officer of the guard using tender endearments such as *"mein liebes Kind"* and *"mein Schatz."*[6] Voltaire, after spending several years as Frederick's guest at Potsdam, fled the Prussian court and published a critical pamphlet filled with double entendres describing the king's penchant for well-built officers and young pages.[7] When Frederick the Great died in 1786 he was not surrounded by members of his family; instead he took his last breath literally in the arms of his personal military retainers.[8]

Whatever Frederick and his Hussars might have been doing behind palace walls, the king's public stance against homosexuality remained unambiguous. Death remained the penalty for sodomy throughout Frederick's long forty-six-year reign, despite his Enlightenment-inspired liberality on other subjects. It was not until 1794, under the reign of Frederick's nephew and heir Frederick William II, that the punishment was changed to imprisonment for not less than one year, flogging upon entering and leaving prison, and banishment upon release. Steakley believes the credit for this legal reform should actually be given to Frederick the Great, as it was the result of extensive legal discussions begun under his reign, and may in fact have reflected the de facto judicial practice for some time prior to the law's promulgation.[9]

If there is still some doubt about Frederick's overt sexual behavior, there is little question that his brother Prince Henry was emotionally and erotically drawn solely to other men. His passionate affairs with a long series of aristocratic lovers have been extensively documented.[10] Prince Henry is of interest to Americans primarily because he appears as a footnote in our constitutional history. In 1787 as the new republic debated what form of government it should adopt, a party led by Alexander Hamilton favored a constitutional monarchy on the English model. The problem, of course, would be deciding which member of European royalty should be invited to become king of the United States. With the country having just thrown off an English monarch, no one could seriously propose a member of the British royal family. The aristocracy of France, Spain, and Austria were unfortunately Catholic, and therefore beyond consideration. That left the most respected Protestant military power on the Continent: Prussia. Baron Friedrich Wilhelm von Steuben, hero of the American Revolution, wrote to his old friend Prince Henry with a tentative offer of the American throne. Prince Henry responded with caution, saying that he doubted that the American people would accept a new monarch, but he offered to rendezvous in Paris with a duly-accredited American agent. Before matters could develop further, the Constitutional Convention decided on an elected president with a fixed term of office, and the idea of an American monarchy quickly faded. It is impossible to determine how much the Americans knew about Prince Henry but (as will be explored in a later chapter) Baron von Steuben clearly was aware of the prince's sexual interests.

It was not just at the German royal courts that same-sex romance flourished. Berlin during the Enlightenment saw the publication of the first German journal dedicated to the new science of psychology: *Magazin zur Erfahrungsseelenkunde*. In the pages of this journal for the first time men who were sexually attracted to other men could find their condition discussed rationally, even empathetically. In 1791 the *Magazin* published a letter from a university student describing the plight of "a friend." The friend had long been known for his cold aloofness, and for the determination with which he "refused to allow his head to be influenced by his heart." Then an attractive new (male) student enrolled in his classes, and for the self-possessed and highly controlled friend, it was "as if he had been struck by an electric shock." He became infatuated, his studies suffered, and he eventually dropped out of the university, even moving to another town where he now lived alone, "quiet and extremely melancholy." The letter ended with a pleading, "Does anyone have further examples of such a peculiar aberration of human nature? And how is my friend to be helped?"[11] While the tone of the letter is one of confused concern, the fact that the topic was being discussed sympathetically in print at all is significant. The *Magazin* certainly served the unintended function of linking like-minded young men to one another.

This Golden Age of *Brüdershaft* in Germany ended shortly after the close of the eighteenth century. "The relevant date appears to be around 1806," Richter writes, "a time when Napoleon invades Prussia and an enlightened, cosmopolitan, homosocial culture accepts him, while in Romantic circles a conservative, homophobic national-ism takes hold."[12] In the various German duchies and principalities the popular image of France underwent a sea-change. Where before the word "French" had conjured up an effete, silk-stockinged fop of the Court at Versailles, after the Napoleonic invasions "the French" were the brutish foot soldiers out to rape German women and butcher German children. German manhood became redefined to the point that only those who were willing to take up arms to defend hearth and home could be considered true men. Nationalism was equated with heterosexuality and the family, and the sexual tolerance of the En-lightenment was quickly extinguished.[13]

In the same way that the growth of Berlin allowed for the develop-ment of a German homosexual network, the emergence of Paris as the major cultural and intellectual capital of Europe during the eighteenth century provided a setting for a community of like-minded French-men. More is known about this community because its activities were chronicled in lurid detail by the *Police des Moeurs* which employed a corps of spies popularly known as *les mouches*.[14] Using the extensive archives of reports filed by the *mouches,* historians Michel Rey, Claude Courouve, and others have been able to reconstruct same-sex social patterns in some detail, and to document that Paris had a well-developed homosexual subculture from at least as early as the 1720s.

The reports reveal that many men who were seeking other men would cruise for sex partners in the Tuileries, Palais-Royal or Luxem-bourg Gardens, or along the *Champs-Elysées*—the same locations frequented by female prostitutes. The police were well aware of the favorite locations and kept them under surveillance almost daily, with increased intensity in the spring and summer, and on Sundays and holidays. As with the female prostitutes and their customers, male-male encounters led either to an assignation in a private room or to sex exchanged on the spot in the more remote parts of the parks. The *mouches* were not expected to make arrests; they merely observed ac-tivity (or sometimes encouraged it) and then reported it to the police. At a later date the *mouche*—this time accompanied by a policeman—would wait at the entrance to the Tuileries or the Luxembourg Gar-dens to point out the suspect and secure his arrest. The men arrested in these entrapment schemes were overwhelmingly from the working class. Some expected money from their sex partners, but most were seeking only sexual gratification. The record of arrests for 1723, for example, indicates that of the nineteen men whose marital status is listed, thirteen were unmarried, and nearly all of the unmarried men were at least thirty years old.[15] With such a large percentage of unmarried men who were beyond the average age of marriage for the period, the records imply the growth of a community of men for whom heterosexual sex was not an object of active pursuit. This floating community continued to grow in Paris throughout the eighteenth century; by the 1780s the authorities had over 40,000 "sodomites" under surveillance.[16]

The reports filed by the *mouches* were written in the slang of the streets, an indication that the police were employing agents with a low level of education. Little attempt was made to prettify the accounts with euphemisms:

> I was picked up by an individual who had his cock *[son vit]* in his hand, and asked me if I had a hard-on and approaching me wanted to put his hand in my breeches. He said that he shouldn't expose himself in this spot, and asked me if I had a room, where we could go to jack off *[branler le vit]* or to screw. He also told me that for the last 20 years he had been involved in the gay life *[la bardacherie],* and that he knew many footmen with whom he amused himself very often, jacking off or screwing them as often as they wanted it.[17]

While public parks were a popular homosexual meeting place, other encounters took place in taverns. A report from 1736 reads:

> Being in a tavern, he had me go into a toilet and he had me close the door and started to uncover himself, asking me if I was in the mood; he threw himself on me wanting to put his hand in my breeches; he showed himself to me entirely uncovered in front and I saw that he was shaved there; I asked him why he was shaved in this spot; he told me that it was because people said he was a eunuch because nature had been very ungenerous to him down there. I said to him, "Let's go to your place instead, we're not safe here"—and that was part of the plan to arrest him—He asked to see my bottom, I said to him: "You'll see it as soon as we are at your place"; he said that we really couldn't go to his place because he was married, and he asked to go to my place instead. I told him I had a partner, he told me, "You could see if

your partner is there, and you could stop down in the street to tell me." He suggested that I consummate the act with him, and that he would be the passive one *[le patient],* that he really liked that, and that that would put him in the mood to then be the active one *[l'agent].*[18]

Surveillance by the *mouches* was not the only way that offenders came to the attention of the authorities. Many were denounced (in some instances by their own families) and were taken into royal custody under the power of a *lettre de cachet.* These men were usually confined in the notorious "hospital" of Bicêtre where they were closely watched for evidence of penitence or religious conversion. In pre-Enlightenment France sodomitical offenses were considered to be as much a sin as a crime. From 1697 until 1718, Marc-René de Voyer d'Argenson served as *Lieutenant général de Police* in Paris. The registers he maintained of men confined to Bicêtre indicate that some men came to the attention of the police because they were members of homosexual groups whose participants had been arrested in a police sweep, a tactic which would be possible only if large numbers of men had established well-publicized methods of meeting one another. D'Argenson made no attempt to eradicate sodomy completely, but he believed that incarceration could rehabilitate—or at least intimidate—inmates to the extent that they would refrain from corrupting others. "Action was taken," writes historian D. A. Coward, "only when specific complaints were laid, when behaviour outrageous to public decency was reported and when offences were committed which involved the corruption of minors. It was a policy of containment which directed its sternest measures against the corruption of the nation's youth."[19] D'Argenson was not adverse to releasing men after a period of good behavior, but only on the condition that they either immediately enlist in the army or return to their villages under the recognizance of their family or local religious leaders. One condition of the release was that they were never to return to Paris, where they had picked up such "bad habits."[20]

Police surveillance of male-male sexual activity in Paris continued throughout the eighteenth century, until in 1807 the police were told to stop pursuing sodomites because "the law can't make provision for this crime."[21] Even when monitoring was at its height there were relatively few prosecutions and even fewer convictions, since most Parisians felt that the prescribed punishment—burning at the stake—

did not fit the crime. When in 1726 a man named Deschouffours was convicted and executed his public immolation was denounced by a wide range of citizens, both those appalled by the cruelty of the punishment and those who objected to calling public attention to a crime which most people (it was presumed) did not even know existed. The moralist Luc de Clapiers, marquis de Vauvenargues declared, "That which doesn't offend society is not within the purview of its justice," a sentiment which in 1789 made its way into the Declaration of the Rights of Man.[22] As a result, the Parisian authorities concentrated on preventing sex acts performed in public, those which corrupted minors, and those which were violent or coercive.

For men seeking a more social environment—and one less likely to come to the attention of the police—private clubs known as *sociétés d'amour* sometimes catered to a homosexual clientele.[23] According to the research conducted by Michel Rey, by 1748 at least eight Parisian taverns functioned as gay bars, providing private spaces for men to come together in groups of anywhere from fifteen to thirty participants.[24] The gatherings usually took place in the evening, when the men would close the shutters to dance, sing, eat, and flirt. Most often the space had two rooms, one for general socializing and a backroom for sexual activities. A typical party was described by a witness:

> This past summer, he found himself in several gatherings of people from la Manchette, either in la Courtille or at the sign of the *Six Sparrows* in the rue aux Juifs (in the central Marais district). In these assemblies the conversation is almost always in the same vein. Some members with napkins on their heads imitate women and mince about like them. Any new young man in their midst is call the bride *(Mariée),* and they all try for him. People pair off in order to touch and to perform infamous acts. Sometimes that also takes place after leaving the tavern.[25]

These men created a group identity by adopting the fiction that they were members of the royal court or a convent or a secret society which required initiation rites before a novice could gain full membership. Though a few nobles and members of the *grande bourgeoisie* sometimes took part in the festivities, the lower classes—servants, immigrants, beggars, and prostitutes—were rarely welcomed. "The assembly," Rey writes, "thus seems to have been a rather coherent social group of small merchants and tradesmen, which fantasized about the freedom of manners and the festivities of the court—as if, in order to fashion a transgressing identity and to become organized, some social demarcation was necessary."[26] This social demarcation and the resulting strong group identity helped to assure discretion, and discretion was vital in order to escape prosecution.

Male-male sexuality was also prevalent at the universities, which led to a popular expression of homosexual slang. "Il n'entend pas le latin" ("he doesn't understand Latin") was well-recognized code for "he is not gay, like us." Claude Courouve has traced the etymology directly to a parallel between the use of the neuter gender in Latin and the existence of male-loving men.[27] Courouve mentions the expression in passing but fails to explore the richness of its implications. In this case the verb *entendre* means "to understand" but its more common definition is "to hear." Taken literally, what the expression is saying is that a man who is not a homosexual is incapable of hearing the gay subtext of a conversation, so it is possible for two gay men to communicate in front of him without having him catch on. This new notion pushed the concept of "the unspeakable crime" into an entirely new dimension, one in which homosexuals were able to speak to one another freely because a wall of incomprehension prevented others from hearing their words.

For the students, merchants, and tradesmen who played at being members of the aristocracy, the charade may have been an attempt to draw around themselves the cloak of immunity enjoyed by members of the royal court, who were able to practice "le beau vice" without provoking the full fury of the law. Writes Coward,

> By the end of 1784 there was reputed to be a male seraglio at Versailles itself and the King was of a mind to exact full retribution. But he was restrained by the traditional argument that to invoke the statutes would ruin families and draw attention to a vice which should be left in the dark. Louis XVI reluctantly acquiesced and exiled the ring-leaders to their estates.[28]

Parisians whose blood was less than blue received no such royal indulgence. While prosecutions were few, they did occur. In 1750 a cabinet-maker of eighteen and a pork-butcher of twenty were arrested by a night watchman when he observed them engaging in a sexual act in public. The courts decided to make an example of the two young men, and they were burnt at the stake in the Place de Grève. In an act of mercy they were strangled before the kindling was ignited. The grisly public execution proclaimed the official position on homosexuality: act with discretion or suffer the consequences.

In the wake of the French Revolution, the revised French Penal Code of 1791 dropped all references to "crimes against nature" and the Civil Code (both in the 1790s and under the Empire) made no mention of homosexual acts carried out in private. The Penal Code adopted under Napoleon, however, once again specifically criminalized public homosexual acts, labeling them offenses against public decency. Article 330 set penalties of imprisonment from three months to a year and fines of 16 to 200 francs. The French Enlightenment attempted to break the monopoly on virtue which it felt the Catholic Church had been claiming for itself. The *philosophes* made a conscious attempt to separate the concept of "sin" from that of "crime," using the principle of "nature" as a guide to correct behavior. "The nature they referred to," writes Michel Delon, "is either a normative principle that replaces divine order, or a principle of reality that accepts the world's contradictions. In the former, homosexuality remains an unnatural but social, not religious, sin. In the latter, it is accepted."[29] While the vast majority of French citizens retained a more conservative view of homosexuality, it was the free-thinkers of Paris who had the greater impact on legal and social policy—and therefore on the lives of gay Frenchmen.

By the closing years of the eighteenth century sodomy was no longer punished as a capital crime in the Russia of Catherine the Great, the Prussia of Frederick William, or the Holy Roman Empire of Joseph II. In 1791 France decriminalized same-sex relations entirely. While the clarity of the Enlightenment was flooding minds on the European continent and sodomy laws were being relaxed or even repealed in many countries, in England the law was frozen in the time of Henry VIII. Not one execution for sodomy is known to have taken place on the European continent during the entire nineteenth century; in England sixty homosexuals were hanged in the first three decades alone, and another twenty were executed aboard ships in the Royal Navy.[30]

The first mention of homosexuality in English jurisprudence occurred in the thirteenth century, when a collaborative legal treatise known as *Fleta* stated that persons "who have [sexual] connexion with Jews and Jewesses or are guilty of bestiality or sodomy shall be buried alive in the ground. . . ."[31] In 1376 in the reign of Edward III a law was passed banishing foreign artisans and traders, especially Jews and Saracens, who were (among other things) accused of importing "the too horrible vice which is not to be named." But it was not until 1533 that a statute was enacted specifically criminalizing homosexuality. In that year Parliament passed the Buggery Act as part of Henry VIII's plan to gut the power of the ecclesiastical courts. Prior to 1533 sodomy had been viewed primarily as a sin, and was therefore in the purview of the Church. Henry (always looking for ways to increase his power and wealth) shared a widely held belief in the venality of the clergy, and recognized that if a man in Holy Orders was denied the right to be tried in the ecclesiastical courts, a conviction in the secular courts could result in the forfeiture of his property in favor of the Crown. The Tudors found in sodomy a convenient charge to levy against Catholic clergy, and by equating sodomy with Catholicism they were able to make it tantamount to treason. "Of Chastity they made great outward shew," reads one diatribe against priests and monks,

> but very litle was fownd amonge them, for it plainlie appered their filthie lusts were not satisfied with maidens wifes & widows but also they practised one with another that detestable sodomitishe & Romishe unnatural Acte whereof St Paul in the first to the Romans writeth which was the Cause that horrible vice was made by parliament felonie without helpe or benefitt of Clergie.[32]

The Buggery Act was repealed during the reign of Mary Tudor, and jurisdiction over sodomy was returned to the ecclesiastical courts. In 1563, five years after ascending the throne, Elizabeth I revived her father's law, asserting that since the 1553 repeal, "divers ill disposed persons have been the more bold to commit the said most horrible and detestable Vice of Buggery aforesaid, to the high displeasure of Almighty God."[33] The law remained on the books during succeeding reigns, but there were few sodomy prosecutions until the eighteenth century.

Before the Age of the Enlightenment, men who engaged in sexual acts with other men were, in the words of Netta Murray Goldsmith, "mythologized as monsters, akin to werewolves and basilisks, outside a divinely appointed, natural order of things, believed by some to be literally the offspring of Satan."[34] There were few sodomy prosecutions over the centuries, in part, because the crime was believed to be so rare and bizarre as to be nearly unthinkable. But at the dawn of the eighteenth century London experienced the same sharp rise in population experienced by Berlin and Paris (by 1700 London's population was over half a million) and the corresponding rise in the number of homosexual men living in one place led inevitably to the formation of small coteries or communities. These men began to designate certain areas of the city as meeting places; at least twenty locales in London have been identified as having been popular for sexual cruising.

The emergence of a gay community in London coincided with a new public mania for information about all things sexual. The eighteenth century saw a sudden rise in the study of venereal diseases, birth control, hermaphroditism, and all types of sexual curiosities. Theatre-goers flocked to plays which discussed adultery, prostitution, and fornication. It was the golden age of literary and pictorial pornography. This atmosphere of heightened sexual curiosity emboldened men who were seeking other men as partners, and they became less discreet in their activities. As their increasing numbers and boldness came to the attention of the average Londoner, a disapproving spotlight was shone on male-male sexuality. *Hell Upon Earth: Or the Town in an Uproar,* an anonymous pamphlet published in 1729, complained:

> They also have their Walks and Appointments, to meet and pick up one another, and their particular Houses of Resort to go to, because they dare not trust themselves in an open Tavern. . . . It would be a pretty scene to behold them in their clubs and cabals, how they assume the Air and affect the name of Madam or Miss, Betty or Molly; with a chuck under the chin, and "Oh, you bold pullet, I'll break your eggs," and then frisk and walk away.[35]

Taking their cue from the *mouches* of Paris, the London police in the 1720s began an organized program of entrapment which included the recruitment of men previously arrested for homosexual violations. One such agent was Thomas Newton, who was released from jail on the condition that he aid police in tracking down his former sexual partners. In July 1726 Newton testified at the Old Bailey about

taking two policemen to an alehouse in Moorfields which was frequented by homosexuals, and described how he caught the attention
of a patron, gave him an enticing look, and then headed for a nearby
pathway well-known as a trysting spot.

> In a little Time the Prisoner passes by, and looks hard at me, and
> at a small Distance from me, stands up against the Wall, as if he
> was going to make Water. Then by Degrees he sidles nearer and
> nearer to where I stood, 'till at last he comes close to me. *'Tis a
> very fine Night,* says he; *Aye* says I, *and so it is.* Then he takes me
> by the Hand, and after squeezing and playing with it a little (to
> which I showed no dislike) he conveys it to his Breeches, and
> puts—into it. I took fast hold, and called out to Willis and
> Stephenson, who coming up to my Assistance, we carried him
> to the Watch-house.[36]

Newton continued to cooperate with the police in their efforts to ap-
prehend other members of the homosexual community, and at least
one man betrayed by Newton was eventually executed.

The increased publicity concerning male-male sexual activity led
eventually to a demand for the enforcement of the long-dormant anti-
sodomy laws. *The London Journal* for May 14, 1726, carried a drastic
proposal for dealing with the emerging problem:

> '[T]is humbly propos'd that the following Method may not only
> destroy the Practice, but blot out the Names of the monstrous
> Wretches from under Heaven, viz. when any are Detected, Pros-
> ecuted and Convicted, that after Sentence Pronounc'd, the Com-
> mon Hangman tie him Hand and Foot before the Judge's Face in
> open Court, that a Skillful Surgeon be provided immediately to
> take out his Testicles, and that then the Hangman sear up his
> Scrotum with an hot Iron, as in Cases of burning in the Hand.[37]

The driving force behind this frenzy to punish was the morality
crusade being conducted by the Societies for the Reformation of
Manners, formed in the Tower Hamlets in 1690 with the original goal
of suppressing brothels and profanity. The Societies established a
network of moral guardians with four stewards in each ward of the
city of London who were charged to gather and disseminate information on offending neighbors. By 1701 there were nearly twenty sepa-

rate organizations, all in communication with one another, all sniffing out various forms of sin and exchanging lists of names and addresses of suspected miscreants. In their fervent campaign to root out inequity, the Societies for the Reformation of Manners soon alienated most Londoners (particularly because of the questionable tactics of their network of informers) and in 1710 the Society for the Promotion of Christian Knowledge was chartered in an effort to reform the Reformers. Using written guidelines and specimen forms, the Society for the Promotion of Christian Knowledge sought to curb the worst abuses of the informants—while promoting the same ultimate goal. The moral crusade received support from the highest level of society when King William declared, "We most earnestly desire and shall endeavour a general reformation of manners."[38]

King William had good reason to make a show of support for the Society's efforts. After Queen Mary's death in 1694 women were rarely seen at his court, and the exclusively male enclave had begun to cause eyebrows to be raised. In France it was rumored that the English court had turned into a "chateau de derriére."[39] Invited to come from Holland to assume the English throne, William and Mary had always been considered outsiders. After Mary's death, William's court was increasingly viewed as "foreign, expensive, and rather sodomitical," in the words of Dennis Rubini. "William's two principal favorites gained over a quarter-million acres of land," Rubini writes, "allegedly in part for sodomitical sexual services rendered to the monarch."[40]

The various societies dedicated to moral reform ignored the irregularities of the royal court, primarily because William's support was needed to assure the continued success of their efforts. They concentrated instead on a campaign of innuendo and intimidation aimed at common folk. The societies hired informants to infiltrate London's homosexual subculture to entrap individuals and to pass along intelligence to the constabulary about times and places of homosexual gatherings. In 1707 alone they entrapped nearly 100 men. Unable to encounter every practicing sinner, the societies extended their intimidation by issuing religious tracts such as *The Sodomites Shame and Doom* which claimed that they had compiled lists of known sodomites which would be published—along with their "places of abode"— if the men did not immediately repent and reform.

As is frequently the case with moral crusades, the reformers succeeded only in encouraging the very vices they were seeking to re-
press. By publishing the names of areas of London where sexual
cruising was rampant, the societies unwittingly created guidebooks
for homosexual socializing. Men unfamiliar with London (or Londoners new to the scene) were instructed that they could find like-
minded men merely by going to the Royal Exchange, Moorfields,
Lincoln's Inn, the south side of St. James's Park or the arcades of
Covent Garden. The increased danger of being arrested and prosecuted created a bond and a sense of common identity for an otherwise
diverse group of men, and led many to join together in informal private clubs to meet in less public places. By 1738 the reforming zeal of
the societies had run its course and they were disbanded, but they left
behind a newly energized homosexual community.[41]

Just as in Paris certain taverns became identified as homosexual
gathering places, in London there were pubs as early as 1700 which
had a primarily homosexual clientele and were known as molly houses
("molly" had originally been a slang expression for a female prostitute, but by the eighteenth century it was the most common term for
an effeminate man who engaged in sex with other men). The existence of the molly houses was brought to the general public's attention in February 1725/26 after a raid on an establishment in Field
Lane, Holborn, run by Margaret "Mother" Clap. Mother Clap's molly
house had many bedrooms and a main room large enough to accommodate fiddling and dancing for the thirty to forty men who would
gather there, particularly on Sunday evenings. A constable who infil-
trated the social group reported on what he saw the evening of November 14, 1725:

> I found between 40 and 50 Men making Love to one another, as
> they call'd it. Sometimes they would sit on one another's Laps,
> Kissing in a lewd Manner, and using their Hands indecently.
> Then they would get up, Dance and make Curtsies, and mimick
> the voices of Women. *O, Fie, Sir!—Pray, Sir.—Dear Sir. Lord,
> how can you serve me so?—I swear I'll cry out.—You're a
> wicked Devil.—And you're a bold Face.—Eh ye little dear Toad!
> Come, buss!*—Then they'd hug, and play, and toy, and go out by
> Couples into another Room on the same Floor, to be marry'd, as
> they call'd it.[42]

The mollies developed their own slang, which they called the Female Dialect. Sexual cruising grounds were known as "the markets" where one could go to "pick up" partners or "trade," or perhaps "put the bite" on someone (arrange for sex). The men took on feminine names which were campily at odds with their actual professions: Princess Seraphina was a butcher, Queen Irons was a blacksmith, the Countess of Camomile was a waiter, Fanny Murray was a bargeman, and Lucy Cooper was a coal-heaver. The molly houses in London seem to have followed the pattern of their counterparts in Paris, being the preserve primarily of middle-class merchants and tradesmen who created an elaborate fictional world which both mocked and emulated elegant court society.

For men of wealth and social standing (and for those young, attractive, and resourceful enough to attach themselves as companions) London offered private clubs where homosexual liaisons could be carried out in relative safety behind sedate mahogany doors and thick velvet curtains. Herman Melville offers a fictional peek inside one of these secret retreats in his novel *Redburn: His First Voyage, Being the Sailor-Boy Confessions and Reminiscences of the Son-of-a-Gentleman, in the Merchant Service*. As with all of Melville's novels, the homoerotic subtext is so deeply encoded that the average reader might be unaware of what is being described; the American sailor-boy's "confession" is almost inaudible to anyone not possessing the proper code. In one dizzying chapter titled "A Mysterious Night in London" the narrator is whisked to the capital by the elegant but secretive Harry Bolton, a young man of apparently good breeding whom Redburn encounters in one of Liverpool's seedy dockside taverns. Bolton, in newly acquired clothes and a false beard, drags his companion on a puzzling adventure to a private men's club.

The location of the London club is a secret—Bolton mutters the address to the cabdriver "in an under tone"—and the building can be identified primarily by the purple light illuminating its high steps. Bolton parks Redburn in one of the ornate halls and disappears. "While I thus sat alone," the narrator recalls,

> I observed one of the waiters eyeing me a little impertinently, as I thought, and as if he saw something queer about me . . . all the time I felt my face burning with embarrassment, and for the time, I must have looked very guilty of something. But spite of this, I kept looking boldly out of my eyes, and straight through

my blushes, and observed that every now and then little parties were made up among the gentlemen, and they retired into the rear of the house, as if going to a private apartment.[43]

Most dazzling of all to the young man are the paintings hung in a secluded chamber upstairs:

They were such pictures as the high-priests, for a bribe, showed to Alexander in the innermost shrine of the white temple in the Libyan oasis: such pictures as the pontiff of the sun strove to hide from Cortez, when, sword in hand, he burst open the sanctorum of the pyramid-fane at Cholula: such pictures as you may still see, perhaps, in the central alcove of the excavated mansion of Pansa, in Pompeii—in that part of it called by Varro *the hollow of the house:* such pictures as Martial and Suetonius mention as being found in the private cabinet of the Emperor Tiberius: such pictures as are delineated on the bronze medals, to this day dug up on the ancient island of Capreæ: such pictures as you might have beheld in an arched recess, leading from the left hand of the secret side-gallery of the temple of Aphrodite in Corinth.[44]

These images from the left hand of Aphrodite are not described in any further detail, but Melville knew that a segment of his reading public would encounter the description, and understand.

Melville's elegant men's club had a real counterpart that was the center of a scandal which rocked London and provided ample grist for the tabloid mill. The White Swan on Vere Street, Clare Market was not as elegant as Melville's fictional "Aladdin's Palace," but it drew its clientele in part from the higher levels of London society. Early in 1810 two Londoners, James Cook and a man known only as Yardley, opened a combination tavern and male brothel. Their interest was strictly financial. Such clubs had proved to be extremely lucrative to their owners (at least four other similar clubs were operating in different parts of London); the two men hoped to make a large amount of money from men willing to pay to enjoy a private meeting place. At his subsequent trial Cook, a married man, declared to the court, "I own I participated in all the guilt except the final completion of it, which is abhorrent to my nature. I am, therefore, the more criminal, because I had no unnatural inclinations to gratify: I was prompted by *Avarice* only."[45]

While the White Swan was a brothel staffed with male prostitutes, not all of the encounters on the premises were of a financial nature. Many men patronized the club simply as a way of picking up other men, and then either rented a room or retired elsewhere. Where the molly houses of the early- and mid-eighteenth century tended to draw men from a similar social class, establishments such as the White Swan in the early nineteenth century attracted the patronage of all levels, from wealthy aristocrats to unemployed servants. This mixing of the social classes was a particular source of public ire, as was the perceived attack on the family unit. In his 1813 pamphlet *The Phoenix of Sodom, or the Vere Street Coterie,* Robert Holloway fumed: "It seems that many of these wretches are married; and frequently, when they are together, make their wives, who they call *Tommies,* topics of ridicule. . . ."[46]

The White Swan had been open in Vere Street for only six months when on July 8, 1810, it was raided by constables, and the owner James Cook, one of the waiters, and at least twenty-five patrons were arrested. Most were eventually set free, either for lack of evidence or because they could afford to bribe the authorities. All of the patrons who were eventually convicted and punished were from the lower-middle class. Six of the convicted men (including Cook) were sentenced to prison terms of one to three years, and exposure at the pillory.

During the course of the eighteenth century a change occurred in the London public's perception of homosexual activity. The change was gradual, with no clear demarcations, and it was neither uniform nor universal, but it had a profound effect on the way men involved in the homosexual subculture lived their lives. Prior to the persecutions instigated by the Societies for the Reform of Manners, most Londoners accepted the European pattern which recognized that certain aristocratic rakes could enjoy sexual relations with both women and adolescent males without loss of masculine status. This type of bisexual libertinism presupposed that the rake's homosexual encounters were restricted to liaisons with prepubescent boys, and that in these encounters the rake always took the active role. (The onset of puberty in males was around age fifteen in the eighteenth century.) Such men were considered scandalous, but they forfeited none of their male or class privilege. By 1750, however, a shift had occurred in the public's perception. The rake (dandified, dashing, perverse) had become the fop (effete, effusive, perverted).[47] Effeminate aristocrats found themselves tolerated socially but excluded from any real political power, and they were frequently the target of blackmail by poorer men. While the aristocrats usually won out over their blackmailers when a case came to trial, an accusation of sodomy—even if disproved—could be enough to cause a man to lose his place in society, and men who had sufficient resources often fled to the Continent or were sent there by embarrassed relatives.[48]

Without the widespread revelations about molly culture it is likely that aristocratic rakes could have maintained their high lifestyle throughout the eighteenth century. A certain liberty in the choice of sex partners was, after all, one of the entitlements of the aristocracy, and so long as their partners also included women (a wife, mistresses, and prostitutes) the men could escape most public censure. The social status of the men, and their evident small numbers, encouraged indulgence on the part of the common people. Even though the laws officially prescribed draconian punishments for sodomy, it was fully *expected* that the upper classes would make homosexual overtures to some segments of the lower. It was assumed, for example, that a valet would be sexually available to his master if the master was so inclined. In 1765 a drunken brawl resulted when two young noblemen, Sir Thomas Gascoigne and the future Lord Dorchester, made sexual advances to the wrong type of servant: "Exacting such offices from their coachman as the *valets de place* only are used to render. . . ."[49] Central to this general tolerance was a belief that gender roles were not being violated when an active rake took to bed a passive (and socially inferior) adolescent.

When the molly house scandals hit the headlines, Londoners were shocked to learn that men of their own social class frequently engaged in sexual relations with other men of the same age and class, and that grown men not only took the receptive role in sexual relations, but they also reveled in assuming an exaggerated female persona. That a burly butcher could become Princess Seraphina was a transgression with complex social consequences (if carried to its logical extreme) in a society in which class and gender played such a prominent role. As the stories of the cross-dressing revels at molly houses made the rounds, the London public gradually came to the recognition that male-male sexuality was more widespread—and therefore potentially more disruptive—than a few isolated incidents of anal intercourse committed by jaded lords on their adolescent servants. With the realization that an entire subculture existed, the focus shifted from the act itself to the people committing the act, and the result was outrage at the confusion of gender roles. Temporary or situational man-boy homosexuality could be ignored as a perverted but acknowledged aristocratic privilege. Sustained aping of the female role was simply an outrage.[50]

Complicating this attempt to define and police gender roles was the rise of the so-called cult of sensibility, a movement among the educated elite (and those who aspired to refinement) to encourage a heightened awareness of an individual man or woman's place in society and in the natural world. As Maximillian E. Novak and Anne Mellor describe it, the notion of sensibility covered a wide range of responses: "as civility and politeness, as refined moral virtue, as compassion and sympathy, as the restraint of passion in the face of bestial bodily desire, or, in its more negative connotations, as sentimentality, as affectation, as excessive passion, even as cruelty."[51] What the cult of sensibility did *not* countenance or privilege was transgressive sexuality between men, which remained a separate issue, unconnected to such responses as sympathy for the suffering of the poor or elation at the beauty of a sunset.[52] Men who found themselves emotionally and sexually drawn to other men may well have located those feelings in the realm of sensibility as a way of explaining (to themselves or to others) their strong attraction, but the link to homoeroticism was by no means imperative. A man could ardently pursue a life of sensibility while having no homosexual tendencies at all. Many of the tenets of male sensibility sound like the modern concept of "getting in touch with one's feminine side," but sensibility did not manifest itself in the eighteenth century in a multiplication of fops and mollies. The Man of Feeling sought to become not more feminine, but less brutish.

Because it was fashionable for men to gush over a field of daffodils or weep at the plight of orphans, it is at times difficult to parse the language of sensibility where male-male affection is concerned. Modern readers who wish to dismiss the apparent homoeroticism in some eighteenth-century correspondence are quick to subsume under the rubric of mere "sensibility" any rhetoric which suggests male-male passion, yet as George Haggerty argues in his contribution to the collection *Passionate Encounters in a Time of Sensibility,* such language may at times have reflected the "erotics of friendship"—not a fashionable literary convention but a true expression of love and desire.[53] Perhaps not homosexuality as we currently conceive it, but something moving in that direction.

While the cult of sensibility dealt primarily with the inward response to outward phenomena, another movement arose concurrently which focused almost entirely on ostentatious show manifested in a lavish pageant with distinctly *political* overtones. In London in the mid-1760s a group of rich young members of Almack's Club returned from their Grand Tour enamored of everything Italian and appalled by the coarse jingoism of the average Englishman. The young men founded the Macaroni Club in satiric rejection of the Anglophilia of roast beef eaters. Though it began as an elaborate joke on the part of a small coterie of friends, the club by 1772 had taken on an unanticipated social significance thanks to the popular press. The term "Macaroni" was quickly applied to anyone who pursued a lifestyle of luxurious consumption, particularly the younger members of the aristocracy who seemed increasingly un-English in their swooning over Continental fads and fashions.

Publications such as *The Town and Country Magazine* played to the prejudices of both the urban bourgeoisie and the country gentry in ridiculing the fastidious pretensions of the fashionable young elite. Central to the rejection of everything that the Macaronis represented was a feeling that England was being overwhelmed by the products of her colonies, that the country was losing its "Englishness" in its pursuit of ever more exotic articles of consumption. Around 1773 a publication titled *The Macaroni Jester, and Pantheon of Wit* lamented:

> A man who has money, may have at once every delicate, every dainty, and every ornamental Beauty of the four Quarters of the World. Asia, Europe, Africa, and America, are cultivated and ransacked to indulge the Inhabitants in every luxury; and when this Island shall be conquered and depopulated, how will the rising World wonder at the luxurious Lives which English Peasants led, when they are informed, that their common Drink was composed of a Plant which grew in China, drawn with hot Water, and mixed with the Juice of the West India Sugar-cane made into a hard Consistence; and that Liquor is called *Tea!*[54]

Men who pursued the lifestyle of the Macaroni defined themselves by an obsessive, effeminate display of fashion which was paraded in a competitive spectacle intended only to impress other men. They wore Parisian suits of rich patterned velvet, closely fitted with tight sleeves and elongated waists, and flamboyant hats festooned with dramatically swooping feathers. The feathered hats in particular became synonymous with "private, venal and luxurious consumption."[55] *Town and Country Magazine* reported with disgust that a Macaroni "renders his sex dubious by the extravagance of his appearance."[56] Moreover, the fad quickly spread beyond the elite confines of the young male aristocracy. "The infection of St. James's was soon caught in the city," warned a contemporary critic, "and we have now Macaronies of every denomination, from the colonel of the Train'd Bands down to the errand boy."[57]

This effeminacy was considered to be as great a threat to the nation as was the pursuit of exotic luxuries, for without a sufficiently manly military force England had little hope of retaining its preeminence in Europe or of controlling the insurrections which threatened its colonies. In 1775 *The Matrimonial Magazine* looked at the state of the English military and lamented, "Our modern monkey of manhood, is by name a soldier; but never felt any ball but a wash ball; nor ever smelt powder, but hair-powder; who never saw any service but that of the table and the toilet; who never had any wounds but from minikin pins and Cupid's darts; who never marched further than the gay parade."[58]

The Macaroni phenomenon of eighteenth-century London found its way into American popular culture by way of a jaunty song still sung by every American school child. One otherwise incomprehensible verse of the patriotic "Yankee Doodle Dandy" declares:

> Yankee Doodle came to town
> Riding on a pony,
> Stuck a feather in his hat
> And called it Macaroni.

The origins of "Yankee Doodle" are obscure, but it is generally believed to predate the American Revolution by several decades. It is frequently attributed to Dr. Richard Shuckburgh, who emigrated from England sometime before 1735. The song appeared in different

versions over time, its many verses adapted and supplemented to reflect current events, but it played an especially prominent role during
the American Revolution. British troops under Lord Percy are said to
have played it when they marched out of Boston in April of 1775. The
words clearly mock Americans as country bumpkins, and many historians have therefore assumed that the lyrics were of English origin.
J. A. Leo Lemay has made a persuasive argument that the words are
American, and intentionally ironic. "From the seventeenth century to
the mid-twentieth," Lemay writes, "Americans have been keenly
aware of English criticisms of their supposed barbarism. Colonial
Americans learned to reply to English snobbery by deliberately pos-
turing as unbelievably ignorant yokels. Thus, if the English believed
the stereotype, they would be taken in by the Americans. And, of
course, if they were taken in, the Americans had reversed the snobbery and proven that the English were credulous and foolish."[59]

Lemay explains in a footnote that the best known verse of "Yankee
Doodle" "probably dates from the vogue of the macaroni in the early
1770s," but fails to explore the implications. If we assume that the
words are American and written as ironic self-mockery, what does
that tell us about the colonists who made the song so popular? On a
literal level they are saying that the bumpkin was foolish enough to
believe that by sticking an ordinary feather in his hat he could cut a
figure as a fashionable London "swell" despite his tattered home-
spun. But if we presume irony, a whole new vista of other implications arises. How is it that an ignorant yokel could be so familiar with
the cutting edge of British fashion? Clearly here is someone very *au
courant* despite his distance from Europe. Lemay estimates that the
verse was added to the song in 1774, only two years after the image of
the Macaroni emerged in the popular press of London. But why
would the American Yankee Doodle *want* to be identified as a Macaroni?

One of the chief objections to the Macaronis was that they rejected
good English roast beef and instead ran after all the exotic imports
that an expanding trade offered. In other words, the Macaronis delighted in the sugar and tobacco and rum which were the basis of the
colonial economies. Moreover, the anti-Macaroni faction was composed primarily of the country gentry and the merchant class, the very
people who had driven many of the colonists to emigrate in the first
place. Probably most persuasive, though, was the connection with the

opposition British Whig party, many of whose members were considered to be followers of the Macaroni fad. The Whigs supported the rights of the American colonies against the king. So closely did they associate themselves with the revolutionary cause that the Whigs adopted as their official colors blue and buff, the colors of the Continental Army uniforms.

All of which aligned the American colonists with the British Macaronis—and placed them uncomfortably close to the befeathered modern monkeys of manhood, the luxury loving exotics of dubious gender. Just how much of a dandy was Yankee Doodle prepared to become? The answer may be found in the rousing call—and barely-concealed ribaldry—of the chorus which immediately follows the most famous verse:

> Yankee Doodle, keep it up
> Yankee Doodle dandy
> Mind the music and the step
> And with the girls be handy.

One of the attractions of the Macaroni fad was that it allowed its adherents to flirt with the trappings of transgressive sexual behavior without actually making an irretractable statement about their own proclivities. This convenient ambiguity was captured in the *Oxford Magazine* of June 1770 in its censorious description of the movement:

> There is indeed a kind of animal, neither male nor female, a thing of the neuter gender, lately started up amongst us. It is called a Macaroni. It talks without meaning, it smiles without pleasantry, it eats without appetite, it rides without exercise, it wenches without passion.[60]

Observers might wonder about a Macaroni's lack of passion in wenching, but they did not necessarily assume that his sexual interests lay elsewhere.

With the public's attention fixed on the ambiguous conduct of the Macaronis and on the outrageous, flamboyant behavior of the fops and mollies, it was relatively easy for less effeminate men to pass undetected. A man who felt sexual interest in other men but who had never dressed in velvet and lace nor taken part in the revelries in the backroom of Mother Clap's tavern did not think of himself as a "fop" or a "molly," convinced that such conduct had nothing in common with his own sexual activities. The law courts aided in this self-deception. The convention of silence surrounding the *crimen innominatum* restricted judges, barristers, and magistrates from giving any details of the crime being tried (lest innocent minds learn of things they would otherwise never consider in the first place). The law writers expended their rhetoric instead in describing their disgust at the very *idea* of the crime: an

> abomination that shocks our Natures, and puts our Modesty to the Blush, to see it so commonly perpetrated, is the *Devilish and Unnatural Sin of Buggery,* a Crime that sinks Man below the *Basest* Epithet, is so Foul that it admits of no Aggravation, and cannot be expressed in its Horror, but by the *Doleful Shrieks and Groans of the Damned.*[61]

The crime was obviously grievous, but it was difficult for a layperson to understand just which acts fell under its interdiction.

A man who occasionally enjoyed a pleasurable fumble with a male bedmate would find it difficult to believe that his gin-soaked fun might bring down God's wrath in a hail of fire and brimstone. What he was doing must, therefore, not be this foul practice which the courts were (obscurely) describing. Such men could easily reject the label of "molly" or "bugger" or even "sodomite"—but then there was nothing else to call themselves. Without the words to describe what it was that they were doing—much less to label their inherent sexual natures—most of these men simply stopped thinking too deeply about the topic.[62]

At times when the persecutions of the overtly effeminate became too intense, the more masculine-acting men took care to stay away from the public cruising grounds for fear of being exposed. Some of them even joined in the persecutions by denouncing other men and cooperating with police entrapment operations. As the stereotype of the effeminate molly became more firmly fixed in the public's imagination, it provided a shield behind which masculine-acting men could hide from outraged citizens—and perhaps even from themselves. In the words of historian Richard Davenport-Hines:

The alternatives [in the eighteenth century], then, were to be so discreet as to be invisible, or to practice self-deception in a way that sometimes could only [be] maintained by acts of violence against one's sexual partners, or to conform to a stereotype (quaintly dressed, physically weak, giggly) that satisfied outsiders that one was powerless.[63]

When these unattractive alternatives were transported to a country of revolutionaries, nonconformists, and rugged free-thinkers, the peculiarly American species of man-loving men was born.

The origins of the word "gay" as a synonym for homosexual may be found in this evolution of English popular opinion concerning sodomites. Lexicographers have been unable to trace with any certainty the exact route of this now-common meaning, but evidence suggests that it occurred at the time that the molly subculture first came to public consciousness. The *Oxford English Dictionary* includes in the definitions of gay, "Addicted to social pleasures and dissipations. Often *euphemistically:* Of loose or immoral life . . . a man given to revelling or self-indulgence."[64] While the editors give an example of this use as early as 1637, it is not until the eighteenth century that a truly pejorative sense is attached to the word. The *beau monde* or the *ton* were denounced for their sexual promiscuity, extravagant couture and conspicuous consumption. In these fervent denunciations of the fashionable world, "gay"—which had previously carried the morally neutral meaning of light, airy, and joyful—took on a distinctly negative connotation, being used to describe everything which was *not* sober, pious, and morally straight.

Almost by definition, it was impossible to be "gay" in the early years of the eighteenth century without having substantial monetary resources (or without living beyond one's means), but as social and political developments in England replaced the influence of the aristocracy with that of the wealthy merchant class, the close link between money and profligacy began to weaken. The voracious, bisexual aristocratic rake became a laughable anachronism, out of place in the new morality of the mercantile bourgeoisie and the cold rationalism of the Enlightenment. It fell to the sexual underworld to step forward and seize the banner of extravagance and exuberant licentiousness—and with it, the term "gay" as a boastful description of itself. Though their finery was more stage costume than haute couture, and

their decadence more playfulness than depravity, the sexual underworld used sham extravagance as a way of setting themselves apart
from the dull, oppressive bourgeois world. In the process "gay" became an encoded term for "homosexual."

America lagged behind England in this process, but not by far. In
1830 when Nathaniel Hawthorne published his story "My Kinsman,
Major Molineux" he demonstrated that the link between "gay" and a
flamboyant theatricality was already in place. The story's narrator,
young Robin, encounters "many gay and gallant figures" dressed in
"embroidered garments of showy colors, enormous periwigs, gold-
laced hats, and silver-hilted swords." Less than twenty years later
when Herman Melville published his novel *Redburn* (discussed previously) the term was understood by at least some readers in its new encoded homosexual meaning. When Redburn brings his handsome,
sexually ambivalent friend Bolton to Captain Riga to ask for a job,
Melville can hint at the reason for the old man's eagerness to employ
Bolton by calling the Captain that *"gallant, gay deceiver"* and "that
gay Lothario of all inexperienced, sea-going youths."[65] Melville uses
italics in the original, calling attention to the fact that he is not merely
describing the Captain as light-hearted and joyful. Since Melville
was drawing on his personal experiences as a sailor from thirty years
earlier, we can assume that "gay" had been adopted by the sexual subculture of America by the early years of the nineteenth century. Certainly by mid-century, the author could use the word in the new sense,
confident that at least a certain subset of his readers would understand
the implication.

Chapter 3

Rum, Sodomy, and the Lash

His Excellency the Commander in Chief approves the sentence and with Abhorrence & Detestation of such Infamous Crimes orders Lieutt. Enslin to be drummed out of Camp tomorrow morning by all the Drummers and Fifers in the Army never to return.

Court-Martial of Lt. Enslin

Don't talk to me about tradition. Tradition in the British Navy is nothing but rum, sodomy and the lash.

Winston Churchill

Of Churchill's trilogy of military tradition—rum, sodomy, and the lash—much has been written to document the extent to which the United States armed forces during the early years were steeped in the first and the third. Less has been written about the prevalence of male-male sexuality, but the historical record yields ample evidence that this, too, was part of the military experience.

Drunkenness was a way of life in the military, the way most men dealt with the deprivations which were part of being a soldier or a sailor. Alcohol was also employed by the military brass as a way of controlling the men. It was used as a sedative to dull their discontent and as a reward for good conduct—both stick and carrot. In his exploration of the many reasons why men fought so valiantly during the Revolutionary War, Robert Middlekauff lists liquor as one of the motivating factors. Officers on both sides of the conflict sometimes helped their men by issuing a gill (one-quarter pint) of liquid courage just before an engagement, and as a result some men entered combat "with their senses deadened by rum."[1] But as effective as alcohol proved to be in stiffening resolve and numbing discontent, it also led to innumerable discipline problems. The vast majority of courts-martial during and after the war were for offenses directly or indirectly linked to drunkenness.

In his journal detailing his tenure as surgeon's mate at Fort Defiance in 1795, Joseph Gardiner Andrews describes a drinking binge indulged in by soldiers when a barrel of "Cyder" arrived from Detroit. Nine men pooled their money to buy the entire barrel, and proceeded to drink about four gallons each. "It may well be imagined," Andrews writes, "that Madam Cloacina did not want for Devotees this day."[2] The reference to the Roman goddess of public toilets is suggestive, but it appears to be Andrews's own coining and not a generally used reference to men who frequent such places for sexual purposes. Still, the choice of words is curious. Andrews was a Harvard graduate (Class of 1785) with the usual background in classics, and if he is referring to vomiting brought on by too much alcohol consumption, one might expect a reference here to the Roman vomitoria. The term "devotees" certainly implies repeated action, rather than an isolated incident of overindulgence. However, in the absence of other references to Cloacina it is probably best to assume a nonsexual reference in this case.

Andrews goes on to supply a vivid picture of Christmas festivities among officers on the frontier. His entry for December 26, 1795, reads:

> Major Hunt & myself having promised to our waiters a frolic if they conducted well at Christmas, gave them their whiskey & necessary provisions; & sending the relics of yesterday up to Mr. McDougall's, in Compy. with Capt. Gaines, dined there very happily; Mr. QM Wilson arrived just after dinner & we drank 4 bottles of wine at McDougalls & took 4 others at Capt. Gaines'; it may be supposed that at 9 oClock pm we all felt lively.[3]

In time continued alcohol consumption was much more damaging to military discipline than a few hangovers from lively parties. Many men found themselves reduced to a craven dependence and were willing to go to any length to procure a drink. The commandant at Fort Bellefontaine was forced to issue a stern warning:

> The Commanding officer is under the necessity of adopting Strenuous Measures to put a Stop to the intemperance and

discipation in which his Soldiers have of late indulged in an unusual degree—He observes with disgust, a disposition in many,
to lurk about the Stores, ready to undertake any piece of Service,
however dirty, for the Consideration of a dram—To prevent this
practice, So mean & degrading to the profession of a Soldier, he
forbids his men undertaking or performing any Jobs of work,
wating on or attending any Citizen, without Special permission
from the Commanding officer of the Company.[4]

If the United States Army during this period was a place of anomie
and isolation relieved occasionally by drunken male bonding, the
Navy was much, much worse—and for similar reasons. Naval historian James E. Valle has described naval life in the early period as
"stultifying, lackluster, and boring," with life aboard ship in particular "physically exhausting, drab, [and] claustrophobic."[5] The average
seaman had little chance of developing esprit de corps while on active
duty. Sailors signed on for duty aboard a particular ship for a cruise of
three years; their enlistments terminated at the end of the cruise and
they were paid off—even if the cruise lasted less than the full enlist-
ment period. Ships were crowded and conditions were harsh. Because of the tremendous manpower required to work the guns, the
crew of an American warship averaged around 500 men, though only
50 were required to sail her at any one time. This left 450 men with
little to do but make-work projects for long periods on a voyage. Control was maintained by a handful of officers who hoped to keep the
crew in line through the liberal use of the lash and by fostering a mild
state of alcoholic stupor.

As in the army, the navy distributed a daily ration of alcohol—
a half pint of whiskey or grog for each sailor, or twenty-three gallons
per man per year by one estimate—which resulted in the same discipline problems. When the men supplemented the official ration with
their own contraband rum, the mild stupor frequently turned into aggression and violence. It was nearly impossible for the army to stem
the sale of illicit intoxicants, but a ship provided a circumscribed
venue in which (theoretically) it was possible to monitor and control
access to alcohol. A ship at sea was relatively secure, but once in port
it faced the same challenges as a land-based army. Sutlers could be
forbidden to bring whiskey or rum aboard when they set up their temporary stores, but once the sailors were released on shore leave, all
control was lost. Giving up hope of preventing binge drinking in port,

the officers tried instead to prevent the sailors from smuggling alcohol aboard for later consumption. It became necessary to search each man when he returned from a visit ashore in order to intercept as many bottles as possible. Wily sailors quickly devised alternate modes of transportation for their libations. One of the most popular was to fashion a "snake"—an animal's intestine which had been cleaned, tied off, and filled with liquor. These could be easily hidden from pat-down searches, particularly if they were strapped to the sailor's leg, extending from his crotch to his calf. Though the men were (as a traveler observed in 1842) "always examined by passing the hand over every part of their bodies," they could be reasonably sure that their loose bellbottoms and the officers' modesty would allow the snakes to pass undetected if placed near their groins.[6]

Another popular smuggling method was to send casks of alcohol on board disguised as barrels of paint, turpentine, or linseed oil. Chaplain Charles Rockwell described an incident in which sailors filled several casks with a mixture of whiskey, olive oil, and white paint, a concoction that could pass the inspection of even the nosiest officer. Once the casks were stowed in the paint locker, the olive oil rose to the surface while the lead-based paint settled to the bottom. The men then inserted a straw into the cask to draw off the whiskey from the middle. The sailors called this practice "sucking the monkey." The etymology is unclear. A "monkey" was a small cask for grog, but the expression originally referred to the sailors' practice of sipping rum out of a hairy coconut that had been emptied of milk, which would give the appearance of fellating a monkey.[7]

The deleterious effects of alcohol were recognized from the very early years of the navy's establishment, but no clear consensus could be formed on how the problem should be attacked. Some members of Congress, although concerned about alcohol abuse, also saw the benefits gained from moderate use. The chairman of the House naval committee felt a complete ban on drinking among sailors would reduce their efficiency and impair their bravery.[8] Some feared that the sailors were so profoundly addicted that any attempt to keep them from liquor would result in mutiny and shipboard riots. Dr. Thomas Harris suggested that a gradual introduction of temperance might work. Young boys aboard navy ships were traditionally issued a full grog ration along with more seasoned sailors, almost assuring that they would eventually become habitual drinkers. Harris suggested abandoning the older sailors to their vice while striving to save the boys and young men by refusing the grog ration to anyone under the age of twenty-one. Some reformers suggested that sailors might be willing to accept the substitution of strong tea, or perhaps a mixture of rice and molasses.

The arguments of the naval temperance crusaders fell on deaf ears throughout the antebellum period. It was not until the summer of 1862, at the height of the Civil War, that Abraham Lincoln signed into law a bill abolishing the grog ration and offering sailors as a substitute a pay increase of five cents a day.

The abuse of alcohol was inextricably linked to the frequent flogging of soldiers and sailors. Winston Churchill was not exaggerating when he spoke of the central role played by the lash in Britain's efforts to discipline its men. British courts-martial could impose sentences of as many as 2,000 lashes—enough to cause death. In an effort to be more humane, the Articles of War adopted by the Continental Army in 1775 limited the number to thirty-nine, the number prescribed by Mosaic law. Unfortunately, this nod to the principles of humanitarian reform proved an ineffective means of controlling the men; Washington complained to Congress that many of his soldiers were so inured to pain that they "declared that for a bottle of Rum they would undergo a Second operation."[9] As a response Congress revised the Articles in 1776, raising the flogging limit to 100 stripes.

Milder punishments usually involved some sort of stigmatization or humiliation—wearing one's coat inside out, a sign around the neck reading "Thief" or "Deserter," digging vaults or latrines, wearing a log attached to one's leg, partial shaving of the head and eyebrows, or branding. The ultimate punishment of death was inflicted either by hanging or by a military firing squad. One particularly severe punishment entailed both humiliation and great pain. Some men were sentenced to "ride the wooden horse," which meant they were seated astride a narrow horizontal board or pole suspended above the ground, the upper edge of which was sometimes sharpened. The soldier's hands were tied behind his back and sometimes extra weight was attached to both legs, increasing the pressure on the groin. Although this penalty was rarely inflicted for longer than fifteen minutes, one court-martial sentenced a man to ride the wooden horse for three days in succession, two hours each day with a musket tied to each foot.[10]

By far the most frequently used punishment was the lash. In the army the standard punishment was 100 lashes, though sentences of fifty or even twenty-five lashes were handed down for some minor offenses. A court-martial could adjust the severity of the standard 100 lashes by ordering that they be laid on slowly or especially hard, or (more commonly) that they be administered twenty-five a day for four days in succession, thus assuring that the soldier's back was only partially healed and therefore particularly tender. A few courts ordered the wounds to be doused with salt water. The typical cat-o'-nine-tails consisted of thick cords, each with several knots tied into it. The man inflicting the flogging would swing the cat twice around his own head, then bring it down sharply on the victim's back. He would then draw the tails through the fingers of his left hand to rid them of lacerated flesh and blood, pause, and strike again. The ritual was gruesome and impressive, and was almost always carried out with great ceremony before the entire assembly of men. In his diary British Lieutenant John Le Couteur recorded one of his early observations of a flogging:

> The lash lacerated his back speedily and the blood flowed freely. He stood close in front of me, the inward groan, at each lash, from being stifled, went sufficiently to my heart but, soon after, the Drummer, in swinging his Cat of Nine Tails, switched a quantity of his blood over my Face and Belts. I fainted away like a Sick girl to my own great horror and Confusion but it was not unnatural after all. The Officers laughed at me but the men did not.[11]

To be able impassively to observe—or, especially, to endure—a flogging was a sign of manhood and a mark of inclusion in the military brotherhood. Joseph Gardner Andrews recorded in his journal in 1795 about the establishment of the "Damnation Club" at Post Vincennes (Fort Knox) "where an essential requisite was to be ever ready to receive 100 lashes if it might be the means of procuring a pint of whiskey for the good of said society."[12]

Sometimes the beating was inflicted by the entire military unit. When a man was sentenced to run the gauntlet, his fellow soldiers lined up in two rows armed with rods or switches. The prisoner was required to walk the length of the rows, his pace regulated by two soldiers with bayonets, one pointed at this chest and one at his back.

Sentences usually called for running (or more accurately, walking) the gauntlet two to four times, though more severe punishments were sometimes imposed. Flogging and the gauntlet were used with about equal frequency by the United States Army, but the two methods of punishment reflected two very different social dynamics. To understand the message being delivered, we need to view the military rituals involved in what Foucault labels "the festival of punishment" or "the theatrical representation of pain."[13] In submitting to the gauntlet a man was being punished by his peers in expiation for a crime committed against the military unit as a whole (theft of community property, cowardice under fire, etc.). The whole unit had been transgressed against; the whole unit would be the agent of punishment. Neither the number of people wielding lashes or switches nor the fervor of the punishers was the crucial factor. As a result of enduring the gauntlet, a soldier expiated his crime by submitting himself to the comrades he had offended, and through their punishment he was welcomed back into the group.

An entirely different ritual was being played out through flogging. Flogging was a more severe penalty not because the individual applying the lash might do so with greater vigor than a host of fellow soldiers, but because the rank of the punisher brought about an even greater degradation in the status of the person being punished. No institution in American society had (and has) a more rigorously observed social hierarchy than the military. In the army of the eighteenth century that hierarchy was composed of four distinct strata. On the highest level were the three ranks of regular uniformed personnel: officers, noncommissioned officers, and enlisted men. Below these were two groups of noncombatant male employees: artificers (carpenters, ironworkers, gunsmiths, etc.) and waiters (the personal servants employed by the officers). Next came the musicians—the drummers and fifers used for mass communication (sounding reveille, providing the cadence for marching, signaling attack or retreat, etc.). Finally, at the bottom of the hierarchy, were the women employed to wash the unit's clothes, nurse the sick, and cook much of the food.

As Lieutenant Le Couteur recorded in his diary, the lash was usually applied by a drummer. The enlisted man being flogged submitted himself to punishment from someone who was his inferior in rank, and therefore during the administration of the flogging the prisoner was effectively lowered in status beneath that of his punisher. The only people lower than drummers were the washerwomen and female cooks. Flogging by a drummer was in effect a form of social emasculation, a very public degradation which was almost always performed in front of the entire military unit. The punishment could be adjusted to be even more shame inducing. Lashes were usually applied to a soldier's bare back, but when a court-martial wanted to inflict a particularly severe humiliation, they would order the whipping to be applied to his "posterior" or "naked breech."

When the prisoner was himself a drummer (and particularly if he was very young), the punishment might be mitigated even if his crime was of a serious nature. William Walker was convicted of repeated drunkenness, insolent language, and mutiny in striking a sergeant. Though he was sentenced to "ninety-nine Lashes on his bare Back" his commanding officer reduced the punishment to fifty lashes, "the Corporal punishment to be inflicted on Walker to take place in one of the private rooms of the Barracks."[14] Walker was spared the full brunt of the punishment and sheltered from public humiliation, but he was also thereby denied the status inherent in being treated as a mature soldier. By denying him a man's punishment, his commanding officer also denied him full manhood.

The military's theater of punishment reflected a world that was profoundly misogynist—or rather, so profoundly andro-centric that women were relegated to a periphery almost beyond serious consideration. Men who broke the rules of the military brotherhood exiled themselves beyond the pale into a quasi-feminine status, and only a very public ritual of pain and humiliation could redeem them and allow them to rejoin their brothers. The offended brothers recognized and acceded to this redemption by standing dutifully at attention to observe the abasement. This ritual emasculation and regendering was perhaps most clearly demonstrated in 1776 when under the orders of Francis "Swamp Fox" Marion four soldiers convicted of going AWOL before a battle were flogged while wearing lace caps and petticoats, or again the same year when an officer accused of cowardice at the Battle of Harlem Heights was drummed out of the army dressed in women's clothing.[15] It is perhaps no coincidence that in both of these cases the crime in question was cowardice in the face of an advancing enemy. Failure to stand shoulder-to-shoulder with one's brothers under attack was the ultimate betrayal of the male bond. George Washington himself denounced cowardice as, "A Crime of all others, the most infamous in a Soldier, the most injurious to an Army, and the last to be forgiven."[16] The rhetoric is curiously close to that used to describe "the infamous crime against nature," and the implication of a similar violation of gender roles is no doubt intentional.

Since flogging was usually not inflicted on officers, the most humiliating ritual available to military justice required that an officer convicted of cowardice wear his uniform jacket inside out and be expelled from the camp mounted backward on his horse, sometimes with a halter or noose around his neck. The practice harkened back to the sixteenth-century practice of the "skimmington," a public debasement inflicted on men and women who violated gender norms (the domineering wife, the henpecked husband) in which the offenders would be paraded around the village riding backward on a broken-down horse or donkey.[17] When an officer was driven from the camp looking literally the reverse of a gentleman, when a soldier was drummed out of the army in women's clothing, the message being sent was unambiguous: as far as the army was concerned, he was condemned to a feminine status beyond the redemptive power of punishment.

The military was slow to embrace the idea of penal reform, and it took legislative action to halt the practice of flogging. When Congress passed laws in April and May of 1812 forbidding the use of the lash in the militia and in the army, the army responded by substituting the practice of "cobbing" or paddling the men with a board or a strap. The punishment, inflicted in public and at times on a soldier's bare buttocks, was perhaps less painful than flogging but was no less profoundly humiliating. Whether the army was fully aware of the symbolism inherent in its punishment rituals is certainly debatable. That the army merely replaced the prohibited cat-'o-nine-tails with the less painful paddle but kept the rest of the punishment/redemption ritual intact is a strong indication that on some level they understood the dynamics of what they were doing.

A somewhat different dynamic reigned during the early years of the Republic aboard the men-of-war of the United States Navy and on the burgeoning fleet of merchant and whaling ships. Here, in the absence of women, the communal testosterone was undiluted and punishments were both less highly stylized and more explicitly sadistic. Absent was the formality of a panel of officers dispassionately weighing the evidence and arriving at a verdict which was then either approved, amended, or overturned by a commanding officer. The captain of the ship—at his sole discretion—could order a sailor to be flogged as long as the punishment was no greater than twelve lashes. More severe sentences—up to several hundred lashes—could be delivered by a court-martial.

Just as a "musician" (the drummer) usually delivered the flogging in the army, in both the navy and the merchant service the designated flogger was the boatswain, the man whose pipe welcomed men aboard ship and provided various aural commands. One writer has observed that the "efficiency of the boatswain was gauged to some degree by the quality of the notes that he blew on his whistle and the way that he swung a cat."[18] In the navy under Article XXX of the Articles of War the captain alone was authorized to sentence a sailor to a flogging, but the rules were more lax in the merchant service. Though the boatswain was usually the punisher, any officer—including the captain—could and did wield the lash. As a result, the army's model of the controlled, dispassionate administration of justice was replaced in the navy and merchant service by corporal punishment that was frequently cruel, personal, and idiosyncratic. There were very few complaints about the way the army drummer did his job, but the contemporary literature is filled with charges of sadism on the part of ships' officers.

In *Two Years Before the Mast,* Richard Henry Dana's description of his voyage to California aboard the merchant ship *Pilgrim* in 1834-1836, the author gives a chilling account of an unjustified flogging. When Captain Thompson believes that a sailor has demonstrated a lack of proper respect, he has the man stripped and hauled up. The captain himself delivers the merciless lashing and then, worked up into an ecstacy of sadism, he turns on the crew and erupts in orgiastic glee. "As he went on," Dana writes,

> his passion increased, and he danced about the deck, calling out as he swung the rope,—'If you want to know what I flog you for, I'll tell you. It's because I like to do it!—because I like to do it!—It suits me! That's what I do it for!'[19]

Dana himself ups the psychosexual ante by admitting that the prospect of seeing a man stripped and spread-eagled to be whipped momentarily "excited" him. That excitement quickly turns to disgust and horror with the first thud of the lash, and the author is filled with determination to do what he can to end the cruel practice. Dana was in a unique position to fight for justice for his fellow seamen, having graduated from Harvard Law School shortly before shipping out on the *Pilgrim,* and his chapter "The Flogging" was an important contribution to the literature calling for a reform of naval discipline. But the book's impact was undercut somewhat by its concluding chapter in which Dana tempers his opposition to corporal punishment, and in the process perhaps unintentionally acknowledges the disturbing momentary frisson of anticipation he felt before the whipping began:

> Those who have followed me in my narrative will remember that I was witness to an act of great cruelty inflicted upon my own shipmates; and indeed I can sincerely say that the simple mention of the word flogging, brings up in me feelings which I can hardly control. Yet, when the proposition is made to abolish it entirely and at once; to prohibit the captain from ever, under any circumstances, inflicting corporal punishment; I am obliged to pause, and, I must say, to doubt exceedingly the expediency of making any positive enactment which shall have that effect.[20]

Dana felt it was inexpedient to abolish flogging without having some other means for a captain to control his crew.

While ordinary sailors lived under constant threat of the lash, all officers—including even new midshipmen—were exempt from corporal punishment. The "young gentlemen" of the ship were frequently a rowdy and troublesome bunch. They ranged in age from teenagers to men in their early thirties who were waiting for an opening in the lieutenant's list. Most of them owed their nominations to congressional patronage, and they tended to be the wilder sons and nephews of prominent gentlemen who had used their political influence to send the family's embarrassment to sea while he sowed his wild oats. The British Navy, which had a similar apprenticeship program, had no rule forbidding the corporal punishment of midshipmen. Minor faults were addressed by bending the youth over a cannon and whipping him with a rattan cane, a penalty referred to (in a further sexualization of punishment) as "kissing the gunner's daughter." American midshipmen could be punished only by confinement or suspension from duty; more serious offenses resulted in dismissal from the service.

The antiflogging movement grew in intensity in the early years of the nineteenth century, and as the debate raged, a few naval captains voluntarily chose to adopt other forms of punishment, some of which were not approved by official regulations. Commander Uriah P. Levy found himself before a court-martial for his treatment of a sailor named John Thompson (variously described as sixteen or eighteen years old). Thompson had been put on report for mimicking an officer of the ship. Not wanting to flog the young man, Commander Levy instead devised a punishment he considered to be more appropriate for the crime: he ordered the boy tied to a gun and his trousers lowered so that a small quantity of tar could be applied to his backside, along with half a dozen parrot feathers. A court-martial found the punishment to be "highly scandalous and unbecoming the dignity of an officer to inflict." (It is interesting to note that the navy considered the exposure unbecoming the dignity of the officer, but not the sailor.) Levy was sentenced to dismissal from the navy, but President John Tyler overruled the court-martial and reduced the sentence to a twelve-month suspension. Tyler felt that the young sailor's humiliation was well within the spirit of a circular issued by Secretary of the Navy Levi Woodbury suggesting that "badges of disgrace" be substituted for flogging whenever possible, but he agreed that "Levy erred by resorting to an entirely disgraceful punishment."[21] The president approved of the "badge of disgrace"—the feathers—but objected to the method of its placement. Sailors themselves took particular umbrage in such cases of forced public exposure. In 1812 the crew of HMS *Centaur* circulated a petition of grievances, one of which was to protest "exposing the private parts of a man's body to public view and flogging on the posterior instead of the back. . . ."[22]

In a recent essay exploring what she terms "the pornography of pain" in Anglo-American culture, Karen Halttunen raises an important objection to much of the current homosexual-focused writing on the history of corporal punishment, pointing out that "this special scholarly attention to presumed anxieties about homosexuality suggests some particular, essential connection between homosexuality and sadomasochism that is assumed rather than argued or demonstrated."[23]

Her point is well taken, but an argument could be made that the theatrical presentation of corporal punishment which was mandated by military regulations evoked erotic images that were de facto homosexual, since they involved the emotional responses of men viewing the semi-naked body of another man. The psychosexual dynamics of the drama were difficult to block out, given the ritual stripping off of clothing, the public humiliation before a stern authority figure, the enforced voyeurism of requiring the entire unit to view the writhing body. Melville caught the whiff of homoeroticism as he described the flogging of a handsome teenage sailor: "As he was being secured to the gratings, and the shudderings and creepings of his dazzling white back were revealed, he turned round his head imploringly; but his weeping entreaties and vows of contrition were of no avail."[24]

The erotic allures of flogging—for the flogger, the floggee, and the voyeuristic onlooker—were explored in lurid detail in eighteenth- and early nineteenth-century pornography. Iain McCalman describes flagellation as "almost an élite pornographic sub-genre, distinctive in its stylistic sophistication, lavish production and likely upper-class readership."[25] Lt. John Le Couteur's observation ("He stood close in front of me, the inward groan, at each lash, from being stifled, went sufficiently to my heart. . . . I fainted away like a Sick girl. . . .") could have been lifted directly from the century's most popular pornographic novel, John Cleland's *Memoirs of a Woman of Pleasure*. Given the omnipresence of flagellation as a theme in literary and pictorial erotica (men whipping women, women whipping men), it is unlikely that military personnel observing a flogging could manage a total erotic disconnect simply because every body involved was male.

Sadomasochism almost by definition plumbed deeply hidden and conflicted corners of the eighteenth-century psyche, and concern about "unwholesome" feelings being aroused in the breasts of viewers was one of the motivating factors in the penal reform movement in America at the end of the eighteenth century. When Benjamin Rush delivered a paper in 1787 calling for a new criminal justice system, he included as one of his primary tenets that all punishment should be inflicted privately, not publicly, and that corporal punishment should be replaced by isolation and hard labor.

The abolition of flogging was by no means universally supported by the average sailor. The crew of the naval steamer *Union* wrote to the secretary of the navy requesting that he use his influence to prevent the prohibition of the lash, and a similar petition was drawn up by the crew of the frigate *North Carolina*. Some men viewed flogging as the only way of keeping "foreigners and lazy vagabonds" in check. Some were alarmed that the alternative penalty being considered was the stoppage of the miscreant's daily supply of grog. (They preferred to be flogged rather than lose their liquor ration.) Some sailors waxed almost nostalgic, viewing the lash as one of the time-honored traditions that set seamen apart from the common landlubber. When given the opportunity to express their opinion, "some of the seamen even voted for the retention of corporal punishment on the ground that it was 'manly.'"[26]

Members of the various sailors' benevolent societies brought to this abolition movement a more subtle understanding of the problem. Unlike congressmen, clergy, or social reformers, the mission workers in the flop houses and soup kitchens down by the docks came in daily contact with sailors and understood the psychological complexities of the issue. When *The Sailor's Magazine* declared that flogging was evil because it turned sailors into "brutish" creatures who "wallowed" in "shameful dissipation" and "licentiousness" it was making its argument with a small but important distinction: not that it was unnatural to treat sailors as beasts, but that treating them so brought out their inherent "beastly" natures.[27]

These writers knew that sailors themselves held ambivalent views about flogging. While few perhaps viewed the situation in terms that we would now call sadomasochism, on some level they understood the meaning of the male-male ritual of dominance and submission which was being enacted on the decks of America's ships, the interweaving of authority, rebellion, manhood, pain, endurance, and brotherhood. While others tackled the issue of flogging as a strictly theoretical construct with clearly defined ethical principles, the sailors' benevolent societies understood the life experiences of the sailors who were navigating the murky waters of unresolved tensions among fathers, sons, and brothers.

The issue of the navy's responsibilities in loco parentis became an important theme in the flogging debate, since sailors—unlike soldiers—were frequently considered to be immature to the point of being infantile. Naval chaplain Walter Colton wrote of the sailors he encountered as "innocent, childlike creatures, governed by feelings of generosity, kindheartedness, credulity, and improvidence."[28] The question of how best to guide a sailor to maturity became the central issue of the debate, with some believing that flogging robbed a sailor of his manhood, and others viewing it as an important part of the maturing process. While Congress banned flogging in the army in 1812, it did not even begin debating the use of the lash in the navy until 1820, and did not vote to abolish it until 1850. The disparity in treatment between the two branches of the military is inextricably tied to differing views concerning the nature of soldiers and sailors. While soldiers were considered to be men fully possessed of the rights of all adult male citizens, sailors were viewed either as being childishly naive or dangerously depraved. In either case a guardian/ward relationship was necessary in order to instill character and maintain control.

The eventual change in the rules governing naval discipline were to a great extent brought about by changes in broader societal attitudes toward the corporal punishment of children. Senator Robert F. Stockton was sketching a new view of fatherhood when he declared that

> the secret of good discipline in the service, is to be found in that spirit of Kindness which regards the Comforts and the welfare of the Sailor, and the Confidence which springs from a conviction in his mind, that he has a friend in his Commander, who will stand by him while he stands by his duty, and is true to his honor and his flag.[29]

Here the equation of sailor and child was maintained, but the idea of what it meant to be an officer/father had been adjusted to reflect changes in the American public's attitude toward parenting.

If the United States military had a long and well-documented tradition of rum and the lash, what then of the tradition of sodomy?

In the exhaustive research for his doctoral dissertation "The Administration of Military Justice in the Continental Army During the American Revolution, 1775-1783," Robert Harry Berlin was able to locate only one court-martial on a charge of sodomy, the case of Lieutenant Frederick Gotthold Enslin. From the slim documentation that has survived it is possible to reconstruct only the barest outline of the case. On February 27, 1778, Ensign Anthony Maxwell was brought before a court-martial charged with "propagating a scandalous report prejudicial to the character of Lieutt. Enslin." The General Orders recorded by George Washington on March 3, 1778, report, "The Court after maturely deliberating upon the Evidence produced could not find that Ensign Maxwell had published any report prejudicial to the Character of Lieutt. Enslin further than the strict line of his duty required and do therefore acquit him of the Charge."[30] Maxwell had evidently reported that Enslin was a sodomite. Two weeks after Maxwell's court-martial, Lieut. Enslin himself was brought to trial.

> At a General Court Martial whereof Colo. Tupper was President (10th March 1778) Lieutt. Enslin of Colo. Malcom's Regiment tried for attempting to commit *Sodomy*, with John Monhort a soldier; Secondly, For Perjury in swearing to false Accounts, found guilty of the charges exhibited against him, being breaches of 5th. Article 18th. Section of the Articles of War and do sentence him to be dismiss'd the service with Infamy. His Excellency the Commander in Chief approves the sentence and with Abhorrence & Detestation of such Infamous Crimes orders Lieutt. Enslin to be drummed out of Camp tomorrow morning by all the Drummers and Fifers in the Army never to return;— The Drummers and Fifers to attend on the Grand Parade at Guard mounting for the Purpose.[31]

The scribe copying the General Orders into Washington's official papers showed his distaste for the crime by underlining the word Sodomy and writing it in a bold, dramatic hand. No record survives of whether the sentence was executed or what happened to the dismissed lieutenant.

Of the 3,315 cases listed by James C. Neagles in his index of Revolutionary War courts-martial, only two can be identified as sodomy prosecutions.[32] One is the Enslin case recorded by Berlin, the other involved John Anderson of the Maryland Line. Anderson's court-martial appears in the orderly books of General Mordecai Gist for April 13, 1792.

> At the same Court held the 9th Instant, was tried—John Anderson private in the Maryland Line—For Sodomy—The Court are of oppinion, that he is guilty of an attempt, to commit Sodomy, and do sentence him to Run the Gauntlope three times thro' the Brigade—The General approves the Sentence, and orders it to take place this Evening at Roll Call.[33]

Two cases among over 3,000 prosecutions. The slim evidence of sodomy among soldiers in the Army can be explained in several ways. Perhaps homosexuality did not exist to any significant extent in the military during the American Revolution and the early years of the Republic, or perhaps most sexual contact between men was private and consensual, and came to the attention of courts-martial only when a complaint was filed. Both the Enslin and the Anderson cases appear to be cases of sexual assault. Perhaps the military chose to treat such acts of sexual misconduct on the subjudicial level, as an internal matter not to be shared outside the confines of the unit. Unwillingness to bring shame and infamy on a unit might have motivated commanding officers to deal with homosexual transgressions in ways that skirted the usual procedures of military justice. If such conduct resulted in a court-martial, it was certainly possible to hedge and obfuscate in such a way that the official record revealed little about the true nature of the proceedings. This intentional reticence may explain some of the more puzzling entries in the surviving orderly books.

One way of avoiding mention of the unspeakable crime was simply to call it something else. Prosecutions for violation of the rule against fraternization between officers and men may have been used in place of the more inflammatory (and more difficult to prove) charge of sodomy. In Vermont, Capt. Isaiah Doane was charged (inter alia) with "immoral and unofficer like Conduct in appearing in parade at Swanton on the 6th Day of March, 1809, in a state of intoxication and Sleeping with his servants in the kitchen on the same Evening."[34] In Boston, Lieut. Alden G. Cushman was charged (inter alia) with "sleeping with the waiter during most of his Residence at Fort Independence."[35] (Perhaps significantly, both of these officers were dismissed from the service by their respective court-martial, a punishment unusually severe for the stated infractions.) Courts could use strong but vague terms such as "filthiness," "scandalous behavior," or the all-encompassing "conduct unbecoming an officer and a gentleman." The Cantonment Washington was the site for a court-martial on a charge of lewdness in the barracks—described as "great habits of indecency."[36]

The records of court-martial proceedings in a few cases seem to be straining to avoid all mention of the crime being prosecuted, which inevitably leads to speculation about the nature of the offence. In the volumes of Anthony Wayne's general orders on deposit in the archives at West Point, for example, are two puzzling entries concerning Lieutenant Hastings Marks. The first, dated May 6, 1795, reads:

> At the Particular request of Lieut. H. Marks of the first Sub Legion a Court of Inquiry to consist of Three Members will sit tomorrow Morning at 10 O'Clock to enquire into certain facts relating to assertions said to have been made by a late Serjeant Bartlet ["]derogatory to the Character of Lieut. Marks as an Officer" and report the facts and their Opinion thereon—

There is no official record of the hearing presumably held on May 7; it may have been suppressed. The next entry, immediately following, is dated May 10, 1795:

> Lieutenant Hastings Marks of the 1st Sub Legion, having requested to be liberated from his Arrest, upon Certain charges exhibited against him by Major Winston and that he may be permitted to resign his Commission and Command in the Legion of the United States—The Commander in Chief has thought proper to grant him those indulgences, & his resignation is accepted accordingly.
> The Pay Master General will Settle his Pay, and Subsistence, up to this Day inclusive—Lieutenant Marks, being a great distance from his Family and Friends, is hereby allowed two Rations per Day, to subsist him on his Route, for One Month, from and after the date hereof.[37]

Clearly, whatever Marks was guilty of was of major significance, yet he was treated with respect and compassion and allowed to leave the army with his dignity intact. The court-martial even made an effort to preserve his privacy by making sure that no written record of his transgression survived. A similar act of discretion is revealed in the case of Ensign William T. Payne:

> At a General Court Martial held in Camp on the 13th and 14th Instant, inclusive whereof Captain John Pierce was president, Ensign William T. Payne was tried upon certain Charges exhibited against him, which charges were fully established in the opinion of the Court.—But in Conformity to what appears to be wishes of the Court, The Commander in Chief is induced to accept the

resignation of Mr. William T. Payne as Offered by him on the 12th Inst., which resignation is hereby accepted, with permission to Mr. Payne to Depart Camp immediately after Settling his Accounts with the Publick.[38]

Compare the vagueness and decorum of Marks's and Payne's reports with ones entered into other volumes of the same set of orderly books. When the transgressions in question involved women of easy virtue, the court could be almost pruriently specific. Captain Ballard Smith was brought before a court-martial:

> 1st for behaviour unlike a Gentleman and Officer, and repugnant to the dignity of the army, by keeping a woman, claim'd and known to be, the Wife of Sergant Sprague of his own Company, which Conduct produced discontent to the Sergant and encourages the woman to be riotous, abusive and is destructive to discipline and in particular in the abuse of Sergant Sharpe of the same Company on the night of the 3d instant, which noise, fighting and abuse ended in the Captains own tent—
> 2nd for a Direct violation of Good order, and Contrary to Common decency by suffering the aforesaid woman, to take refuge in his tent in the face of all the encampment, when she was ordered to be confined for having threatened to take the Captains Pistols, with an intent to take the life of Sergant Sharpe.[39]

Captain Isaac Guion was charged with disobedience of orders and mutinous conduct, "In refusing to obey the Orders of Major Doyle, to leave a certain Woman, and not take her below the falls of the Ohio, and for pointing to the Boat she was in, and saying there she is, and no Person shall take her out."[40] In another case, a Sergeant Hopkins had been carrying on an affair with one of the women hired to nurse the sick. He was court-martialed "for riotously beating a Woman kept by him as a Mistress to the great injury of the Sick in the Hospital, and disturbance of the Garrison, for abusive language and with using Menancing words and gestures to Doctor Carmichael."[41] A Lieutenant Kreemer was charged with "behaving in a scandalous, infamous, manner such as is unbecoming the character of an officer & a Gentleman. . . . In keeping & Cherishing in his hut a most abandon'd *Whore*, treating her more like a wife than a *whore*."[42]

Given the repeated descriptions of drunkenness, desertion, cowardice, theft, and heterosexual licentiousness that appear in volume after volume of the army's orderly books, when a court chooses not to specify the crime in question it inevitably becomes a case of "the dog that did not bark." In 1793 Lt. Daniel St. Thomas Junifer was brought before a court-martial, charged by Lt. William Devin "with making use of and uttering in the Company of Officers, Ungentleman And Unsoldierly expressions, with a View to induce a Suspicion that Lieut. Devin is capable of the commission of Felonious Acts." The court-martial in its decision chose not to reveal what Lieut. Devin was suspected of being capable of doing, though it could barely conceal its disgust with the entire matter:

> The foregoing Charges exhibited by Lieut Devin, against Lieut Junifer, appear to be only the counterpart of those exhibited by Mr. Junifer against Mr. Devin, before a Genl. Court Martial held at Legion Ville on the 26th December 1792. Neither having for its Basis either the Honour or Dignity of the Legion, or the Benefit of the Service, but evidently founded in Malice, and personal Resentment, and which had been better settled by some other Mode, than that of a Court Martial; The Commander in Chief therefore hopes, that the times of the Officers, will be no longer taken up, or their feelings tortur'd in hearing and recording Charges and Proceedings, that tend only to disgrace the Orderly Books of the U: States of America.[43]

Junifer was evidently very sensitive about aspersions on his manliness. Only three months later he was dismissed from the service for refusing to subject himself to the authority of a superior officer. The court-martial report for that proceeding concludes with the observation, "It is a false Notion that Subordination and Prompt Obedience to Superiors is any debasement of a Mans Courage or a Reflection upon his Honour, or Understanding but the reverse."[44]

The United States Navy was no less concerned with guarding its reputation against charges that it was a haven for sodomy. On March 20, 1846, Lieutenant Henry B. Watson, the commander of the marines aboard the *Portsmouth,* reported that Midshipman Frederic Kellogg was allowed to resign in order to avoid the publicity of a court-martial. Kellogg "was charged with a most unnatural, and diabolical crime, the charge was Arson, or in nautical parlance it is called buggering."[45] In one of those ironic twists with which history is rife, less than four months after Kellogg was driven off his ship for engaging in homosexual activity, the *Portsmouth* sailed through the Golden Gate and claimed for the United States the sleepy Mexican settlement of Yerba Buena. Under its new name—San Francisco—the place would become the major locus of gay culture in America, spreading out from a central plaza named (in honor of the ship) Portsmouth Square. Marine Midshipman Frederic Kellogg would perhaps appreciate the irony.

The Kellogg case demonstrates the puzzling use of "arson" to refer to buggery, sometimes falsely attributed as a variation of the slang word "arse." Actually the term has much deeper roots in British jurisprudence. The link between sodomy and the burning of buildings was made in an ancient treatise on the laws of England, known as *Fleta* (noted above in the discussion of the history of English law). The treatise was based on the writings of Henry de Bracton and Ranulf de Glanville, and is believed to have been written by an anonymous judge or lawyer during the reign of Edward I. Chapter 35, "Of Arson," begins with the standard definition of the term: "If anyone in time of peace maliciously burn the house of another, through enmity or for the sake of spoil, he should be punished with a capital sentence." The second paragraph of the chapter, though, has no apparent logical connection with the first:

> Apostate Christians, sorcerers and the like should be drawn and burnt. Those who have connexion with Jews and Jewesses or are guilty of bestiality or sodomy shall be buried alive in the ground, provided they be taken in the act and convicted by lawful and open testimony. Traitors, who slay their lord or lady, or who lie with their lords' wives or daughters or with the nurses of their lords' children, or forge their lords' seals, or who administer poison secretly to anyone whereof he dies, and are convicted thereof, shall be drawn and hanged, and, if they be women, they shall be burnt.[46]

Since it covers a wide range of crimes—from sodomy to adultery, from treason to murder—it was possible to cite the general chapter "Of Arson" without mentioning specific unspeakable practices.

While the records of courts-martial in the navy are at times couched in obscure and equivocal language, a few records of sodomy prosecutions during the period are largely unexpurgated and leave no doubt about the crime in question. For readers unfamiliar with terminology used in these naval proceedings, one historical study provides a glossary, which includes, "Frig: Slang. To masturbate another person at his request," and "Chicken: Slang. The regular partner of an aggressive homosexual."[47] For the specifics of most sodomy prosecutions, however, no glossary is necessary.

Four court-martial cases listed in the Judge Advocate General's index for the period under review are unambiguously sodomy prosecutions. The Navy's first recorded court-martial for sodomy occurred in 1805 aboard the *Constitution,* the famous "Old Ironsides" still docked in Boston harbor. Marine Private George Crutch was charged with attempting to sodomize a seaman known only as Geregano. A friend of Geregano alerted Marine Sergeant James P. Mix who, together with Sergeant James Reynolds, discovered the crime in progress. Sergeant Mix testified before the court-martial that he had found

> George Crutch on the Spars between the boats, with his Pantaloons down, and shirt above the Navel, on top of Geregano; he [Mix] immediately run his hand down between them & felt the Penis of George Crutch—it appeared to him by the feel that Crutch had no connection with Geregano but was about making the attempt and that Geregano had his shirt above his waist.[48]

Following the tradition set by the army when dealing with such a distasteful and disturbing topic, the matter was swiftly swept out of sight. The ship's officers hearing the case asked only if Crutch appeared to be drunk when he was apprehended. When they received a reply in the negative (meaning that the conduct was conscious and intentional and not the aberrant result of too much grog), they cut off all further discussion. Fearful of where the testimony was leading, the officers brought the court-martial to an abrupt conclusion and found Marine Private Crutch (despite the graphic testimony) not guilty. They were relying perhaps on a strict definition of sodomy, which required both penetration and emission.

The second sodomy case grew out of an incident which had been treated at first on the subjudicial level. Thomas Cumming and Andrew Hansen, two novice seamen (or ship's boys) aboard the *Potomac* in Naples Harbor in 1835, were discovered between two cannons on the gun deck engaging in intercourse. Cumming was immediately discharged without a court-martial and put ashore, while Hansen was temporarily retained. The commanding officer planned to discharge Hansen at the next port of call as a way of separating the two boys, whom he believed to be lovers. Cumming received a simple discharge and so technically was not guilty of any offense, and his case would not have been recorded in any official record except for his subsequent conduct. Unwilling to let the ship sail away with his beloved aboard, Cumming began to circulate stories that Lieutenant Owen Burns was having sexual intercourse with two of the *Potomac*'s boys, including young Hansen. Cumming hoped in this way to delay the sailing of the ship, and perhaps to have his lover set ashore at Naples with him. At a court of inquiry both boys testified that Burns had ordered them to "frig" or masturbate him in his cabin. Hansen admitted that he had complied five or six times, but only after being threatened with punishment; the other boy testified that he had steadfastly refused Burns's advances. A ship's boy from Burns's previous ship, the schooner *Shark*, testified that he too had spurned the officer's attentions, although he "asked me almost every night to do it."[49]

Lieutenant Burns testified in his own defense that the ship's surgeon was treating him for a venereal infection and had prescribed genital baths in cold water. Burns insisted that he had merely called the boys to his cabin for the purpose of having them administer the medicinal baths for his infected penis. The court again found the case distasteful and did its best not to look too deeply into the charges.

> We now approach the subject with great diffidence and with great regret, as we are led to believe that Lieutenant Burns must, from his conduct [have] laid himself liable to improper impressions as well as improper remarks from those of his inferiors who have been permitted to approach him to discharge their domestic duties; and we take leave to observe that an officer ought at all times in our opinion, be placed above suspicion or the shadow of reproach.[50]

Commodore Daniel T. Patterson sought to dispose of the matter by merely furnishing Burns with a letter authorizing him to leave the squadron, a letter which expressed the commodore's belief that Burns was entirely innocent of the charges, or was guilty only of poor judgment for engaging in conduct which might too easily be misconstrued. But the members of the court-martial were convinced that the lieutenant was in fact guilty of sexual misconduct. They protested the light sentence, and Commodore Patterson eventually ordered Burns to be publicly reprimanded.

The third sodomy case in the Judge Advocate General's index is a complex case with much contradictory testimony. In 1840 Seaman Daniel Lupenny was charged with sexual assault on a second-class apprentice boy named Henry Phinney. Phinney, who slept in a hammock next to Lupenny, testified that Lupenny had awakened him "and asked me to let him bugger me." Phinney had refused, and an argument had ensued which awoke two other sailors, Flint and Dyer. The next day Flint and Dyer reported the attempted assault on the boy, and Lupenny was arrested and consigned to the brig. Eight days later Lupenny escaped from his confinement, returned to the hammock where young Phinney was sleeping, and stabbed him twice but did not cause serious injury.

At the trial the court-martial panel asked Phinney if he was Lupenny's "chicken" and the boy replied that he was not. Perhaps the ship's officers had begun to suspect that they were dealing with a lovers' quarrel since young Phinney contradicted the assault charges, saying that Lupenny had in fact never threatened him nor consummated the act of sodomy. (It was Flint and Dyer, not the boy himself, who had brought the charges in the first place.) Flint then testified that he knew nothing about any attempted sodomy, that he had reported Lupenny only for making a disturbance on the berth deck. Dyer further muddied the waters by claiming that he was aware that Lupenny and Phinney had engaged in sexual intercourse on an earlier occasion. Thoroughly confused by this point, the court-martial sought the easiest way out. Since there was no clear evidence of rape, and since the stabbing took place in the dark with no one able to identify the assailant, Lupenny was found guilty merely of overpowering the sentry and escaping from the brig. He was sentenced to fifty lashes and dismissal from the navy.[51]

Five years later, in 1845, another sodomy case found its way into the official records. Midshipman Joseph Miller reported that he had received an anonymous note that the other midshipmen on the frigate *Savannah* were aware of his conduct which took place "under cover of night" a year earlier, and they were prepared to report him to the ship's executive officer. The following day he received another anonymous note, which read:

Sir: At your request we herein state the charges, which we lay against you—

You are charged sir with having (during our stay in this port [Callao] about the ninth of may—1844—Crept Staethily & under cover of night) to Mr. Griffin's hammock—and, while that gentleman was asleep, removed the bedclothes—from his person and taken his Penis—as it appeared—in your hands—for what purpose, we are at a loss to imagine.

Respectfully, the
Steerage Officers.[52]

Eager to clear his name, Miller petitioned Commodore John Sloat to convene a court of inquiry. The commodore in reviewing the request noted that the event referred to had taken place nearly a year earlier, and suspected that this was not a case of moral outrage but rather petty squabbling among his midshipmen. He instructed the court of inquiry to scrutinize the *accusers* closely and to be prepared to move against them if the unsavory charges they had brought appeared to be unfounded. Midshipman Griffin testified that he had been visited in his hammock on several occasions by an unknown person who had handled his genitals while he was sleeping and then disappeared. On the final occasion he had awakened in time to see Miller ascending a hatchway ladder. Under intense grilling by the court of inquiry, the midshipmen's story was exposed as a plot to discredit an unpopular shipmate.

Commodore Sloat's clear distaste for the topic was not lost on his junior officers. When later that year a very similar case was brought against Yeoman Joseph Downey (accused of being "overly friendly" with one of the ship's boys), the officers declined even to look into the matter.[53] Officers in the United States Navy were well aware that opening the hatch and peering into the putrid quarters below deck would in effect be opening Pandora's box, exposing horrors best left undisclosed. Wherever possible they chose to look the other way.

The lengths to which a naval commander was willing to go to avoid dealing with the topic of homosexuality aboard his ship is revealed in the final case indexed by the Judge Advocate General, this one from April 1856. William Kieth, captain of the top, was tried for "Indecency and drawing a knife on a boatswain's mate." Kieth had gotten drunk and was attempting to climb into the hammocks of various ship's boys on the berth deck when he was confronted by Boatswain's Mate John Oliver. The two men began a shouting match, which ended with Oliver striking Kieth. Kieth then went on deck to report Oliver to the marine sentry on the quarterdeck, and Oliver reported Kieth to the berth deck sentry. The two men confronted each other again; Kieth drew a knife but was disarmed and taken to the brig.

The officers on the ensuing court-martial ignored the indecency charge and found Kieth guilty only of pulling a knife. In reviewing the proceedings, Commander William Lynch agreed with the court's finding. "I think it proper also to remark," wrote Lynch, "that if Oliver had struck Kieth at the moment when he thought he detected him in the attempt to commit an unnatural crime, it would have been [a] palliation of his infringement of the law," but since Oliver had testified that he struck Kieth for his offensive language and not in an attempt to stop him from committing sodomy, Oliver was also at fault in the action.[54] Lynch reduced Kieth's punishment to five days' solitary confinement on bread and water, and ordered Oliver—who had first reported the sexual transgression—to be put in double irons (hands and feet). The message being sent to the ship's crew was clear: handle homosexual disputes in private, outside of officials channels, or risk finding yourself punished for your role in bringing the offense to light.

Beyond these indexed cases, an official report to Congress on naval floggings for the year 1846 includes notations of punishments for "improper conduct too base to mention," "filthy and unnatural practices," "gross misconduct to boys," and "improper conduct on the berth deck."[55] Another report, this one covering the year 1848-1849, includes, "Scandalous conduct," "Filthiness," and "Taking indecent liberties with boy in hammock."[56] It is not surprising that little more survives in the official government records for the period. In his analysis of sodomy prosecutions in the Old Navy, James E. Valle describes a pattern of intentional ignorance, which was the official military policy where consensual male-male sexuality was concerned. Officers were expected not to look too closely at what their men were doing, and to intervene only when avoidance was no longer an option.

> When rumors of berth deck homosexuality began to circulate within a ship or when an incident was reported, it was always petty officers who were sent to investigate—never commissioned or warrant officers. When the guilty parties were appre-

hended, they were supposed to be quietly reported to the commanding officer, who either gave them twelve lashes, logging the punishment vaguely as retribution for "filthy conduct," or discharged them and put them ashore at the first opportunity without recording anything on paper. In those instances when homosexual activity, for some reason or other, was officially reported so that it became a matter of record, a court-martial was held. In these cases, the officers comprising the court-martial boards betrayed their disgust and loathing for the duty assigned them by simply refusing to grapple with the issue of homosexuality. They either voted to acquit without waiting to hear much of the evidence, or they found the defendant guilty of some other charge and assigned him a punishment for that.[57]

Herman Melville in his 1850 novel *White-Jacket* describes exactly this policy of official blindness in the U.S. Navy:

> The sins for which the cities of the plain were overthrown still linger in some of these wooden-walled Gomorrahs of the deep. More than once complaints were made at the mast of the Neversink, from which the deck officer would turn away with loathing, refuse to hear them, and command the complainant out of his sight.[58]

The court-martial proceedings recorded in garrison orderly books and in ship's logs give an obscured view of male-male sexual relationships in the military, and necessarily focus only on those that led to public charges of wrong-doing. The diaries and private correspondence of soldiers and sailors reveal a very different picture of daily life, providing a record of consensual relations, most of which never came to the attention of the superior officers and were never subject to the glaring light of a court-martial. Perhaps the most frank and revealing of these records is the diary of Philip C. Van Buskirk, a member of the United States Marine Corps whose journal was analyzed by B.R. Burg in his book *An American Seafarer in the Age of Sail*. Van Buskirk began his diary in 1851 while serving as a drummer in the Marine Corps. The thirty-six surviving volumes of the diary contain an extended, detailed, and critical look at moral conditions aboard various ships of the American Navy, and in the course of recording his own trials and failures, Van Buskirk paints a lurid picture of shipboard life. "There is no school of vice comparable to the Navy," he wrote in 1855. "Certainly ninety per cent of the white boys in the Navy of this day . . . are, to an extent that would make you shudder, blasphemers and sodomites."[59]

Van Buskirk describes an all-male world in which masturbation— solitary, with a partner, or in a group—was a common and accepted practice. Van Buskirk, product of an upper-middle-class family and avid consumer of the antimasturbatory literature which poured from the presses of antebellum America, fought a losing battle with his own sexual appetite, yet he could never accept the prevalence of self-pollution among his shipmates. "Even after regularly observing them masturbating and writing of what he saw," Burg comments,

> Van Buskirk failed to comprehend that they practiced the activity openly, talked of it, created coarse jokes about it, watched others engage in it without being scandalized, and considered it a convenient activity for passing idle days and weeks in the barracks or at sea.[60]

Mutual masturbation was one of the most frequent sexual activities aboard ship; it was known as "going chaw for chaw." (In an era when most American men were uncircumcised, a penis when withdrawn into the foreskin resembled a chaw or twist of tobacco.) Mutual masturbation was popular for several reasons. While many of these sexual encounters were open to the view of other sailors, they needed to be hidden from the officers in charge. Crowded conditions below deck and lack of privacy throughout the ship made sexual intercourse problematic, while mutual masturbation could be effected standing up, fully clothed. Two men interrupted in the practice could quickly hide the activity by turning away and buttoning up. Mutual masturbation was not viewed as a sodomitical practice, neither by the men nor by the courts. Moreover, by its very mutuality masturbation made moot the question of gender role violation. Neither man could be designated as the "woman" in the encounter. Van Buskirk's disgust with the sexual practices of his shipmates mirrored his own struggle with self-abuse. It was the potentially detrimental expense of bodily fluid which appalled him, not the fact that two men were engaging in sexual activity.

Anal intercourse (buggery) was not unknown, but it appears to have played a secondary role among American sailors and marines.

There were few places on the ship where two men could engage in the practice unobserved, though one or two locations were designated as appropriate hiding places. The existence of the "boom cover trade" was well-known. The range of sexual activity available to those who crawled under the boom cover was not limited to buggery, but the cover provided a modicum of privacy when needed.[61]

Anal intercourse was usually limited to an arrangement known as "chickenship" in which a younger sailor (usually a boy) was taken as a sexual partner by someone larger, older, or of a more senior rank (frequently all three). This was understood to be a commercial arrangement—the boy provided sexual services in return for small gifts or cash—but it was not necessarily viewed as a form of prostitution or sexual exploitation. The arrangement was mutually agreed to and there was frequently an exchange of affection. Sailors even noted sometimes that an unscrupulous chicken was taking advantage of his older partner, accepting gifts and pretending to fidelity while engaging in sexual activities on the side.[62] Chickenship was an open and accepted institution among the sailors, so much so that it led to a popular adage concerning the employment of female prostitutes while on shore leave: there was no point in paying three dollars on land for what cost a quarter afloat.[63]

The remark, though largely facetious, is significant in that it puts the lie to the notion that men aboard ship engaged in sex with one another only because no women were present. Yet it cannot be said that the majority of men who went to sea were "homosexual." Here the binary view of sexual orientation simply breaks down. Although a certain amount of self-selection was involved—men who were more comfortable in all-male communities were likely to seek out all-male communities—life aboard a crowded ship was awash in testosterone, and the patterns of shore-based communities inevitably rearranged themselves to accommodate this altered set of circumstances. In evaluating male-male sex acts during this period it is important to avoid inferring that the men involved came to these encounters with the same cultural baggage imposed on their later Victorian brothers. Nor should we assume that in these encounters one man necessarily played the "male" role while the other played the "female," or that one partner came away from these sexual acts feeling he had been unmanned. Homosexual acts when performed in a context of mutuality served to reinforce feelings of masculine self-worth, particularly when the men involved had been deprived of female referents for long periods of time. To be an object of desire—to be prized for one's manliness by an "other"—was positive and ego affirming regardless of the gender of the admirer. To have the skill and the means to bring pleasure to another person—particularly someone whose strength and masculinity were evident and unquestioned—was an act of empowerment for the pleasurer.

This is not to say that male-male sexuality was always viewed as a positive good, or even an activity that was morally neutral. In particular, anal intercourse—with its association with an angry Jehovah raining fire and brimstone on the Cities of the Plain—caused some men pause. Yet male-male sexual activity aboard ship was common, expected, and accepted. It was joked about and denigrated. It was deplored yet eagerly pursued. But it was rarely analyzed too deeply. As Burg writes in his discussion of the Van Buskirk diary:

> These mariners did not extend sexual encounters into broader contexts that emulated the heterosexual roles and duties subscribed to by the rest of society, nor did they divide their labors into masculine and feminine spheres. Involvement in homoerotic encounters implied no negative correlation with masculinity. Sexual contact among males was simply another of the immoral facets of life among seafarers. Being known as a sodomite or as a sailor who would masturbate or be masturbated by a friend did not imply physical weakness, fear, effeminacy, or a dependent character.[64]

The average sailor's view of his own sexuality to some extent reflected society's views of it—which in turn had been molded by the average sailor's conduct while in port. The image fed the reality, and vice versa. All men who went to sea were suspected of dissipation and debauchery, the common merchant seaman even more so than members of the United States Navy or Marines. Sailors led lives that were irregular—literally, outside the rules. Most port cities developed a "Sailortown"—a maritime ghetto adjacent to the docks where vice was carefully segregated from the rest of the community, giving the local population protection from contact with such an unsavory element (unless, of course, they sought that contact). The solitary, transient nature of their mode of living made sailors attractive sexual objects for landlubbers seeking quick and unencumbering liaisons. The docks of most ports were notorious cruising grounds, particularly for men of a higher social class seeking sexual contact with their social inferiors.

The seductive allure of men who went to sea inevitably found its way into the popular culture of early America. The folk song "The Jolly Waterman" captures the easygoing sexuality of the sailors whose small boats ferried goods and passengers around rivers and harbors. The lyrics are anonymous, but the tune was written by Charles Dibdin, who first performed it in 1774. Dibdin's handsome young waterman uses his good looks and charm on both the ladies *and* the gentlemen, to equal effect:

> He look'd so neat, and he row'd so steadily,
> The maidens all flock'd in his boat so readily,
> And he eyed the young rogues with so charming an air,
> That this waterman ne'er was in want of a fare.

The fashionable young girls who hire him to row them around flirt shamelessly, but the working-class waterman is stolidly unimpressed.

> And oftentime would they be giggling and leering;
> But 'twas all one to Tom, their gibing and jeering;
> For loving or liking he little did care.
> For this waterman ne'er was in want of a fare.

It becomes clear that the "fare" that handsome Tom is never in want of is a sexual partner, male or female. In the last verse he falls in love with one of his (female) passengers and looks forward to marrying her so that there will always be someone in his bed: "And how should this waterman ever know care,/When he's married, and never in want of a fare?"[65]

We may also turn again to Herman Melville and his novel *Redburn* which presents a sort of "rough trade" trawler in the character of Harry Bolton. Melville was drawing on his own experiences as a novice merchant seaman when in the voice of the title character he describes the seedy brothels and louche gin joints of Liverpool and the epicene young gentleman he encountered there:

> I made the acquaintance of a handsome, accomplished, but unfortunate youth, young Harry Bolton. He was one of those

small, but perfectly formed beings, with curling hair, and silken muscles, who seem to have been born in cocoons. His complexion was a mantling brunette, feminine as a girl's; his feet were small; his hands were white; and his eyes were large, black, and womanly; and, poetry aside, his voice was as the sound of a harp.

But where, among the tarry docks, and smoky sailor-lanes and by-ways of a seaport, did I, a battered Yankee boy, encounter this courtly youth?

Several evenings I had noticed him in our street of boarding-houses, standing in the doorways, and silently regarding the animated scenes without. His beauty, dress, and manner struck me as so out of place in such a street, that I could not possibly divine what had transplanted this delicate exotic from the conservatories of some Regent-street to the untidy potato-patches of Liverpool.[66]

Redburn overhears Bolton chatting up a sailor in one of the neighborhood taverns and, believing that Bolton is expressing an interest in visiting America, he steps forward and offers to provide him with any information he needs. "He glanced from my face to my jacket, and from my jacket to my face, and at length, with a pleased but somewhat puzzled expression, begged me to accompany him on a walk."[67]

This is one of the earliest depictions of homosexual cruising in an American novel. After their brief adventure at a London men's club, Redburn finds the penniless Bolton a position as a "boy," or inexperienced sailor, aboard his ship on its return voyage to New York, and Bolton needs to fend off the unwanted attentions of Captain Riga. As in all his novels, Melville here sails as near to the edge of homoerotic explicitness as he dares, then veers off at the last moment and turns the tale into a standard boy's coming-of-age-at-sea yarn.

Bolton has good reason to be wary of the captain. A boy—or a young man who signed on as "boy"—faced the likelihood of receiving sexual attention from a ship's officers. This sexual dynamic was so common that it was the subject of ditties and sea chanteys sung by sailors well into the nineteenth century. Some of those songs (no doubt in expurgated versions) found their way into print in the form of song sheets or broadsides sold for popular consumption. Handsome young sexually ambivalent boys who prove their bravery are a staple of this genre. Songs such as "Harry Bluff" (a name certainly suggestive of transgender role-playing) celebrate tender sailors who have ambiguous gender presentation:

> Like a sapling he sprung, he was fair to the view,
> He was a true Yankee Oak, boys, the older he grew;
> Though his body was weak, and his hands they were soft,
> When the signal was given, he the first went aloft.[68]

Another standard theme of these sea songs is cross-dressing, with its resulting gender confusion. Almost always it is a woman who dresses as a man in order to go to sea, usually in pursuit of the man she loves, though in "The Female Sailor" the reasons for cross-dressing are somewhat obscure. In this song the girl leaves home to follow her sailor lover, but she dresses at first in female clothing. It is not until she discovers that her lover has been drowned that she decides to stay at sea and to begin passing as a man.

> With great grief and anguish this lady did mourn,
> She thought to her parents, she would not return;
> Her golden locks she cut off, as you will understand,
> Blue jacket and trowsers, she quickly put on.
>
> She went on board the Hero, without more delay,
> And inquired for the captain, as you may plainly see;
> He enter'd her as cook, and steward likewise,
> But little did he think she was a maid in disguise.
>
> For three years and better, she sail'd on the main,
> And still there were none could to the secret obtain;
> For when in port, she was as jolly as a sailor could be,
> Her grog she would drink, and kiss the girls merrily.

Her manly drinking and girl-kissing does not protect her from the unwanted sexual advances of the captain, who believes she is a man. In a passage which is so obscure it is probably the result of expurgation, the captain discovers that the young man he is pursuing is actually a woman:

> This ship was for Liverpool, and near to the port,
> The captain was inclin'd to pass away a joke;
> And to his great surprise, he found she was a maid,
> When he arrived in Liverpool, the secret he betray'd.[69]

Up until the cross-dressing incidents, the song follows a strict a-a-b-b rhyme scheme, but when the girl begins to pass as a boy the rhyme scheme falls apart—strong evidence that the verses have been tampered with for publication as a popular song sheet. When the girl resumes her female clothing (and marries the captain!) the regular a-a-b-b rhyming returns.

In "The Handsome Cabin Boy," the cross-dressing charade is taken to even greater lengths. In this case it is not a missing lover but "a mind for roving" that motivates the girl to dress like a boy and go to sea. Things quickly become complicated, since the captain's wife is on board and she is as sexually interested in the cabin boy as is her husband. The girl-as-boy soon finds herself fending off advances from both sides:

> She engaged with the captain, his cabin boy to be,
> The wind it being favorable they soon put out to sea;
> The captain's lady being on board, who seemed to enjoy
> The favorable appearance of the handsome cabin boy.
>
> So nimble was the cabin boy and done his duty well,
> But mark what followed after the thing itself will tell:
> The captain with this pretty maid would often kiss and toy,
> And he soon found the secret of the handsome cabin boy.[70]

The narrator expresses no shock or surprise that the captain would "kiss and toy" with his cabin boy, unaware of her gender until the intimacies had progressed to a point where a revelation was inevitable. Even after the captain is aware that his cabin boy is a girl, the masquerade is continued in front of the other sailors. "Her cheeks were like roses, and with her side locks curl'd,/The sailors often smil'd and said, she [he?] looks just like a girl." The cabin boy's secret is dramatically revealed one night when "he" goes into labor and gives birth to the captain's child. The captain's wife is philosophical as she sums up the dizzying gender confusion: "The captain's lady to him said; my dear, I wish you joy,/For either you or I've betrayed the handsome cabin boy."

These songs—even in their published, censored versions—reveal a world that holds heterosexuality to be the norm, but which allows for a wide swath of sexual ambiguity. Sailors seem to have been granted a special dispensation to behave in ways that would bring condemnation to a landsman. In *Redburn* the effete Bolton cruises the docks of Liverpool because he is enticed by the popular image of the sailor as outlaw or rebel. Something inherent in the nature of men who went to sea both made them unfit for the shackles of conventional morality *and* freed them to pursue avenues of conduct closed to most other men. This concept of the *innate depravity* of sailors was shared by much of the American public, and toward the end of the period under review the leaders of the great antebellum reform movements began to shine their crusading lamps on the moral delinquency of the men who went to sea. Organizations such as the American Seaman's Friend Society, the Boston Society for the Religious and Moral Improvement of Seamen, and the Society for Promoting the Gospel Among Seamen in the Port of New York sought to raise these men from their lives of debauchery by teaching them how to fight the temptations which seemed an inevitable part of a life spent among sailors, lest those poor souls "lapse into barbarism."

The seamen's mission movement fought an uphill battle, not only because the men resisted Christian moralizing, but also because established churches shunned contact with sailors. Evangelist Ward Stafford, in an 1817 pamphlet titled *Important to Seamen*, took his fellow Christians to task for their inhospitality:

> [Sailors] regard themselves, and they are regarded by others, as an entirely separate class of the community. They do not mingle with other people. Their very mode of life excludes them from all society, except that of their companions. . . . As they have generally become vicious in consequence of being neglected, and as no distinction is made between the sober and the profligate, they are strangers whom all feel at liberty to despise. . . . Another barrier is their dress. Their dress is generally different from that of other people. When they enter a church, they are known and marked as sailors. . . . It is a fact, and one at the recital of which the persons concerned ought to blush, that they have been virtually turned out of our churches when they have

entered! They have received no invitation to take seats—the pews have been closed against them—and they, in some cases, have been informed, that there was no room for sailors.[71]

William Maxwell Wood offered a dissenting view. In his pamphlet denouncing the daily grog ration Wood suggested that sailors were not innately depraved, but were merely acting the part expected of them whenever they cruised the docks, reeling in drunkenness:

[P]opular opinion has seemed willing to tolerate gross propensities and vices in men of this class on account of the virtues, not belonging so extensively to mankind in general, which is attributed to them by the popular imagination. Boldness, recklessness, generosity, are among the supposed peculiarities of seamen as a body, and for these sensuality, ungoverned impulses, low appetites, and a disregard for rule and order, are to be tolerated and justified. . . . The popular impression respecting nautical character and the indulgence with which its irregularities are regarded, do much to keep up the affectation of peculiarity in the public eye, by men who, under other influences, would have no disposition to exhibit an assumed recklessness, nor to descend to low vice. The sailor, during his short sojourns ashore, is on exhibition—he is only dramatizing the part allotted to him by public expectation.[72]

Whether a sailor was indeed morally depraved or merely faking it—incorrigibly sinful or slyly taking advantage of the license his professional reputation afforded him—this widely held assumption of sinfulness had an inevitable effect on the self-images of those men presumed ipso facto to be living lives of drunkenness and sodomitical licentiousness. For an American sailor in the early Republic it could take only a few psychological steps to achieve something very much like a modern liberated gay identity: (1) I am a sailor; (2) Sailors are popularly believed to be innately depraved, particularly because of our sexual conduct; (3) I enjoy having sex with my shipmates or with men I encounter on the docks; (4) Having sex with other men is an innate aspect of life for a man like me; and (5) Therefore male-male sexuality is a natural part of who I am. How many American sailors took this psychological journey toward self-awareness we will never know.

Chapter 4

Gone for a Soldier

Oh! My friend how often I think of our friend, how would he be pleased could he see us enjoying the comfort which surround[s] us, the decency perhaps I might say, the respectability with which we move down the hill of life—but He is gone—& by & bye you and I shall follow it will be better for the one who goes first It is comfortless to be left alone in a desert.

Col. William North to Col. Benjamin Walker

So far only a few surviving American letters and diaries have been uncovered that describe in detail the type of sexual encounters included in Philip Van Buskirk's diary of life among the United States Marines, but some writings allow readers to track the lives of men whose youthful intimacy survived into adulthood. Not surprisingly, the letters rarely include explicit sexual references, but ample evidence shows that the intimacy extended well beyond mere friendship. One detailed narrative is provided by the extraordinary body of letters exchanged during and after the Revolutionary War among three men: Friedrich von Steuben, Benjamin Walker, and William North. The written record of their complex, interwoven emotional bonds extends for nearly forty years and gives one of the most complete pictures of male intimacy during the period. Today few Americans are familiar with the life of Baron Friedrich Wilhelm von Steuben, but at the close of the War of Independence he was one of the most famous men in the United States. In 1783 George Washington paid him a great tribute by addressing the last letter he wrote as commander of the American forces to the man he felt was greatly responsible for changing the course of the war.

Altho' I have taken frequent Opportunities both in public and private, of Acknowledging your Zeal, Attention and Abilities in performing the duties of your Office: yet, I wish, to make use of this last Moment of my public life to Signify in the strongest terms, my entire Approbation of your Conduct, and to express my Sense of the Obligations the public is under to you for your faithful, and Meritorious Services. . .

This, is the last letter I shall ever write, while I continue in the Service of my Country—the hour of my Resignation is fixed at twelve this day—after which I shall become a private Citizen on the Banks of the Potomack, where I shall be glad to embrace you, and testify the great Esteem and Consideration, with which I am My Dear Baron Your most Obedt. and Affectn. Go. Washington.[1]

The Baron was born in 1730 in Magdeburg, Prussia, and christened with the ungainly name of Friedrich Wilhelm Ludolf Gerhard Augustin von Steuben, which he eventually changed to the (presumably) more dignified Friedrich Wilhelm Augustus Henry Ferdinand von Steuben. The penchant for improving personal names was an inherited trait. It was Friedrich's grandfather, Augustin Steube—son of a tenant farmer—who assumed the aristocratic-sounding but unmerited "von" and changed the family name to von Steube. An ambitious and diligent student, Augustin entered the ministry, became chaplain at the castle of Schmalkalden, and eventually married the Countess Charlotte Dorothea von Effern. Their son Wilhelm in turn invented an ancestor whom he named Ludwig von Steuben, Knight of St. John, and he changed the family name once again in order to bring it into accordance with the falsified genealogy. Wilhelm married Maria Justina Dorothea von Jagow, who brought to the marriage a noble lineage but unfortunately very little ready cash. Their first child, Friedrich Wilhelm, therefore spent his early years in an atmosphere of shabby-genteel poverty.

After attending the Jesuit school at Breslau, Friedrich Wilhelm entered the Prussian army of Frederick the Great in 1746 at the age of sixteen. He fought in the Seven Years' War, and was twice wounded in the Battle of Prague. By 1758 he had been promoted to the elite "free battalion" of General Johann von Mayr, and upon von Mayr's death was assigned as staff officer to General von Hülsen. It was through this appointment that von Steuben first met the king's brother, Prince Henry, who was renowned as a military leader (and notorious as a lover of men). The two soldiers remained friends throughout their lives.

At the end of the Seven Years' War, Frederick the Great established a special school which would eventually develop into the *Kriegs Akademie*. Its first class was comprised of thirteen officers who had shown exceptional military ability during the war; one of the thirteen elite was Captain von Steuben. The king was the sole instructor for the class, which he used as a means of passing on to the next generation of military leaders his extraordinary grasp of the art of warfare. Under the king's personal tutelage von Steuben learned the craft that he would eventually bring to the aid of the beleaguered Continental Army.

Through the course of the Seven Years' War and the peace which followed von Steuben's star continued a slow, steady ascent, until suddenly and mysteriously it fell. He was relieved from his duties at the royal headquarters, transferred to the *Ultima Thule* of the lower Rhine, and then summarily discharged. The reasons for the precipitous fall are unclear. In one of von Steuben's autobiographical essays he gives only a vague account:

> Soon my commanders and my thoughtful King took notice of me and preferred me. Of my service in the Seven Years' War I have no reason to be ashamed. At the close of this war an inconsiderate step and the rancor of an implacable enemy frustrated my expectation of an appropriate reward. To say it in one word, I found myself compelled to quit the Prussian Service.[2]

What that inconsiderate step was von Steuben never specified, but the change in his status was profound. There is even evidence to suggest that Frederick the Great ordered him to leave Prussia. He was penniless and in debt; since the age of sixteen he had been in the army and had few other skills. With the help of a written testimonial from Prince Henry and the intercession of Henry's niece, Princess Frederica of Württemberg, von Steuben found a position as Grand Marshall at the court of the Prince of Hohenzollern-Hechingen. The post was essentially that of majordomo: he was responsible for the smooth operation of the court and burdened with the unenviable task of stretching the prince's ever-shrinking finances to cover the expense of running a royal household. The principality had been hovering near bankruptcy for more than a century; when von Steuben took up his duties the court's elegance and dignity had become more and more a pantomime of smoke and mirrors.

Von Steuben ran the prince's shabby pageant for eleven years, but by 1775 the finances of the Hohenzollern-Hechingen court had become so precarious that he felt that he needed to find more secure employment. At the age of forty-six he decided to try once more for a military career. Despite several promising leads—including the possibility of a commission in the French army—he was unable to find anyone willing to pay for his services. Finally an unexpected opportunity arose when at Karlsruhe he met P. P. Burdett, an Englishman who was an old friend of Benjamin Franklin. Burdett was sympathetic to the American cause, and he revealed that France was secretly supporting the insurrection in the colonies by sending over military advisors. None, Burdett sighed, had the necessary experience in army administration to take charge of military training. Von Steuben casually mentioned that "a friend"—an experienced officer who had trained under Frederick the Great—might be interested in helping out the Americans, if the proper arrangements could be made. Burdett passed this information along to Benjamin Franklin and Silas Deane in Paris. Von Steuben soon received a reply that the Americans would be very much interested in meeting his "friend."

In June 1777 von Steuben arrived in Paris and met first with the French war minister the Comte de Saint-Germain, who enthusiastically supported his cause and promised not only to introduce him to the Americans, but also to assure them of the strong (though secret) endorsement of the French government. The Baron was invited to meet with the Americans at Franklin's house in Passy. Though Franklin and Deane were impressed by what they saw and heard, their offer to him was somewhat less than he had anticipated. So many foreign officers had been arriving to join the Continental Army that they were becoming a source of discord among the American officers, jealous of their commissions. Congress had ordered the American commissioners in Paris to make no more promises concerning rank or pay. His finances having dwindled to an alarming level, the Baron was willing to volunteer his services and to hope that Congress would later reward him according to his merits, but when he learned that

Franklin and Deane were not empowered even to pay his travel expenses, he had no choice but to withdraw. Franklin's attitude during the negotiations did not help. The Baron later wrote that when Franklin declined to make a firm offer, "He told me that with an Air & manner to which I was then little accustomed, & I immediately took leave without any further Explanation." He was "disgusted by Dr. Franklin's declaration."[3] Word arrived of a possible opening in the service of the Margrave of Baden, and the Baron left Paris to return to Germany.

But before von Steuben could secure the position with the margrave, a disturbing allegation was raised. An unnamed source at the court at Baden wrote to von Steuben's former employer the Prince of Hohenzollern-Hechingen to find if there was any truth to a rumor being circulated:

> It has come to me from different sources that M. de Steuben is accused of having taken familiarities with young boys which the laws forbid and punish severely. I have even been informed that that is the reason why M. de Steuben was obliged to leave Hechingen and that the clergy of your country intend to prosecute him by law as soon as he may establish himself anywhere. . . . Has the Baron de Steuben been accused of the crime in question?[4]

The prince's response (if there was one) has not yet been discovered, but whether he supported von Steuben or not, the damage had been done. Though this is the earliest explicit reference to von Steuben's sexual practices yet found in German archives, it cannot be the first time the issue was raised. Given his subsequent actions, von Steuben must have felt this charge hanging over him for some time. No evidence indicates that he was in fact a pedophile—his subsequent interest seems to have been directed entirely toward young men, not boys—but perhaps he felt the distinction would be difficult to explain. Rather than stay and provide a defense, rather than call upon his friends in the Prussian army and in the minor European courts to vouch for his reputation, von Steuben chose to flee his homeland, never to return. He immediately hurried back to Paris and finding the Americans still interested, accepted their original offer in its entirety—no guaranteed salary, no guaranteed rank, no guaranteed commission.

Did the Americans know the reason for von Steuben's abrupt about-face? Benjamin Franklin was the most worldly and most sexually sophisticated of the Founding Fathers, and as the darling of the freethinkers in French society he surely would have heard the court gossip swirling around the Baron. Worldly as Franklin may have been, he probably shared the prejudices of most Americans when it came to charges of men having sex with young boys. Perhaps his distaste accounts for the coolness von Steuben sensed from a man otherwise renowned for his easy humor and deft diplomacy. But Franklin was also a hardheaded businessman with few illusions about human nature. If he disapproved of the Baron's sexual practices, he was willing to overlook them if circumstances required it. The Continental Army was in desperate need of both tactical know-how and international prestige, both of which would come from a perceived alliance with the Prussian military machine. The Baron was to some extent "damaged goods," but he was the best Franklin could acquire at the moment, and if von Steuben was not exactly the personal envoy of Frederick the Great, King of Prussia, no one in America need know that. Franklin welcomed the Baron to the American cause, and the marketing of Friedrich Wilhelm von Steuben began.

First, it was necessary to improve his rank. Despite the honor of being chosen to attend Frederick the Great's elite military school, von Steuben had never been promoted beyond the rank of captain. Franklin and Deane sent ahead letters that described him as a lieutenant general and aide-de-camp of the King of Prussia. Once the Baron landed in America the "error" was officially corrected but not widely publicized. Some explanation was needed for von Steuben's sudden availability, and the groundwork needed to be laid for an eventual military commission and salary. The official story circulated for popular consumption was that von Steuben had left behind his vast wealth and exalted position in Europe in order to volunteer his services in the American struggle for independence. Though an aristocrat by birth, he was inflamed by the call of freedom for the common man. He asked for no rank or military honors. He asked for no immediate compensation for his immense sacrifices, but was willing to trust that Congress would—should the Americans be victorious—award him some small recompense for his trouble. The Baron's biographer John McAuley Palmer asks,

Could a Prussian soldier of fortune, completely ignorant of our language, create a plot and a role so informed with intimate understanding of the American character and of the whole American scene? Impossible. In my opinion we find here the unmistakable stagecraft of Benjamin Franklin.[5]

The Baron set off to meet Washington at Valley Forge. He carried with him a personal letter from Henry Laurens, the president of Congress, to his son John Laurens, who was one of Washington's aides-de-camp. Because von Steuben spoke German and French but little English, and his personal interpreter Pierre Duponceau knew little about military affairs, Washington lent him two of his own aides-de-camp who were proficient in French: the young John Laurens and Alexander Hamilton (future secretary of the treasury). The choice of Laurens and Hamilton from Washington's staff is an ironic one, since the two young men were at the time deeply involved in a romantic friendship. The following spring, when Laurens was in South Carolina hoping to organize battalions of black slaves to fight against the British, Hamilton wrote to him:

Cold in my professions, warm in [my] friendships, I wish, Dear Laurens, it m[ight] be in my power, by action rather than words, [to] convince you that I love you. I shall only tell you that 'till you bade us Adieu, I hardly knew the value you had taught my heart to set upon you. Indeed, my friend, it was not well done. You know the opinion I entertain of mankind, and how much it is my desire to preserve myself free from particular attachments, and to keep my happiness independent on the caprice of others. You sh[ould] not have taken advantage of my sensibility to ste[al] into my affections without my consent. But as you have done it and as we are generally indulgent to those we love, I shall not scruple to pardon the fraud you have committed, on condition that for my sake, if not for your own, you will always continue to merit the partiality, which you have so artfully instilled in [me].[6]

Parts of this letter were obliterated, with words crossed out so that it is impossible to read them. The first page of the letter is annotated in pencil, presumably in the hand of John C. Hamilton, an early editor of

Alexander Hamilton's correspondence. The note reads, "I must not publish the whole of this."[7]

Hamilton's nearly ungovernable libido was legendary and would lead him into a heterosexual scandal which almost destroyed his career. But that was all ahead. In 1780 Hamilton made an advantageous alliance, marrying into the prominent Schuyler family. "Next fall completes my doom," he wrote his friend. Laurens congratulated him on moving on to this new stage of life, but Hamilton assured him that his affection would not be altered:

> In spite of Schuyler's black eyes, I have still a part for the public and another for you; so your impatience to have me married is misplaced; a strange cure by the way, as if after matrimony I was to be less devoted than I am now.

As the war wound down Hamilton urged Laurens to join him in building the new republic.

> Quit your sword my friend, put on the *toga,* come to Congress. We know each others sentiments, our views are the same: we have fought side by side to make America free, let us hand in hand struggle to make her happy.[8]

John Laurens and Alexander Hamilton never had the opportunity to struggle hand in hand in the new republic. Laurens was killed in a minor skirmish with a British foraging party. Hamilton's last letter never reached him.

Once installed at Valley Forge, von Steuben set about familiarizing himself with the Continental Army by conferring with the heads of each brigade, division, and regiment. He spoke with the common soldiers in their drafty huts, saw their ragged clothes, battered weapons, and meager rations. What he saw touched him to his core. He reported to Washington that no European army would have held together and endured what the Americans were accepting with grit and determination. Von Steuben was appointed Acting Inspector General, with responsibility for devising a method of drill that could forge the various colonial contingents into a national military force. Because some units followed some parts of the French drill, others some parts of the Prussian drill, and still others some parts of the English drill, the Baron had little choice but to write his own drill manual, adapting it as necessary to the capabilities of the American army.

There was no time to have a drill manual composed and printed, so each day von Steuben would write a portion of the manual in French, and give it to his aide Pierre Duponceau to translate into English. Duponceau would pass the translation on to Laurens and Hamilton to edit into proper military form. The Baron would then commit the new English version to memory, though he could understand very little of the actual words and grammar. The new portions of the manuscript were copied again and again by hand, and the written sheets distributed to each of the fourteen brigade inspectors. Each morning as the men began to follow the new drill procedures, von Steuben was busily at work writing out the next day's chapter.

The drill manual eventually found its way into print, and it remained the official United States military blue book until 1812. To a modern reader the Baron's instructions have an oddly salacious ring, sounding more like a sex manual than a drill manual:

> Bring the right hand briskly, and place it under the cock. . . . Quit the butt with the left hand, and seize the firelock at the swell. . . . Bring the left hand down strong upon the butt. . . . Bring the butt of the firelock under the right arm, letting the piece fall down strong on the palm of the left hand, which receives the swell, the muzzle pointed directly to the front, the butt pressed with the arm against the side. . . .[9]

Although it is tempting to read the drill manual as an elaborate homosexual joke devised by von Steuben, Laurens, and Hamilton at the expense of the unwitting military brass, a comparison with other drill manuals of the period reveals that the language is very much in line with what might be expected of the genre. The double entendres that are so striking to a modern ear were probably unheard in the eighteenth century.

The drill manual was a necessity, but it was not sufficient as an instructional tool. Von Steuben next created a model company and drilled the soldiers himself. They could be used to supplement the written word by demonstrating the maneuvers to the rest of the men, and each would in turn instruct his own unit, with careful corrections given by the Baron. The method worked well—except whenever a complicated march-and-wheel maneuver collapsed into confusion and von Steuben's meager store of English failed him. He would begin to shout in French and then German, and eventually fall back on the one English word he could always remember: "Goddam! God-dam! Goddam!"[10]

It was during one of these fiascos that a handsome young officer stepped forward and, speaking to the Baron in flawless French, offered his services as an interpreter. "If I had seen an angel from Heaven I should not have more rejoiced," the Baron later recalled. The angel was Captain Benjamin Walker. Walker was born in London in 1753 but had emigrated at an early age to New York City. He was twenty-five years old when he first met von Steuben, strikingly handsome, self-possessed, and intelligent. Within weeks of appearing as the Baron's "angel" Walker was appointed as his aide-de-camp.

It was also during these first months in America that the Baron met Captain William North, who was to become his second aide-de-camp, his closest companion, and (with Benjamin Walker) his heir. North was born in 1755 at Fort Frederick, Maine, where his father had been stationed as a captain in the army. When he was eight years old, his father died and he and his mother moved to Boston, where North received his education. There is no indication that Walker and North knew each other before being assigned as aides-de-camp to von Steuben, and they served together for nearly two years before their romantic friendship blossomed. For a while, North was apparently involved with another of the Baron's aides-de-camp, James Fairlie, but sometime after the entourage joined Washington's encampment at Tappan, New York, North realized that his regard for Ben Walker had grown into a deeper love.

At a distance of over 200 years, with only the evidence of a large but scattered and incomplete body of correspondence, it is impossible to prove the nature of the relationships which developed between North and Walker, and between von Steuben and each of the two young men. It appears that North and Walker enjoyed a romantic friendship which included sexual intimacy. North was more deeply emotionally involved in the relationship than was Walker, but during the early years (at least) the feelings were mutual. North was also emotionally drawn to von Steuben, but their relationship more closely followed the model of a romantic mentorship. Fatherless from a young age, William North sought out the love and regard of the older man. Von Steuben was clearly infatuated with North, and it is probable that the relationship at some point included sexual intimacy. Von Steuben was also attracted to his "angel" Benjamin Walker, but while

Walker held the Baron in high esteem, and perhaps loved him as a father figure, he does not appear to have been sexually interested. An element of flirtation in von Steuben's letters to Walker indicates that the relationship had never quite developed along the lines the Baron desired.

From early in their association Benjamin Walker had no scruples about exploiting the Baron's sexual interest in him to his own advantage, even though he had no intention of reciprocating. While von Steuben was in Philadelphia overseeing the publication of his drill manual, Walker wrote to him from headquarters where he had temporarily joined Washington's staff,

> If it would not be taking too much Liberty, I should be extremely obliged to you to desire Du Ponceau to get me a good Hat & send it by the first Opportunity that Offers the price of which I will reimburse you with thanks on your arrival in Camp.[11]

The Baron must have responded promptly and generously, sending underwear as well. Two weeks later Walker wrote him again:

> [Nicolas] Fish deliverd me the Linnens you was so kind as to send, for which accept my thanks you are determined to keep me your Debtor in every respect, however I shall not attempt to say much on this subject as all I can say or do will fall far short of the repeated Instances of Friendship you have honor'd me with—Of this however I can with Confidence assure you, that I could remain easy under so many obligations *from you alone* & that I shall never be more happy than in an Opportunity of convincing you that I am with greatest respect & Esteem, Dear General, Your very humble Obdt. Srvt. Ben Walker.[12]

Two weeks later he wrote once again, this time with a more extensive shopping list:

> Accept my D[ea]r General my thanks for your kind offer of procuring me a few necessaries—with respect to the Uniform I shall only want a Coat Blue—turned up & faced with Buff[,] white Lining & plain white buttons[,] a Cockade for the Hat with a black silk cord & tassell—two or three Yards of Hair Ribbon, a pair of Gloves & a Sword belt with Swivels—

> These my D[ea]r General are all the articles I stand in need of &
> with which I should really be ashamed to trouble you had you
> not indulged me in the pleasing thought, of regarding you in the
> double capacity of my General & my Friend. . . .[13]

The letter ends with a postscript which indicates that von Steuben had
offered to supply favors for Washington's other aides-de-camp, an offer they had declined: "The Family desire their Compliments to you,
they thank you for your kind offer but have no Commissions."

"Family" was indeed the preferred term for the group of younger
officers who were assigned as aides-de-camp to senior military leaders. The young men could look to their commanding officer for privileges and advancement as if he were an indulgent parent, and they in
turn lent status to the commander largely based on their number, rank,
and familial connections. Even an officer's staff of "waiters" (personal servants) could add to his lustre, not by their social status but by
their personal appearance. The archives at West Point include a petu-
lant letter written to Commandant Henry Burbeck in 1807 from an officer seeking to block the transfer of one of the servants,

> It has been hinted to me that Lieut. Leonard has made applica-
> tion for his waiter to be transferred from my Company to Captn.
> Stille's, this I hope will not be granted him, as he is one of the
> best looking soldiers that I have in my Company.[14]

Being part of an officer's military family—or even the servant of a
member of the family—brought with it privileges and immunities
that are amazing by modern standards. After the battle at Blandford,
British General William Phillips sent a note to von Steuben requesting that the standard etiquette of warfare be observed concerning a
captured British waiter:

> My Aide de Camp's Servant John Portuit was taken yesterday. I
> request you will have the goodness to send him back as soon as
> possible. I conceive nothing but the little hurry of yesterday
> could have prevented this being done without application, as I
> imagine you are a Gentleman who perfectly understand[s] these
> civilities, which have been practiced by the Kings Officers on all
> occasions, particularly in the instance of General Steubens Ser-

vant and others taken by Lieutenant Colonel Simcoe in the last expeditions, who were sent back immediately.[15]

Von Steuben responded with equal punctiliousness:

> Before I received your letter, left at a Tavern, relating to your aid-de-camps servant, orders had been given to send him in. Be assured, Sir, that I know and that I wish to observe that politeness from Gentleman to Gentleman and from Officer to Officer. If I was difficient in not sending him in the same day as he was taken, yourself have been happy enough to find my excuse—A Retreat before three times my number, commanded by Gen. Phillips, certainly demanded all my attention.[16]

Once a young officer was assigned to a senior officer, he was regarded by all as an intimate part of that officer's entourage, even when an assignment temporarily took him elsewhere. When Walker wrote to von Steuben from Washington's camp he provided a sardonic view of life with the great man:

> I am not negligent in my attendance at Head Quarters, tho' to little purpose—you who know with what reserve the General conducts himself with those in much higher Stations than myself will hardly suppose he enters into Conversation with me, except at Table, his inquiries are confined to, "when did you hear from the Baron?"[17]

So identified was Walker with von Steuben that he considered himself to be the Baron's surrogate whenever they were apart:

> I enclose a letter from General Schuyler—his Daughter is now in Morris Town—I have not yet seen her tho' she acknowledges she came recommended to your protection. As all that is left of you in Camp, I should not have neglected so fair an Opportunity of supplying your absence, but Alas! my Old Coat & Hat forbid my associating but with my Brethren in affliction whom I endeavour to console as much as in my Power by giving one or two of them every night a good Supper.[18]

The letter served a double purpose: to assure the Baron that Walker was avoiding the enticement of female company, and to remind him of his request for new clothes.

Having overseen the publication of his *Regulations,* in the spring of 1780 von Steuben rejoined the army at Middlebrook, New Jersey. Shortly after the Baron's return, twenty-four-year-old William North was assigned to him as an aide-de-camp, and North and Walker (along with James Fairlie) became von Steuben's family. After over two years of service in the Continental Army, the Baron fully comprehended the enormous handicap he had assumed by signing onto the American cause without a firm arrangement for financial support. Despite the dramatic change in troop discipline brought about thanks to his drill manual, despite the improvement in supply distribution which resulted from his careful system of returns, despite the high regard in which he was held by the American troops from General Washington down to the most ragged foot soldier, Congress held the purse strings and Congress begrudged every penny spent on the Baron's maintenance. For four years he found himself fighting both the British and the Congress. After the victory at Yorktown von Steuben wrote to General Nathaniel Greene announcing that he had come to the end of his resources and he had no choice but to resign. He stayed on until the end of the war, but soon enough learned that the cessation of hostilities with the British would not bring an end to his monetary woes.

After the American victory a grateful nation settled money and land on its war heroes, but a congressional committee voted to award von Steuben only a gold-hilted sword and two thousand dollars, less than one-twentieth of the amount he had anticipated. Biographer John McAuley Palmer speculates on why the Baron was treated so shabbily:

> Here the committee was probably influenced by its chairman, Arthur Lee. Lee was one of the American Commissioners in Paris when the Baron sailed for America. He had been ignored and humiliated by Franklin and Deane and was rarely consulted by them. He resented their attitude and considered them unscrupulous intriguers. Their conversion of Steuben, a poverty-stricken captain, into a well-to-do lieutenant general was a case in point. Lee had had no part in the transaction but he probably

knew the facts. He had returned from a mission to Frederick the Great shortly before Steuben's second journey to Paris.[19]

Palmer discounts the German charges of sexual misconduct against the Baron, and credits Lee's animus against von Steuben primarily to outrage that the Baron was pretending to a military rank he had not earned. It is much more likely, however, that Lee learned at the Prussian court of the Baron's sexual practices, and although Lee was loathe to raise such a distasteful topic, he was determined that von Steuben not be treated as an American hero.

How many people knew of the accusations against von Steuben that led to his flight from Europe? While in Philadelphia supervising the publication of his *Regulations* the Baron stayed at Belmont, the estate of Richard Peters, a member of the Board of War. During his visit he showered attention on Peters's little boy, playing soldier with him and appointing him as his honorary aide-de-camp. When he left to return to General Washington's headquarters he sent a note to Duponceau which included the instructions, "Go to Mr. Peters' house and give three kisses to my little aide-de-camp and as many to his mother if Mr. Peters offers no objection."[20] To Richard Peters himself he wrote: "My respects to Mrs Peters, and an hundred kisses to my Rake of an Aide de Camp, repeat often my name to him, that he may not forget me quite."[21] It is unlikely he would have written in this tone if he believed that Peters and his wife were aware he had been accused of taking sexual liberties with young boys. The social prohibition concerning the unspeakable crime against nature in this case worked to von Steuben's advantage. Opposition from those in the know was implacable, but it was also largely silent.

The war brought the Baron, William North, and Benjamin Walker together, but they spent only around two years of it sharing the same quarters. Temporary missions sometimes separated them, and in January 1782 Walker was permanently transferred to General Washington's staff to become one of his aides-de-camp. Walker found life at army headquarters stultifying:

> We are here in the Center of dullness, HeadQts you know was always the last place in the World for mirth—and unhappily, there being only two of us, I cannot go out to take my share of the little that is circulating abroad—At home the occupations of each day are so much alike from one end of the Month to the

other, that the life is really disgusting—I had two disciples at Chess—Mrs. Washington & my Colleague [poet Colonel David Humphreys]—but unhappily one is thinking too much of her home & t'other is making verses during the game—their progress therefore was so little that both are tired of it—and so I have been obliged to learn Back Gammon—of which I am equally tired—in fact I have only one resource left to prevent my dying of *Ennuy*—to seek some neighbours daughter *pour passer le temps*—you know my dear General how much this is against my conscience and will judge how hard I must be drove before I could bring myself to seek this Expedient to <u>amuse myself</u>.[22]

Walker's letters are often tender and affectionate: "I was exceedingly glad too to hear that North was again with you—your situation was too solitary, and wanted his gaiety to make it tolerable—but tell him, that he has another friend besides his General—as he passed on to you he had forgot it."[23] He sometimes closed his letters with a wistful, "Adieu my dear Baron tell North I love him."[24]

With Walker's transfer to General Washington's staff, the carefully balanced tension of their triangle collapsed. Walker and North appear to have been deeply in love. The Baron was physically attracted to North and flattered by his boyish devotion, but he had also been a little jealous of the emotional closeness of the two younger men. He was intrigued and frustrated that Walker was unwilling to enter into the same type of intimate relationship with him that he shared with North. In his letters to Walker, the Baron was not above playing one friend against the other if he felt it might advance his own cause with either. In February 1782 he wrote (in French) a letter in which he both flirted with Walker and attempted to suborn him into criticizing North:

This wretched [*chienne de*] ministerial correspondence has cost me infinite trouble. You know that I am without help even for my English correspondence. What shall I do, my friend, if I must make another campaign? I do not believe Popham wishes to rejoin me; at least I have not had a line from him. Where shall I find a W——— [Walker] but I must not make you too vain. But seriously, where shall I find a man who can conduct my correspondence? See a little if you can suggest me a good fellow. You know what I want. I always count on my North, nevertheless you know his strength does not lie in the pen. You know too that he is as lazy as he is good.[25]

North in turn wrote from Mount Vernon, where he and the Baron were guests of George and Martha Washington. The letter includes sniggering gossip about Washington, his wife, and his niece, Fanny Bassett (". . . but she has no breasts Ben!"), and he flippantly assures his friend that he has not fallen into low Southern habits: "Will you believe it—I have not hump'd a single mulatto since I am here. . . ."[26]

As the war wound down, von Steuben and North were drawn into a social whirl as the giddy prospect of peace spread across the country. With Walker gone, North took on the full burden of being the Baron's companion, and it is probably during this period that they became physically intimate. His letters take on a strained and frenetic tone: "We are frequently in town," he wrote to Walker,

> but receive no pleasure. We dine & surfeit, we dance & are tired, wish for solitude, & retire to the country, are sick of ourselves & sigh for the noise and bustle of the City. We go—we return. This is a most infamous world, would to God I was out of it.[27]

With the coming of peace, the Baron insisted on living like a European nobleman and military hero, even though he lacked the financial resources to support an elegant lifestyle. He had full confidence that the Americans would grant him a fair recompense for his contribution to the war effort, and he saw little reason to wait until the money was in his bank account. It fell to North to try to reason with him, to get him to realize the seriousness of his money woes. In exasperation North wrote to Walker:

> Used to a country where whatever a Nobleman did was always right & a rascally peasantry dare not call to him to an account, he forgets that here all men affect to be equal & that no man is independent except by being free of debt, & that a Nobleman who owes can neither be screened from paying or from that legal insult which the creditor (tho ever so mean) offers to his debtor.[28]

In his soberer moments, von Steuben understood that his young companion was right in urging caution, and he made many solemn promises to mend his ways—only to turn around and order another five

cases of fine French wine. Gentle chiding and sincere repentance
soon escalated into messy domestic quarrels. The Baron would lose
his temper and denounce North as a "miser" and a "*bougre*" [faggot]
and then abjectly apologize and seek forgiveness.[29] A few weeks of
probity would follow, but then North would once again find himself
trying to placate the hordes of irate tradesmen who pounded on their
door with fists full of unpaid bills.

Early in the winter of 1783-1784 von Steuben leased a run-down
but spacious estate on Manhattan known as the Louvre. Here he could
provide an elegant home for his family: William North, Benjamin
Walker, James Fairlie, and any of the other ex-soldiers who chose to
join him. The fashionable young men came, lived off his hospitality
for a while, and then left. Only North remained, though he was frequently on the road. Together with Walker and Alexander Hamilton,
North did everything in his power to goad Congress into granting von
Steuben at least a portion of the money he deserved, but to little avail.

The Baron remained incapable of living frugally, and North found
himself in the unenviable (and draining) position of both fighting the
government for more funds and fighting von Steuben to stay within a
budget. Their relationship degenerated into one long argument over
money. In a chastened mood, the Baron wrote:

> Ah, Billy, I am too proud of you not to suffer through your ab-
> sence. But what folly [for me] to be attached to a man who is so
> often in a bad humor, scolding and disagreeable. This is what
> my reason tells me. But hush, my reason, you are mad. . . . It is
> true that he often scolds me. But it is because he wants me to be
> better than I really am. He wishes for order in my business af-
> fairs and I have none. He would have me be prudent, but my im-
> pulsive nature too often leads me to folly. He wishes that I were
> one of the seven sages of Greece, but my passions often make a
> fool of me. . . . Scold me, Billy, as often as I deserve it—that is to
> say, scold me always.[30]

In June 1786 the state of New York granted von Steuben a quarter
township of land on the Mohawk River, and he eventually transferred
his household to a small farm in the wilderness. By this time, however, the von Steuben-North-Walker triangle had been irrevocably
broken. Walker, too, had come to the limits of his patience. "I sometimes wish," he wrote to North, "I had never seen or never loved the

Baron. If he makes his friends happy by his goodness and amiable qualities, he also makes them miserable by his want of management and misfortunes."[31] Both men still loved and respected their mentor, but they were no longer under the spell of his worldly charm. With the conclusion of their military service, von Steuben, North, and Walker lost their defined role of "family" and there was nothing to take its place, no acceptable social structure that would allow them to retain their intimacy. Even if the Baron's profligacy had not alienated his companions, the triad could not have continued. North and Walker were ready to move on in their lives, and "moving on" for them meant finding a wife and settling down. In the eighteenth century there were few other choices.

Benjamin Walker married shortly after the end of the war. Little is known about his wife other than that her name was Molly and she is believed to have been a Quaker. William North began to court a young lady named Polly Duane, daughter of James Duane, a prominent lawyer and one of New York's most eminent citizens. With North on the road on various assignments for the new government, the courtship was carried on largely through correspondence—at least on William North's side. Polly Duane felt it was improper for a lady to write letters to a gentleman she hardly knew, and so von Steuben was drafted to act as intermediary.

> Why do you not make the girl write to me? Custom! Delicacy! Phsa! Would I not break through custom for her. Miss D— knows what is delicate & if she can in her conscience say that she thinks it indelicate to write to me, why I must give the matter up & notwithstanding I have written her four letters, I will write her again and not expect an answer.[32]

Playing the Marschallin to North's Octavian, von Steuben acted as go-between, delivering letters and making a laconic attempt to present North's case as an eligible suitor. As he felt his companion slipping away, the Baron's letters to North became more florid and less discreet. He would address them to *"Mon tendre et Cherissime Billy"* and close them with a passionate *"Adieu mon cher et tendre ami—je suis j'usquà mon dernier soupir votre bien affectionné et sincere Ami."*[33] The Baron's intercession was nevertheless effective and

Polly Duane finally relented; she and William North were married on October 14, 1787. The following spring they settled on a farm near Duanesburg, New York, a wedding present from Polly's father.

North was in high spirits and wrote to Walker: "The Baron arrived here about fourteen days after he left New York [City], & stayed with us only four or 5 days. . . . I wish we could live all together Ben!"[34] It would be a common theme in his letters for years to come. The Baron's short visit—traveling for two weeks and staying for only four or five days—is a good indication that he realized he could play only a minor role in North's new life. As both Billy and Ben pursued their new roles as husbands, von Steuben found himself alone and unwilling (or unable) to replace them. He rehired his former butler from the flush days at the Louvre, Mitchell, and began to shower him with expensive presents. North considered Mitchell to be a "worthless rascal," and particularly objected to the fact that the Baron was dressing him "like a beau with his silk stockings & waistcoat"—more like a pampered companion than a servant.[35] Walker remained silent, perhaps remembering the blue coat, underwear, and hair ribbons he had received from the Baron in their early years together. The relationship between von Steuben and Mitchell appears to have been based on the model of erotic employment, with Mitchell nominally serving as the Baron's valet, but also perhaps providing sexual services.

The Baron traveled extensively, staying for periods of time with both North and Walker. He wrote to North relating how he savored his young friend's letters; especially on those evenings when Molly Walker gave them only an old crust of cheese for dessert, they provided him with the equivalent of "Poudin & Mince Pey."[36] Despite some additional funds from Congress and generous grants of land from a number of grateful states, the Baron's finances remained perilous. Finally, in 1792, he decided to settle permanently in upstate New York to try to make a go of his farm. The "worthless rascal" Mitchell was replaced by John Mulligan, a recent graduate from Columbia College. Mulligan was hired to be von Steuben's "secretary and companion," but clearly their relationship included a deep personal component. More than employer and employee, the two men lived together with a certain degree of intimacy, but it is impossible to determine from the surviving evidence whether it was a romantic mentorship or merely erotic employment. Perhaps it shared elements of both. North made an attempt to counsel the new companion on how to handle the Baron's addiction to high living, but to no avail. "I talked to Mulligan about it," he wrote to Walker, "—but he is but a boy."[37]

The Baron made a few short journeys from his cabin, but his life became more and more isolated, and his privacy more guarded. Whenever von Steuben and Mulligan were away, the servants were forbidden to enter the Baron's bedroom for any reason. The two men focused their attentions on each other, socializing little, and North and Walker found it increasingly difficult to keep in touch with their old friend. The Baron was sixty-four years old, and a lifetime of military campaigns and excessive indulgence had taken their toll. On November 29, 1794, Mulligan wrote to Benjamin Walker to inform him that von Steuben had died of a stroke the day before. "O, Colonel Walker," the young man wrote in distress,

> our friend, my all. I can write no more. Come if you can. I am lonely. Oh, good God, what solitude is in my bosom. Oh, if you were here to mingle your tears with mine, there would be some consolation for the distressed.[38]

North attended the funeral, but Walker did not. Mulligan and North walked together in the funeral procession. "A few tenants and servants," North wrote, "the young gentleman, his late companion, and one on whom for fifteen years his eye had never ceased to beam with kindness [North himself], followed in silence and in tears."[39] It is perhaps significant to note that to North, Mulligan was von Steuben's "companion"—not his secretary or valet.

An odd proviso in the Baron's will may provide an insight into the intimate aspects of his relationship with Mulligan. After listing his bequests to his household staff he added a stipulation:

> I do hereby declare that these legacies to my Servants are on the following conditions, that on my Decease they do not permit any person to touch my Body, not even to change the shirt in which I shall die but that they wrap me up in my old military cloak and in twenty four hours after my Decease bury me in such spot as I shall before my Decease point out to them and that they never acquaint any person with the place where I shall be buried.[40]

That he specified in particular that his shirt not be removed may be an indication that he was engaging in practices which left scars or marks on his torso.

In his will the Baron left Mulligan his library, maps, and charts, "and the sum of Two Thousand and five hundred Dollars to complete it." After bequeathing one year's wages to each of his servants, he left the remainder of his estate equally to North and to Walker. To Benjamin Walker he also specifically left three thousand dollars and the gold-hilted sword given to him by Congress. To North he left a silver-hilted sword and a gold box presented to him by the City of New York. In a slip of the pen which can be described only as "Freudian" the holograph will reads, "To the said William North I bequeath my silver hilted North. . . ."[41]

Baron Frederick Wilhelm von Steuben was buried under a hemlock tree near his cabin. Several years later a work crew laying out a new road broke open the grave and exposed part of the coffin. There is a story that neighbors opened the coffin to take scraps of his uniform as souvenirs. When Benjamin Walker heard of the desecration he had the remains moved to a more secluded spot and arranged for security and perpetual care for the grave site.

William North's life after his marriage to Polly Duane was not an easy one. He was not cut out to be a farmer, and the land in Duanesburg never prospered. As early as January 1789, less than two years after his marriage, he was writing to the Baron,

> My wife is the best Woman possible, my boy is good but I am not happy. . . . I shall come to New York, kiss you & Ben, go to Boston [to] comfort my old Mother & return here to drudge on in getting my living. . . . Give my love to Ben & his Wife—I am not the best of husbands—but I will endeavour to be as good as I can.[42]

In his letters to Benjamin Walker he was philosophical about their respective marriages, tacitly acknowledging that taking a wife had been the only option available to them:

> Which of us had the most courage [in marrying] I won't say— our heads had more to do in our marriages than our hearts, our hearts have now more to do in the business than our heads—We

began by esteeming [our wives] & end with loving—I believe the women went on the same way. I am sure neither my wife or I loved each other half so well a Year ago as we do now. I wish the Good God would give you a child, but if he does not, you shall have one of mine, *if we have more*. it shall lay in your bosom & be unto you as a son, & you will not love it the less if it is not called Ben—which is a name my wife never would be prevailed on to give it.[43]

North had wanted to follow the convention of naming a son after his beloved friend, but his wife would not permit it. To object to naming one of her sons Ben, Polly North must on some level have been aware of the nature of the relationship between the two men. Billy suggested that further pregnancies were in any case doubtful; this may be an indication that the sexual side of their marriage had already broken down.

As the years passed Polly became more and more of a recluse, and was increasingly unwilling to allow her husband out of her sight. "I never have attempted before this time to go from home & stay a night," North wrote to Walker, "& now I find its impossible—If I was married to Mother Duane I could sleep out as many nights as I pleased. . . ."[44] (North's relationship with his mother-in-law had evidently also soured.) A dozen years later, when Ben invited the Norths to visit him and his wife in Utica, Billy explained that his wife never leaves the farm. "As for me," he offered,

I will come & see you, whether you come here or not—I am more attached to you than I ought to be, not that you don't deserve my attachment—but because it is folly to have much regard for any thing in this World, where the good is only a smaller evil—in which, during 40 years I have not found more than three or four men to love sincerely—two of whom I have lost & the other lives at 100 miles distance. . . .[45]

One evening in November 1792 William North got profoundly drunk and wrote a letter to Benjamin Walker which is so extraordinarily revealing that it deserves to be quoted in its entirety:

My dear friend,
The table at which I ate my morsel—morsel!—by heaven I have

eaten most monstrously, an hogs head baked with liver, heart & lights (lites, for 'twas not on the light of heaven I dined) You will say, or if you will not, I will, tis a most excellent dish, nay, two dishes—grog have I drank for three days, but as an accompaniment to *this dinner* I slipt'd down the pantry stairs without any ones knowing it, unlocked the door of my little repositary & brought up (at the moment I had half dined) one bottle of your port. It was not for fear the grogg would grow upon me, & yet "let him that standest take head [heed] lest he fall." but it struck me that I should relish it—the idea of my friend struck me & I was ashamed to prefer grogg because it was in the closet, to wine because it was in the cellar. The first glass I drank formally to the health of my wife & little children—I wish I could have only thought of them when I drank it, but Walker, his wife (I love her Ben, for her own sake) & the Baron, crowded into my mind & the devil could not put them out again. So that every glass I have drank, & I have been drunken, the whole squad, & even Eustis, & Major Edwards have cheek by jowl brought themselves along side of my wife & children—at the 3d glass, I cried, 'tis damn'd hard, I felt I was alone—I felt—but in an instant, I felt thankful to God (seeing my barn which stands in full view of my table) that I was so well off as I was. Poor sad[?] Wissenfell, passed over my imagination & I was happy—I have known you, Ben, for twelve years—When I began to love you, I know not—the first motion of disregard to Fairlie, I remember—'twas at Tappan—I lay on straw with one blanket—but tis no matter—I loved you, Ben, before your letter respecting my wife's laying in at your house—I do not forget your wifes coming two hundred miles to see us—& if the Baron should not stay with me an hour at his next visit, or should he never visit me again, I will not forget when he did—You will, on reading this, exclaim, the fellow was drunk! But to show you that I am sober, I shall leave a blank space   for a wafer—I drink another glass of wine not to all the saints in heaven but to all those on earth whom I love—so God bless you

W North

[P.S.] Tuesday Mrn—I shivered a little & froze more last night—[46]

The postscript is perhaps both an embarrassed apology for the drunken scrawl and an invocation of the cold night in Tappan when they had only a straw bed and a single blanket. "Poor sad Wissenfell" is probably Lt. Charles Frederick Weissenfels, a fellow officer from New York. Walker served briefly under Weissenfels's father, Lt. Col. Frederick Weissenfels, in the 1st New York, and both Ben Walker and James Fairlie served with the younger Weissenfels in the 2nd New York Regiment.[47] Why Weissenfels was "poor sad" is unknown; given the context in which he was called to mind, perhaps he represented for North someone who had failed to make the transition to the role of settled married man.

In the years ahead both William North and Benjamin Walker held political office. North represented New York in the United States Senate from 1789 to 1799, and Walker served in the House of Representatives from 1801 to 1803. In 1811 the two men had a falling out when North spoke out against a bill to create the Seneca turnpike, a measure which Walker strongly supported (and perhaps in which he had a financial interest). For nearly two years all communication ceased, but then North wrote to break the impasse:

> My dear friend, for so I shall continue to think & believe & feel that you are notwithstanding the silence which has reigned between us for so long a time that I don't know whether one or two years have passed without my writing to, certainly without being written to by you—You have never been for a month out of my mind, I have wished to write—to write on common place subjects was not to write, to speak of the unhappiness which has fallen to the lot of a man whose course of life has passed in making others happy & who has not deserved the ills which are inflicted on him—God knows, not at least from those who inflict them—to tell your friend whom you love in *a letter* what you feel for him—how can it be done what is it worth, if done—I could embrace you Ben, & weep with you in silence over your griefs—but such a subject one who feels, can not write—[48]

North suffered the loss of two sons—Frederick (named after the Baron) in 1789 and James (named after Polly's father) in 1792—and in 1813 both his eldest son William and his daughter Adelia were gravely ill. While his daughter was still in the process of recovering, his wife Polly died. North was devastated. "I am alone," he wrote to

Walker, "tis lonesome, but I must remain alone through life. . . . I fear God may take my remaining children from me and I am more than half undone already."[49] Although his loss was profound and unsettling, North realized that he needed to plan for the future. With the death of his reclusive wife he was freed from the tether that had bound him to the frustrating and profitless life of a Duanesburg farmer. For two more years he stuck at it, and then finally decided he had had enough.

His thoughts turned to New York City and the social life he had fled so many years ago, a life filled with books and dinners and the company of witty, literate, like-minded men. He visualized exactly where he wanted to be: sunk into a comfortable leather chair in Kirk's Reading Room. Unfortunately family obligations intervened yet again. When his daughters heard of his plans to move the family to the city, they balked. Having been raised in rustic simplicity they realized they would be no match for the sophisticated New York debutantes. Despite their kinship with the oldest and most respected families in America, they had little money to launch themselves in society and next to nothing in the way of refined social skills. City life was out of the question. With apparently little struggle North gave up his dream of an urban lifestyle. In writing to Walker about his change of plans he explained the advantages of buying a large house in the suburbs, adding that it would allow him to provide a home for his son who was just completing his studies at New Haven, a strong incentive since "boarding houses & boarding house companions are not the best for a young man."[50]

The farm in Duanesburg was placed on the market and the girls began the exhausting task of packing up the household in preparation for the move east. At the age of sixty-two William North found himself at a crossroads, resigned to the life he had chosen yet still longing for the road not taken and unsure of what lay ahead. But before events could proceed further, fate placed one more twist in that road. In June 1817 Molly Walker unexpectedly died, and suddenly Ben *also* was freed from a marriage he had entered into more with his head than his heart. North sincerely mourned Molly's passing; she had always had his respect and affection and he felt true empathy for his friend's grief. And yet as they both faced major life changes they were also presented with a new opportunity. Now that they had faithfully fulfilled their obligations to society as husbands and fathers, might it be possible after all these years to share a life together? For William North the ember that had been damped down thirty years earlier had smoldered but never died.

He was unsure, however, of how Ben now felt, and he decided to approach the topic gingerly. He wrote an eloquent letter of sympathy ("There is nothing to be said, my dear friend, but there is enough to feel") and assured Walker that he was aware that the loss of a wife was a pain that would never heal. But then he hinted about the future:

> You have society, & valuable society around you—but, I think you should look to a speedy removal elsewhere—Where a total change of scene would present it self & where new food for the mind could every moment be procured.[51]

He stopped short of suggesting New York City, but the thought was obviously there.

Walker agreed that a change of scene was in order—and announced that he was planning a trip back to England for a visit, after which he would settle in Utica and live the life of a retired gentleman. "I think you will not, that you ought not to go to England," North replied.

> Who is there now, whom you can call friend—every thing is changed, & those you once knew[,] you will no more find—here you are not alone in the World—you are known & respected, & at least by more than one, beloved—You can live you say like a Gentleman at Utica—Yes, but what is this living like a Gentleman worth? What does it amount to? to giving dinners to people, one of whom, possibly, out of 20, would alone go to see you if you had no dinner to give—however I will say nothing further on this, habit is not easily changed—& yet I am about changing an habit of 30 years—but I can't stay here longer—I think I shall not stay any where long—I am frequently astonished by the state of my body & even mind, that the machine is decayed, & the wheels almost worn out.[52]

William North still clung to the dream of sharing his life with Benjamin Walker, but Walker seems to have put their past intimacy behind him. The last surviving letter between the two men was exchanged in October 1817, thirty-seven years after the young soldiers first met. "I will, God willing, next Winter make you a visit in January as I think," North wrote, "William [his son] will tell you how & where we are—What I am to do & where I am finally to retire next Spring, next Spring will show."[53] But in January 1818, before Billy North could see his old friend once more, Ben Walker died. The list of Walker's personal property filed in probate includes a painting of George Washington and bust of Alexander Hamilton, his two heroes. The bulk of his estate was left to his daughter and his two sisters; William North was not mentioned at all in the bequests.[54] North lived on alone for another eighteen years, and died in 1836 at the age of eighty-one.

Chapter 5

Sodomites in America's Libraries

The punishment of buggery is death without benefit of clergy, by the laws of this commonwealth. . . . For the honor of human nature it must be observed that this crime is seldom committed.

The New Virginia Justice (1795)

It is quite impossible to express my admiration for [Ossian's] Poems; at particular passages I felt my whole frame trembling with ecstacy; but if I was to describe all my thoughts, you would think me absolutely mad.

Andrew Erskine

On an April evening in 1782 the Marquis de Chastellux visited Thomas Jefferson at his hilltop home of Monticello accompanied by a small party of fellow Frenchmen traveling through North America during the closing months of the Revolutionary War. After dinner Mrs. Jefferson withdrew, leaving the men to their tobacco and punch. The room was hazy with smoke and candlelight, and the conversation was wide-ranging—philosophy, natural history, art, politics. The talk drifted easily, sometimes in English, sometimes in French. Then the topic turned to the poems of Ossian, and the desultory tone of the after-dinner talk changed abruptly.

In his memoirs the marquis recorded that he and Jefferson suddenly connected in a profound and dramatic way.

> It was a spark of electricity which passed rapidly from one to the other; we recalled the passages of those sublime poems which had particularly struck us, and we recited them for the benefit of my traveling companions, who fortunately knew English well and could appreciate them, even though they had never read the poems.

Jefferson called to have the volume of Ossian's poems brought to the room, where it was placed next to the bowl of punch. "And, before we realized it, book and bowl had carried us far into the night."[1]

Jefferson was passionately moved by the poems, first published in London in 1761 under the title *Fingal, an Ancient Epic Poem, in Six Books: Together with Several Other Poems, Composed by Ossian the Son of Fingal.* According to the book's title page, the poems had been translated from the original third-century Gaelic by a Scotsman named James Macpherson. So entranced was Jefferson by the power of the ancient epic that he wrote to an Edinburgh bookseller named John Macpherson (whom he believed to be related to the translator) asking if it would be possible to purchase a copy of the poems in their original language. He was willing to pay handsomely to have the manuscripts copied, if no printed version was available. With typical Jeffersonian thoroughness, he also requested a Gaelic-English dictionary and a grammar to help him in his reading of the originals. The bookseller eventually responded that no printed version of the Gaelic originals was available, and that the translator was, unfortunately, too busy to provide a copy of the manuscripts in his possession.

James Macpherson was unable to provide copies of the manuscripts because the "originals" did not exist. The poems were an elaborate literary hoax: Macpherson was not the translator of the poems; he was their author. A Highlander deeply resentful of the British suppression of Scots culture and fearful of its eventual loss, Macpherson as a young schoolmaster began to transcribe the traditional oral ballads recited by the old people of the region. In 1759 he was approached by the Scottish playwright John Home (who knew no Gaelic, but was fascinated by the ancient stories) and was asked to provide an English translation of one of the poems he had gathered. Macpherson complied, delivering in a few days an English version of a story about the death of Oscar, son of Ossian. Home was thrilled and asked for more. Before Macpherson quite understood what was happening, the partnership had snowballed into a publishing contract, and Macpherson, the poor schoolmaster, overnight found himself a national hero and the toast of literary London. Somewhere along the line the passive "translator" inevitably became a very active "poet." To cover his tracks Macpherson adopted the name of a third-century bard named Ossian and ascribed his modern poems to the ancient poet. Though his ruse was almost immediately detected, many readers—including Jefferson—continued to believe in the authenticity of the writings well into the nineteenth century.

In Europe and in America Macpherson's Ossian prose poems created such a sensation that the reaction of some readers has been described as "virtually an obsession."[2] In Germany they caught the imagination of Goethe and inspired him to write *The Sorrows of Young Werther,* the melancholy 1774 poem which touched off a wave of adolescent male suicides on the Continent. Ossian's audience was overwhelmingly young or middle-aged men, who responded on a visceral level to the wild and passionate landscape of the poems.

> The clouds of night come rolling down. Darkness rests on the steeps of Cromla. The stars of the north arise over the rolling of Erin's waves: they shew their heads of fire, through the flying mists of heaven. A distant wind roars in the wood. Silent and dark is the plain of death![3]

Here is an elemental world, one of prime principles. Man's place in the Universe is unambiguous, and his proper duty is unquestioned. Ossian's world is a place with a strong, clear social hierarchy, where the bonds between men are paramount, where loyalty is expected and breeches of trust inexorably punished. It is a world where men resolve their differences on the field of battle, and where the victor can not only generously spare his opponent's life, but also hold a banquet to honor the vanquished man's valor in fighting the good fight.

In Ossian's world women play a decidedly secondary role. They have two primary plot functions: to inspire valor or to incite mischief. Good women are uniformly beautiful, virtuous, and silent. They glow in their father's court, stand wistfully on hills overlooking battlefields, give their hearts, and then die on cue—leaving behind the necessary male heir. Ossian's women are always "white-handed" or "white-armed" or "white-bosomed." All that is seen or imagined about them is pure and unsullied; nothing below the waist exists. They are sometimes treated as booty in war in ways that show their nullity as personalities. Swaran offers to let Cuthullin leave the battlefield alive—if he will turn over his lands, his wife, and his dog.

When women take an active role in the epics, it is usually to cause strife and dissension among the men. Cuthullin forms a close bond with his friend Ferda. ("Ferda, son of Damman, I loved thee as myself! . . . We moved to the chace together: one was our bed in the heath!") But Ferda falls under the spell of Deugala, the fickle wife of Cairbar. Deugala tells Cairbar she is leaving him for "that sun-beam of youth" (Ferda), and insists that she be given half of her husband's herd. Not wanting to be accused of giving her the inferior half, Cairbar asks Cuthullin to divide the herd evenly. Unfortunately, when the division is complete there is one extra snow-white bull, which Cuthullin assigns to Cairbar. Deugala is enraged that her ex-husband has gotten more than she, and orders her lover to kill his friend Cuthullin, but the young man demurs.

> "Deugala," said the fair-haired youth, "how shall I slay the son of Semo? He is the friend of my secret thoughts. Shall I then lift the sword?" She wept three days before the chief, on the fourth he said he would fight. "I will fight my friend, Deugala! but may I fall by his sword! Could I behold the grave of Cuthullin?"

Ferda and Cuthullin begin to fight, but their hearts are not in it. Seeing that her lover is unlikely to prevail, Deugala chides him, "Thine arm is feeble, sun-beam of youth! Thy years are not strong for steel. Yield to the son of Semo. He is a rock on Malmor." With tears in his eyes, Ferda apologizes to Cuthullin for having to kill him, and begins to fight in earnest. Cuthullin has no choice but to slay his best friend.[4] It is easy to see in the Cuthullin-Ferda-Deugala conflict a permutation of Eve Kosofsky Sedgwick's concept of triangulated desire as explored in *Between Men: English Literature and Male Homosocial Desire*.[5] In Ossian the two men are not sublimating their forbidden desire by fighting over the same woman; the woman herself incites conflict between the two friends because she senses that the best way to punish Cuthullin for the perceived slight is to cause him to lose either his life or the man he loves.

The Ossian poems are certainly chauvinistic by modern standards, but they are no more antifemale than Jane Austen. They describe a world in which the options for women are few, freedom is nonexistent, and life is stressful and short. Whether they accurately portray society in ancient Scotland and Ireland is, of course, moot since they are a product of the eighteenth century. The more cogent question is why they were so wildly popular with the men of Jefferson's time. One way of answering the question is to look at the context in which they were created. James Macpherson was born in 1736 and grew up in Scotland, which was being brutally stomped into submission by the British army. It was a country divided between Highlander and Lowlander, with the former believed to be wild, trouble-making barbarians and the latter viewed as weak, materialistic collaborators. Macpherson grew into a deeply conflicted young man. He loved the Highlands, but also had an immense thirst for learning, and he realized that the only way he could secure an education and add any scope to his world was to descend to an urban area. In 1752 he entered the university at Aberdeen, a bustling city riding the first crest of the Industrial Revolution, its woolen industry, linen factories, and paper mills turning it into a major manufacturing center. In Aberdeen Macpherson's internal conflicts multiplied tenfold. Here he was both drawn to the splendor and ease brought by the city's new wealth and appalled by how quickly and completely the old Scots way of life was being abandoned and trampled in the rush for riches.

In 1756 he began a long poem titled "The Hunter," a fairy tale about a Highlander who accidentally kills a faun belonging to a fairy princess. The princess avenges the death by planting seeds of ambition in the hunter's soul, causing him to abandon his beloved Highlands and flee to Edinburgh where he hopes for worldly success. In the poem's searing indictment of the city can be read all of the young Macpherson's discontent:

> On rocks a city stands, high-tower'd, unwall'd,
> And from its scite the hill of Edin call'd,
> Once the proud seat of royalty and state,
> Of kings, of heroes, and of all that's great;
> But these are flown, and Edin's only stores
> Are fops, and scriveners, and English'd whores.[6]

Here in a few bitter lines is a view of the world that the Ossian poems oppose: a world filled with effeminate poseurs, writers who copy out other people's words for wages, and women who have prostituted themselves so frequently that they have become the enemy. The Ossian poems recall a purer world, one with truer values, one filled with heroic men and virginal women. It is this world that inspired a passionate cult following, and which kept Jefferson and the Marquis de Chastellux quoting verses at each other late into the night at Monticello.

Ossian had a tremendous following in England and on the Continent, but his impact in America was perhaps strongest of all. The poems spoke especially to men of Jefferson's generation, to the men who were young at the outset of the Revolution and who had lived to see the Spirit of 1776 slowly eroded by the petty politics of the early years of the Republic. These men were mired down in the internecine wars between the Federalists and the Republicans, disgusted by the backroom shenanigans of the election of 1800, and increasingly uncomfortable as they saw their dream of an agrarian utopia slowly eaten away by a few metastasizing cities (dominated, particularly in Philadelphia, by a merchant oligarchy with little concern for the rights of the laboring classes). To these readers Ossian provided a halcyon vision of a lost world which spoke to something deep within their souls. The poems became the "foundation myth for a cultural identity based upon muscular sensibility," in the felicitous words of Dafydd Moore.[7] How to find a balance between aggressive muscularity and refined sensibility was the challenge faced by many men in the no-holds-barred tumult of post-Revolution America. The redefinition of gender roles (particularly in areas where the gender balance was uneven) raised troubling issues for men struggling with issues of aggression and sensibility. The Ossian poems provided many men with an elegiac glimpse into a world where these two opposites had been effortlessly meshed. No wonder, then, that Abigail Adams called out to "remember the ladies." The ladies played a decidedly marginal role in this misty vision of primal male bonding.

If a book of Ossian's poems was given pride of place beside Jefferson's punch bowl, the novels of Tobias Smollett were in no less favor. While Ossian merely hinted at a world that was romantically homosocial, Smollett holds the distinction of creating the first English-language novel with identifiably gay characters: *The Adventures of Roderick Random*. (Thomas Jefferson owned the 1763 London edition.[8]) First published in 1748, the picaresque novel includes four characters who are unambiguously meant to portray homosexual men.

The novel's hero first encounters "Captain Wiffle" when the naval officer takes command of the man-of-war on which Random is serving as an assistant to the surgeon. Smollett describes the lavender-scented Captain as a tall, thin, young man, dressed in this manner; a white hat garnished with a red feather, adorned his head, from whence his hair flowed down upon his shoulders, in ringlets tied behind with a ribbon.—His coat, consisting of pink-coloured silk, lined with white, by the elegance of the cut retired backward, as it were, to discovered a white sattin waistcoat embroidered with gold, unbuttoned at the upper part, to display a broach set with garnets, that glittered in the breast of his shirt, which was of the finest cambrick, edged with right mechlin. The knees of his crimson velvet breeches scarce descended so low as to meet his silk stockings, which rose without spot or wrinkle on his meagre legs, from shoes of blue Meroquin, studded with diamond buckles, that flamed forth rivals to the sun! A steel-hilted sword, inlaid with figures of gold, and decked with a knot of ribbon which fell down in a rich tossle, equipped his side; and an amber-headed cane hung dangling from his wrist:—But the most remarkable parts of his furniture were, a mask on his face, and white gloves on his hands, which did not seem to be put on with an intention to be pulled off occasionally, but were fixed with a ring set with a ruby on the little finger of one hand, and by one set with a topaz on that of the other.[9]

A vision in pink, white, and gold, glittering with garnets, diamonds, rubies, and topazes, Captain Wiffle is the embodiment of the effeminate fop. He is surrounded by "a crowd of attendants, all of whom, in their different degrees, seemed to be of their patron's disposition."[10] Wiffle's entourage includes his valet de chambre, Vergette (the French word for a clothes whisk, but also the diminutive of *verge*—slang for a penis) and his personal physician, the aptly named Mr. Simper. The latter is described as "a young man, gayly dressed, of a very delicate complexion, with a kind of languid smile on his face, which seemed to have been rendered habitual, by a long course of affectation."[11]

For any reader who has not yet picked up on just what exactly is being described here, Smollett adds that the captain insisted that only his servants and Mr. Simper could enter the cabin without first sending in to obtain leave, a regulation which "gave scandal an opportunity to be very busy with his character, and accuse him of maintaining a correspondence with his surgeon, not fit to be named."[12] Random soon leaves Captain Wiffle's ship, electing to stay in the West Indies rather than sail home to England under his command.

Random eventually does return to London, where he persuades some new friends to introduce him to Earl Strutwell, a lord whom he believes to have high connections in the royal court. Bribing his way past belligerent footmen and valets, Random is ushered into the presence of the great man, who receives him dressed in morning gown and slippers. Strutwell is immediately taken with the young man and promises to help him secure a lucrative position in a foreign embassy. "I could not even help shedding tears, at the goodness of this noble lord, who no sooner perceived them, than he caught me in his arms, hugged and kissed me with a seemingly paternal affection."[13] This seemingly paternal affection is revealed to be something quite different on a return visit, when Earl Strutwell tests his protégé by slipping into his hand a copy of a book by Petronius Arbiter (probably the *Satyricon*), slyly asking his opinion of the author. When Random replies that he considers the writing lewd and indecent, Strutwell launches into a defense of homosexuality:

> I own (replied the Earl) that his taste in love is generally decried, and indeed condemned by our laws; but perhaps that may be more owing to prejudice and misapprehension, than to true reason and deliberation.—The best man among the ancients is said to have entertained that passion; one of the wisest of their legislators has permitted the indulgence of it in his commonwealth; the most celebrated poets have not scrupled to avow it at this day; it prevails not only over all the east, but in most parts of Europe; in our own country it gains ground apace, and in all probability will become in a short time a more fashionable vice than simple fornication.—Indeed there is something to be said in vindication of it, for notwithstanding the severity of the law against offenders in this way, it must be confessed that the practice of this passion is unattended with that curse and burthen upon society, which proceeds from a race of miserable deserted bastards, who are either murdered by their parents, deserted to the utmost want and wretchedness, or bred up to prey upon the commonwealth: And it likewise prevents the debauchery of many a young maiden, and the prostitution of honest men's wives; not to mention the consideration of health, which is much less liable to be impaired in the gratification of this appetite, than in the exercise of common venery, which by ruining the constitutions of our young men, has produced a puny progeny

that degenerates from generation to generation: Nay, I have been told, that there is another motive perhaps more powerful than all these, that induces people to cultivate this inclination; namely, the exquisite pleasure attending its success.[14]

Roderick fears that the earl may be under the misapprehension that he (Roderick) having traveled "might have been infected with this spurious and sordid desire abroad." He denounces homosexual activity as "unnatural, absurd, and of pernicious consequence," and Strutwell quickly retreats, insisting that he was merely testing the young man's virtue by pretending to extol such a loathsome practice. In time Roderick learns that Strutwell is a scam artist with no power to win him an appointment, and his footmen are merely pimps sent out to lure young men into the presence of the light-fingered earl. The hero loses his watch, a diamond ring, and most of his money before he learns about the game, and although he makes a half-hearted attempt to retrieve his property he eventually goes away poorer but wiser.

Besides the amazing frankness of these early portrayals, the characters of Wiffle, Vergette, Simper, and Strutwell are significant in that the plot does not require them to be punished for their sexual transgressions. Captain Wiffle and his entourage merely sail off toward the horizon, while Earl Strutwell retires behind his gates and burly footmen. At a time when pamphlets such as *Satan's Harvest Home* were calling down the retribution of an angry Jehovah on such purveyors of abomination, the narrator in Smollett's wildly popular novel merely sniffs and shrugs. These are, certainly, negative stereotypes without the slightest hint of a redeeming virtue, but they are not portraits of monstrous villains. Smollett seems to be saying that a young man out in the world is bound to encounter such creatures and—like street vermin or the pox—they are to be avoided whenever possible. That he includes not one but two homosexual encounters in the novel is a good indication that such men were not rare occurrences in the world of eighteenth-century adventurers.

Jefferson had, of course, one of the largest and most distinguished libraries in America and it is not surprising that it included a copy of *The Adventures of Roderick Random*. What is striking to contemplate is how popular and widely available the novel remained throughout the colonial, Revolutionary, and post-Revolutionary periods. Hundreds of Americans must have been acquainted with these explicit portraits of male homosexuals. The novel was particularly popular in

Virginia. George K. Smart's survey of around 100 private Virginia libraries covering the period 1650-1787 revealed that the works of Smollett—in particular *Roderick Random, Peregrine Pickle,* and *The History of England*—were well represented in a wide variety of collections. "[T]he owners cover all phases of life in the colony," Smart writes, "for doctors, churchmen, lawyers and legislators, planters large and small, music teachers, and dancing masters are to be found among them."[15] An advertisement was published in the *Virginia Gazette* on November 25, 1775, offering a two-volume set of *Roderick Random* available from the Williamsburg booksellers Dixon & Hunter.[16] James Napier's study of book sales in Dumfries, Virginia, for the period 1794-1796 shows *Roderick Random* as the fifth most popular work of fiction (*Peregrine Pickle* was number three). Smollett was, in fact, the best-selling author of fiction on Napier's list, besting both Shakespeare and the Bible. He was nosed out of the very top position by the sale of one extra copy of Webster's *Spelling Book.*[17] A copy of *Roderick Random* even appears in an inventory of books owned by Baron von Steuben's "angel," Benjamin Walker, which was filed with the New York courts at the time of Walker's death in 1818.[18]

In a recent article Clare A. Lyons has charted a similar record of popularity for the book among readers in Philadelphia:

> *Roderick Random,* with its homoerotic characters Lord Strutwell and Captain Whiffle, was one of the most popular English novels in mid- to late eighteenth-century Philadelphia. Advertisements for it appeared nineteen times in the city's newspaper, the *Pennsylvania Gazette,* between 1748 and 1778; ten different booksellers included it in their lists of books "just arrived from London and for sale." It was also advertised in the book catalogues issued by the city's booksellers, owned by the city's new lending libraries, and reprinted in a Philadelphia edition in 1794.[19]

From the perspective of the twenty-first century it is difficult to measure the impact on American readers of the homosexual characters in *Roderick Random.* Some perhaps read these portraits and failed to understand what Smollett was describing, but those readers must have been in a minority, for Smollett's depictions are extensive and explicit. They depend for their comic effect on the reader's recognition of a particular identifiable persona: the sexually voracious, foppish sodomite. The depictions of Captain Wiffle and Lord Strutwell are certainly over-the-top, but Smollett bases the exaggeration on a type that must have been familiar to his readers. *Roderick Random* was an immediate best seller because it offered a palatable morality tale spiced up with the type of rollicking bawdiness found in *Tom Jones* and *Tristram Shandy,* its neighbors on the best-seller list. Certainly there is no evidence of either widespread puzzlement about what was going on in the narrative or any effort to censor or inhibit sales of the novel. The overwhelming popularity of *Roderick Random* demonstrates that early American readers could be presented with a depiction of homosexual behavior and be neither puzzled nor outraged.

An intriguing mystery surrounds Jefferson's personal copy of *Roderick Random.* In the catalog of Jefferson's library printed in 1815 when the former president sold his collection to the Library of Congress, a manuscript notation reveals that volume two was missing. Later catalogs indicate that volume one is missing also. When E. Millicent Sowerby began the monumental task of producing an annotated catalog of the library as part of the 1943 celebration of the bicentennial of Jefferson's birth, she discovered that the entire novel was indeed nowhere to be found. It is in the second half of the novel— the part reported missing in 1815—that Random meets Wiffle and Strutwell, but it is impossible at this point to discover whether the volume was disposed of by Jefferson or whether it was borrowed by someone and not returned.

Jefferson's library also contained a copy of a book that was the most popular (and probably the *only*) volume of gay pornography published in English in the eighteenth century: a pseudo-medical text titled *Onania: or, the Heinous Sin of Self-Pollution, and All Its Frightful Consequences, in Both Sexes Consider'd, &c,* which appeared first as an anonymous pamphlet published in London around 1710. It was an immediate best seller. Robert H. MacDonald estimates that it was republished in at least nineteen editions, with a total print run of around 38,000 copies—an amazing sales record for a humorless, scolding lecture on the evils of masturbation.[20] It is easy to understand its popularity, however, if one looks at the later editions, which include testimonials from readers who supposedly have been helped by reading the book. From the fourth edition on, the testimonial letters become a significant part of the volume—in Jefferson's fifteenth edition (London: 1730) they constitute more than half of the total 344 pages of the text.

Though a few of the letters are from women, the overwhelming majority are from young men. They all sound as though they were written by the same person (as they well may have been), and they usually follow a standard pattern: a brief biographical description of the writer, followed by an unnecessarily detailed description of his former masturbatory practices, and concluding with an expression of gratitude for having been saved from a life of physical and spiritual degeneracy. Some of the letters sound like screenplays for the improbable fantasies of gay porn videos, such as one describing the sex play shared by twin brothers:

> Two Twin-Brothers, among the many of your Scholars and Patients, make bold to trouble you with the following Lines. 'Twas but very lately since we happen'd to see an Advertisement in the daily Paper, of a Book entitled ONANIA, which led us to a farther Curiosity of buying it; and having diligently perused it, are thoroughly convinc'd how great our Error has been, in thinking the Sin you so finely treat on, but an innocent Diversion: There has been so mutual a Love between us even from our Infancy, which obliged us not to keep or conceal any thing from each other.

> We were about 17 Years of Age when first we practis'd the Sin of SELF-POLLUTION, we being now full 20 ; it came to us at first entirely thro' Nature, not by any evil Conversation : The first Time we perceiv'd our Seed, it surprised us very much, yet the uncommon Titillation was pleasing to a great Degree; but then it growing Customary to us, and our Manhood riper, we use it more frequent, and thought it much better to quench our lustful Desires that way, than carnally having to do with the Female Sex, and we believe that was the only Motive that induced us from that Since, and we were willing (as we thought) of two Evils to chuse the least; we have neither of us used it to Excess, but are both of weakly Constitutions, (except in our Manhood) : We do verily believe, had not your excellent Book been publish'd, we had always been ignorant of the Prejudice we did

our Bodies as well as our Souls, by committing that so heinous
(yet undesigned and unknowing) a Sin.[21]

The cumulative effect of these hundred-plus descriptions of young
men masturbating is prurient if not pornographic, and the immense
popularity of the book obviously stemmed not from the stern lecture
of the text but from the titillation of the testimonials. *Onania*'s anonymous author was aware that his book was being employed by some
people for the express purpose of being aroused by the tales of young
lust and (while continuing to add more and more sexual scenarios
with each edition) he feigned disgust for anyone looking to be sexually aroused by these true stories of moral awakening. "They study
Cases of Conscience," he thundered, ". . . not to avoid, but to learn
Ways how to offend God, and to pollute their own Spirits, and search
their Houses with a Sun Beam, that they may be instructed in all the
Corners of Nastiness."[22]

Any young man who diligently searched the library at Monticello
for nastiness could indeed find a few corners where it lurked, but dispassionate information on homosexuality would be hard to find. Jefferson's personal feelings about same-sex relations were not recorded, but he did discuss briefly the legal aspects in his writings on
law reform. He felt it was important that the law clarify two distinct
crimes which had been conflated under the heading of buggery: sodomy and bestiality. Bestiality, he believed, should be decriminalized
entirely. Because "it can never make any progress" (i.e., there was no
possibility of pregnancy), bestiality could not cause any permanent
injury to society and therefore should not be severely punished. Sodomy, of course, can never make any progress either, but Jefferson felt
that it was enough of a threat to public welfare that it should remain a
criminal offense. He did suggest, however, that the penalty be reduced from hanging to simple castration.[23]

Jefferson was listed as a subscriber to *The New Virginia Justice,* a
1795 manual for Virginia magistrates written by William Waller
Hening. Intended to be used as a vade mecum for the commonwealth's legal procedures, it includes boilerplate language for drawing up indictments, including one for a charge of buggery:

The jurors for the commonwealth upon their oath do present
that   of the county of   aforesaid, labourer, not having the fear of God before his eyes, nor regarding the order of

nature, but being moved and seduced by the instigation of the
devil, on the   day of   in the year of our lord with
force and arms, at the county aforesaid, in and upon *one   a
youth about the age of   years,* then and there being, feloniously did make an assault, and then and there feloniously, wickedly, diabolically, and against the order of nature, had a venereal
affair with the said   and then and there carnally knew the
said   and then and there feloniously, wickedly, and diabolically, and against nature, with the said   did commit
that detestable and abominable crime of buggery (not to be
named amongst *Christians*) to the great displeasure of Almighty
God, to the great scandal of all human kind, against the form of
the statute in such case made and provided, and against the
peace and dignity of the commonweath.[24]

This blank indictment is instructive not only because of what it says
about the reason for society's objections to buggery, but also for what
it implies about who is likely to commit the crime and how it is likely
to be committed. Although this is a skeletal form intended to be filled
out in constructing an indictment, the profession or social status of
the accused has already been supplied: labourer. It assumes that a
gentleman would not be a buggerer (or, perhaps, would not be indicted for it). The crime is presupposed to be an assault; consensual
anal intercourse is unimaginable. Finally, it is assumed that the sexual
act will be intergenerational, with an older man assaulting a youth. It
should be noted that the Virginia statute being violated actually says
nothing about social status, assault, or age. The law reads simply:
"That if any do commit the detestable and abominable vice of buggery, with man or beast, he or she so offending, shall be adjudged a
felon, and shall suffer death, as in a case of felony, without benefit of
clergy."[25] (The inclusion of women as violators and beasts as the violated reflects the common conflation of sodomy with bestiality,
which Jefferson sought to change.) Hening's additions to the sample
indictment probably reflect the generally accepted assumptions of
Virginians of the period. Certainly an educated gentleman reading
Hening to determine whether his consensual coupling with a fellow
gentleman fell into the category of "buggery" could assume that under Virginia law he had committed no offense.

    The information on human sexuality included in Jefferson's li-
brary was about as extensive as would be available anywhere in

America until well into the early years of the Republic, yet there was no information at all about same-sex activity in any of the six medical treatises listed in bibliographies of his collection.[26] That is not to say that the topic was never raised elsewhere in print during the Jeffersonian era, however. A few medical treatises (mostly those addressed to an audience of physicians) did mention the subject, albeit briefly and always accompanied by a stern lecture delivered in a tone of barely controlled disgust. Jean Astruc in his book *Traité des Maladies Vénériennes* (Paris: 1740) explained that excrescences around the anus often indicate syphilis and "l'infamie des Efféminés."[27] Rhagades (anal fissures) are frequently caused by "le crime des Effeminés," and tissue erosion may be caused by the virulence of the "Humeur Séminale" of men addicted to "une Débauche infâme." Astruc felt it necessary to apologize for even mentioning such distasteful subjects:

> One is ashamed, it is true, to keep bringing up such sordid things; but in a work like this one, one cannot spare oneself from reporting a cause of venereal disease which, to the embarrassment and the disgrace of human kind, is only too true and too frequent. The interest of good morals seems even to demand that one bring it up often; in order to frighten those who dare abandon themselves to such debauchery, and that, if they are insensible to the voice of disgraced Nature, and incapable of being stopped by the terror of the judgments of God, they will be [stopped] at least by fear of the illnesses which follow their criminal actions.[28]

Nikolai Falck was even more passionate in his denunciation. In his book *A Treatise on the Venereal Disease* (London: 1772) he fumed:

> This [venereal disease] is [usually] the consequence of wenching, and the abuse of the gifts of nature; but there are other causes, from debaucheries, of the most heinous, unnatural, and diabolical nature; sum up all the vices which human ideas can possibly conceive of Satan, and they are all comprised in that unnatural monster, and scandal to human nature, a Sodomite. What a deplorable wretch! . . . The Sodomites have at times made it their plea, that they were not subject to the venereal disease; but they have been griviously mistaken; for of all infections, theirs is of the most shocking, and the most obstinate kind of any, and as to

the catamites, they have at times exhibited [a] most horrible specta[c]le. I am ashamed to discribe the ideas, I have of such an unnatural and horrid act; nor can I conceive, what can induce these monsters to a passion, for such filthy pleasure.[29]

Falck even suggested that homosexual anal sex *causes* syphilis to appear in the first place. "[I]f we add the violent friction in this diabolical act, we need not wonder, that the most pernicious virus may become generated."[30]

Falck's treatise is particularly important for reconstructing the homosexual milieu of the eighteenth century because of what he implies about the formation of a gay community. "The Sodomites have at times made it their plea . . . ," presupposes a group of men who not only were labeled on the basis of their shared interest in same-sex relations, but also felt so strongly and defiantly identified with that group that they could dare to launch a public defense of their conduct. Despite theories that homosexuality is a social construct created by medicolegal authorities in the late nineteenth century, Falck's text indicates that as early as 1772 a group of men recognized that they were different from the majority of people, and that the sole basis of that difference was their sexual response.

Some writers on venereal disease took the role of social reformers. William Buchan in his *Observations Concerning the Prevention and Cure of Venereal Disease* (London: 1796) called for an increase in London police patrols in order to halt the proliferation of streetwalkers, though he warned city officials that they should not be *too* vigorous in their suppression of heterosexual desire, activity which is "dictated by nature and reason" and is therefore to be expected. "Indeed," he counseled, "all undue restraints on that intercourse do mischief. They lead to the commission of unnatural crimes, and to the formation of connexions which prove injurious to the dearest interests of society."[31]

Most of the medical denunciations of homosexual activity focus on anal sex, but John Marten in his work *A Treatise of All the Degrees and Symptoms of the Venereal Disease* (London: 1708) gave one of the few—and certainly the longest—descriptions of male oral-genital contact. Marten dropped all pretext of scientific objectivity about the topic and delivered a tirade filled with disgust and disbelief. Marten's text is perhaps the strongest evidence available that eighteenth-century writers on venereal disease were aware that their books circulated beyond the medical community and were sought out by lay readers try-ing to learn more about sexuality. Speaking over the heads of his pro-fessional colleagues, Marten delivered a tongue-lashing to anyone even contemplating homosexual activity:

> I had almost forgot to acquaint the Reader, that there is yet an-other way of getting the *Venereal* Infection . . . and this is by one Man's conversing with, or having the Carnal use of another Man's Body, *viz.* B_____y, an abominable, beastly, sodomitical, and shameful Action; an Action, as its [sic] not fit to be named, so, one would think, would not be practis'd in a Christian Coun-try, more especially since the Laws of God and Man, are so di-rectly in force against it; but I say by that means have we known the Distemper to have been contracted, and I am afraid is what is too commonly practis'd in this dissolute Age, and the Distemper by that means very frequently gotten, as it was lately by one (as I was told) that I had in Cure.
>
> And which is still worse, this Distemper is also gotten after another manner of Conversation, *viz.* by a Man's putting his erected *Penis,* into another Persons (Man or Woman's) Mouth, using Friction, &c. between the Lips; a way so very Beastly and so much to be abhorr'd, as to cause at the mentioning or but thinking of it, the utmost detestation and loathing; but by that means also has it been gotten, and a Man so Infected . . . had I in Cure not long since, who assur'd me (tho' with seeming concern for the committing [of] so foul a Crime) that he contracted it no other way; and that the Person from whom he got it (being a Man) had at the same time . . . several *Pocky* Ulcerations, &c. in his Mouth; but in such a woful pickle was this Patient of mine, and indeed (as I told him) very deservedly, that I never in my Life before, saw one (both for Pox and Clap together) worse.

Having delivered a strong condemnation, and having assured his pa-tient that he was suffering exactly what he deserved for engaging in such disgusting conduct, Dr. Marten's curiosity got the better of him and he insisted on knowing all of the most intimate details of the pa-tient's sex life:

> I being desirous to know the whole of this abominable Encoun-ter, (having never known, tho' before had heard, that such

beastly Abominations were practis'd) ask'd him if 'twas any Pleasure to him, and how he dispos'd of his *Semen?* he told me 'twas great Pleasure, and that he ejected it into the Person's Mouth he had to do with, who both willingly receiv'd it, and assisted, as he said, in this foul Act, by sucking his *Penis.* O monstrous! thought I, that Men, otherwise, sensible Men, should so vilely debase themselves, and become so degenerate; should provoke God so highly, contemn the Laws of Man so openly, wrong their own Bodies so fearfully; and which is worse (without sincere Repentance) ruin their own Souls eternally.[32]

These frank and explicit discussions were addressed to a European reading public. Any American citizen seeking information about homosexually transmitted diseases needed to rely on these European imprints; if his local bookseller could not provide access to foreign publications, he remained in ignorance, since American writers strenuously avoided any mention of same-sex activity. The current author surveyed twenty-nine medical books on venereal disease published in the United States between 1787 and 1820 but was able to find only one treatise that even hints at homosexuality: the English translation of a French text by Frantz Swediaur published in Philadelphia in 1815.[33] Swediaur gives a minimum of detail and dismisses the topic with the required condemnatory language. In his chapter "Of Syphilitic Excrescences and Rhagades" he writes: "A depraved and an unnatural appetite is among the most frequent causes of these diseases, especially when seated at the anus. . . . I repeat that these complaints were not infrequent among the Greeks and Romans."[34]

American medical writers avoided the topic of oral sex entirely, and when discussing anal disorders adopted a neutral vocabulary, which did not address with any specificity the activities involved, thereby sidestepping the question of same-sex encounters. In his work *Observations on Some of the Principal Diseases of the Rectum and Anus* (Philadelphia: 1811) Thomas Copeland merely acknowledged that illnesses may arise from "venereal mischief in the system."[35] Cosmo Stevenson, in *Observations on the Disease of Gonorrhœa* (Philadelphia: 1803), avoided discussing the homosexual etiology of some anal disorders but recommended that leeches be applied to the scrotum and perineum to give temporary relief from anal discomfort, and assured his readers that "Mucilaginous injections thrown up the rectum, are of great benefit; especially if opium be combined with them."[36] The frequency with which similar medical advice appears in American treatises indicates that such diseases were not uncommon, yet a layman—or a physician—would be hard-pressed to extract any information about homosexuality from these domestic texts.

It was not until the antebellum period that American medical writers began to discuss homosexual activity with the degree of frankness with which it had been treated by Europeans for nearly a century. Frederick Hollick, in his book *A Popular Treatise on Venereal Diseases in All Their Forms* (New York: 1852), alludes to male-male sexuality in his section on "Blennorrhagia of the Anus" by assuming the usual stance of condemning the patient while describing the disease. "This is a disgusting affection, both in its nature and from the unnatural way in which it is sometimes contracted, but still as it is occasionally met with, it ought to be treated." He then adds a compassionate aside: "Besides, it *may* arise accidentally, and is then a real misfortune."[37] For those who have brought misfortune on themselves through their own illicit conduct, Hollick has very little sympathy:

> But what shall be said of other modes of contracting this form of disease? Some people will ask if it is *possible* that such instances of the effects of depravity are ever seen? Most assuredly they are, as every one extensively acquainted with hospital practice well knows. I have also known cases of Sailors being so affected, after a long voyage.
>
> This subject may sometimes be important in a *Medico Legal* point of view, and that is the principal reason why I refer to it. . . . It is requisite to take other circumstances into consideration, and especially to observe if there be any of those peculiar indications of unnatural crimes with which surgeons are acquainted.[38]

Although European writers on homosexually acquired venereal diseases adopted a negative tone when discussing the subject, few if any suggested that physicians should actively aid police departments in detecting sex crimes, as Hollick here urges.

Hollick's book is particularly interesting because it includes a case study of what surely must have been a homosexually conflicted man. The patient's sad story provides some insight into the mental distress and isolation such a man could experience in America in the early years of the nineteenth century. The patient, referred to as "R. H—" was an Englishman who experienced a great deal of anguish when the "large mercantile establishment" that employed him filed for bankruptcy due to excessive speculation in foreign bonds. Mr. H— began to suspect his fellow employees of dishonesty, and the suspicions quickly grew to hallucinations of persecution:

> Emissaries were constantly on the search for him to arrest him for *unnatural* crimes committed in London; every one who met him in the street, read in his countenance the crimes he had committed; tailors made his coats with the sleeves the wrong way of the cloth, in order to brand him with infamy; the sight of a policeman in the street alarmed him beyond measure; and often, if a stranger happened to be walking for some little time in the same direction as himself, he would exclaim that he was one of the emissaries sent to seize him. [Italics in the original][39]

Other than this paranoia, the patient was perfectly normal:

> When led away from his disorder into any discussion on public matters, he was, however, a most amusing and instructive companion; as a man of business he was equally acute, and to a stranger as long as nothing was done to offend him he was, to all appearance, a man of observation and experience.[40]

After treatment in England met with little success, the patient decided to emigrate hoping that he could escape the imagined emissaries by fleeing to America. There he lapsed into silence. In September 1843 his family received a letter from an American physician who had tried unsuccessfully to treat him for the recurring symptoms, and in 1845 his friends received an anonymous letter and a newspaper clipping with the headline "Death of a Hermit in West Jersey."

> It was stated that he had lived on a small farm, entirely alone, with the exception of a dog, and that he had shunned all intercourse with his neighbors. He was taken suddenly ill, applied to a neighboring farmer for assistance, but died in the course of the following day. From information subsequently obtained by his friends, it is believed that he died of apoplexy, or perhaps, in one of the attacks of congestion of the brain, from which he frequently suffered before he left his native country. . . . Mr. H—'s insanity at first, constantly had reference to his having either

committed or been accused of committing unnatural crimes, and this idea never entirely left him, although during the later part of his life, his more prominent hallucinations had reference to imaginary persecutors constantly watching him, and endeavoring to ruin him by spreading false reports, and to poison him by adulterating his food, and infusing noxious gases into the air. There can be little doubt, on taking into consideration his complaints of weight between the rectum and bladder, with darting pains, &c., in the same region, that the pollutions [involuntary ejaculations] arose from irritation in the neighborhood of the prostate; and I think, that if at an early period of his disease this had been relieved, there would have been considerable hope of his recovery from the hallucinations he manifested.[41]

American doctors were so far from understanding sexual psychology that they could diagnose severely conflicted homosexual desire as a simple prostate infection.

Some American medical writers approached even the topic of *heterosexual* venereal disease with a high degree of discretion, as if fearful of giving offense. *Medical Advice* by William Hayne Simers (New York: 1805) included in its subtitle the promise of a wide range of popular medical knowledge: "chiefly for the consideration of seamen, and adapted for the use of travellers or domestic life; containing practical essay[s] on diseases in general, gun-shot wounds, dislocations, and on the venereal disease, with plain and full directions for their prevention and cure."[42] The "Appendix on the prevention and cure of the venereal disease" was, however, published and sold separately so that readers interested in gunshot wounds but not sexually transmitted diseases could thereby be accommodated.

American medical texts avoided the topic of homosexuality, but they were vehement in their denunciation of masturbation. The campaign against self-pollution created a cottage industry in anti-masturbatory books and pamphlets which promised illness, insanity, and death to any young man indulging in the private vice. Perhaps more surprisingly, many writers also painted an unsavory picture of heterosexuality by warning men of the dangers of intercourse with women. In his thesis submitted in 1801 to the medical school at the University of Pennsylvania, James Tongue rejected the idea that venereal disease was sent by God as a punishment for sexual transgressions. "I would rather suppose," Tongue wrote, "the venereal disease was caused by copulating too frequently, thereby stimulating the vagina to such a degree, as to make it take on an action capable to secreting this poison."[43] Women, it seemed, *generated* venereal contamination. Swediaur (Philadelphia: 1815) warned that men can be infected without having complete congress with a woman: "To receive the infection it is not necessary that the penis should be introduced with the vagina, as many patients imagine; the most superficial contact will sometimes produce the effect."[44]

Felix Pascalis Ouvière (New York?: 1811?) took the matter one step further, warning men that a woman's vagina emits an invisible vapor which can transmit venereal disease if a man even comes near her. "[I]nfected parts of female generation, whether contaminated with matter or not, produce a peculiar effluvium, or *aura syphilitica,* which is equally dangerous."[45] Any American man reading these books would certainly think twice before engaging in heterosexual intercourse, given the scientifically demonstrated perils of female genitalia. The "cult of true womanhood" which rose to prominence during this period included the belief that "good" women were entirely passionless, and that men—even husbands—were brutish despoilers. Anti-sex literature suggested that even within the bonds of sacred marriage, sexual intercourse should be strictly limited to no more than once a month.[46]

The peculiar combination of scientific fervor, moral rectitude, and personal disgust with which American medical writers treated human sexuality may have led to an entirely unintended phenomenon: the encouragement of homosexual activity. By raising the alarm against the lures of diseased women, by insisting that sex within marriage be restricted to infrequent attempts at procreation, and by condemning masturbation (and even involuntary nocturnal emissions), medical experts left men with few approved sexual outlets. American physicians' prudish unwillingness to discuss homosexuality in any public forum created a serious breech in the overall effort to contain and channel obstreperous libidos. The average American man might by default be left with the impression that the only safe form of sexual expression must be through discreet male-male activity, the one outlet rarely condemned because it was rarely discussed.

Chapter 6

Racism and Homosexual Desire in the Antebellum Period

> *Oh, Sally is de gal for me,*
> *I wouldn't hab no udder,*
> *If Sal dies to-morrow night,*
> *I'll marry Sally's brudder*

Minstrel song

We explored in the opening chapter the ways in which a stereotype developed suggesting that American Indians possessed very weak libidos. Just the opposite was the case for African Americans. Sexual depravity was a common charge, leveled especially against black slaves. Medical treatises since at least the 1600s had warned nursing women that they could transmit venereal diseases to their children through breast milk, but the anonymous Virginia physician who published *A Treatise on the Gonorrhoea* (1787) took the warning one step further. He suggested that black nursemaids take advantage of young boys who at the age of three, four, or five are capable of maintaining an erection, and warned parents to be vigilant lest their sons be venereally infected through sexual intercourse with their nurses,

> especially in this country where, for the most part, the care of children is left to slaves, who have no character to lose, and unawed by the fear of shame, or loss of subsistence, are guided by no principles but those of their appetites.[1]

Given this common perception of the sexual rapaciousness of blacks (both free and slave), one might assume that the racist literature of the period would contain ample allegations of sodomy. This is not the case. There is little documentation of male-male sexuality oc-

143

curring under the auspices of the institution of slavery or among free
men of color, whether between blacks or between a white man and
black man (or a man of mixed race). Recently, Charles Clifton has attempted to decipher homoeroticism in published slave narratives, and
in presenting his research has pointed to one serious barrier to our understanding. In an attempt to claim for themselves the dignity of
white-defined manhood, male former slaves needed to suppress references to their sexual degradation. Black women could describe in
gripping detail their rape by white slave owners without losing their
inherent vulnerable femaleness, but black men needed to remain silent about the sexual invasion of their own bodies. For a black man to
admit that his bodily integrity had been breached was ipso facto to assume the status of less-than-a-man.[2] White abolitionists—who ex-
ploited the issue of rape for all its emotional power where women
were concerned—skirted warily around the topic of homosexuality,
only occasionally hinting that the dispersal of slave families left men
with no alternative but to pursue "unnatural" activities.[3]

Little documentation survives on which to reconstruct male-male
sexuality under slavery during the early years of America's history,
but remnants of the complete story may be located in a few places, especially in the antebellum period. Where better to start than with the
best known, most widely read description of American slavery: *Uncle Tom's Cabin.* Harriet Beecher Stowe's portrait of the pious and
long-suffering Uncle Tom would appear to be an unlikely locus for a
homosexual narrative, but the entire center section of the book focuses on a sexually ambiguous white man and his fey, dandified
slave. Stowe's novel has been unjustly denigrated as sentimental abo-
litionist propaganda, when in fact it displays a nuanced understanding
of the moral complexities of life under slavery, as well as a surprisingly sophisticated appreciation of sexual psychology. It is particularly interesting to note that the book struck a resonant chord with the
American reading public and dominated the best-seller list in the
mid-nineteenth century the way *Roderick Random* had in the mid-
eighteenth. Stowe's description of lush, homoerotic New Orleans
was familiar reading in most literate American households for nearly
a hundred years.

In the novel's middle section, Stowe tells the story of two brothers—Alfred and Augustine St. Clare—who were born to a Louisiana
planter and his Huguenot wife. Augustine inherits from his mother

"an exceeding delicacy of constitution," so he is sent to his uncle in Vermont in hopes that he will be strengthened by the more bracing climate. While his health is improved only slightly by the New England winters, he is innoculated with just enough of a Yankee conscience to make him uneasy in his subsequent life as a southern slaveholder. In Augustine St. Clare, Stowe creates a character of ambiguous gender presentation. "In childhood, he was remarkable for an extreme and marked sensitiveness of character, more akin to the softness of woman than the ordinary hardness of his own sex," and as a young man he revealed a preference for the "aesthetic"—"his whole nature was kindled into one intense and passionate effervescence of romantic passion."[4] We encounter here all the code words associated with the effeminate fop or sissy. St. Clare himself is aware of the gender confusion:

> My brother and I were twins; and they say, you know, that twins ought to resemble each other; but we were in all points a contrast. He had black, fiery eyes, coal-black hair, a strong, fine Roman profile, and a rich brown complexion. I had blue eyes, golden hair, a Greek outline, and fair complexion. He was active and observing, I dreamy and inactive. . . . [H]e was my father's pet, and I my mother's.[5]

Augustine returns to Louisiana to help run the family plantation, but the twins soon come to a parting of the ways when Augustine cannot accept the brutality inflicted on their slaves.

> Alf and I came to about the same point that I and my respected father did, years before. So he told me that I was a womanish sentimentalist, and would never do for business life; and advised me to take the bank-stock and the New Orleans family mansion, and go to writing poetry, and let him manage the plantation.[6]

If sensitive, womanish Augustine was out of his element in the snows of Vermont or the cotton fields of the plantation, he is very much at home in the voluptuous sensuality of the city of New Orleans.

Though he has pledged his heart to a pure and chaste woman, he is tricked into marrying someone else, and on his wedding day he begins to rue his attachment to someone whose nature is so obviously uncongenial with his own. Husband and wife settle into a domesticity of parallel lives, each secretly loathing the other while still going through all the polite marital rituals. Somehow (Stowe makes us suspect it must have been asexually) they propagate, bringing forth the insufferably cheerful and pious little Eva. It is Eva who first notices the slave Tom and, recognizing in him a fellow Christian soul, insists that her father purchase him for her.

St. Clare takes possession of Tom with a gesture of striking intimacy between a master and a male slave: "He stepped across the boat, and carelessly putting the tip of his finger under Tom's chin, said, good-humoredly, 'Look-up, Tom, and see how you like your new master.'" Stowe feels constrained to assure her readers (in a tangle of negatives) that while Tom's reaction to St. Clare's intimate touch is emotional, it is definitely not *unnatural:* "It was not in nature to look into that gay, young, handsome face, without a feeling of pleasure; and Tom felt the tears start in his eyes as he said, heartily, 'God bless you, Mas'r!'"[7]

St. Clare's New Orleans mansion shimmers with all the oriental splendor of a seraglio, and it is presided over by a majordomo who is quite different from the other slaves in the household. "Foremost among them was a highly-dressed young mulatto man, evidently a very *distingué* personage, attired in the ultra extreme of the mode, and gracefully waving a scented cambric handkerchief in his hand." Adolph greets his master dressed in a very unslavelike couture: "conspicuous in satin vest, gold guard-chain, and white pants, and bowing with inexpressible grace and suavity."[8] When St. Clare recognizes that the satin vest is one that Adolph has "borrowed" from his own wardrobe he accepts the theft with indulgent good humor, and the slave considers it all as merely his due. "And Adolph tossed his head, and passed his fingers through his scented hair, with a grace."[9]

Without drawing an explicit comparison between the pampered, hankie-waving Adolph and the popular stereotype of the mulatto mistress, Stowe makes it clear that St. Clare is unusually—perhaps unnaturally—indulgent with his valet and she sets up a contest for the master's soul, pitting the scented minion against the Christian laborer. The outcome is, of course, foreordained. From Tom's first appearance in the household, effete Adolph recognizes that in the brawny new acquisition he has a serious rival:

> As St. Clare turned to go back his eye fell upon Tom, who was
> standing uneasily, shifting from one foot to the other, while
> Adolph stood negligently leaning against the banisters, examin-
> ing Tom through an opera-glass, with an air that would have
> done credit to any dandy living.[10]

In the debates between Augustine St. Clare and his Yankee cousin
Miss Ophelia, slavery is the ostensive topic, but throughout the narrative the subtext seems to be a more general moral issue with broader
implications: Should people be held accountable for sinful actions
arising from weak natures? "Are you such a sweet innocent," St.
Clare chides her, "as to suppose nobody in this world ever does what
they don't think is right? Don't you, or didn't you ever, do anything
that you did not think quite right?"[11] He sums up his philosophy of
life in words which make it clear that he prefers to keep conflicting
urges carefully segregated, and to go through life without thinking
too deeply about who he is or what he is doing.

> "In short, you see," said he, suddenly resuming his gay tone, "all
> I want is that different things be kept in different boxes. The
> whole frame-work of society, both in Europe and America, is
> made up of various things which will not stand the scrutiny of
> any very ideal standard of morality. It's pretty generally under-
> stood that men don't aspire after the absolute right, but only to
> do about as well as the rest of the world."[12]

Finally, St. Clare compares the South under the curse of slavery to the
guilt of Sodom and Gomorrah, and the sexual subtext, which Stowe
seems to have been flirting with ever since St. Clare placed his finger
under Tom's chin, at last comes out into the open.[13]
    Uncle Tom's muscular Christianity and simple faith inevitably win
St. Clare for God, and the fey Adolph is vanquished. But also inevitably St. Clare dies (transported to heaven on a beatific vision of his
saintly mother). The cruel widow Marie then decides to sell her husband's seraglio and his slaves, and both Tom and Adolph end up on
the auction block at the New Orleans slave market. Tom is bought by
the infamous Simon Legree, with his bullet head and course mouth
and dirt under his fingernails, but a very different fate is in store for
the dandy Adolph:

"Hulloa, Alf! what brings you here?" said a young exquisite, slapping the shoulder of a sprucely-dressed young man, who was examining Adolph through an eye-glass.

"Well, I was wanting a valet, and I heard that St. Clare's lot was going. I thought I'd just look at his—"

"Catch me ever buying any of St. Clare's people! Spoilt niggers, every one. Impudent as the devil!" said the other.

"Never fear that!" said the first. "If I get 'em, I'll soon have their airs out of them; they'll soon find that they've another kind of master to deal with than Monsieur St. Clare. 'Pon my word, I'll buy that fellow. I like the shape of him."[14]

Stowe's interest is in Tom, and the narrative continues to follow his fate, leaving the reader to speculate about what Adolph's future will be with the young man who—together with his exquisite friend—looked at St. Clare's "—" (catamite is perhaps the indelicate missing word) and liked the shape of what he saw.

In the slave Adolph and the master St. Clare, Stowe has set up a psychomachia between Femininity and Masculinity, the two powerful forces who fight for dominance in the sexually ambivalent characters. For St. Clare the contest is especially complex. His father is a slaveholder (cruel, dissipated) and his mother is a Christian (gentle, pious), but St. Clare wavers between the two roles because their respective requirements are not at all clear. To reject the floating life of a debauched fop (feminine) and assert himself as the head of an upright household (masculine), he must turn from the life of a cruel slaveholder (like his father) and become a pious believer (like his mother). St. Clare's confusion reflects Stowe's own ambivalence toward the male Creole population of New Orleans, an ambivalence common among Yankees since long before the Louisiana Purchase. With the slave Adolph the struggle includes the further complication of race. Adolph is a mulatto, and we are to assume that his father is white and his mother is black (since the alternative is unthinkable). His struggle, then, is between his black/slave/feminine side and his white/master/masculine side, and when he both scents his hair *and* orders around the other slaves in the household it is clear that the struggle will be a close one. But the slave laws stipulated that one drop of black blood made a person legally black, and that a child's slave or free status followed that of his or her mother, so Femininity must win this battle. We last see Adolph on the auction block being ogled by an exquisite dandy, and the implication is clear: he will be both enslaved and unmanned.

This unexpected fictional equation of slavery with homosexuality raises intriguing questions. Herman Melville drew on his brief career as a sailor when spinning his homoerotic tales, but Stowe placed her characters in a world she had never seen. How close did she come to reality? Certainly there were slaves like Adolph who lived in intimate familiarity with their master. The son of a plantation owner was usually assigned his own slave as a valet or—in a term that reflects the intimacy of the relationship—as his "body servant." When the match was made at an early age the two boys might grow up together, and when they became men and began to assume their very separate roles in life, confusion and emotional turmoil could arise on both sides. It was relatively easy for a young master to view field hands as semi-human chattel, but it was more difficult to dehumanize someone he had come to trust with his most intimate thoughts. A South Carolina slaveholder expressed this cognitive dissonance when he cried out in confused frustration to his body servant, "Why weren't you white! Why weren't you white! Why weren't you white!"[15] The desire for emotional intimacy across the color barrier was as transgressive in male-male relationships as in male-female, but a white man who took as his sexual partner a woman of color was at least participating in a cultural phenomenon that was widespread and to some extent condoned. A white man taking a black man was not.

Even when a slave like Adolph was pampered and indulged, the relationship with his white master was never consensual. The power to force sexual relations was always held by the slave owner, and the slave was always subject to punishment if he resisted. Given the reluctance of male former slaves to discuss their sexual degradation, it is perhaps not surprising that the most detailed description of male sexual abuse comes from the narrative of a female former slave: Harriet Jacobs. In her classic *Incidents in the Life of a Slave Girl,* Jacobs tells the story of a slave named Luke, who was inherited by the son upon his old master's death. "This young man," Jacobs writes of the new master,

> became a prey to the vices growing out of the "patriarchal institution," and when he went to the north, to complete his education, he carried his vices with him. He was brought home, deprived of the use of his limbs, by excessive dissipation.[16]

The exact nature of the vice and dissipation is never stated, but Jacobs' description of Luke's treatment makes a clear implication of sexual perversion. Luke was assigned to attend his bedridden young master, but was allowed to wear no clothing except a shirt. The master kept a whip nearby, and when Luke displeased him he was forced to strip and kneel naked beside the bed to be flogged until the master collapsed from exhaustion. When the master was too weak to deliver a lashing, he would call in the constable, and Luke would be flogged while the master watched.

> As he lay there on his bed, a mere degraded wreck of manhood, he took into his head the strangest freaks of despotism; and if Luke hesitated to submit to his orders, the constable was immediately sent for. Some of these freaks were of a nature too filthy to be repeated.[17]

When Jacobs runs away from her bondage, she leaves Luke chained half-naked to his master's bed. Jacobs writes at length of the sexual harassment she herself endured from a cruel master, but the story of Luke's abuse is told in sketchy outline, carefully crafted to hint at the unspeakable while not giving offense to the tender sensibilities of her readers.

In a recent study of sexuality and race in colonial North Carolina, Kirsten Fischer raises a further issue that complicated interracial homosexual contacts, and no doubt gave impetus to efforts to obscure the historical record. Fischer explains that

> a sodomized white man had apparently lost (or relinquished) mastery over his own body and hence also an important aspect of white male privilege. . . . Both de-masculinized "blackness" and "female" passivity represented inappropriate uses of white men's bodies, and sodomy symbolically combined aspects of "femininity" and "blackness" in ways that blurred the distinctions between white men and black men.[18]

A white man might engage in a sexual act with a black man and still retain his privileged status as long as he was the active, insertive partner; for a white man to be the receptive partner was to reverse the power dynamic—an unacceptable inversion.

Another window into male-male relations (albeit obscured and racist) is provided by the lyrics of the wildly popular minstrel shows. Blackfaced minstrel show performers created a new form of entertainment which has been described as evolving "out of the racial fantasies of northern urban whites," and although the picture is highly unreliable, it does tell us something about black-white relations during the period.[19] To the modern ear these songs, plays, and skits sound irredeemably racist, but they were not necessarily viewed in that way by either the (white) performers or the (white) audience. The actors prided themselves on their authenticity as "Ethiopian delineators" bringing to the theater-going public the lively dances and amusing songs of the colored race. Participants on both sides of the footlights viewed black people as unquestionably inferior to whites, but it was not until late in the antebellum period that racial ridicule began to overwhelm genuine (if misplaced) cultural appreciation. Not until plantation slavery became a national issue—and runaway slaves a northern urban problem—did the performances become both purposely malicious in their stereotyping and pointedly reassuring in their depiction of a folksy, romanticized South where the increasingly irksome urban blacks, it was felt, obviously belonged.[20]

In the early years (beginning in the 1830s) minstrel shows were rowdy, raucous affairs—definitely not family entertainment. "Even the verbal humor, which today appears so chaste in the acting editions," writes Gary D. Engle, "could be richly larded with sexual innuendo by the simple addition of gestures and vocal emphases."[21] When the blackfaced singer of "My Love He Is a Sailleur Boy" lamented that a young lover—"tall as a flag-staff"—had sailed away, and worried "that his *affections* don't still *point* to me," a little body language helped to get the idea across.[22] As early as 1843 an advertisement in the New York *Herald* assured its readers that the Virginia Minstrels' performance would be "entirely exempt from the vulgarities and other objectionable features, which have hitherto characterized negro extravaganzas."[23]

For most of its history the minstrel show employed only male performers, with men in drag playing "wench parts." The audience was also at first almost exclusively working-class males. Walt Whitman recalled seeing Thomas D. "Daddy" Rice, one of the first big minstrel stars, performing before an appreciative crowd, and he reminisced

about those evenings as a youth at the theaters on the Bowery where
stag audiences cheered everything from slapstick to *Othello*.

> Pack'd from ceiling to pit with its audience mainly of alert, well
> dress'd, full-blooded young and middle-aged men, the best av-
> erage of American-born mechanics . . . bursting forth in one of
> those long-kept-up tempests of hand-clapping peculiar to the
> Bowery—no dainty kid-glove business, but electric force and
> muscle from perhaps 2000 full-sinew'd men. . . . For types of
> sectional New York those days . . . the young shipbuilders,
> cartmen, butchers, firemen . . . they, too, were always to be seen
> in the audiences, racy of the East River and the Dry Dock. Slang,
> wit, occasional shirt sleeves, and a picturesque freedom of looks
> and manners, with a rude good-nature and restless movement,
> were generally noticeable.[24]

It is those full-sinew'd (white) men whose prejudices and expectations shaped the songs and skits of the minstrel show. In order to understand the subtext of the performances, it is important to keep in
mind that during the early years the performers were blackfaced
white men aiming their humor at an audience of working-class white
men. The genre was so spectacularly successful because (along with
toe-tapping music and side-splitting jokes) the minstrel show fed the
psychic needs of this nearly homogeneous audience. With its ludi-
crous racial stereotypes it reminded the working-class men that—
grim and degrading as their daily lives might be—at least they were
white. For a period of a few hours with their buddies in a crowded theater, they were on top. That illusion of superiority was enhanced by
one of the stock minstrel situations: the trickster Negro who by clever
manipulation puts one over on "Massa" or turns the tables on a rich,
powerful, well-educated snob. Here for a moment the audience experienced the vicarious pleasure of seeing a common enemy humiliated. It is in the intersection of this perceived racial superiority *and*
momentary kinship that the complex dynamic between free urban
blacks and working-class white males must be viewed.

Not surprising, given that the audience was overwhelmingly young
and male and the general tone rowdy and crude, a primary theme of
the minstrel show was sex. Although the majority of songs and comic
situations in a typical show were based on the assumption of heterosexuality (of both the characters and the audience), quite a few songs

and skits flirted with the idea of male-male sexuality. Performing in
blackface provided an entertainer with a mask—doubled in the case
of a white man pretending to be a black woman—that allowed him to
say and do things that would otherwise be too salacious for the public
stage. Many jokes fixated in particular on the size of a black man's
penis. Humor is often the signifier of fear, and the white man's fear of
sexual inadequacy revealed itself as subtext again and again in the
minstrel songs. Even the most obtuse in the audience got the reference when a blackfaced white man sang:

> I don't like a nigger,
> I'll be dogged if I do,
> Kase him feet am so big
> Dat he can't war a shoe.
> . . .
> I was coloured by de smoke,
> In de boat war I war borned,
> And de gals say my gizzard,
> Am as white as de corn.[25]

Nor is it necessary to be a practicing Freudian to understand what is
really being described in the song called "Astonishing Nose":

> Like an elephant's trunk it reached to his toes,
> An wid it he would gib some most astonishing blows
> . . .
> He used to lie in his bed, wid his nose on de floor
> . . .
> De police arrested him one morning in May,
> For obstructing de sidewalk, having his nose in de way.
> Dey took him to de court house, dis member to fine;
> When dey got dere de nose hung on a tavern sign.[26]

Although sly allusions to large black penises may be explained away
as rather adolescent straight male humor, some of the songs contain
much more explicitly homosexual themes. (It should be kept in mind
that the lyrics available for analysis today are only those that made it
into print; others of a more unexpurgatable nature were no doubt rejected by potential publishers.) The audience was certain to catch the

allusion when a male singer praised a jug of rum with double entendre lyrics:

> My mouth around him cling,
> Close as de rum ole friend.
>
> . . .
>
> Niggar, put down dat jug,
> Touch not a single drop,
> I hab gin him many a hug
> And dar you luff him stop . . .
> I kiss him two three time,
> And den I suck him dry
> Dat jug, he's none but mine
> So dar you luff him lie.[27]

"The primary effect of these lines, rendered in blackface," writes
Alexander Saxton, "would have been to attribute masturbation or homosexuality to black males."[28] The reference seems to be more to fellatio than masturbation, but the inference of homosexual sex is inescapable, and it was perhaps designed to conjure up in the audience's
mind the idea of an alcoholic black man sexually servicing another
(white?) man in return for a drink. When the ersatz black man is not
performing fellatio, he is receiving it, or inviting attention to his en-
dowments. Music sheets of the period frequently showed characters
with their coattails hanging suggestively between their outspread
legs, or with walking sticks, poles, or banjoes placed near their groin.
"In short," as Eric Lott writes, "white men's investment in a rampa-
geous black phallus appears to have defined the minstrel show."[29]

A white man fantasizing about being fellated by a black man might
well experience castration anxiety, faced with the cartoon stereotype
of thick lips and a cavernous mouth. In an alternative version of the
classic "Jimmy Crack Corn" the blue tail fly hides in the master's
shoe, and when the white master attempts to slip his *toe* into the opening of the black *shoe*, the fly eats him whole—all but a last bit dangling from the hungry fly's mouth: "An all ob de ole Massa dat we
could spy/Stuck out ob de troat ob de Blue Tail Fly."[30] The image of
the remnant of a white man in the throat of a black man was a potent
sexual image. Nor was the minstrel show unique in its depictions of
black-white oral-genital contact. In 1837 when Davy Crockett boasted
in his popular *Almanac* that he could "swallow a nigger whole with-

out choking if you butter his head and pin his ears back," the entire body of the black man has become a lubricated phallus.[31]

On the palimpsest of the minstrel show genre we may be able to read something about black-white male intimacy (or perhaps only fantasy or fear) during the early years of American history. Oral-genital sex, penis envy, alcoholism, taverns, and arrests: these are the fragments of a story assembled for popular entertainment. Minstrel shows dealt in exaggeration and stereotypes, yet those excesses had a comic effect only to the extent that they were grounded in something immediately recognizable to the audience, a base on which to build the exaggeration. A close reading of the literature of the minstrel show genre reveals at the very least that the young white men in the audience were interested in—indeed, fascinated by—black male sexuality. Whether and with what frequency that interest was carried into action is a question more difficult to answer.

There is one more potential source of information about black gay lives: police and court records from the period. Unlike Paris or London, American cities did not have vice squads, police spies, or large-scale entrapment schemes aimed at controlling male-male sexuality, so researchers do not have available to them the detailed descriptions preserved in European public records. Still, given the usual messiness of daily life, citizens who were brought into court for other reasons sometimes revealed details of the personal lives not directly related to the crime in question. In 1836 Peter Sewally, a black thirty-two-year-old New Yorker, was charged with grand larceny. Sewally, dressed in women's clothing, would walk the streets looking for interested men. In the process of enticing or engaging a man in a sexual act, Sewally would lift the person's wallet (technically not prostitution, since there was no intended exchange of money for sex). Sewally lived and worked in a brothel on Greene Street performing domestic duties and greeting customers, and he sometimes used the alias "Mary Jones." In court, though dressed as a woman, he identified himself as a man and testified that he frequently engaged in cross-dressing, both while living in New York and while visiting in New Orleans.[32] It is unclear whether Sewally was a transvestite or a transsexual, or whether the victims were aware of Sewally's biological sex, but the court case offers an intriguing glimpse into the life of a free person of color who

was living a life somewhat outside the norm of accepted gender behavior.

Also intriguing is the story of Louis Hart, a black hairdresser living
in New York City in 1803. According to a report filed with the District Attorney's Indictment Papers, Hart was standing outside his
house on Water Street when a white sailor named Lewis Humphrey
began beating the black woman who lived in Hart's cellar. The
woman managed to escape into her apartment, but Humphrey took
out a knife and attempted to jimmy the lock. At this point the hairdresser stepped in to protest and the sailor struck him. "[T]he depo-
nent . . . not being willing to fight with him went into the House."[33]
The sailor stormed off, but the encounter still rankled him and he
soon returned with six of his shipmates. They broke into the cellar
and assaulted the woman, and then proceeded upstairs where they
beat the hairdresser, smashed up his room, and stole from him a number of silver teaspoons. Nothing in the police report specifies the hairdresser's sexual orientation, and it is perhaps only through the lens of
modern stereotypes that we can read this narrative as homosexual.
Such an intentionally "queered" reading can never be determinative,
but it may at least provide us with a place to start to fill in the gaps of a
part of black history that will otherwise remain hidden.

It is not surprising that Harriet Beecher Stowe set the St. Clare seraglio in New Orleans, nor that Peter Sewally testified that he frequently walked the streets of that city in female drag. New Orleans
had a well-deserved reputation for decadence. Prostitution, gambling, and intoxication were pursued with an openness that became
part of the city's mystique. In the popular imagination that moral lax-
ity included toleration of male-male sexuality, even though from
Spanish colonial times the laws of Louisiana strictly prohibited the
pecado nefando and punished it with burning at the stake.[34] When the
territory was incorporated into the United States with the Louisiana
Purchase, it brought with it an uneasy tradition of very conservative
sex laws which were rarely enforced.

In 1821 the Louisiana state legislature commissioned former New
York mayor Edward Livingston to rewrite completely the code of
criminal law for the state. Because of Louisiana's complex colonial
history a jurisprudence had evolved that was a "medley of Spanish
and French laws and usages, English common law and contradictory
statute laws, which made the interpretation of the criminal law per-

plexed and doubtful . . . and the consequent miscarriage of justice frequent and inevitable."[35] The proposed new code was particularly radical, in that it was designed to prevent rather than punish crime, and its publication brought Livingston an international reputation as a legal reformer. Although it would be a mischaracterization to say that the code presaged the concept of "victimless crime," it is noteworthy that (among other innovations) Livingston dropped all mention of sodomy or buggery. His reasons for doing so had nothing to do with support of male-male sexuality, but rather reflected his opposition to the incursion of religious beliefs into a secular code. Livingston assumed also that discussion of this unpleasant topic was simply unnecessary. In his introductory report to the Louisiana legislature he explained:

> Another species of offence is also omitted, though it figures in every code, from the Mosaic downward, to those of our days, and generally with capital punishments denounced against its commission; yet I have not polluted the pages of the law which I am preparing for you by mentioning it; for several reasons:

> First. Because, although it certainly prevailed among most of the ancient nations, and is said to be frequently committed in some of the modern, yet, I think, in all these cases it may be traced to causes and institutions peculiar to the people where it has been known, but which cannot operate here; and that the repugnance, disgust, and even horror, which the very idea inspires, will be a sufficient security that it can never become a prevalent one in our country.

> Secondly. Because, as every crime must be defined, the details of such a definition would inflict a lasting wound on the morals of the people. Your criminal code is no longer to be the study of a select few: it is not the design of the framers that it should be exclusively the study even of our own sex; and it is particularly desirable, that it should become a branch of early education for our youth. The shock which such a chapter must give to their pudicity, the familiarity their minds must acquire with the most disgusting images, would, it is firmly believed, be most injurious in its effects: and if there was no other objection, ought to make us pause before we submitted such details to public inspection.

Thirdly. It is an offence necessarily difficult of proof, and must generally be established by the evidence of those who are sufficiently base and corrupt to have participated in the offence. Hence, persons shameless and depraved enough to incur this disgrace, have made it the engine of extortion against the innocent, by threatening them with a denunciation for this crime, and they were generally successful: because, against such an accusation, it was known that the infamy of the accuser furnished no sure defense.

My last reason for the omission was, that as all our criminal proceedings must be public, a single trial of this nature would do more injury to the morals of the people than the secret, and therefore always uncertain, commission of the offence. I was not a little influenced, also, by reflecting on the probability, that the innocent might suffer, either by malicious combinations of perjured witnesses, in a case so difficult of defense, or by the ready credit that would be given to circumstantial evidence, where direct proof is not easily created by the very accusation.[36]

At 444 words this is the most extensive discussion of the *crimen innominatum* in American legal literature to date, yet in his desire to screen tender pudicity, Livingston refrained from employing even the most common circumlocutions used to refer to sodomy. He might as well be denouncing pinochle. Yet in his discussion of why he had decided not to discuss that which should not be discussed, Livingston said quite a bit about his own beliefs, and perhaps those of his peers. First, he acknowledged the possibility of consensual adult homosexual relations. Livingston assumed that most male-male sexual encounters would occur in private and be witnessed only by those "sufficiently base and corrupt to have participated [willingly] in the offence." Compare this to William Waller Henings's sample indictment in *The New Virginia Justice* of 1795, where it is assumed that a predatory sodomite would be assaulting an innocent young boy. Livingston also understood that a man of position and wealth might find himself at the mercy of a partner who threatened to reveal (or fabricate) a sexual encounter. In a warning which foreshadowed the trials of Oscar Wilde at the end of the century, Livingston predicted that shameless rent boys might be called on to give evidence in a court of law. It is curious that Livingston ignored entirely what in Europe was the central objection to sodomy: the gross indecency of public sexual encounters. Perhaps we can infer from this that—at least in Livingston's New York and perhaps even in louche New Orleans—taverns, public parks, and privies were not used as they were in Paris or London. That Livingston felt compelled even prior to publication to defend the absence of sodomy laws under his penal code is a strong indication that he understood that this was an area in which others might point out a serious lacuna. Clearly, male-male sexuality was perceived to be occurring with sufficient frequency in Louisiana that some citizens felt the necessity for prohibition. Though Livingston insisted that the crime of sodomy "can never become a prevalent one in our country," his detailed four-point explication is an odd response to something of little importance.

Even odder is the code's discussion of prostitution, solicitation, and pandering. Title XVI ("Of Offences Against Morals"), Chapter II ("Of Offences Against Decency"), Article 343 reads: "Whoever shall, for hire, procure the means of illicit connexion between persons of different sexes, or shall solicit or procure a woman to prostitute her person to another, shall be imprisoned not exceeding three months in close custody."[37] To state specifically under this penal code that the crime of prostitution involves two people of the opposite sex implies that it might otherwise involve two people of the same sex. Livingston's code would have had the paradoxical effect of legalizing homosexual prostitution.

In the end the Louisiana legislature rejected the entire code, since it would have required a restructuring of the penal system of the state and a complete rethinking of the concept of crime. Still, Livingston's contemporaries were quick to praise him for his efforts. Thomas Jefferson wrote to the author that the code "will certainly arrange your name with the sages of antiquity."[38]

Chapter 7

The Nation's Capital Under Jefferson: Four Case Studies

Mr. Jefferson . . . was playing a game for retaining the highest offices in the state where manners are not a prevailing feature in the great mass of the Society being, except in the large towns, rather despised as a mark of effeminacy by the majority who seem to glory in being only thought men of bold strong minds and good sound judgement.

Augustus John Foster

Washington City during the presidency of Thomas Jefferson provided an unusual opportunity for the country to sort out its shifting attitudes about gender roles, in particular American expectations about masculinity. Washington was an artificial instant city, a tabula rasa without the encumbering social legacies of New York, Boston, or Philadelphia. Although it was a Southern city, it was filled with representatives from all parts of the new country as well as the diplomatic corps from abroad, diluting any strong regional prejudices. It was also a strange hybrid: a population center with fervent cosmopolitan aspirations but with a decidedly skewed gender ratio. Like a small camp on the roughest edge of the frontier, Washington had a population that was transient and predominately male. Three politicians came to Jefferson's capital handicapped by somewhat ambiguous gender presentations, and their stories reveal much about the options available to men who were ill equipped to follow the standard heterosexual path. A fourth man used accusations of sexual irregularity as a weapon against men of influence, but ended by having the weapon turned on himself.

History has not been kind to Anthony Merry, the British minister to America during part of Jefferson's tenure as president. He has been judged to be "the least well bred and among the stupidest" of the many envoys from the Court of St. James, a "thin-skinned, almost stupid man," "self-important," and a "vain, irascible, weak man, as poor a diplomat and ambassador as Great Britain had ever sent from her shores."[1] He might more charitably be viewed as a man whose diligence and fastidious loyalty to the crown raised him to a position beyond his natural talents. He certainly served the king to the best of his ability, even though he lacked the self-confidence needed to cope with the communications difficulties inherent in a posting so far away from London, and he was ill equipped to flourish in the messy democratic leveling that Jefferson brought to the social functions of the nation's capital.

Merry was born in London in 1756, the son of a merchant in the Spanish wine trade who was declared bankrupt when Anthony was eighteen. Because of the nature of his father's business Merry was fluent in Spanish, and he began his own career as a business associate of the British consul at Málaga. In 1783 he entered the diplomatic service, using his slim life savings to obtain the post of British consul at Majorca. The Majorca posting led to a more prestigious appointment as British consul general at Madrid, and after two years he was named chargé d'affaires in the absence of the British ambassador. The highly stylized, almost operatic formality of the Spanish court proved to be the perfect atmosphere for a hothouse plant like Anthony Merry. With the zeal of a lowborn arriviste he steeped himself in the nuances of court etiquette and protocol, quickly memorizing the arcane shadings of honor, dignity, and precedence of each count and grandee.

The Foreign Office next posted him to Denmark, Prussia, and Sweden, and with each assignment he confirmed his reputation as someone who was hardworking though unimaginative, diligent but rather dull. In the autumn of 1801 he served as aide to Lord Cornwallis in the peace negotiations being conducted at Amiens. Cornwallis praised Merry's efficiency but complained that he did not "conduce much to our amusement" at embassy social gatherings.[2] Merry proved to be a more able diplomat than Cornwallis himself, however, and the latter wrote a glowing recommendation of Merry's work during the negotiations. As a result of his capable service at Amiens, he was named British minister ad interim in Paris, presenting his credentials to Napoleon in 1802.

Merry had by this time reached a point in his career at which a wife was a valuable asset—perhaps even a necessity—if he wanted to climb higher on the diplomatic ladder. Ministers were expected to host elaborate dinners and balls, and a gracious wife to serve as hostess was as important to a man as good china and silverware. The connubial requirements for the forty-six-year-old bachelor were few but they were nonnegotiable. First, she must have money. The salary of British ministers rarely covered the cost of the lavish entertaining expected of them; it was assumed they would supplement the meager budget by drawing on their own family fortunes. Unfortunately, Merry, the son of a bankrupt wine merchant, had none. Next, the woman must be seeking a calm, companionate marriage, not a passionate union. Certainly, she must be beyond childbearing age. Finally, she must want to marry quickly and with a minimum of fuss. He needed a competent wife, not a blushing bride.

The perfect candidate presented herself in the person of the widowed Elizabeth Leathes (née Death). Mrs. Leathes was not beautiful, but she did have an impressive presence. She was a large woman who towered over the diminutive Merry, but she carried herself with a hauteur that demanded attention if not deference. Like Merry, she came from a humble background (she was rumored to be the daughter of a Herringfleet farmer), but she had raised herself through an advantageous marriage and worked hard to put her inauspicious youth behind her. One historian has described her as a "slightly faded society hostess of fragile emotional balance."[3] Her emotional balance was perhaps the only thing fragile about her. After fourteen years of childless widowhood she saw her options shrinking; a quick marriage to a mature diplomat would provide her with a wider, more worldly platform on which to live out the remaining years of her life. Merry was pleased with the prospect of acquiring a formidable and loquacious hostess capable of making heads turn, but he had some doubts about her financial situation. He asked his friend Francis James Jackson to investigate the terms of her marriage settlement and was disappointed to learn that she possessed only a life interest in the Leathes estate. He considered pursuing instead the daughter of Sir Philip Stephens, a woman who was rumored to be wealthy and available, but in the end settled on Mrs. Leathes. Her fortune would provide nicely for them during her lifetime, and she had the added advantage of being childless and likely to stay that way.

Anthony Merry married Elizabeth Death Leathes in January 1803, and eight days later it was announced that he had been appointed as His Britannic Majesty's envoy extraordinary and minister plenipotentiary to the United States of America. Their arrival in Washington the following November was inauspicious; they were delayed for two weeks at Norfolk due to bad weather (during which time Mrs. Merry developed a fever from being bitten by mosquitoes), and the voyage up the Chesapeake and the Potomac to Alexandria took a grueling six days. They were then taken by carriage to Georgetown on winter roads which were nearly impassible. Mrs. Merry later wrote that her new husband's "*quiet* astonishment and *inward groaning*" as the coach jolted over the frozen landscape moved her to "mirth and risibility."[4] She found nothing to laugh about, however, when the two were formally presented to Washington society.

When Merry came to present his credentials, he arrived at the President's House in full diplomatic regalia, prepared for a solemn and dignified investiture ceremony. Instead he encountered President Jefferson for the first time in a hallway, wearing disheveled clothing and slippers worn down at the heels (his "usual morning-attire," Merry sniffed in his report to the Foreign Office). Further indignities were soon to follow. At a dinner given (he supposed) in his honor to welcome him to America, Merry was discomfited to discover that Louis André Pichon, the French chargé d'affaires, was among the guests. France and Britain were at war, and protocol dictated that the two men not be invited to the same functions. Even worse, when dinner was announced the president offered his arm to Dolley Madison, led her into the dining room, and seated her at his right, a honor that should have gone to Mrs. Merry. The wife of the Spanish minister was then seated on Jefferson's left, and the Marqués de Casa Yrujo himself sat next to Mrs. Madison. Elizabeth Merry, livid at the slight, grabbed the seat next to Yrujo for herself. Merry in turn tried to gain the place next to Señora Yrujo, but a more agile congressman slipped into the chair ahead of him. Merry maneuvered himself into the next available space, ate dinner, and then immediately called for his carriage. When a similar contretemps occurred a few days later at a dinner hosted by Secretary of State James Madison, the Merrys decided that they had had enough. They withdrew from official Washington society functions, sent an indignant report to the Foreign Office, and awaited instructions from London.

Augustus John Foster, the secretary to the British legation from 1804 to 1808, saw in Jefferson's informal dining arrangements a deliberate attempt to disparage and ridicule Anthony Merry. From his days in Paris Jefferson was, of course, very much aware of conventional diplomatic protocol and of the expectations of aristocratic society. Jefferson, Foster believed, was "playing a game" with Merry by stripping the tradesman's son of his only effective weapon: his diplomatic dignity. Good manners were not considered to be essential in America, Foster wrote, where they were "rather despised as a mark of effeminacy by the majority, who seem to glory in being only thought men of bold strong minds and good sound judgment."[5] Merry was obviously neither bold nor wise, and now Jefferson—shrewdly aware of his opponent's limitations—was changing the rules so that even "effeminate" good manners were of no advantage at all. Jefferson tried to explain that at social events in a democracy the principles of "pele mele" and "next the door" took precedence over diplomatic rank, but the Merrys declined to accept the excuse. At the insistence of the Foreign Office, Anthony Merry resumed his place at official functions, but his wife continued to boycott any gathering where she was not assured the dignity of her proper place.

Though she refused ever again to attend a function at the President's House, Elizabeth Merry threw herself into Washington's nascent social life. She would have nothing of Jefferson's "democratic" simplicity and instead always dressed as though she carried on her ample bosom the majesty of the entire English nation. She sailed into one diplomatic ball with the bravado of a British man-of-war, looking somewhat like an elaborately decorated Mardi Gras float. Society hostess Margaret Bayard Smith described the arrival:

> Mrs. Merry was there and her dress attracted great attention; it was brilliant and fantastic, white satin with a long train, dark blue crape of the same length over it and white crape drapery down to her knees and open at one side, so thickly cover'd with silver spangles that it appear'd to be a brilliant silver tissue . . . , her hair bound tight to her head with a band like her drapery, with a diamond crescent before and a diamond comb behind, diamond ear-rings and necklace, displayed on a bare bosom. She is a large, tall well-made woman, rather masculine, very free and affable in her manners, but easy without being graceful. She is said to be a woman of fine understanding and she is so entirely

the talker and actor in all companies, that her good husband passes quite unnoticed; he is plain in his appearance and called rather inferior in understanding.[6]

The Merrys impressed most of Washington society as a couple who were oddly mismatched. Few people warmed to Elizabeth Merry and most blamed her for the disruption in British-American relations. Jefferson dismissed her as a "virago" (a mannish woman) and wrote that she had "established a degree of dislike among all classes which one would have thought impossible in so short a time."[7] She frightened and fascinated most of the women she encountered, and elicited a bemused appreciation from most of the men for her garrulous and hearty fellowship. Anthony Merry had wanted a wife who would be a helpmate with the chores of diplomatic entertaining; what he got was something much, much more. Merry was uncomfortable in an assertive role; he always preferred to be the efficient and capable assistant working quietly behind the scenes accomplishing whatever needed to be done. If his wife had pushed him into the spotlight more Merry might have become a more effective minister, but Elizabeth craved attention and when her meek husband hung back she forged ahead, her diamonds and silver-tissue blazing. She made it easy for the minister to sink back into a subordinate role by undermining his frail confidence, making him reluctant to take any decisive action. John Randolph of Roanoke quipped that if anyone asked Anthony Merry what time it was, he was apt to reply, "I will write to my government for instructions."[8]

It is impossible at this distance to reconstruct their private lives, but their public images hinted that theirs was a marriage of mutual convenience and not a passionate love match. If Elizabeth Merry struck some observers as "masculine," her husband was widely believed to be old womanish. When his secretary, Augustus John Foster, wrote letters home he almost always referred to his superior as "Toujours Gai," a reference to the motto inscribed on Merry's personal seal (a pun on his surname). Foster had great respect for Merry's diligence but found the motto to be somewhat at odds with the minister's fussy, humorless demeanor. A comparison of other uses of "gay" in Foster's correspondence reveals that it is unlikely that the word carried for him a specifically homosexual connotation; rather, the humor came in picturing his boss as a member of the *ton*, the debauched clique of rakes, libertines, and wits who ruled fashionable English society.

Foster was not the only contemporary to find humor in Merry's motto. Napoleon added a twist, referring to him as "Monsieur Toujours Rire." It is unclear what the First Consul meant by the jest. Perhaps he was pointing out what a silly man he found the minister to be, abbreviating the expression *"il me fait toujours rire"* (he always makes me laugh), or he may have been making a bilingual punning reference to Merry's perceived sexual proclivities: always in the rear. The jibe might also be a reference to the chronic case of inflamed hemorrhoids that plagued Merry for many years. The affliction became so serious during Merry's stay in Washington that he was forced to endure the rigors of a carriage ride to Philadelphia to undergo anal surgery. Augustus John Foster wrote to his mother about Merry's illness, adding that the minister "bears it like a woman."[9]

Merry continued to serve in Washington with only moderate success until December 1806, when he was replaced by David Montagu Erskine. With the exception of two brief, unexceptional assignments, Merry's diplomatic career was at end, and in 1809 the Merrys settled into a quiet life at Herringfleet Hall in Suffolk, the Leathes' ancestral home. When Elizabeth Merry died in 1824 the estate passed to John Francis Leathes, a nephew of Mrs. Merry's first husband. Anthony Merry moved to the village of Dedham in Essex, where he spent the last ten years of his life living with his spinster sister. To the local villagers he was a cipher: a quiet gentleman who never allowed anyone to get to know him very well. After his death they described him as ceremonious and refined, an old man "walking about with the most impenetrable face possible."[10]

Anthony and Elizabeth Merry provide an interesting case study of the gender expectations of the inhabitants of the new capital. Anthony represented everything that the Americans despised in British diplomats. He was officious and toadying. He was constrained in his entertaining and overly concerned with his own personal dignity. Above all, he was effeminate without the saving grace of style. The Americans were prepared to be dazzled and would have forgiven him much if he had put on a better show. Elizabeth provided the proper diplomatic theatricality, but because of her masculine gregariousness she was denounced as a virago. If the couple had been able to exchange— or even to blend—some of their personality traits, their stay in Washington might have been a success. As it was, their gender nonconformity doomed them to a short, frustrating tenure.

"I have at last reached this soi disant City as you perceive," Augustus John Foster wrote to his mother upon reaching America's raw new capital, "& am settled with *Toujours Gai*, but such a Place!"[11] He arrived in Washington in December 1804, posted as secretary to the British legation to assist Anthony Merry in his attempts to navigate the treacherous diplomatic waters of Jeffersonian America. Thirty years later he wrote a detailed memoir of his visit, which he titled "Notes on the United States," and through this memoir (which survives in two differing manuscript versions), his notebooks, and his voluminous personal correspondence we are able to reconstruct a picture of a young man who encountered in America a unique, appalling, and ultimately seductive new world.

Foster has been unfairly described as foppish and oversexed.[12] A contemporary sneered that he was a "very pretty young gentleman" who "looks as if he was better calculated for a ball room or drawing room than for a Foreign Minister."[13] Yet he did not fit the stereotype of the effete fop or the Regency rake, and it is perhaps only in comparison with the soporific dullness of Anthony Merry that he appeared flamboyant. During his two stays in America, first as legation secretary during Jefferson's presidency and then as British minister under James Madison, his most memorable accomplishment seems to have been hosting Washington's most elegant and stylish dinner parties—though he is also sometimes blamed for the outbreak of the War of 1812. It is certainly true that he was no more astute than Anthony Merry in his understanding of the American political terrain, and he unfortunately lacked Merry's diligence and dronelike work ethic.

If he was shallow, vain, and easily distracted, it was perhaps largely due to his unorthodox upbringing. Augustus John Foster was the son of an Irish squire, John Thomas Foster, and the former Lady Elizabeth Hervey, daughter of Lord Bristol. His parents separated shortly before his birth when Elizabeth discovered that her husband had seduced her own maid, though it appears that adultery was merely the latest woe in four long years of unhappy married life. The conditions of the separation were harsh: Elizabeth lost custody of her two sons (including the infant Augustus) and Foster would grant her only £300 a year in maintenance. She was rescued from a life of genteel poverty by a chance encounter with Georgiana, Duchess of Devonshire, who was immediately attracted by her charm and wit. Elizabeth soon entered the Devonshire household, ostensibly in the role of governess to the duke's illegitimate daughter. In time she became the duke's mistress, bearing him two children—while at the same time, apparently, enjoying a passionate lesbian relationship with the duchess.[14] Bisexuality was something of a Hervey family trait. Elizabeth's grandfather, Lord Hervey, was so ambiguous in his sexuality that Lady Mary Wortley Montagu is alleged to have said, "When God created the human race, he created men, women, and Herveys."[15]

John Foster did not want his wife to have custody of their children, but he had no great interest in the boys himself. They were removed to Ireland and placed in the care of their paternal grandfather, the Rev. Dr. Thomas Foster, where they spent a lonely, rather spartan childhood. Everything changed in 1796 when John Foster died and the two boys were returned to their mother's care. For the sixteen-year-old Augustus, it was like waking up on another planet. The Duke and Duchess of Devonshire were the center of a swirling world of fashion and politics, inhabiting a realm of lush, baroque splendor that could not have been farther in time and place from the stern piety of his grandfather's house. It was a world of masked balls, elaborate coiffeurs, and cutthroat gaming (the duchess at one point owed over £60,000 in gambling debts, the modern equivalent of six million dollars). Adultery was a casual pastime. When her sons were finally returned to her, Lady Elizabeth Foster was deeply enmeshed in this world of complex sexual entanglements in which a trip abroad almost always indicated a pregnancy that needed to be concealed. Like tourists bringing home Belgian lace or Venetian glass, the women in the Devonshire Circle always seemed to be "adopting" the "foundlings" they encountered during their stays on the Continent.

It is unknown how much the young Augustus was aware of the sexual irregularities of his mother and her circle (at the time he arrived from his Irish exile, Lady Elizabeth was the mistress of both the Duke of Devonshire and the Duke of Richmond). It would have been difficult for his mother to shield him from the nearly pornographic depictions of the Devonshire set which were sold for a shilling in London print shops and circulated freely around coffeehouses. It was not until after Georgiana's death and Lady Elizabeth's subsequent marriage to the duke that she revealed to her son the truth about her "adopted" son and daughter. Foster, by then living in America, wrote to her expressing his surprise and pleasure in learning that Clifford and Caroline were actually his half-siblings.

The elaborate sexual charades of the Devonshire set had no immediate impact on the young Augustus. His older brother Frederick entered Christ Church, Oxford, where he studied law, but Augustus had little interest in pursuing an education. He was instead commissioned a cornet in the Royal Horse Guards, and in two years rose to the rank of lieutenant. He abandoned his military career for an education at Oxford, but after only a few months of desultory study took off on his Grand Tour. While in Berlin he wrote to his mother to let her know that he had decided on a career in diplomacy and that he planned to stay abroad for a few years studying foreign languages. He returned to England in 1800 and rejoined his regiment for another two years. Then once again he went abroad as a tourist, this time traveling as far as Constantinople. Back in England after eighteen months of leading the life of an aristocratic *flâneur,* he hoped for a diplomatic appointment, but not until the summer of 1804 did an opportunity arise. At twenty-four he was rapidly attempting and discarding all of the various careers open to a young man of his class; if the American experiment failed, there was little left but the Church.

His mother had grave doubts about his appointment in the United States. Lady Elizabeth Foster was worried that her son, once set adrift in a strange country, might enter into an inappropriate marriage. He seemed to lack the facility of weighing the consequences of his actions and was likely to act based on what was immediately expedient or pleasurable without looking too far down the road. She, on the other hand, was all too aware of her own precarious social and financial situation, and though she had managed to keep herself and her children afloat at the highest levels of society, it was only at the cost of constant worry and calculation. Augustus had inherited none of her keen mind for strategy and was likely to stumble into some foolish alliance that would bring him neither money nor social position. Critics called him shallow; gossips called her scheming. In any case she was reluctant to send him abroad where he might make a disastrous alliance; before he left London she extracted from him a solemn promise that he would not marry an American girl.

In a New Year's letter written a year after his arrival in Washington, Foster assured his mother that he was having no difficulty keeping the *"Promesse sacrée"* that he had made to her in London. Lapsing into

French he told her *"le Peril n'est pas grand ici, hors l'Attrait de le jeunesse et quelque fraîcheur, il n'y a guère d'autres dans les filles de cette partie de l'Amérique."**[16] It was about the kindest thing he had to say about the ladies he encountered. "The Women here are in general a spying, inquisitive, vulgar & most ignorant race," he wrote in disgust.[17] "Money, & not Cupidon, is their God. Bashfulness and Simplicity have not yet crossed the Ocean, at least I have not yet found them in these States."[18] By the time he wrote his *Notes on the United States* he had mellowed into a more charitable mood, but he still criticized the shallowness of American women:

> Unfortunately, however, maugre the March of Intellect so much vaunted in the U. States especially, the literary education of these females is by no means worthy of the age of Knowledge, and Conversation flags, tho' a seat by the Ladies is always much coveted. Dancing & Music, nevertheless served to eke out the Time but one got heartily sick of hearing the same Song every where, even when it was "Just like love is yonder rose," : no Matter how this was sung, the words alone were the men-traps, the belle was declared to be just like both & People looked around as if the listener was expected to become very tender & to propose on the instant."[19]

Although he was able to make some allowances for feminine ignorance, he had less tolerance for lapses in personal hygiene.

> Others I have seen contract an aversion to water in supposing it to be injurious to their Skin, & cover their faces & bosoms with Hair Powder in order to render the same smooth and delicate. This was the case with some Virginian Ladies who came to the Balls, & who in Consequence were hardly less intolerable than Negroes.[20]

His disdain was not limited to the women of America. Men, too, were the targets of his barbs and sarcasm. "Meanness, Vulgarity & Selfishness without one grain of feeling are the most striking Features of the People whom as yet I have seen here," he wrote after four

---

*The peril isn't great here, besides the attraction of youth and a kind of freshness, there are hardly any others among the girls in this part of America.

months in America.[21] "The Scum of every Nation on Earth is the active Population here."[22]

> Imagination is dead in this Country. Wit is neither to be found nor is it understood among them. . . . I have frequently attended their Congress. There are about five persons who look like gentlemen all the rest come in the filthiest dresses & are well indeed if they look like farmers—but most seem Apothecaries & attornies.[23]

He was as distressed as were the Merrys about the promiscuous mingling of classes in America. "I believe it would be my ruin to remain a year longer," he wrote in the fall of 1806, "in this mean disgusting Country, where you may have to dine with your Footman."[24] Foster might easily be dismissed as a snob and a thorough misanthrope, except for an intriguing note that unexpectedly creeps into his correspondence and memoirs: he appears to have had conflicted feelings about the people of color he encountered in America. His first impressions, though, were decidedly negative:

> There are a great many Negroes in and about Washington and Slaves are advertised for sale frequently in George Town, most Families having them for Servants, nor could I find that they are often worse treated here than Domestics in Europe, they are dressed as the whites are yet I cannot help thinking that if the Moorish or Eastern Costume were given to the Blacks they would not only look better and more cleanly but be less offensive, the rank smell that they carry about with them, and which is no doubt promoted by a woollen Livery, being at Times so intolerable that I have been obliged to take my Leave at a Ball or Party in Consequence of my utter Inability to bear it.[25]

From at least his days at Oxford, Foster had been waited upon by a white manservant named Robert who appears on the periphery of his story, silent and without a surname. While Foster's ship languished in port waiting for better weather before sailing for America, he wrote to his mother, "Robert [lies] with the pigs, sailors, geese, goats & broken glass" below deck.[26] When his appointment as secretary to the British legation was over and he was ready to return to England, he wrote her, "I have packed up to be ready & removed Robert & the

Rest of my heavy baggage to Philadelphia. . . ."[27] But from time to time the fog of habit appears to have lifted and his servant's humanity seems to have dawned upon him, particularly on occasions when the man's presence proved to be awkward:

> Robert poor fellow has had a melancholy Sejour in this dreary Place when I have been obliged to leave him each Time I have gone to Philadelphia on account of the mean Footing. Servants out of Livery are put upon in travelling in America, being considered by all Shopkeepers as beneath them, & it not being possible for them to associate with Blacks or the lower lot of white Servants.[28]

This is an odd observation, given that Foster had earlier sneered at the social leveling in America, where he might be required to eat with his footman. In any case, he used the excuse of alleged ill treatment to explain why he chose to replace the manservant who had accompanied him since his teenage years. "Poor Robert," he wrote on another occasion,

> il s'ennuye ici même plus que son Maître,* the meanest refugees from Europe here affect to look down upon all Servants confounding white with black—which makes it impossible for me to take him with me when I make a Tour, so that I am obliged to keep a mulatto Groom.[29]

Foster evidently thought better of the idea of costuming his groom in Moorish robes, but instead outfitted him in the clothes of an English gentleman, and the two rode together throughout Washington. The misanthropic minister, who was barely able to conceal his distaste for Euro-Americans of all social classes, found in his mulatto groom a pleasant and—perhaps more significant—an *exotic* new companion.

Foster appears to have been a man whose attraction to other males was deeply repressed and could be expressed only in relation to someone coming from a completely different culture. Only someone outside of the familiar pattern of the British social hierarchy could intrigue him enough to lower his guard; only someone absolutely be-

---

*He is bored here even more than his master.

yond the pale of the Devonshire set could engage those parts of his sexuality that he kept hidden, perhaps even from himself. Foster's reaction to the exotic Other was not unique, and it may be located squarely within a well-documented tradition of white male encounters with indigenous peoples during the age of colonial expansion. As Edward Said has explored in great detail, Western Europeans encountered other cultures in complex ways which were "governed not simply by empirical reality but by a battery of desires, repressions, investments, and projections."[30] G. S. Rousseau and Roy Porter write in their Preface to *Exoticism in the Enlightenment,* "Containing an element of the forbidden, though without its correlate, the abominable, the exotic is the realm of the excluded which is not absolutely prohibited, but merely signposted by danger lights."[31]

For many of Foster's close contemporaries, a fortuitous encounter with the excluded but not absolutely prohibited helped to uncover hidden wells of homosexual desire. Removed from the strictures of white Christian heteronormative culture, these men found themselves aroused by contact with men whose skin was of a darker color. The writer Charles Warren Stoddard, for example, found ecstatic release among the young men of Polynesia. "Was I not seized bodily one night," Stoddard wrote,

> one glorious night and borne out of a mountain fastness whither I had fled to escape the sight of my own race? Was I not borne down the ravine by a young giant, sleek and supple as a bronzed Greek god, who held me captive in his Indian lodge till I surfeited on bread-fruits and plantain and cocoanut milk? And then did we not part with a pang—one of those pangs that always leave a memory and a scar?[32]

Theodore Winthrop, a descendent of the Ur-Puritan governor John Winthrop, fictionalized his encounters with Indians after his sojourn in the American West.

> "The Adonis of the copper-skins!" I said to myself. "This is the 'Young Eagle,' or the 'Sucking Dove,' or the 'Maiden's Bane,' or some other great chief of the cleanest Indian tribe on the continent. A beautiful youth! O Fenimore, why are you dead! There are a dozen romances in one look of that young brave. One chapter might be written on his fringed buckskin shirt; one on

his equally fringed leggings, with their stripe of porcupine-quills; and one short chapter on his moccasons, with their scarlet cloth instep-piece, and his cap of otter fur decked with an eagle's feather. What a poem the fellow is! I wish I was an Indian myself for such a companion; or, better, a squaw, to be made love to by him."[33]

Leslie A. Fiedler has explored the homoerotic allure of the American Indians in James Fenimore Cooper's novels. Fiedler describes this interracial male bonding as a unifying theme in Cooper's narratives:

> an archetypal relationship which also haunts the American psyche: two lonely men, one dark-skinned, one white, bend together over a carefully guarded fire in the virgin heart of the American wilderness; they have forsaken all others for the sake of the austere, almost inarticulate, but unquestioned love which binds them to each other and to the world of nature which they have preferred to civilization.[34]

This archetypal relationship was also acted out beyond the realm of fiction. John W. Hallock in his biography of "the American Byron" Fitz-Greene Halleck describes the poet's infatuation with the Cuban youth Carlos Menie, whose exotic Latin eroticism melted the cold Yankee's natural reserve. The biographer writes, "Halleck learned to associate his sexuality with otherness to the point of changing his name, seeking out foreigners, and shedding his hometown. . . . His attraction to foreign men persisted beyond his infatuation with Carlos Menie and beyond his formative years."[35] For Halleck (and Stoddard and Winthrop) the exotic Other was mostly a fantasy projection, but it was no less powerful for being unreal. Many American men found their emotional and sexual lives opened in unexpected ways when they traveled to a place where "sex was neither penalised, nor pathologised, nor exclusively procreative."[36]

For Foster, the first glimmer of warmth toward his mulatto manservant was succeeded by an even stronger fascination with a young American Indian. In the wake of the Lewis and Clark expedition several groups of Indians journeyed to meet the Great White Father on the Potomac. From 1805 to 1807 delegations of Mandans, Osages, Sacs, Sioux, and Pawnees traveled to the nation's capital. In his memoirs Foster describes one visitor in particular:

There was one very handsome young Man with black Hair and on the forehead a broad Streak of light green Paint, highly rouged Cheeks and green Ears : he could not be more than 16 or 17 years old and wore a Crest of red feathers on the Head. When arrived at the House appropriated for them, he sat down on a Chair and smoked out of his Pipe Hatchet with great apparent Indifference & the Paint really looked well upon him.[37]

His name was Wa Pawni Ha, and he was a member of the Sac (or Sauk) tribe. Foster quickly became obsessed with the young man, studying his every gesture and mood. The fascinated Englishman sought Wa Pawni Ha out whenever he could, and on one occasion found him in a room apart from his companions, "making his toilette." Foster's memory of the Indian's preparations is almost photographic in its detail:

He laid on the red Powder with a small lath on his Cheek & Nose, taking Care not to colour with it the Drop of the Nose which remained yellow & was pierced for a Ring. He powdered with his own Hands the Hair & [metal] case behind, with the same rouge, all the while having the looking glass before his face. The Ears were painted with a verdigris green, & the under Lip red. The young Sac had changed the design of his Painting, instead of the whole but one half now left green, of his forehead & he had an undulating Stream of verdigris down the left Cheek with a Cross (X) on the right.[38]

During one visit Wa Pawni Ha expressed admiration for the fashionable buckskin gloves Foster was wearing, so Foster removed them and placed them himself on the young Indian's hands. Both were delighted when the gloves fit perfectly. The next day was Christmas. Foster noticed Wa Pawni Ha at a church service and went over and tapped the young Indian on the shoulder to give him greetings of the holiday season; they shook hands warmly. "He had the gloves on," Foster noted with pleasure. He arranged to have the young man's portrait painted the day after Christmas, but Wa Pawni Ha's companions were beginning to tease him about the white man's obvious interest in him—"he had had some vexation from the older Indians," Foster wrote. Wa Pawni Ha cancelled, only to reschedule the sitting for a day later. "He cried a good deal and was vexed he could not visit me."[39]

In later years Foster would speculate that the Jefferson administration had exerted pressure on Wa Pawni Ha to avoid the British embassy, fearing that he might make an alliance with a foreign power. Given the young Indian's age and lack of stature in the tribe, as well as Foster's poor diplomatic reputation even in the minor post of personal secretary to the minister, it would appear that Foster was flattering himself to assume that the president was particularly alarmed by the friendship. It is more likely that Foster's first impression was correct: that Wa Pawni Ha was being teased by the other members of the Sac delegation.

Wa Pawni Ha may have worried that Foster, by seeking him out and giving him gifts, was assuming that he was a berdache or "Two-Spirit," and he was torn between his attraction to the Englishman (and his desire for more gifts) and the fear that Foster's continued attentions might compromise his tribal status.

The Sac and Fox Indians are among the tribes for whom the berdache tradition has been documented in some detail. George Catlin, in his *Letters and Notes on the Manners, Customs, and Conditions of the North American Indians* (1844) describes a Sac and Fox berdache as

> a man dressed in woman's clothing . . . and for extraordinary privileges which he is known to possess, he is driven to the most servile and degrading duties, which he is not allowed to escape; and he being the only one of the tribe submitting to this disgraceful degradation, is looked upon as *medicine* and sacred. . . .[40]

Catlin describes the annual celebration in which the Sac and Fox warriors who have been the sexual partners of the berdache perform a ritual dance in the man's honor. His painting of the dance shows sixteen young men with shaved heads surrounding a tall demure figure in women's clothing, whose hair is long but whose large feet and hands reveal that his sex is male. Catlin makes the berdache's tribal role unmistakable, but he holds back from describing the actual homosexual acts. For one long untranslated sentence he switches from English into what was believed to be the Sac and Fox language, apparently giving details too obscene for nineteenth-century readers. Recent scholarship has suggested that the sentence is neither Sac and Fox nor Dakota, but is rather "meaningless gibberish."[41] If this analysis is true, it raises interesting and perhaps unanswerable questions about why Catlin added the sentence in the first place. Catlin concludes his description with a prim denunciation of Sac and Fox homosexual practices:

> This is one of the most unaccountable and disgusting customs, that I have ever met in the Indian country, and so far as I have been able to learn, belongs only to the Sioux and Sacs and Foxes—perhaps it is practiced by other tribes, but I did not meet with it; and for further account of it I am constrained to refer the reader to the country where it is practiced, and where I should wish that it might be extinguished before it be more fully recorded.[42]

It is unknown whether Foster was aware of this particular Sac custom, but he certainly threw himself into learning everything he could about Wa Pawni Ha's people. For a brief period he was able to put aside his peevishness and express some real admiration for the people of the United States. With uncharacteristic enthusiasm he wrote to Lady Elizabeth Foster about his new friend:

> I have formed an Acquaintance with a young Man of the Sac Nation who is very good looking about 17 & who is son to a very principal Chief of that Country. I got him to come to me today for Three hours to have his Portrait taken, & I had an opportunity of studying a little his Character which is very reserved & timid. however he became by degrees at his Ease more & more, & I amused him extremely by shewing him Caricatures. . . . His name is Wa Pawni ha or White Hare, we are great Friends & he shakes my Hand with a smile of Content when he sees me. He has four men to attend on him, & is now occupied in learning to write English, the first Lesson I saw him taking today, & he really seems very intelligent. None of them have the ferocious Countenance which I had been led to expect & they behave very decently & with perfect Propriety.[43]

Foster, with some trouble, persuaded Wa Pawni Ha that it would be proper to visit the Englishman at the Merrys' home as long as he did not come alone, and indeed each subsequent meeting of the two men appears to have been chaperoned. For his portrait sitting he was accompanied by a Chippewa named John Riley who (according to Foster) was the son of a Flemish man and an Indian woman. Riley spent the entire day with Foster and Wa Pawni Ha at the British legation, but in the Englishman's memoirs Riley is marginalized to the point of near invisibility.

> Wa Pawni Ha at last after sitting for two Hours, yawned & I took him up Stairs to see the House. He was surprised at seeing a Mocking bird in a Cage & always expressed his Surprize by a Laugh, which he did particularly at a little Hand organ, to which he had listened for a Time with great attention, on seeing the Lid open and the work move. He appeared less embarrassed when Mrs. Merry was gone and he was alone with me & Riley. I took him to my Room & gave him a military Plume . . . I showed him my Uniform and Sword which he appeared pleased to handle, and I asked him for a Lock of his hair which he allowed me to cut which is nearly as fine as mine.[44]

Riley was not asked for a lock of *his* hair.

Foster did everything he could think of to entice the young Indian to continue his visits. "On the 31st December, 1805, Wa Pawni Ha came to me again," Foster wrote, "& he and a Companion that he brought with him ate of oranges & raisins in great Quantity and were particularly delighted with the oranges which they had never seen before."[45] Later, when the entourage of Indians was taken on a tour to Philadelphia "in order that they might be properly impressed with a conviction of the power and population of the United States," Wa Pawni Ha stayed behind, and he and two companions came to visit Foster. Foster was pleased and flattered to see that Wa Pawni Ha was wearing a hat decorated with the plume which he had given him. The Englishman had now given the "young chief" presents of a pair of gloves and a hat feather (as well as an impressive array of food), but as yet he had received no gifts in return. The visit of the Indian delegation was drawing to a close and Foster was beginning to feel keenly the imminent loss of his new companion. He wanted something tangible as a remembrance.

> After they had eaten a few Cakes of which they seemed to be very fond, I took them up Stairs to my room and made the young Chief sit down with a Pencil in his hand, where after some little Time he drew two uncouth figures of men, one, he said, to repre-

sent a Sakai Chieftain & the other an Osage—the former with a Sword in his Hand, and the Osage upon his Knees.[46]

In a letter to his mother written at the time, Foster was even more explicit than in his later memoirs. "I took him up to my Room," he wrote her, "& made him draw me a Figure—which he did of himself with a sword, in the Act of killing his Enemy. The Figures are very gross of course—but as his, worth preserving."[47] And preserve them he did. In the manuscript of his "Notes on the United States" which now resides at the Library of Congress, Foster placed an x after his description of the drawing, and in the margin inscribed "vide appendix." It is clear that, if the book had been published during his lifetime, he planned to include Wa Pawni Ha's drawing as an illustration. Foster had carefully guarded the gift during the intervening thirty-three years.

This ritual depiction of dominance and submission was a rather gruesome keepsake, but with it Wa Pawni Ha (probably unwittingly) touched on the very quality that drew Foster to him in the first place. It was the young Sac's "savageness" that entranced the Englishman; he was attracted by the untamed animal lurking just beneath the surface of the well-behaved guest. With ill-concealed fascination Foster described in detail the various methods of torture employed by Wa Pawni Ha's people:

> Mr. Barron told me that he had been present at the tormenting of Prisoners among the Sacs, that they were burnt with Cedar wood, their Fingers & Toes having been first smoked, that is, each Finger having been placed in the Bowl of a Pipe full of burning Tobacco and smoked until it cracked, at the same time red hot Irons with sharp Points are driven thro' different Parts of the Body, particularly the pudenda.[48]

With a frisson of feigned horror, Foster related that the Sacs practiced cannibalism, the victorious members of the tribe eating the "men's meat" of their enemies.

> This I am sorry to say was the Case with my friend Wa Pawni Ha whose father was killed by the Osages & who was obliged by the Customs of his Tribe to partake of this species of Revenge, tho' he assured me he had only put a bit in his Mouth & had not swallowed it.[49]

Here for Foster was the perfect "noble savage"—savage enough to eat the flesh of his enemies, but noble enough not to swallow.

With the death of prime minister William Pitt early in 1806, a new coalition came to power in London. The new foreign secretary, Charles James Fox, was displeased with Anthony Merry's performance as minister to the United States, and in February notified him that he was being recalled, ostensibly because of his chronic ill health. Despite his hemorrhoids and his unhappy wife, Merry had plugged along at a job for which he was obviously unsuited. He was more than ready to leave Washington, but he was all the same discomfitted by a vague feeling that his accomplishments had not been properly appreciated. Augustus Foster also felt that his superior was being treated unfairly, but saw in the recall an opportunity for his own advancement. Custom dictated that he would be promoted from secretary to chargé d'affaires, overseeing the running of the legation until a new minister arrived from London. When the news of the recall arrived without any mention of Foster's promotion, both men assumed a clerical oversight. When a second dispatch arrived and it too failed to name him as chargé d'affaires, there could be no doubt that the new administration held Foster also in low esteem.

"It would be difficult to explain in a Letter all the Reasons I have for not wishing to stay longer here if Mr. Merry goes," Foster wrote to his mother.[50] Among the unspoken reasons was the departure of Wa Pawni Ha, who left Washington in early April. Foster's acquaintance with the delegation of Indians was one of the few pleasant incidents of his American visit, and he came away filled with admiration for the noble savages. As he prepared for his departure he wrote that "the Indians here are of the true race well made & dignified & what may surprise you perfectly well-behaved."[51] He was particularly proud that the Sacs had the reputation of being fierce warriors: "The Nation of my Friend Wa Pawni Ha you will find, is said to be very powerful."[52] In this same letter—with only one sentence intervening—Foster adds an apparent non sequitur: "They say I grow tall very visibly—& a little fattish—I am not in Love yet, which accounts for the last—I think if I return in any resonable Time that I shall, I shall go *core intatto* o piutosto *non amazzato*."[53] That Foster declared that he would return to England with his heart untouched is unremarkable, but the contrasting image—*o piutosto non amazzato* ("or rather not murdered")—is certainly odd enough to give one pause. It had been only

two weeks since he received the drawing of Wa Pawni Ha slaying the
Osage; perhaps he was imagining himself as the kneeling warrior
waiting to be slain by the young man's sword.

In July 1806, still waiting for official word about his future, Foster
wrote to his mother of his frustration at the impasse in his career.
There were no immediate openings for him in other parts of Europe,
yet America had lost whatever slight charm it once possessed. Like
Merry before him, Foster realized that to progress up the diplomatic
ranks he needed a wife, yet a protracted stay in America would only
diminish his prospects in the marriage market.

> If I do [stay in Washington] I must look out for an American
> wife which will be the worst thing in the world, for the Ameri-
> can women are miserable anywhere but in their own Country, as
> L[ad]y Afflick can tell you, but that will be the End of it, for who
> in England will have me if I stay till I have paid the Line, & go
> home with my dried up Brains from this parched Country.[54]

Foster made at least one acquaintance who kept his brains from becoming completely desiccated during his first stay in America.
Though Meriwether Lewis had already left on his expedition by the
time Foster arrived to take up his duties as secretary, the two men became friends in 1806 after Lewis's return. Foster peppered the explorer with questions about the Indian tribes he had encountered and
he obtained some rock samples to send to the Duchess of Devonshire,
who was an amateur mineralogist. He even sent his mother, Lady
Elizabeth Foster, a copy of a description of the Corps of Discovery's
journey to the Pacific. The enclosed document has been separated
from the original letter and is perhaps now lost, but this 1806 narrative was one of the earliest descriptions of the journey to reach
Europe.

It was not until 1808 that Foster was finally relieved of his American assignment. For the next two years he served as chargé d'affaires
at Stockholm. When he was once again posted to the United States, it
was in the role of full-fledged minister. He arrived in Washington at
the age of thirty-three, acutely aware of his youthful appearance and
of his unmarried status—an embarrassment that did not dim with
time. Four years later he was still writing to his mother:

An English Minister really plays a great part, but he should have a larger house & something else larger than is allowed, & he should be married. When I passed thro Baltimore & set off from Philadelphia the Street was crowded for two or three hours with people waiting to see H. M. Representative. Poor I sneaked into the Carriage ashamed almost of my juvenile looks for which I have been greatly abused. They bore me terribly with reports if I pay the slightest attention to any Lady & I am obliged to be cautious. . . .[55]

Foster was truly in need of "something else larger than is allowed" because his ministerial budget could not begin to cover the expense of his balls, dinners, and fancy receptions. He claimed to have spent more than £9,000 on entertainment, and was petitioning the Foreign Office for reimbursement after only six months in America. He quickly gained a reputation as the most stylish and elegant host in Washington, and his invitations were much sought after. But on the diplomatic front he was largely a failure, and by the time he fled the United States on the eve of the War of 1812 he had earned for himself the criticism later voiced by a member of Parliament: "he must be a person of little penetration who does not see through the pomposity of Augustus and the shallowness of his mind."[56]

Foster spent the next two years as MP for Cockermouth, and then received diplomatic postings to Copenhagen and to Turin. In 1815 he finally made an advantageous marriage, taking as his wife Albinia Jane, daughter of the Hon. George Vere Hobart and sister of the Earl of Buckinghamshire, by whom he had four children. His post-America diplomatic career was undistinguished. The author of his entry in the *Dictionary of National Biography* reports laconically: "He remained in Denmark for ten years, during which nothing of importance happened . . . and he remained at Turin for no less than sixteen years, until 1840, during which period no event happened to bring his name into notice."[57] On August 1, 1848, he committed suicide by cutting his own throat.

In 1806 Foster wrote to his mother about a "very singular Character" named John Randolph.

[H]e is a good deal at Times at Mr. Merry's—& as he is very Gentlemanlike & full of Imagination I like him very much—as he is certainly the First in point of Brilliancy in either House [of Congress]. . . . he has taken me en Amitié & we often ride together—for about a Fortnight during the Winter Washington was as gay as it can be.[58]

One of John Randolph's attractions for Foster was that he was a descendent of the Indian princess Pocahontas, and thereby carried the double cachet of being both a well-mannered nobleman and an unpredictable savage.

During the early years of the Republic there was no more conspicuous member of Congress than John Randolph of Roanoke (as he called himself). Elected to the House of Representatives from Virginia in 1799, Randolph served almost continuously for the next thirty years. He was defeated in his reelection bid in 1813, returned in 1815, and declined to stand in 1817, but was never quite able to disentangle himself from political life. In 1825 he was elected to the United States Senate to serve out the two remaining years of James Barbour's term, and then he was once again returned to the House. Randolph began his career as a staunch supporter of Jefferson, and as chair of the House Ways and Means Committee he helped pass the Louisiana Purchase. His promising career was dealt a serious blow when he badly mismanaged the impeachment trial against Judge Samuel Chase, and his power and influence thereafter began to falter. By the time of Jefferson's second term, Randolph had broken his ties with the Republican leadership and set off on a political career that was flamboyant, erratic, and highly colorful. Something in Randolph's histrionic self-presentation challenges armchair psychologists to wonder about his aggressive quirkiness, and inevitably historians have questioned what it was that caused him

> to hint at mystery in his own life, some strange, secret, unutterable cause of grief, which cannot be escaped or shaken off. It might be remorse, it might be love, it might be the incapacity of loving. We are only to understand that it is something obscure and terrible.[59]

Randolph enjoyed a reputation as a mesmerizing speaker, and few people who experienced his oratory ever forgot the dazzling display of verbal pyrotechnics. In his diary Thomas P. Cope recorded:

I went to the House Reps. & found Randolph had just commenced a speech which I would not have lost the opportunity of
hearing for the loss of my baggage. . . . Even his youthful & effeminate appearance & voice which, in a man of weak or mean
talents would be disadvantageous, are in Randolph's favor. His
feebleness excites sympathy & his voice, which is clear & sono-
rous, becomes more masculine as his subject rises. His expression is deliberate & solemn & I could scarcely help fancying, as
I saw the meagre sprite before me, like a being tottering to the
grave, that I heard the voice of an angel sent down from Heaven
to warn the deluded from their errors. In the zeal with which he
inspired me, I could gladly have leaped from the gallery to clasp
him in my arms.[60]

No contemporary observer writing of John Randolph of Roanoke
could fail to comment on his odd physical appearance. Even on the
floor of Congress he wore knee-high riding boots and carried a
leather whip, his long frocked coat swirling around him as he made
dramatic entrances and exits. He wore his hair long and swept back
from his forehead "something like the fashion with which women
part theirs," and a bandana around his neck which he sometimes removed with a theatrical flourish and tied around his head as he prepared to launch into a speech which might last for several hours at a
stretch.[61] With a sweeping grasp of Shakespeare and the classics and
an acid tongue that could etch glass, Randolph was famous for skew-
ering his opponents with a bony finger and a vicious mot juste. He
was a gracious host, an amusing guest, and a nasty foe. "Enemies he
could not destroy he never failed to cripple," Josiah Quincy wrote.
"Those he could not conquer, he was apt to leave skinned alive."[62]

But it was his eerie youthfulness that struck people the most. Edward Hooper wrote in his diary of his first encounter with the thirty-
five-year-old Randolph in 1808, "A person rose—to appearances a
boy of about 15 or 16—resembling in countenance young Martin of
the South Carolina College. A voice quite shrill but still boyish, and a
look quite effeminate. . . ."[63] George Ticknor described his 1815
meeting:

His long straight hair is parted on the top and a portion hangs
down on each side, while the rest is carelessly tied up behind
and flows down his back. His voice is shrill and effeminate and

occasionally broken by low tones which you hear from dwarfs
or deformed people.[64]

Samuel Taggart was even less charitable in his description:

> As to Mr. John Randolph you can scarcely form an idea of a hu-
> man figure whose appearance is more contemptible. He is rather
> taller than middle size, extremely slender, he never had a razor
> on his face and has no more appearance of beard than a boy of
> 10 years old, and his voice is the same. . . . By his appearance
> one would suppose him to be either by nature, or manual opera-
> tion fixed for an Italian singer, indeed there are strong suspi-
> cions of a physical disability. . . .[65]

Randolph's startlingly androgynous appearance has been linked to
a bout of scarlet fever which he suffered during a visit to the city of
Richmond when he was nineteen. Allegedly the disease impaired his
testicles and prevented him from developing secondary male charac-
teristics, though this explanation has always been greeted with some
skepticism. With the onset of male puberty being around the age of
fifteen in the eighteenth century, Randolph (even if he was a late
bloomer) should have begun to mature by the end of his teenage
years. It is well documented that a hormonal imbalance was evident
in him long before his illness in Richmond.

Randolph had been viewed as unusually effeminate from his very
early years. In 1859 biographer Hugh Garland wrote of the young
Randolph, "He was so delicate, reserved, and beautiful, that he attracted the notice of all who frequented the house. His skin was as
soft and delicate as a female."[66] John Randolph himself wrote of his
appearance as a young boy, "Indeed, I have remarked in myself, from
my earliest recollection, a delicacy or effeminacy of complexion,
that, but for a spice of the devil in my temper, would have consigned
me to the distaff or the needle."[67] For Randolph, his caustic tongue
and intimidating swagger were all that saved him from being relegated to the role of a subservient female.

He was a difficult child. By the age of four he would throw temper
tantrums so violent they would cause him to collapse in a faint. He
would subject himself to odd tests, pressing a lump of ice against his
own wrist to see how long he could endure the pain before crying
out.[68] His schooling was erratic, parental discipline haphazard.

He belonged to the *irritabile genus* [Garland writes]—was a born poet, and could not brook the restraint or the gin-horse routine of a grammar school. "I have been all my life," says he, "the creature of impulse, the sport of chance, the victim of my own uncontrolled and uncontrollable sensations; of a poetic temperament. I admire and pity all who possess this temperament." Poor fellow! What could mother or step-father do with such a thin-skinned, sensitive, impulsive, imaginative boy? With his fits of passion and swooning, what could they do?

What they did mostly was give free rein to their strange child. After his father's death and his mother's remarriage, Randolph and his two older brothers moved to a plantation with the apt name of Bizarre. There (and at another family plantation, Matoax) he grew up in a world that can be described only as Southern Gothic. His mother died in 1788 when Randolph was fourteen. His brother Theodorick died in 1792, having drunk and whored himself to death. In the fall of that year (the same year in which John supposedly suffered his emasculating disease), his elder brother Richard was charged with having committed incest with his wife's sister, Nancy, and with having murdered the resulting child in order to hide the pregnancy. Richard was acquitted (thanks primarily to a legal team which included Patrick Henry and John Marshall), but his reputation was irreparably damaged. John escaped the squalor by leaving the family circle to indulge in his own round of drinking and dissipation, but he was drawn back in 1796 when Richard suddenly died. In later years John Randolph believed that Richard's spurned sister-in-law had poisoned her lover for returning to his wife after the incest trial—though she nonetheless continued to live with her widowed sister.

At the age of twenty-three Randolph found himself the surrogate head of a family that included his bitter, grieving sister-in-law Judith, Judith's sister Nancy (who allegedly next engaged in an affair with one of the family's black slaves), and his two nephews, St. George and Tudor. Richard had died deeply in debt, and John Randolph took on the daunting task of dragging the family back from the edge of financial disaster. Dividing his time between Bizarre and his own plantation, Roanoke, Randolph tried to act the role of dutiful father to the two young boys. St. George was from birth both deaf and mute, but Randolph cherished hopes that he might live a normal life, at least to the extent of getting married and having children. Then in 1814, in

quick succession, Bizarre burned to the ground, and St. George suffered a mental breakdown, becoming "a frantic maniac." Tudor was
called home from New York to help deal with the deepening family
crisis, though Randolph dreaded the young man's homecoming:

> His birthplace in ashes, his mother worn to a skeleton with dis-
> ease and grief, his brother cut off from all that distinguishes man
> to his advantage from the brute beast. I do assure you that my
> own reason has staggered under this cruel blow. I know, or
> rather have a confused conception of what I ought to do, and
> sometimes strive, not altogether ineffectually I hope, to do it.[69]

Tudor—Randolph's only hope for carrying on the family line—died
the following year of consumption, and the widowed Judith died the
year after, leaving her deaf-mute and deranged son committed to the
care of a Philadelphia mental asylum. Randolph's attempt at the role
of paterfamilias was a spectacular failure.

As his immediate family sank into illness, insanity, and death,
Randolph retreated into a fervent practice of the Anglican religion he
had learned at his mother's knee. He pored over his Bible and struggled at times with the moral dilemma of being a slaveholder (although not until his death did he free his slaves). With his election to
the House of Representatives his life gained a new scope, but there
was little increase in personal happiness. His social position as a
Randolph opened many doors in gentry-conscious Washington, but
he was too antagonistic to be an effective legislator and as his tenure
in Congress lengthened he became increasingly conservative to the
point of opposing anything for the mere sake of being in opposition.
He suffered from violent chronic diarrhea and insomnia, and to numb
the pain he drank heavily and took opium. "I am fast sinking into an
opium-eating sot," he wrote, and though he considered suicide he rejected it, not wanting "to rush into the presence of our Creator in a
state of drunkenness, whether produced by opium or brandy."[70] He
feared that he too was going insane, and increasingly as the years
passed he experienced periods of mental instability characterized by
manic behavior and aberrant speech. During the long hot summer of
1819 he lay in a darkened room at Roanoke, and in sadness wrote to
his friend John Brockenbrough, "Perhaps a strait waistcoat would not
be amiss."[71]

Though the annus horribilis of 1792 plunged Randolph into a prolonged family tragedy, he enjoyed a brief spell of happiness in 1795
and 1796 due to his friendship with Henry M. Rutledge of South
Carolina, a young man he had met while they were both college students. Randolph described Rutledge as "my closest friend." During
the summer of 1795 Rutledge made an unexpected stop at Bizarre on
his way to Charleston and, finding Randolph not at home, left a note
inviting him to come for a visit. "I burned with desire to see him once
more," Randolph later recalled, and immediately set out on horseback
after his friend.[72] He was determined—despite the rigors of winter
travel and his continued ill health—to visit Rutledge again only six
months later. Shortly after Christmas he wrote to his friend of his im-
pending visit:

> In the anticipation of seeing you is every other idea absorbed. In
> ten days or a fortnight, I shall commence my progress toward
> Charleston. No child was ever more impatient than I am of this
> delay. Adieu, my very dear Henry. Believe me with a sincerity,
> which you will never have reason to question, your friend. If
> there is any other term more expressive of a pure affection be-
> tween man and man, supply it.[73]

Though Randolph struggled to find a word to describe the type of
"pure affection between man and man" he felt toward Rutledge, their
intimacy did not survive beyond this second visit to Charleston. The
two men continued to correspond, but they met face-to-face only
once in the next thirty years. As an old man Randolph wrote to
Rutledge, "Let me know your future movements, and, perhaps, I may
contrive a meeting; when you will see an old, withered, weather-
beaten, shrivelled creature, and look in vain for him you once
knew."[74] By then the beautiful, boyish twenty-three-year-old had
shrunk into an odd wizened doll.

Rutledge was succeeded by other young men. Randolph was described as an intimate friend of naval hero Stephen Decatur, and when
Decatur was killed in an 1820 duel, Randolph suffered one of his
more deranged episodes. His aberrant behavior at Decatur's funeral
drew public comment, but little is known about the nature of their relationship. His friendship with fellow Congressman Nathaniel Macon
was also uncommonly close. "More like the love of a woman for a
man or a woman, than a man for a man was that which Randolph and
Nathaniel Macon bore for each other," wrote biographer William

Cabell Bruce in 1922.[75] The feelings were, at least for a time, mutual. "Jonathan did not love David more than I have Randolph," Macon wrote, and they remained close friends for many years. But the intensity and passion of these early romantic friendships could not survive beyond young manhood. Rutledge, Decatur, and Macon all went on to marry and start their own families, leaving the preternaturally youthful Randolph to languish at Roanoke, where time seemed to move at a slower pace.

Given the sordid debacle of his brother's marriage, it is not surprising that Randolph maintained a somewhat jaundiced view of the institution. His attitude toward women was always courtly and respectful, but he kept them at a distance. A romantic story sprang up to explain his apparent lack of interest in the ladies. Some believed he was carrying a life-long torch for Maria Ward, whom he had supposedly loved desperately as a young man but who had instead married his cousin Peyton Randolph. One version of the story described how John rode up to the Ward plantation one day, heard Maria singing to Peyton a song she had once sung to him alone, and rode off—sobbing inconsolably. An even more implausible story was circulated by his descendants. In 1930 Beverley Randolph Tucker insisted that sometime between 1790 and 1794 John Randolph seduced and then secretly married the daughter of a Philadelphia washerwoman. The marriage was not a success and his wife, the former Hester Hargrove, decided to leave Randolph and return to her native Ireland. Since she was a Roman Catholic, divorce was not possible and Randolph was never free to marry again (and was therefore forced to assume a life of regretful celibacy).[76]

Issues concerning appropriate conduct for men and for women, or the distinguishing markers of masculinity and femininity, are returned to again and again in Randolph's correspondence. Women are almost always cast in an unfavorable light.

> Brought up from their earliest infancy to disguise their real sentiments (for a woman would be a monster who did not practice this disguise) it is their privilege to be insincere, and we [men] should despise [women] and justly too, if they had that manly frankness and reserve, which constitutes the ornament of our character, as the very reverse does of theirs. . . . A woman who unsexes herself deserves to be treated and will be treated as a man.[77]

As Randolph grew older he continued to hold women as a gender at arm's length, but nonetheless appropriated metaphors that cast himself in a traditionally feminine—or at least subordinate—role. In 1823 he described his delight in a brief respite from his chronic insomnia: "My feelings next day were as new and delightful as those of any bride the day after her nuptials, and the impression (on memory at least) as strong."[78] In his isolation at Roanoke he compared himself to a dryad, one of the female divinities that presided over forests and woodlands.[79] He characterized his health problems as "the incubus that weighs me down." An incubus is an evil male spirit believed to descend upon and have sexual intercourse with sleeping women, in contradistinction to a succubus, a female spirit which has intercourse with sleeping men. Randolph wrote gratefully of the devotion of his slave, John: "His attention and attachment to me resemble more those of a mother to a child, or rather a lover to his mistress, than a servant's to a master."[80] In writing to his friend John Brockenbrough about a particularly intense lobbying effort, he wrote that Vice President John C. Calhoun "has actually made love to me."[81] His rhetoric in the debate over the formation of the National Bank revealed a longing for a strong male force to dominate his life: "If I must have a master let him be one with epaulettes, something that I could fear and respect, something I could look up to—but not a master with a quill behind his ear."[82] For a time he thought he had found that dominant master in Andrew Jackson. During one of his mentally unstable periods he wrote a bizarre letter to the president, fawning over him and comparing Jackson to Alexander the Great and himself to Alexander's homosexual lover Hephaestion. "I trust," Randolph wrote, "that I am something better than his minion (the nature of their connection, if I forget not, was Greek love). . . ."[83]

In his later years Randolph's behavior became so erratic—and when sane he was so irascible—that he drove away most of his neighbors and many of his former friends. "At times," an acquaintance wrote,

> he is the most entertaining and agreeable; and, at other times, he is sour, morose, crabbed, ill-natured and sarcastic, rude in manners and repulsive to everybody. Indeed, I think he is partially deranged and seldom in the full possession of his reason.[84]

He retreated to the isolation of Roanoke where for weeks at a time his only companions were his slaves. During his lucid periods his loneliness was intense. "I yearn to see and speak to somebody who is not indifferent or distrustful of me, and there are moments, when the arrival of anyone for whom I feel regard, would give me as much pleasure as the drawing of the great prize in the Lottery," he wrote. "I sometimes look toward my gate . . . with a sense of privation of human intercourse and a gushing of the heart toward the individual whom I picture to myself as riding or driving up." In another letter he added a potent metaphor to this image of a friend entering through his private gate: "I would rather see the face of a friend than fill a throne; but I am so unused to the voice of kindness that it would unman me."[85] For someone who struggled with issues of virility and masculinity, the image is of particular significance.

From his earliest days at school Randolph was bullied and taunted about his effeminacy, and as he entered the rough-and-tumble world of politics his opponents did not shrink from making pointed observations about his lack of virility. His comments reveal the frankness with which issues of sexual potency were discussed on the floor of Congress:

> The honorable gentleman . . . has pronounced, with an arrogance unusual even with him, that I, Sir, am never to be blessed with any of those pledges of domestic happiness of which true value he knows so little as to expose them without regard to the delicacy of sex, or the tenderness of infancy (a piteous spectacle), to the public eye. . . . Does the honorable gentleman mean to boast *here in this place* a superiority over me in those parts of our nature which we partake in common with the brutes? I readily yield it to him. I doubt not his animal propensities or endowments.[86]

On a similar occasion he shot back at an opponent, "You pride yourself upon an animal faculty, in respect to which the negro is your equal and the jackass infinitely your superior."[87]

The exact nature of John Randolph's sexual abnormality is unknown. In 1955 William Stokes suggested that he might have suffered from advanced syphilis. (Since Maria Ward's purity cannot be impugned, Stokes pointed to the Catholic washerwoman's daughter as the probable culprit.[88]) Syphilis could account for Randolph's periodic dementia, but it would not explain his life-long effeminate appearance. Historian William Bruce recorded that the doctor who administered a postmortem "communicated to the world the fact that an examination of Randolph's sexual organs after his death had demonstrated his impotence, and was severely criticized by public opinion for doing so."[89] One report stated that his testicles were "mere rudiments." The public censure that followed this revelation resulted in a quick suppression of further information, and it is not known whether the examination revealed him to be a hermaphrodite, or a sufferer from undescended or malformed testicles or some other disease or trauma.

Randolph was buried at his beloved Roanoke, as he had directed. In 1879 his body was exhumed for reburial at Richmond's Hollywood Cemetery. With a touch of the macabre which would have delighted the squire of Roanoke, the gravediggers reported that the roots of the great tree under which he had been buried had pierced the coffin, entwined themselves through the dead man's long black hair, and then filled his skull with their tendrils. In death he was as fascinatingly grotesque as he had been in life. Historian Robert Dawidoff's summary of Randolph's career is perhaps the most cogent:

> For a long time, Randolph seemed a touch of comic relief, an oasis of the fantastic in the grim story of tariffs, canals, and politics that seemed to be the stuff of history. Later he came to seem a dire example of the degenerate weirdness of the gothic south, proof of what had gone wrong.[90]

None of these three men—Merry, Foster, or Randolph—can be labeled as a "gay man" in the modern sense of the word, yet each in a different way evidenced gender-nonconforming behavior. They were effeminate in their self-presentations in ways which drew comments from their contemporaries and which brought down upon them mild ridicule and, at times, overt contempt. Their gendered behavior was considered remarkable for their time and place and (to varying extents) it even became an integral part of their public personas, the odd quirk which set them apart from others. Merry was described as womanish even by his strongest supporters; Foster was criticized for being shallow and effete; Randolph was sneered at on the floor of Congress for his lack of male virility. What is important for the current study is the effect that this manifestation of gender nonconfor-

mity had on the public careers of the men under discussion. They
were mocked and denigrated for their feminine self-presentations
(privately and sometimes publicly), but they were not barred from
taking a leadership role in Washington during the early Republic.
Both Merry and Foster served as the chief representative of the British Crown, and Randolph was given the high-profile position of
chairman of the House Ways and Means Committee—and he was repeatedly returned to Congress by a Virginia public who evidently
cherished his flamboyant eccentricities. What these men did not do
was cross the line into overt espousal of homosexual sex (unlike some
of their European counterparts). The unspoken rule seems to have
been that a public life was possible as long as one's conduct in the
bedroom never aroused more than vague speculation. Although not
enough evidence survives to declare with certainty that any of these
three men actually experienced homosexual desire, the ambiguity of
their sexual presentations provides ample evidence of how someone
who might have been labeled a "gay man" under current definitions
could have lived a public life in the nation's capital.

Given the social opprobrium attached to homosexuality and the severe legal consequences of a criminal conviction, it is not surprising
that allegations of "unnatural" sexual proclivities became a common
means of denigrating a political enemy, and in the mudslinging contest between the Federalists and the Jeffersonian Republicans, insinuations of this sort were all too common. In the center of the fray was
the archetypical scandalmonger: James Thomson Callender. Callender was a Scot who fled Britain in 1793 to escape an indictment for
sedition. In America he found a patron in Thomas Jefferson, who was
impressed by Callender's fierce writings in defense of republican ide-
als. He was soon hired by the *Philadelphia Gazette* to report congressional proceedings, but while his anti-Federalist tirades at first delighted the Republicans, his vivid pen proved to be too intemperate
for the times and he was dismissed.

Callender next worked briefly for the Richmond, Virginia, *Examiner,* but his frequent bouts of drinking made him an unstable and unreliable contributor. He found greater success as a writer of political
pamphlets. His book *The Prospect Before Us* so outraged the government of President John Adams that Callender was indicted under the
Sedition Act of 1793. On June 6, 1800, in a kangaroo court presided

over by the Federalist judge Samuel Chase, he was convicted, fined $200, and sentenced to nine months in the Richmond jail. When Jefferson was inaugurated the following March, he pardoned Callender (who had by that time served most of his sentence anyway). Callender assumed that he would be reimbursed for his heavy fine, but the money was not forthcoming. He also assumed that he would be rewarded for his contribution to the defeat of Adams's reelection bid and the triumph of the Republicans, but he soon learned that his former colleagues no longer wished to be associated with his brand of invective.

Unable to find employment on a Republican newspaper, he turned instead to the Federalist Richmond *Recorder,* and although he never became a Federalist himself, he promptly used his acid pen against his former patrons. Callender is perhaps best remembered as the journalist who spread the stories about Jefferson and his slave Sally Hemmings, but although Jefferson was by far his most prominent target, Callender spared no one in his campaign of rumor and insinuation. Hints of sexual irregularities were among his favorite rhetorical weapons. He called former President John Adams a "hideous hermaphroditical character which has neither the force and firmness of a man, nor the gentleness and sensibility of a woman."[91]

More subtle calumny was reserved for his fellow newspaper editors. In the cutthroat world of the popular press during the Jefferson administration, even journalists—or perhaps *especially* journalists—were not safe. Callender exposed the fact that Meriwether Jones, his former boss at the *Examiner,* kept a slave mistress and frequented brothels and black dances. "I have heard him, at his own table," claimed Callender, "and before his own lady, boasting that he never had any pleasure, but in a certain kind of woman; and that it was the custom of his family to be fond of the other colour."[92] Unable to dig up any comparable scandal on the mild-mannered and bland Samuel Harrison Smith (editor of the Jefferson administration's mouthpiece, the *National Intelligencer*), Callender decided instead to impugn Smith's manhood. In a letter to the president he warned "that it is not by beaux, and dancing masters, [or] by editors, who would look extremely well in a muslin gown and petticoats, that the battles of freedom are to be fought and won."[93] On May 26, 1802, an article appeared in the Richmond *Recorder* under the title, "A LITTLE MORE about Mr. Bayard, Mr. Jones, and MISS SMITH."[94] The article criticized Callender's rival editors but said nothing about Smith's sexuality. In subsequent issues of Callender's newspaper the editor of the *National Intelligencer* was almost always referred to as "Miss Smith" followed by the masculine pronoun—again without elaboration. Callender had learned well how to avoid lawsuits. It was not necessary to made a direct charge of unnatural sexuality. A simple oblique insinuation, repeated again and again, could have the desired effect.

His former colleague William Duane, editor of the Philadelphia *Aurora,* was the subject of a more vicious attack. Duane had once lived in Calcutta, where he edited an English-language newspaper, *The World.* The newspaper was written for the resident British ruling class, but its editorial positions became more and more antimonarchist as the American-born Duane grew increasingly disillusioned with political developments in Europe. In 1795 he was arrested and deported by the British colonial government because of the "impropriety and intemperance of various publications" he had edited.[95] Once established in Philadelphia, Duane was disinclined to discuss his troubles in India, and the lack of specific details gave Callender leeway for a little salacious fabrication.

On November 10, 1802, the Richmond *Recorder* published a short, one-paragraph item under the title "The Calcutta Pole" which claimed that Duane had been "paraded on a pole through the streets of Calcutta . . . publickly whipt, [and] sent to England in irons."[96] Ever adept at innuendo, Callender managed to conflate the image of a man astride a pole and a man impaled by a penis. In subsequent issues he repeatedly invoked the image of the pole while making sly references to Duane's *Aurora* as the "Organ of the Public Will." ("Pole" was by this time a slang term for the male sexual organ, as demonstrated in the 1826 letter of Jeff Withers to James Hammond in which Withers wonders, "whether you yet have the extravagant delight of poking and punching a writhing bedfellow with your long fleshen pole—the exquisite touches of which I have often had the honor of feeling?"[97]) The hints that Duane had been convicted of sodomy reached their peak in an impassioned—and probably drunken—tirade against the editor:

> He has hitherto been silent as to the POLE which has been so frequently cast in his face. This silence alone would be a sufficient evidence of his guilt. His newspaper, as now conducted, is a nuisance to all parties. I call upon him for a direct answer. To brag

of his elevated situation cannot be advisable. Every body will think of the POLE. Pray, sir, did the porters permit you to put a truss of straw between that piece of wood and your venerable posteriors? When persons *are astride upon a pole*, is it customary for the populace of Calcutta to pelt them with dead cats, and rotten eggs? Were your hands tied behind you; or your legs tied beneath you? Is there a pillory at Calcutta? Did you stand in it? Did the British drummers cut deep when they flogged you, and how long after each whipping did you find it necessary to sleep upon one side? Did you begin to squall in the first, or was it in the second fifty [lashes]? Were you led to the halberts, like a British soldier; or were you tied to the whipping post, like a common thief? How did you keep your health in the bilboes, and in the hold of a British East-Indiaman, for the six or eight long months? And when you saw your family, after an absence of eight years, how did you *look at your children*?[98]

The invocation of the standard punishment for convicted sodomites (including the pelting with dead cats and rotten eggs) and the image of his deep shame before his own children were intended to imply unspeakable crimes—without, of course, specifying the nature of the offense. In fact, Callender never did state what he believed Duane had been charged with in Calcutta—that was left up to the vivid imaginations of his readers.

Perhaps inevitably, Callender and his co-editor Henry Pace had a falling out, and their differences were (also inevitably) aired in print, with Callender publishing his version of events in the *Virginia Gazette* and Pace responding in the *Recorder*. The newspaper's circulation had increased dramatically thanks to the reading public's hunger for Callender's brand of scandalmongering, and Callender insisted that Pace was withholding his fair share of the profits. For good measure, he charged Pace with being a pimp. Pace responded by alleging that Callender had attempted to sodomize Pace's brother. Meriwether Jones, editor of the rival *Examiner*, gloated over his colleagues' very public dispute:

> Callender accuses Pace of acting as his pimp, and Pace accuses Callender of attempting sodomy with his brother, and the accusations seem equally well supported on both sides. . . . The public are much indebted to them for the complete developement of

their characters. They have told home truths concerning one another which indeed; nobody could previously doubt, but which
they themselves cannot *now* deny. Callender cannot deny that
Pace has pimped for him; nor can Pace deny the attempt which
Callender made on his brother. They dare not here-after to deny
the multiplied crimes, in the commission of which they have
been partners. Their matchless audacity can bear them out no
longer—they must sink under the united contempt and execra-
tion of every creature whose heart palpitates with the feelings of
humanity, or sensations of manliness, and respect for his species.[99]

By this point the mudslinging slugfest had descended into farce, and
there is no way of assessing whether there was any truth to the accusations. In any case, the end came soon. Within days of the published
accusation of sodomy, Callender was found floating face-down in
shallow water in the James River. A hasty coroner's inquest delivered
a verdict of accidental drowning while drunk, and Callender was
quickly buried the same day.

Chapter 8

On the Streets of Philadelphia, Annapolis, and Boston

Cast an eye to the gay world, what see we, for the most part, but a set of querulous, emaciated, fluttering, fantastical beings, worn out in the keen pursuit of pleasure. . . .

Universal American Almanac for 1769

I am not a friend of placing young men in populous cities, because they acquire there habits and partialities which do not contribute to the happiness of their after life.

Thomas Jefferson

Philadelphian Benjamin Rush was one of the most wide-ranging intellects of his era, and he holds the distinction of having written the first comprehensive American treatise on mental illness. In *Medical Inquiries and Observations on Diseases of the Mind* (1812), Rush briefly—if somewhat obscurely—discusses homosexuality. In the chapter titled "Of the Morbid state of the Sexual Appetite," he discusses the evils that result from idleness.

> It is from the effects of indolence and sedentary habits that the venereal appetite prevails with so much force, and with such odious consequences, within the walls of those seminaries of learning, in which a number of young men are herded together, and lodge in the same rooms, or in the same beds.[1]

Rush refrains from specifically mentioning sodomy or buggery, but he considers "morbid" any sexual desire expressed outside of the marriage bed. He recommends that unmarried men pursue a rigorous frontier life as an antidote to excessive interest in women: "The love of military glory, so common among the American Indians, by combining with the hardships of a savage life, contributes very much to weaken their venereal desires."[2]

Dr. Rush needed only to look out the window of his house at the corner of Walnut and Fourth Streets to see ample evidence of people reveling in "morbid" sexual desires. Philadelphia in the post-Revolutionary War period was a raucous city where people quite literally had sex in the streets. In her remarkable doctoral dissertation "Sex Among the "Rabble": Gender Transitions in the Age of Revolution, Philadelphia, 1750-1830," Clare A. Lyons paints a picture of Philadelphia very different from the repressed, pince-nez-and-antimacassar image that came to be associated with the city in the latter half of the nineteenth century. Philadelphia had a well-deserved reputation as an open town with an active and highly visible sexual subculture. Like her older sisters, London and Paris, Philadelphia was a magnet for a variety of social misfits who felt out of place in the country's small towns and villages. Together they created a marginal subculture steeped in sex and floating in alcohol. Taverns and brothels were numerous and were scattered throughout the city, even in those neighborhoods considered to be more refined or fashionable. On the eve of the Revolution the city boasted one neighborhood drinking establishment for every 140 Philadelphians.[3] Authorities made fitful attempts to regulate the liquor and sex trades, but to little avail.

The sex trade was rampant but rarely prosecuted. Moreau de Saint-Méry complained that streetwalkers "swamped" the streets at night, yet during his stay in Philadelphia (1794-1798) there were fewer than two arrests per month for prostitution.[4] Streetwalkers might be prosecuted under vagrancy laws or charged with lewd public behavior, but sex workers in brothels were usually left alone. The law required evidence that commercial sexual intercourse had been actually witnessed on the premises of a bawdy house, and few people who had been watching the illicit activities were inclined to describe them in a court of law. When a brothel owner was convicted, he or she could expect little more than a slap on the wrist. Of the twenty-six convictions for keeping a bawdyhouse recorded between 1805 and 1814, fifteen were sentenced to six months or less in jail, and eleven were fined two dollars or less. Only one person was sentenced to more than a year in jail, and only one was fined as much as a hundred dollars. Two were fined only one penny.[5] Fornication was technically illegal under the Pennsylvania penal code, but during the 1790s there was not a single case in Philadelphia for which it was the sole cause of arrest or prosecution, and only nine cases in which it was included among other charges.[6]

"Fallen" women and illegitimate births were a major social problem, and private charitable organizations developed an extensive safety net to take care of the women during their pregnancies and to protect the fatherless children after they were born. These services were much in demand. During the 1750s, one in 852 Philadelphians parented an illegitimate child; by the 1790s the figure had soared to one out of every fifty-five.[7] Even those not immediately engaged in premarital or extramarital sex were drawn by the city's easygoing attitude toward sexual matters. Pennsylvania's divorce laws were among the most liberal in the nation, and the unhappily married from many states flooded into Philadelphia to establish residency.

This riot of licentiousness was nothing new to the city of Philadelphia, and it certainly was not the result of the tumult of the Revolution or the economic turmoil that followed. As early as 1698 William Penn wrote from London to the Provincial Council about reports he had received concerning the moral climate of his "Holy Experiment" on the Delaware River. Penn had heard that in his absence lewdness had become so prevalent that "there is no place more overrun with wickedness, sins so scandalous, openly committed in defiance of law and virtue." He wrote that he was deeply troubled by "facts so foul I am forbid by common modesty to relate them."[8] (Penn's colony was not unique: Plymouth also experienced a large number of sex crimes during this period, nearly one-quarter of them involving sodomy.[9]) The Council agreed with Penn that there was cause for worry about lewd conduct in Philadelphia. "As this place hath growne more popular and the people more increased, Looseness and vice Hath also Creept in," they admitted, and they placed a great deal of the blame on the profusion of "ordinaries," or taverns.[10]

Philadelphia was a drinking culture, and during the colonial, Revolutionary, and post-Revolutionary periods taverns flourished everywhere in the city.[11] So high was the per capita number of drinking establishments that they began to specialize, attracting very specific types of clientele. There were elite taverns and working-class pubs, sailors' bars and dance clubs. Some establishments offered "Negro" music, while others provided rooms on the premises where sexual liaisons could take place. In 1787 the *Pennsylvania Gazette* warned its readers of "the growing nuisance of the cabins in the suburbs of the city, occupied by free negroes."

> At the last city sessions a negro was tried and convicted for keeping a disorderly house; it appeared upon the occasion, that the offender kept a place of resort for all the loose and idle characters of the city, whether whites, blacks or mullatoes; and that frequently in the night gentlemens servants would arrive there, mounted on their masters horses . . . and indulge in riotous mirth and dancing till dawn, when they posted again to their respective homes.[12]

Masters were warned to beware of their servants' "nocturnal excursions."

As in the streets and molly houses of London, cross-dressing was sometimes observed (and at times prosecuted) in Philadelphia. In 1704 a man drew the ire of the authorities by brazenly walking the streets in drag. "John Smith of the City Strawberry Alley," the arrest report reads,

> for being Maskt, or Disguisd in womon's apparroll, walking openly through ye streets of this city, and house to house; on or about ye 26 of ye 10 month last past, it being against ye Law of Nature, to ye profaining of holy profession, and Icoridging of wickedness in this place.[13]

Given the date, this may have been an early Halloween celebration. Tavern owner John Simes was prosecuted for allowing (another?) John Smith and Edward James to "dance and revel" while dressed in women's clothing—while Sarah Stevee [or Stiver] and Dorothy Canterill looked on dressed as men. Simes was charged with keeping "a disorderly house, a nursery to debauch the inhabitants and youth of this city."[14]

This lax attitude about sexuality was the result of several different currents converging in a particular place at a particular time in the nation's history. The Friends, or Quakers, who founded the colony trusted in an "Inner Light" that would guide an individual's moral development without the need for religious creeds or superintending clergy. By the time of the Revolution the Quakers were in a minority in Philadelphia, but their philosophy of religious tolerance and avoidance of dogmatism pervaded the atmosphere of the entire city. Unlike the Puritans in New England, the Quakers were not driven to enforce a strict code of conduct in their communities or to expel transgressors for fear that a vengeful God might punish the whole for the sins of the few. The Quakers allowed for a free moral economy: some souls would prosper, some would become morally bankrupt, but salvation was an individual matter. Although a Philadelphian might run to the nearest tavern or coffeehouse to gossip about his neighbor, he was profoundly disinclined to meddle in his neighbor's personal life. Throughout the eighteenth century and into the early nineteenth, anyone in a position of authority who attempted to impose rigorous moral standards would meet with utter frustration. When Gottlieb Mittelberger wrote about his 1750 visit he quoted a local saying, "Pennsylvania is the heaven of the farmers, the paradise of the mechanics, and the hell of the officials and preachers."[15]

This philosophical distaste for moral dogma was further supported by the geography of the place. In Philadelphia, city lots were usually only about seventeen feet wide and twenty-five feet deep. Most houses were small, dark, and cramped. Artisans and shopkeepers frequently worked out of their homes, in a front room which opened onto a public street. Since space and light were at a premium, most Philadelphians spent as much time outside as the weather would permit. Women would spin and sew while sitting in front of their houses, and men would frequently leave bench or shop to make leisurely treks to the local tavern.[16] Life was very public and privacy was at a premium. Philadelphians lived their lives very much under one another's noses, so by common consent the community adopted a policy of noninterference.

This good neighbor policy extended even to people in differing social classes. Philadelphia was distinctive for the heterogeneity of its resident population, a mulligan stew of immigrants and native born, slave and free and indentured, representing all races and all segments of the economic spectrum. While outlying neighborhoods such as Southwark, Moyamensing, and the Northern Liberties had a preponderance of the rougher classes, the Middle Ward was tightly packed with citizens of all sorts, the elite living cheek by jowl with the lower orders. Because of this intimate social intermingling, it was a rare

Philadelphian who could stereotype people blindly or hold unreason-
able prejudices without having them challenged on a daily basis. Intermingling was not without tension, and social distinctions were
never totally overlooked, but it was difficult for Philadelphians to accept the idea that their betters were much higher above them or their
inferiors that far below. This may account for the extraordinary network of private charitable organizations providing nonjudgmental
support for unmarried pregnant women. The short distance—physically and socially—between "me" and "thee" encouraged an indulgent understanding of common human weaknesses.

This is not to say that the general population approved of promiscuity or drunkenness. On the contrary, both were considered to be
gravely sinful. But Philadelphians were able to look at sin as a private
failing, not as a dangerous challenge to a wrathful Jehovah. More
concerned with the status of his or her own soul—and ever intent on
getting ahead in the material world—the average Philadelphian had
little taste for sermonizing. The result was an environment extraordinarily tolerant of social deviance, even by the standards of other
comparable world cities.

In short, ample evidence suggests that Philadelphia—America's
metropolis during the eighteenth century—enjoyed a reputation that
would have attracted from all over the country citizens actively engaged in many types of transgressive sexuality. One would expect to
find in the public records of Philadelphia the same evidence of same-
sex encounters that can be found so extensively in Berlin, Paris, and
London during this period. One would be disappointed.

Philadelphia had no equivalent of the *mouches* of Paris sneaking
around the bushes of public parks, taking notes. From its earliest days
as a colony, the city's primary police force consisted of a nightwatch
of citizens drafted to patrol the streets. In 1751 the General Assembly
passed an ordinance "for the better regulating [of] the nightly watch
within the City of Philadelphia and for enlightening of the streets,
lanes and alleys of said City," but its emphasis again was on maintaining nocturnal peace and security, not on the active pursuit of crime.[17]
It was not until the early 1830s that the city established a regular police force along the lines of modern law enforcement. Before that
time, defendants were brought into the criminal justice system in two
ways: either through a complaint filed by a justice of the peace, constable, or sheriff, or by the "oath" or "affirmation" of a private citizen

taking formal action to report a crime he or she had personally observed.[18]

As a result, certain victimless crimes rarely appeared on the court dockets, particularly those of the "unspeakable" nature. As has been noted, even heterosexual sex was rarely the subject of prosecution. When in 1795 a man named William Band and a woman named Hannah Fell were arrested for having sex in the street it was only because in their fervor they had forgotten to keep an eye out for the night watchman making his rounds.[19]

The absence of graphic descriptions of homosexual encounters should not be interpreted to mean that they did not occur, or even that they occurred but were never punished. Salted among the records of arrests for vagrancy, lewd conduct, and public drunkenness in Philadelphia can be found references to crimes that may well have been homosexual in nature but were prosecuted under a different guise in order to avoid public discussion of unspeakable practices. If we keep in mind that public markets were one of the most popular places for homosexual cruising, we must wonder about Joseph Kelly, who on June 24, 1790, was arrested and "Charged with being found lurking about the market & giving contradictory Accounts of himself, etc."[20] Our suspicions are further raised when we read that for the crime of "lurking" he was sentenced to twenty days of hard labor. It was the duty of the nightwatch patrols to maintain the tranquility and security of the streets, so most arrests for drunkenness occurred in open public places, triggered by a public disturbance of some kind. The street patrols rarely entered taverns to drag out drinking men, so it is curious that in 1841 sixteen men—twelve whites and four blacks—were arrested for drunkenness in a bar described as a "beastly haunt" in Moyamensing, a Philadelphia neighborhood notorious for its squalidness.[21]

Of 115 prisoners sent to Philadelphia's Walnut Street Prison in 1795, only one is unambiguously recorded as having been incarcerated for homosexual activity. On June 18, 1795, Toby Morris was imprisoned, charged with "buggery." He was sentenced to ten years of hard labor. According to the prison records, Morris was a mulatto about thirty-seven years old, and a native of Maryland. He was described in brief: "thin visage Ship carpenter by trade." After serving nearly two years of his sentence, Morris was pardoned by the governor and discharged.[22]

Philadelphia may have been a wide-open town in which sexuality played a prominent role, but it would be a mistake to assume that men were therefore able casually to express their attraction to other men. Although prosecutions were few, they did occur, as the case of Toby Morris illustrates. From 1718 until 1786 sodomy was a capital offense in Pennsylvania, and even after the death penalty was removed, all same-sex activity was illegal and soundly condemned by both the judicial and the religious establishments.[23] In 1792 William Bradford was asked by the governor of Pennsylvania to review the state's criminal justice system in light of changing attitudes toward the death penalty. Sodomy was one of the formerly capital crimes that Bradford felt should be punished with greater leniency. "This crime," Bradford wrote in the report he published the following year,

> to which there is so little temptation, that philosophers have affected to doubt its existence, is, in America, as rare as it is detestable. In a country where marriages take place so early, and the intercourse between the sexes is not difficult, there can be no reason for severe penalties to restrain this abuse.[24]

Bradford is one of the legal commentators who, like William Waller Hening in Virginia, maintained that sodomy was an extremely rare occurrence in America, but it is impossible to tell at this distance whether he actually believed the behavior to be rare or whether he was merely defining it in such a way that most common male-male sexual encounters were not included. Certainly his comment about the age of marriage is predicated on a view that men might just as readily (and understandably) seek sexual relations with one another if they did not have access to women. The concept of "sexual orientation" is completely absent.

Bradford argued both that a strong deterrent was unnecessary since the crime was so unlikely and that in any case the death penalty did not serve as an effective deterrent. If a man committed the crime in private, he would have no fear of punishment (whatever that punishment might be) since he would not be observed and arrested. So infamous was the crime that no man in his right mind would commit it in such a way as to risk detection—and a man who is not in his right mind will not be deterred by the threat of the death penalty. He labeled sodomy as "detestable," but Bradford was modern—even daring—in his rejection of biblical teaching on same-sex relations:

These facts prove, that to punish the crime [sodomy] with death would be a useless severity. They may teach us, like the capital punishments formerly inflicted on adultery and witch-craft, how dangerous it is rashly to adopt the Mosaical institutions. Laws might have been proper for a tribe of ardent barbarians wandering through the sands of Arabia which are wholly unfit for an enlightened people of civilized and gentle manners.[25]

Compared to most places in America (and, indeed, in the world) during the eighteenth century, this was very liberal and enlightened thinking.

Men in Philadelphia did not, however, feel completely free to indulge in same-sex relations at will. Sexual desire toward other males could be an extremely troubling affliction for some men, as the story of James Denning suggests. We can reconstruct Denning's story from a diary kept by a woman named Elizabeth Drinker, the wife of Henry Drinker, a wealthy and socially prominent Philadelphian who owned a shipping and importing business. Elizabeth Drinker kept her diary from 1758 until her death in 1807, recording in it the minutia of daily life among the city's merchant class. She was sixty-one years old and a devout Quaker in 1795 when she recorded the troubling story of her coachman, so it is not surprising that we need to read between the lines in order to understand a sequence of events which she found completely puzzling:

> Our James Denning, coachman, has been for some time past very strange in his behavior; sometimes talks of leaving us tho' he says he has no cause for so doing—then changes his mind and appears easy. This evening Ben Oliver asked to speak with H.D. [Elizabeth's husband]—told him James was at his house crying; that he could not find out what ailed him, but said his conduct was very strange.
>
> James came in some time after and asked my husband if he would forgive him. What has thou done amiss? He said he had sometimes overfed the Horses, at another time suffered them to run away. Poor fellow! I fear he has something at heart that we know not of.[26]

Later that day Denning brought in the keys to the coach house and the stable and announced that he was going to leave town.

> I asked him where he was going? Anywhere, he said, where he
> was not known. We were uneasy on his account, as he had eaten
> nothing, or next to nothing, for two days past. I desired him to sit
> down in the window. He did so, and wept much. He told us he
> had acquainted his master with the crime that lay heavy at his
> heart.

Elizabeth later asked her husband what crime Denning had confessed
to committing, but her husband did not enlighten her, either because
the coachman had been so obscure in his confession that Henry truly
did not understand what he was talking about or because (fully com-
prehending the revelation) he felt constrained to protect his wife from
such a sordid topic. Elizabeth wrote of her husband's reticence, "He
said he could not make out what [Denning] would be at; what he said
to him was unintelligible."

Elizabeth and her son, William, gave Denning a drink of watered
wine infused with laudanum, and the distraught coachman retired to
his room. Elizabeth continued to wonder about the nature of Denning's crime.

> He told us that he had been some days ago at ye Swedes Church,
> when the minister said something that pierced his heart. Poor
> fellow! his nerves appear to be much affected; he is but 23 or 24
> years of age, a stout young man, near 6 feet high.

Denning came down to dinner and appeared to be much better, but
later in the evening when William Drinker went to check on him, he
found him on his knees fervently praying. "I feel much for the poor
young man," Elizabeth wrote in her diary, "in a strange land—his parents are, he expects, living in Ireland. He told my husband last night
he was afraid he would break their hearts."

A few days later, the coachman drove Elizabeth's son William and
daughter Molly over to a nearby family property.

> Billy tells me that James went into the woods while they were at
> Clearfield, and staid so long as to occasion their returning home
> rather later than was proper. He is exceedingly low this eve-
> ning—is desirous of going away somewhere, he knows not
> where. He would set off this evening if we would consent; says

his heart is very heavy—that he is a great sinner, and has been too well treated in this house &c.

Later that day another coachman, Ben Oliver, came to the Drinkers' home to check on Denning.

> Ben Oliver came in after 10 o'clock to know how James was. He is his confidential friend; he hinted that James had told him of something, which if it was true was very bad, but he could not believe it; he looked upon it as the effect of his low state of mind, which made the worse of everything. He further said, that he talked of hanging or shooting himself. What the crime was he did not say, supposing, as I thought that we knew it, nor did I urge him, not knowing of what nature it might be. He said Mr. Drinker knew what it was; if that is the case, I trust it is nothing criminal, as H.D. seems to pity him.[27]

The next day Denning left the Drinker home, saying he was going to his brother's house. He left some of his clothes with the Drinkers and some at the home of his friend Ben Oliver. The Drinkers finally accepted his departure as a resignation and hired a replacement coachman. "No intelligence yet of poor James Denning," Elizabeth recorded in her diary for May 18, 1795. Nearly a month passed before she mentioned him again: "James Denning came to town from his brothers; he appears better. We are pleased to see him in the land of ye living." The Drinkers did not reemploy the coachman, however, and he disappears from the diary for nearly a year and a half. Finally, in January 1797 Elizabeth records:

> John Denning, brother of poor James, who now lies in Chester Jail, in irons, accused of murder, tells us that James was at work for one Williams, father of Captain Williams, as he is called: the father and son lived together, James with them. The old man being abroad, the son came home much intoxicated with liquor, and endeavored to go up stairs, but fell repeatedly, and bruised himself. He got up at last and lay on the bed where James also went and lay by him. When the father came home he went up stairs in the dark, and found them both on the bed, but could not awaken his son, and after getting a light discovered that he was dead, and James Denning sleeping by him. This is the incorrect

account he gives, and further says that the [grand] jury has brought it in wilful murder—the man's body being much bruised. We never saw James in liquor when he lived with us.[28]

The grand jury was justified in being skeptical of James Denning's story. The injuries were not consistent with someone who had merely fallen down the stairs, nor was it likely that someone so badly injured would simply walk back up the stairs and go to bed. A few clues in Elizabeth Drinker's sketchy narrative can be used to reconstruct what may actually have happened. Although it was not unusual for grown men to share a bed in eighteenth-century America, it was certainly an occurrence that seemed odd to the elder Williams when he returned home unexpectedly that evening. Rather than let the two men continue to sleep, he attempted to rouse his son and get him out of the bed he was sharing. Denning must have been profoundly drunk to sleep through the father's attempts to wake his son, as well as the bustle of fetching a lamp to get a better look at the scene.

Three possible scenarios present themselves. On an evening when they believed the father to be "abroad" and unlikely to disturb them, the two young men began to drink heavily. A drunken Denning made sexual overtures to Williams, who rebuffed them. Humiliated and enraged, Denning beat Williams to death. Or perhaps, since Denning had been living in the Williams household for some time, the son had picked up on clues that the coachman was sexually interested in him, and the interest was mutual. His inhibitions lowered by the alcohol, the young Williams made a sexual pass at Denning. The coachman, confronted with the opportunity of giving in to impulses he had been struggling so long to suppress, panicked and beat Williams to death. Or perhaps the two men had gone to bed together through mutual desire and had begun to have sexual relations when Denning's panic occurred, and he struck out at the man who had "enticed" him to indulge in activities that had long been a part of his troubled fantasies. He must have beaten the dazed Williams for some time in order to kill him and leave the body "much bruised."

Elizabeth Drinker, still in the dark about the "crime" Denning had confessed to her husband and to Ben Oliver, found it difficult to believe that her coachman would commit such a brutal murder. She could imagine absolutely no motive for an act of such violence.

It has given me some concern, believing him to be, by no means, a wicked man, but rather what may be called of a tender spirit. He must, we think, have been deranged at the time; having been so while with us, at which time he appeared to have no ill will to any one, but thought ill of himself.[29]

Nor could the jury which heard the case the following month believe that such a "tender spirit" could be capable of beating a man to death. On February 25, 1797, Drinker recorded in her diary, "James Denning is acquitted—his general good character was much in his favor." Henry Drinker was called as a character witness, but there is no indication that he shared with the court whatever it was that Denning had confessed to him. Despite the coachman's size ("a stout young man, near 6 feet high") and the extent of young Williams's injuries, the jury could not conceive of a sequence of events in which a sturdy, pious young man like Denning would beat Williams to death and then share his bed. They chose to believe that Williams merely fell repeatedly down the stairs while drunk. The announcement of the acquittal is the last mention in Elizabeth Drinker's diary of Denning or his fate.

In Philadelphia and other cities, throughout the early years of the country's history, various types of male social clubs gained in popularity, an outgrowth of the general movement of separating the male and female spheres of influence. As the male workspace moved from a home-based operation to a neutral place of business, the family home became the undisputed sphere of women. Exiled as it were from the former intimacy of the home-based workplace, men created a new "home" life through crafts guilds, political organizations, fishing clubs, drinking societies, and the like. Clubs helped men to define their masculinity by drawing distinct boundaries between "male" and "female," excluding the participation of women in many gatherings and activities. But as with any attempt to codify gender roles, trouble arose when clubs needed to account for men whose conduct fell somewhere near the gender border.

This struggle is nowhere better documented than in the history of the Tuesday Club of Annapolis, a purely social group which met from 1745 to 1756. The club was formed at the instigation of Dr. Alexander Hamilton (not the more famous patriot of the same name), an immigrant to Maryland who brought with him fond memories of the conversation societies of his native Scotland. Hamilton first joined an established group, the Ugly Club of Annapolis (which, unlike its London namesake, did not require its members to be—or profess to be—physically unattractive). Members of the Ugly Club were merely expected to affect slovenliness of dress and to avoid "foppish and finical airs."[30] The club disbanded in 1744 after a series of rancourous disputes divided the membership into warring factions, so when Hamilton formed the Tuesday Club he insisted on adopting the "gelastic" law:

> That if any Subject of what nature soever be discussed, which levels at party matters, or the administration of the Government of this province, or be disagreeable to the Club . . . the Society shall laugh at the member offending, in order to divert the discourse.[31]

The group met on Tuesday evenings in the homes of its various members in rotation to share conversation, a bowl of punch, a side of bacon, some bread, and a wedge of plain "batchellor's Cheese." We know so much about these meetings because Hamilton (under the pseudonym of Loquacious Scribble) wrote an extensive history of the club, employing a grandiose mock-heroic style to satirize the rambunctious proceedings. Hamilton's narrative is filled with broad double entendres and adolescent puns on male genitalia (the founding group is usually referred to as "the Longstanding members"), and most of the club's hilarity seems to have revolved around food, flatulence, and defecation. Hamilton's *History* is of particular interest because its hyperbolic prose is intended to be read on more than one level. Many of the farcical incidents he describes are (in their unadorned state) actual occurrences in the Tuesday Club's history *and* encoded descriptions of events or trends taking place in the broader Chesapeake society of the period.[32]

With this trope in mind, it is intriguing to read of the rise and fall of the club's foppish president, Charles Cole, who is given the pseudonym "Nasifer Jole." Jole begins his term in office by outlawing the plain "batchellor's Cheese" in favor of more elaborate dishes. "Mr. Jole proceeded gradually in his Schemes," Loquacious Scribble records, "and slap dash, there followed a whole troop of frecassees, ragous, hashes, soups, pasties, pies, puddings, dumplings, tarts, Gellies and Syllabubs. . . ." The cheese is dismissed supposedly because of its offensive smell, Scribble explains, but it is not the first time, that good Laws, ordained for the establishment of frugality and temperance, have been annulled upon the like Specious pretences, and Luxury and Epicurism, have met with Strenuous advocates to support their Cause, and vindicate the practice of these effeminate Vices. . . .[33]

Jole continues to introduce effeminate luxury into the Tuesday Club by dressing himself in ever more elaborate costumes:

[T]he Honorable Nasifer Jole Esqr made his appearance, in a flamming Suit of Scarlet, a magnificent hat, bound round with massy Scolloped Silver lace, a fine large and full fair wig, white kid Gloves, with a gold headed cane, and I cannot be certain whether or not he had a Silver hilted Sword, with a beautiful Sword knot of Ribbons, white Silk Stockings rolld, large Shining Silver Shoe buckles, his coat and vest edged round with gold twist, the buttons gold & gilt Spangles, the button holes trimmed with gold and several brilliant rings upon his fingers, his Shoes shining like a looking glass, his beard close shaved, and his nails close pared, in this luxury of dress did he ascend the chair of state, and looked like a flaming comet in his perihelion. . . .[34]

In short, Jole—the one member of the Tuesday Club who professes no interest whatsoever in women—takes control of the group and reigns in the traditional guise of the effeminate fop, replacing simplicity and hearty masculine fellowship with elaborate pomp and seductive hedonism. He rejects the smelly cheese of mutual brotherhood and installs instead a highly perfumed regime of iced cakes, social hierarchy, intrigue, and favoritism.

On one level the metaphor is, of course, the struggle between American colonists and the oppressive British aristocracy, but Hamilton places far too strong an emphasis on Jole's flamboyant effeminacy to make this merely a political parable. The *History of the Ancient and Honorable Tuesday Club* must be read also as a metaphor for what can happen to all-male societies. Male-male sexual tension is the snake in the garden spoiling the paradise of fraternal gatherings. Jole banishes the manly belches and farts, and instead sets the men on a ruinous path of competitive display and simpering sycophancy, a path that leads eventually to open revolt and to his expulsion. Like the

Ugly Club before it, the Tuesday Club learned the importance of prohibiting "foppish and finical airs."

When Charles Cole (the *History*'s "Nasifer Jole") died in 1757, his obituary read,

> Died here in an advanced Age, Mr. Charles Cole, Merchant, who had resided in this City above Forty Years, and was formerly a very considerable Trader. This Gentleman was a Batchelor, who, it is said, Repented of nothing in his latter Years, so much as that he had not Married while he was Young.[35]

The unsubstantiated assumption that Cole regretted not marrying should, of course, be weighed against the devastating portrait of him in Hamilton's record of the Tuesday Club, and although the portrait is a broad caricature, it (like everything else in the *History*) is probably based on fact. Nasifer Jole succeeds with very little effort in seducing his fellow club members into a life of effeminate indulgence, and the ease of that seduction can be read as a warning to all men who gathered in the absence of women.

The Tuesday Club of Annapolis was merely one of many such social groups that sprang up before, during, and after the Revolution. In Newport, Rhode Island, there was the Society for Promoting Virtue and Knowledge, by a Free Conversation. In New York there was the Monday Club. In Virginia there was the Hickory Hill Club. These were all small clubs with relatively short life spans. Of far more significance was an organization with roots in England and Scotland which quickly spread throughout the colonies and which, by the opening decades of the nineteenth century, many Americans would view as a Satanic cult enticing young men into a secret world of homosexual orgies.

In 1826 a man named William Morgan, a stonemason from Batavia, New York, was arrested on a trumped up charge of stealing clothing. He was thrown into jail but was soon released from custody—only to be abducted on the street outside and dragged into a waiting yellow carriage. Despite his cries that he was about to be murdered, no one came to his rescue. With the help of a cadre of secret conspirators he was whisked to an abandoned military post at Fort Niagara, where it is believed he was imprisoned and then, sometime in the ensuing days or months, murdered. His body was never found. Morgan was probably executed by his former brothers in the Batavia lodge for the crime of revealing Masonic secrets, secrets he had pledged to protect

> under no less penalty than to have my throat cut across, my tongue torn out by the roots, and my body buried in the rough sands of the sea, at low water mark, where the tide ebbs and flows twice in twenty-four hours.[36]

The Masonic Order was established in England in the early eighteenth century, but members sought to legitimize the organization further by tracing its roots to biblical times, claiming as their founder Hiram Abiff, the master workman at the building of Solomon's Temple. Freemasonry quickly took root in colonial America, attracting such eminent members as Benjamin Franklin and George Washington. The order was very consciously elitist, accepting for membership only men of the "better sort," and it became popularly viewed as a desirable—and in some cases, absolutely necessary—step for social and financial success in colonial communities. But in the early years of the Republic the fraternity took on an added function, as described by historian Steven C. Bullock:

> Colonial Masons considered their order a means of entering public life, of teaching the manners necessary for genteel behavior, and of encouraging the love that held society together. The growing post-Revolutionary disjunction between a competitive, impersonal public world and an affective private world, however, changed Masonry. . . . [T]he fraternity intensified affectionate ties between its members that both separated Masonry from the outside world and helped provide the business and political contacts necessary in a rapidly expanding commercial society. Brothers increasingly described the lodge as a haven from a cold public world, a vision of separate spheres that only later became fully attached to women and the home. At the same time, brothers also used their fraternity to pioneer a new romantic vision of the self, an internal identity based on the heart and expressed through emotional outpourings rather than through controlled and polished public self-presentation.[37]

Many men fled to a Masonic lodge because it was a place where they could let down their guard and for a while at least step out from behind the stolid facade they had created to face a hostile world. The lodge was a sealed, secretive place where brothers promised unconditional loyalty and mutual support. Solemn, highly stylized rituals led a man step-by-step into a secret inner world that was with each step increasingly distant from his life outside the lodge, and with each initiation into a more exclusive circle of the Masonic Order a man joined a smaller and more intimate band of brothers.

A central trope of the initiation ceremonies of American fraternal organizations was that the initiate must undergo a second birth, this time through the agency of other men. As Mark C. Carnes writes in *Secret Ritual and Manhood in Victorian America,* "The rituals affirmed that, although woman gave birth to man's body, initiation gave birth to his soul, surrounding him with brothers who would lavish on him the 'utmost affection and kindness.'"[38] Fraternal organizations such as the Freemasons, the Knights of Pythias, or the Fraternal Order of Red Men wove into their ceremonies stories of a mythical time when male bonding was primary and women were of little significance. Although it is unlikely that the homosocial world of the lodge became frankly homosexual to any significant degree, the fraternal movement created a context in which men who were drawn emotionally and sexually to other men could experience what life could be like without the demands of a heteronormative society. Suspended somewhere between sublimation and fulfillment, these men could bask however briefly in a world of male unconditional positive regard.

In 1797 Thaddeus Harris addressed his fellow Masons on the topic of the intimate feelings of brotherhood, employing an image that both appealed to the indisputable tenets of science and alluded to the fate of the biblical Sodom. Feelings of fellowship could, he told them, both nurture and destroy. "Like rays of light," Harris explained, "if widely diverged, they are scattered and lost; if concentrated in a very small focus, they are intense: their real use is a due medium, where they are collected so as to warm, to vivify, and to cheer—not to burn, effervesce, and consume."[39] Here, again, was the snake in the garden. The Masons taught that men are always happiest when they share their affections among a small group of like-minded fellows, but men must be careful that those close personal ties do not become dangerously focused into "particular friendships." For men who had already taken the step of discarding their public mask of unemotional reserve, negotiating that line between brotherly love and unacceptable attachment was sometimes difficult, particularly since Masonic functions usually involved the consumption of large amounts of alcohol. Inhibitions once lowered were sometimes difficult to reinstate, particularly since loyalty to a brother included an indulgent acceptance of his conduct within the confines of the lodge.

"The gay we do not despise," William Bentley assured his brothers in 1797. "The follies which violate no laws of life and manners, we forget." And yet the line between folly and abomination could be fine indeed, especially on those evenings when, secluded in their secret chambers, the brothers sang, the liquor flowed freely, and the men exercised what Thoreau called their "organ of gregariousness." "And if we sometimes exceed the bounds, which decency and good manners appoint," Brother Bentley explained,

> it is not because we do not profess an abhorrence of every thing contrary to the purest laws of life. We lament what we cannot correct. And in a faithful manner, we have the surest restraints upon our gayest pleasure. . . . A master watches over his Lodge: he commands, and he is always obeyed.[40]

Masonic brothers were free, then, to indulge their high spirits, confident that the parental figure of the lodge master would step in if their rowdiness verged on indecency. They were also confident that the bonds of friendship and brotherly devotion would be elastic enough to provide great leeway in their conduct toward one another. Pledges of deep regard—and even gestures of warm affection—could be made freely, without fear of misinterpretation. Yet even here Bentley (despite his sunny view of Masonic indulgence) understood that things could begin to get a little dodgy. In a passage that is so opaque it is difficult to parse, Bentley writes about the love between Masonic brothers:

> Our friendship is not begun in disinterested love. We have an interest in each other. There is too little of this love in the world, not to induce doubts of the strength of it, in many who profess it. The little to be found, which resembles it, agrees too well with the nature of our habits, to be accounted for, more easily, on any other principle.[41]

Bentley found it difficult to articulate the nature of the love between Masonic brothers, yet it is unlikely that this love manifested itself in the vast majority of cases in much more than sublimated homosociability. The Masonic movement was simply too widespread in America (in 1825 New York State alone hosted 450 lodges, with 20,000 members), and it involved a segment of the country's male population much too intent on social and economic success to risk transgressive behavior.[42] Even though the long evenings of revelry sometimes resulted in a few sloppy drunks, the lodge meetings always commenced with a dignified intonation ("Behold how good and how pleasant it is for brethren to dwell together in unity"), and solemn ritual was punctiliously observed—until the jugs began to circulate. This balance of rakish excess hemmed in by strictly observed limits made the Masonic movement such a success in America, for it played to that peculiarly American creation: the sensual Puritan. Within the guarded confines of the lodge, within the closed circle of his brothers, a man could relax a little, confident that his behavior would be judged with tolerance and partiality.

Although a brother would always be given the benefit of the doubt, Masons were ever vigilant, aware that the removal of the usual reserve between American men might lead to undesirable behavior. Part of the Master Mason, Third Degree ceremony was an oath "that I will not be at the initiating of an old man in dotage, a young man in non-age, an Atheist, irreligious, libertine, idiot, madman, hermaphrodite, nor woman."[43] Before the coining of the word "homosexual" in the late nineteenth century, "hermaphrodite" was one of the scientific terms used to describe a man who enjoyed sexual relations with another man; by specifically excluding such men from membership the Masons hoped to assure that brotherly affection flowed only in acceptable channels. The results of such vigilance were sometimes comic in effect. In his illustrated manual *A Ritual of Freemasonry* (Philadelphia: 1831), Avery Allyn included a drawing of the Masonic embrace known as the "Five Points of Fellowship": hand to hand, foot to foot, cheek to cheek, knee to knee, and hand to back. In Allyn's drawing the two men are warmly embracing each other cheek to cheek with their kneecaps and the instep of their right foot touching, yet they are careful to maintain an improbably wide gap between their apron-covered loins.[44]

Masons were well advised to keep their expressions of affection very carefully circumscribed, for the order's hermetic secrecy led outsiders to speculate about the exact nature of their brotherly bonds. Anti-Masonic literature cannot, of course, be used as a reliable guide to actual Masonic practices, but the torrent of abuse leveled against the brothers provides modern readers with a rich source of information about the average American's fears and prejudices about homosexuality. It is significant that most opponents of Masonry during this period assumed that any all-male secret organization would necessarily be involved in same-sex orgies. As early as 1734 in Boston a faithful Mason warned his brothers "that people of dark Suspitious minds, have Imagined that Something Extremely Wicked must be the Cement of our fabrick. . . ."[45]

Homosexual sadomasochism was assumed to be practiced in many Masonic rituals. Bostonian Joseph Green claimed that Masonic brothers chose a master based on his ability to endure the pain of having his nose pulled and his "posteriors" beaten ("nose" being a common transposition for "penis").[46] The *Boston Evening-Post* in 1751 was even more specific, publishing a long poem which suggested that the Masons used their trunnels for erotic purposes.[47] A trunnel is a wooden peg (originally "tree-nail") popular especially in shipbuilding because a wet trunnel swells and makes an excellent fastener for timber. The poem, written as though a Mason is bragging about his order's practices, responds to criticism of a recent Masonic parade through the streets of Boston.

> I'm sure our TRUNNELS look'd as clean
> As if they ne're up A—se had been;
> For when we use 'em, we take care
> To wash 'em well, and give 'em Air,
> Then lock 'em up in our own Chamber,
> Ready to TRUNNEL the next Member.
> You see I have put our ARMS above,
> To shew you that we live in Love.[48]

The supposed Masonic "arms" accompanying the poem is a woodcut showing two men purportedly engaged in a Masonic love ritual. One has pulled down his trousers and is bending over a table. The other man has inserted a trunnel into the first man's anus and is about to drive it home with a wooden mallet. Both of the men are smiling broadly. To one side there is a braying ass with a banner coming out of his mouth that reads, "Trunil Him well Brother."

It is odd that in this case the poet (and artist) selected as tools the trunnel and the mallet, rather than the traditional symbols of the Masonic Order: the trowel and the square. The explanation may simply be that a trunnel is much more phallic than a trowel, but the poem suggests that the participants had paraded through the streets proudly displaying their trunnels in the same way that Masonic brothers usually carried the tools of the stonemason's trade (even though very few were actually stonemasons by profession). The trunnel here appears to carry a symbolic weight much greater than its mere resemblance to a phallus. The poet is perhaps conflating two types of parades: a Masonic procession and the traditional craftsmen's parade popular in America throughout the eighteenth century and well into the nineteenth. In the craftsmen's parade, members of various guilds or unions would celebrate holidays and significant events by marching together while carrying banners and "articels emblemattical of [their] Trade." In the 1825 bank book of New York's Union Society of Shipwrights and Caulkers there is a notation of an expenditure for a "ceremonial caulking mallet."[49] Perhaps, then, the poet is calumniating Masons by evoking a stereotype associated with another group of artisans: shipbuilders. Although no definitive evidence has yet been uncovered to indicate that shipbuilding was considered a profession popular with men of dubious sexual inclinations, it is interesting to note that the only man committed to Philadelphia's Walnut Street Prison in 1795 charged with buggery was Toby Morris—a "Ship carpenter by trade." The close association between shipbuilders and sailors perhaps linked them in the public mind as men who were not adverse to having sex with other men. Certainly the fact that the two professions frequently inhabited the same seedy neighborhood near the docks would make the shipbuilders equally morally suspect.

Allegations of sexual transgression in all-male lodges were a staple of anti-Masonic rhetoric. In language rich in sexual innuendo, one critic charged that Masonry had persuaded young men to "fondle the viper," unaware of the danger to which they were subjecting themselves. "You might as well expect religion in a brothel, as in a Masonic Lodge," warned a Massachusetts newspaper. Former Masons made public confessions of their "uncleanness" due to the sins they had once committed "in the unhallowed orgies of [Satan's] midnight assemblies." Others expressed profound guilt about their "shameful experience and knowledge," and urged their former fraternity members to "come out, and be separate from masonic abominations." Lodges were the site of "unseemly orgies" and "Bacchanalian revels." A typical Mason could be found "till past midnight, in the orgies of the lodge room." Outsiders alleged that Masonic initiation rituals included strip searches and close examination of the young man's genitals. The initiate, wrote Solomon Southwick in disgust, "submits to be stripped naked under the indecent and ridiculous pretense of ascertaining his sex and that he has no minerals or metals about him."[50]

This assumption of sexual impropriety seems wildly at odds with our image of an organization graced by the presence of Benjamin Franklin and George Washington, but Masonry as it was practiced in Washington's time was quite different from its later manifestations. By the early 1800s Masonry began to draw its membership primarily from men in their twenties or early thirties. Lodges frequently included older members also, but members tended to become less active in their lodge over time. Many of the young men were still living at home until they could establish themselves in a profession, and part of the impetus for joining a lodge (particularly their father's lodge) was to declare their separation from the sphere of influence dominated by their mother.[51] At a period when mainstream American Protestant churches were becoming the province of women and effeminate men, Masonry offered a more muscular Christianity wrapped in the cloak of a vaguely defined, very liberal form of deism. The appeal to enlightened reason rather than to received dogma, the ornate chambers and elaborately costumed rituals rather than the stark simplicity of Protestantism, the emphasis on florid masculine bonding rather than the sobriety of Christian marriage and fatherhood—all of these appealed to the young men who stripped and knelt to receive the ancient secrets.

Women played a leading role in the anti-Masonic tidal wave which swept over America following the abduction and murder of William Morgan. One of the chief sources of rancor against the order was its strict exclusionary policy; women who saw their sons and young husbands disappear into lodges where they themselves were not allowed to follow wondered what went on in there, and imagined the worst. The primary objection to Masonry was its secretiveness, an insularity which bred suspicion. At the heart of this suspicion was the tension caused by a reconceptualization of human sexuality and gender roles. The cult of true womanhood had desexualized women and cast men in the role of crude brutes driven by their uncontrollable animal lusts. A man who left his virtuous (passionless) wife at home and went drinking past midnight with his friends in the sealed privacy of the lodge could well be indulging in any number of unspeakable acts. Despite the repeated references to orgies and bacchanals, few if any anti-Masonic tracts accused the order of smuggling female prostitutes into their gatherings. The presumption, usually unspoken, was that the orgies were carried on in the absence of women. Masons themselves argued that it was necessary to exclude all women from the lodges because the presence of any woman in such a secret gathering would necessarily destroy her reputation. Mothers and wives objected that the lodge allowed a man to close the door to a woman's saving influence, shutting her out from her natural role as spiritual guide and domestic savior. In the place of a mother or a wife, the Masonic brother looked to the lodge master for moral guidance. In a world in which a woman's influence was sharply circumscribed at best, Masonry usurped the role of teacher of spiritual truths. It was a bitter theft, and few women took it lightly.

Chapter 9

Spirituality and Sublimation

*I saw a great fire, and a nude man, perfect in his physical organism, standing by it; he stepped into its very midst, the flames completely encircled his whole body. The next thing I observed was, that while he was perfect in **living beauty**, he was so organically changed that no "fig leaf" covering was required.*

Brother Frederick W. Evan

During the early 1800s a wave of religious revivalism swept through America, leaving its mark on many aspects of society. Especially in the "Burned Over District" of upstate New York, the mainstream Protestant denominations were suddenly in competition with a host of new religious organizations, spiritual philosophies, utopian communities, and cults. At least three of these new faiths offered as a part of their theology an alternative to the established "one man-one woman" view of human sexuality, and thereby issued a serious challenge to orthodox beliefs about marriage and procreation. Despite this challenge, homosexual activity was viewed in an unwaveringly negative light, so it is not surprising that same-sex desire posed a moral dilemma for some of the men caught up in the movements of spiritual rebirth. Religious commitment (then as now) varied widely, and while for some homosexually inclined men religion was a nonissue, for others it was central to their struggle to find a way of assimilating their sexual impulses into their faith lives. Men with homosexual yearnings could find in some of the new radical sects and utopian communities models for an alternative way of constructing one's sexuality outside of the expected husband-wife coupling, and for some converts the new religious communities provided a sanctuary from disappointed families and small-town gossip.

For any man ambivalent in his feelings about sexual relations with women, the Shakers offered an attractive refuge. The religious teachings of the Shakers would resonate in many ways with a man who respected women and valued their contributions to American life, but had little or no interest in going to bed with one. The Shakers preached spiritual equality for women (their founder, Mother Ann Lee, considered herself to be the Female Christ), but that spiritual equality was manifested on earth in communities which followed a doctrine of equal but separate. Shaker communities were planned and organized in such a way that men and women had very little contact with one another. Men and women slept in separate dormitories (or at opposite ends of one large building), and they used separate entrances, separate staircases, and separate dining tables. When they died they were buried in separate areas of the cemetery. Life for members of the community was minutely regulated. At the first bell everyone was expected to rise promptly, in a prescribed way: "Put your right foot out of bed first. Place your right knee where your foot first touched the floor in kneeling to pray. . . ."[1]

In stressing the necessity of rejecting worldly ties, the Shakers urged their members to turn their backs on their biological families. Part of pledging themselves to their new spiritual family entailed a severing of the relationships with parents, siblings, and others who they had known since childhood. For Shakers for whom home relationships had been strained or unpleasant, it was a relief to sing:

> Of all the relations that ever I see
> My old fleshly kindred are furthest from me
> So bad and so ugly, so hateful they feel
> To see them and hate them increases my zeal.
>> O how ugly they look!
>> How ugly they look!
>> How nasty they feel![2]

While confirming the spiritual equality of women, the Shakers strongly upheld the prevalent nineteenth-century concept of separate spheres for the sexes. "If woman would work successfully," wrote Shaker elder Antoinette Doolittle, "she must keep within her own sphere. The distinctive lines between the masculine and feminine are clearly defined. . . . The sea and land have their prescribed limits. So with man and woman."[3] Like their counterparts in the secular world, Shaker women were expected to do all the cooking, cleaning, sewing, washing, and other household chores, while men left the communal house during the day to work in the fields, stables, or crafts shops. After an 1843 visit to a Shaker community, Abigail Alcott wrote in her diary, "There is servitude somewhere, I have no doubt. There is a fat sleek comfortable look about the men, and among the women there is a stiff awkward reserve that belongs to neither sublime resignation nor divine hope."[4] A man joining a Shaker settlement did not need to give up much in the way of male privilege in order to blend into the community.

What he did give up was the right (or perhaps the obligation) of having sexual relations with women. The Shakers were celibate communities, and the separation of the sexes was viewed as a necessary aid in overcoming the tyranny of the flesh. By keeping a modest distance from one another, men and women would not be tempted to indulge in base activities that tied them to a fallen world. Surprisingly (since the order was founded by a woman), Shakers believed that women bear the greater fault in sins of the flesh. Women are temptresses who seduce men to commit acts against their better judgment. Women are less rational, more emotional, and more sensual than men. At a time when mainstream Protestant religions were preaching that passionless women were the guiding light of salvation for beastly men stumbling in darkness, the Shakers set the typology on its head. The sexual force itself was seen as feminine and all sexual desire a type of emasculation. One of the basic tenets of Shaker belief was that any yielding to lust, including nonprocreative sexuality within the confines of marriage, "UNMANS the man." All acts of carnality were therefore labeled "effeminate." Given the equation between heterosexual desire and effeminacy, it becomes difficult at times to decipher references to homosexuality in Shaker writings. "I never have had any unlawful connection with any woman," former Shaker Reuben Rathbone vowed,

> and from the time I first knew the Shakers to this time, *I never defiled myself with what is called among you effeminacy....* As to the woman who is now my wife, *I never knew whether she was male or female* until after I was legally married to her.[5]

It is easy to see how life in a Shaker community would have been attractive to a man who was struggling with homosexual desire but prevented by his religious beliefs from seeking sexual relations with another man. Removed from the marriage market and the pressure to procreate, he would receive every support from his surroundings to live a life pledged to celibacy. The women in his universe were there to cook his food and wash his clothes, to make his bed and darn his socks—with no expectation of courtship or marriage. It was possible never to have a private conversation with a female. But the separation of the sexes in Shaker communities could, of course, be a double-edged sword for such a man. While he was spared close contact with women, he was at the same time thrown into a communal living arrangement with several other men. Adding to the temptation would be the practice of hiring non-Shaker men to help out in the fields and the workshops. Although the incest taboo and respect for the deep religious convictions of his brothers might provide a sufficient barrier against unwanted sexual overtures, intimate daily contact with men from "the world" could be a gnawing source of frustration.

Much sexual tension for both men and women was channeled into exhausting work and ecstatic singing and dancing. Helpful also were the dreams and visions that were an integral part of Shaker spirituality, and which the faithful were encouraged to share with other members of the community. The homoeroticism evident in Frederick W. Evan's beatific vision (used as the epigram for this chapter) is a vivid testimony of conflicted sexuality.[6] Perfect living beauty in men could be appreciated, perhaps even embraced, but only if a refining fire had cleansed them of their genitals.

In the twenty-first century, gay men living in rural areas frequently designate a remote wooded area as a locus for sexual cruising, and there is evidence that American men in the eighteenth and nineteenth centuries did likewise. (This could account for Philadelphia coachman James Denning's unexplained disappearance into the woods when he was supposed to be attending Elizabeth Drinker's son and daughter.) The 1818 Shaker "visionary dream" of Garrett K. Lawrence may reveal guilt about a similar practice. Lawrence describes a dream in which he and a number of the other Shaker brothers are looking at a partridge that glitters like gold and sports a long phallic tail protruding from its spotted body. The bird suddenly flies out the door, and Lawrence alone runs after it. Unable to overtake the bird,

Lawrence returns to the house, but on the way he realizes that he is completely naked. He slips "slyly" into the dormitory and dresses, but he forgets to wash his muddy feet. Rejoining the others, he finds them talking to "the most beautiful man I ever saw in mortal clay." When the others ask the man to identify himself, he answers in words that echo those of Christ, "Whom think ye that I am?" Only Lawrence is able to identify the man as Father James Whittaker, the successor to Mother Ann Lee as leader of the Shakers. The stranger turns to Lawrence and noting his muddy feet accuses him of having "given away in your feelings of unbelief—to fleshly affections and lusts." In tears, Lawrence confesses and receives absolution. "I awoke in tears, and continued crying for an hour, feeling God was at work with me."[7]

Another Shaker, James Bishop, related a dream in which he, too, is wandering in the woods trying to follow a strange star which he knows he must not lose sight of or he will be lost forever. He struggles "thro briars and thorns; over logs, rocks, and thro deep mire," until he finds himself in a "wilderness swamp" where the star is revealed to be a woman standing in the doorway of a brightly shining house. Bishop wants to approach the woman, but he feels unworthy.

> There I was brought to a mortifying trial; when the light of steadfast shone upon me, I found my clothes were torn from me insomuch that I was almost naked, and covered with mud from head to foot.
>
> My next exertion was, to find some way around the backside of the house; for I had not confidence to approach such a heavenly looking woman, and in such a bright light; but this would not do; the woman called to me and said: "You must come in at the door; for they that clime up some other way, are but thieves and robbers." Seeing no other way, I complied; and when I came to the door, she took me by the hand and led me to a back room, striped [sic] me of my raggs, and clothed me with a clean new dress; then led me to a table furnished with everything which heart could desire.[8]

Men who enter through the "backside" of a house, those who "clime up some other way," will be lost. Only those who are stripped and reclothed by a pure and shining woman (Mother Ann Lee) will be saved.

Sublimation of homosexual desire was necessary since all such thoughts and feelings were proscribed. "Cease to gratify your carnal desires with your own sex, man with man and woman with woman," warns the Shaker's *Divine Book of Holy and Eternal Wisdom*.[9] To guard against any possible gender confusion, cross-dressing was specifically forbidden: "Brethren and Sisters should not dress in garments belonging to the opposite sex."[10] Shakers were urged to police their own thoughts and actions, and the order instituted auricular confession to help members acknowledge their faults, with women hearing the confessions of women and men those of men. Self-monitoring was at times an insufficient way to assure purity, so communities were closely watched by a cadre of internal informers constantly on the lookout for transgressions and willing to carry reports to the Elders. With the enforced intimacy of communal life it was a rare fault that went unnoticed.

Though Shaker communities were celibate, adult members sometimes arrived accompanied by their offspring. Children, too, were subject to the rule of gender segregation. Girls lived with the women and helped with the household chores, while boys lived with the men and received apprentice training in the various crafts that sustained the community or brought in needed cash. Intimate friendships sometimes grew up between the young apprentices in the Shaker workshops and the older members who taught them. In 1826 apprentice Benjamin Gates wrote to his absent master, Isaac Youngs, "Come home and see me so that I can stroke your head and kiss you once more as I used to." Youngs was thirty-three when Gates longed to stroke his head and kiss him; Gates was only nine. This was perhaps a romantic mentorship, though probably without an overt sexual component. Children were closely watched, and it would have been difficult for a pedophile to hide his activities. Yet a deep emotional tie developed (at least on the boy's part) despite the prohibition against particular friendships, and the relationship between the tailor and his apprentice lasted well beyond Gates's boyhood. Ten years after the 1826 letter, at the age of nineteen, he was again lamenting Youngs's absence: "But the lonely lonesome hours that I have pass'd thro' in your absence have not been verry few I assure you."[11] Despite their spiritual calling (or perhaps because of their rejection of overt sexuality), descriptions of physical touching play a prominent role in Shaker writings. "Here in this lovely valley," one Shaker wrote, "you will find Fathers and mothers to caress you as all Mothers know how to. . . ."[12] The men in Shaker villages, it would seem, could be as physically demonstrative as the women.

Despite the rigors and deprivations of Shaker life during its early years, the rate of apostasy was stunningly low: about 1 percent.[13] At the New Lebanon settlement in New York members who joined before 1830 stayed an average of thirty years in the community, many remaining in the order until their deaths.[14] When a reason for leaving the Shakers was recorded, it almost always involved an inability to adjust to the rules concerning sexuality. The Shaker elders were well aware that the lures of the flesh were great, so commitment to the community was assured by a slow three-step process of gradual incorporation into full fellowship, and those unable to embrace celibacy were usually weeded out early on in the process. For heterosexual men and women the outside world offered the siren song of traditional marriage and sanctioned sexual indulgence, but for men and women attracted to their own sex there was no perceived Christian alternative. This sense that the Shakers offered the last best hope for salvation left some members in abject despair when their sexual desires became overwhelming. For the years 1833 through 1880 the records for the Shaker community at New Lebanon (later known as Mount Lebanon), New York, record seventeen cases of insanity, suicide, or attempted suicide.[15]

Another alternative to traditional American sexual relations was offered on July 12, 1843, when Joseph Smith announced that it had been revealed to him by God that men of the Church of Jesus Christ of Latter Day Saints should be encouraged to engage in plural marriage. The addition of polygamy to Mormon doctrine was accomplished over a long period of time, at first largely in secret, for fear that it would drive some members to apostasy, as well as bring down upon the fledgling religion the wrath of local authorities. During the period from 1839, when the church moved to Nauvoo, Illinois, through the death of Joseph Smith in 1844 and the relocation to Utah in 1847, members of the church were gradually brought to the acceptance of a pattern of sexual conduct jarringly at odds with everything they had previously believed. This sea change in sexual ethics necessarily raised the possibility of a related questioning and reformulation of opinions about other aspects of human sexuality.

It is easy to understand the attraction of strict Shaker celibacy for a man struggling with same-sex desire, but it is perhaps more difficult to appreciate the attraction of Mormonism. Joseph Smith's teachings, after all, involved a theory of salvation that linked redemption to marriage (and eventually, multiple marriages) and to frequent acts of procreation. But this almost regimented, mandatory heterosexuality provided sexually ambivalent men with a strong, unambiguous moral bunker from which to fight their troublesome desires, one which simultaneously blocked off and channeled their libidos, while still offering the tantalizing promise of a new dispensation. If Joseph Smith could challenge the most basic tenet of Christian sexual theology—one husband, one wife—what other acceptable permutations might eventually be revealed?

In the handsome, charismatic Joseph Smith, men with strong spiritual yearnings found a welcome alternative to the effeminate, weak-tea preaching of the typical American pastor, and in his vision for a new type of communal living Smith sent an eloquent message that the traditional structures of society can and must change. Basic to this new society was a strong bond between male friends. In describing the joyous reunions to come at the resurrection, Smith employed a striking image of male intimacy to describe how "the Saints" who had been buried at the blessed site of Nauvoo would enjoy an added benefit over those buried in scattered locations around the globe. As recorded in Wilford Woodruff's diary on April 16, 1843, Smith preached,

> To bring it to the understanding it would be upon the same principle as though two who were vary friends indeed should lie down upon the same bed at night locked in each other['s] embrace talking of their love & should awake in the morning together. They could immediately renew their conversation of love even while rising from their bed. But if they were alone & in separate apartments they could not as readily salute each other as though they were together.[16]

Historian D. Michael Quinn has explored the homosocial aspects of Joseph Smith's teachings and has discovered a revelation from December 1832 which he believes to be a formal male-male pledging ceremony:

Art thou a brother or brethren? I salute you in the name of the Lord Jesus Christ, in token or remembrance of the everlasting covenant, in which covenant I receive you to fellowship, in a determination that is fixed, immovable, and unchangeable, to be your friend and brother through the grace of God in the bonds of love, to walk in the commandments of God blameless, in thanksgiving, forever and ever. Amen.[17]

Joseph Smith took the concept of male bonding well beyond the accepted notion of warm fellowship. In 1840 Robert B. Thompson, a twenty-nine-year-old convert to Mormonism, became Smith's personal secretary. Their relationship was evidently unusually intense, even by the standard of the effusive romantic friendships of the mid-nineteenth century—so much so that Thompson's wife began to complain. "Sister Thompson," Smith rebuked her, "you must not feel bad toward me for keeping your husband away from you so much, for I am married to him."[18] Smith's strong heterosexual orientation cannot be doubted (particularly in the light of his determination to wed multiple wives), but he possessed a sexual magnetism which affected even men who otherwise had little attraction in that direction, and at times he revealed a pansexuality which sent mixed signals to his male followers.

The homoerotic tension simmering just below the surface of the Mormon community at Nauvoo erupted in May 1842 when John C. Bennett was "disfellowshipped" or excommunicated after a break with Joseph Smith. Bennett was charged with immoral conduct for seducing a number of women by assuring them that Smith had received a new revelation concerning biblically sanctioned promiscuity. Supposedly Smith had confided the new doctrine to Bennett, but not yet to others, and Bennett was offering his services to initiate the women into the new spiritual mysteries. The Mormon community's newspaper *The Wasp* (edited by Joseph Smith's brother William) discussed the case against Bennett at length, in the process seeming to level veiled criticism against the prophet himself for his strong support of Bennett during the period when rumors about him became to circulate. "It will be seen by this," the paper concluded after several column inches of criticism of Bennett, "that Gen. [Joseph] Smith was a great *philanthropist* as long as Bennett could practice adultery, fornication, and—we were going to say *(Buggery)* without being exposed."[19] One wonders about the italicized *philanthropist,* and whether the editor was archly using the word in its literal sense: a lover of men. The charge of buggery against Bennett seems to be gratuitous, given the documented heterosexual excesses that were the primary reason for his excommunication, but it might reflect a bisexual orientation. As we have seen, allegations of same-sex misconduct were a standard part of the litany against public figures suspected of moral lapses, so the inclusion of buggery in the list of charges cannot be determinative.

Paradoxically, the aspersions cast on Joseph Smith are more difficult to discount, since they are presented in the form of more subtle insinuations. Criticism of Smith had been circulating throughout the Nauvoo community for some time, so much so that (as the same issue of *The Wasp* reported) on July 22, 1842, a vote was taken "to obtain an expression of the public mind in reference to the reports gone abroad calumniating the character of Pres. Joseph Smith." About a thousand men voted in favor of a resolution affirming that Smith was a "good, moral, virtuous, peaceable man." Two or three men in the assembly voted against the resolution, and one of them, Orson Pratt, spoke at length, explaining his objections to Smith's moral conduct. Smith himself then rose to respond to Pratt. Their exchange—as reported in the Mormon newspaper—might be interpreted as an astute exercise in sophistry. Smith asked carefully, "Have you personally a knowledge of any immoral act in me toward the female sex, or in any other way?" To which Pratt answered with equal care, "Personally, toward the female sex, I have not."

William Smith's support for his brother in the face of these allegations of buggery can be further questioned because of the addition of a note at the end of the article discussing the Smith-Pratt exchange:

> "*Note.* In the Wasp of Saturday last, a mistake occurred in the minutes of the public meeting held in this city, in inadvertently omitting some qualifying words in the question of Pres. Joseph Smith to Elder O. Pratt, and in his reply. The omission was without design and the proper corrections are made in the Extra. [signed] Gustavus Hills, Clerk."[20]

The Wasp of the previous Saturday, however, contains nothing about the Smith-Pratt exchange, and the "corrected" version quoted above, published in the July 22 issue (marked "Extra" on its masthead), appears in fact to be the one with the "inadvertent" omissions—omissions which seem to be hinting at unspoken allegations of homosexuality. Although this may be simply a typographical error caused by the rush to meet a publication deadline, it might also be a "design" on the part of the editor to warn his brother against further questionable conduct. Certainly the fact that the thousand men who voted in favor of the prophet did so with an important qualification—"So far as we are acquainted with Joseph Smith"—leaves the impression that the allegations were not fully resolved and that some doubt remained about the particulars of Smith's misconduct.

Smith would have been an intriguing figure for anyone struggling with the strict sexual prohibitions promulgated by American law and Christian tradition. By presenting himself as a prophet, Joseph Smith arrogated the power to free his followers from long-held moral and ethical imperatives. He could, through divine revelation, reinterpret scripture and bring the Mormons to a new understanding of old religious doctrines. As a Priest of God he could establish a new kingdom in Kirtland, Ohio, or Nauvoo, Illinois, which followed a different set of rules from those of other kingdoms of the earth, and all that was required of his followers was to acknowledge and accept this new dispensation. Wilford Woodruff recorded Joseph Smith's words in his diary on January 22, 1843:

> And whare there is a Priest of God, A minister who has power & Authority from God to administer in the ordinances of the Gospel & officiate in the Priesthood of God, theire is the Kingdom of God & in Consequence of rejecting the gospel of Jesus Christ & the Prophets whom God hath sent, the judgments of God hath rested upon people Cities & nations in various ages of the world, which was the Case with the Cities of Sodom & gomoroah who were destroyed for rejecting the Prophets.[21]

Anticipating modern biblical exegesis by more than a hundred years, Joseph Smith dissented from the common belief that the sin of the Cities of the Plain was homosexuality, and focused instead on their inhospitality to the angels sent by Yahweh.[22] Although never overtly preaching acceptance of homosexuality, Smith reinterpreted one of the standard scriptural passages used for condemnation of same-sex activity.

If the Shakers offered a view of salvation based on celibacy and the Mormons one based on a carefully regulated system of polygamy, a far more liberating sexual theology was offered by John Humphrey Noyes, founder of the utopian Oneida Community. For Noyes, sexual ecstasy was a form of worship, and the exchange of semen a metaphor for eucharist. The Oneida Community practiced not plural marriage, but complex marriage—a system in which every member past the age of puberty was "married" to every other member.

John Humphrey Noyes was born in 1811 in Brattleboro, Vermont. His father, John Sr., was a successful businessman who once served as a Vermont congressman (1815-1817), but who struggled throughout his life with debilitating alcoholism. Because of his political career and his obsession with the family business, the senior Noyes was frequently absent, and John was reared primarily by his three elder sisters and his mother, Polly Hayes Noyes (a second cousin of Rutherford B. Hayes), who was described as "a strong-willed, often overbearing Yankee woman, with a highly idealistic and deeply religious nature."[23] Congressman Noyes hoped that his son would follow in his footsteps, and to please his father John enrolled in Dartmouth and "read the law" with his uncle for a year, but after attending a revival in 1831 (at the insistence of his mother), he experienced a complete religious conversion, and enrolled instead in Andover Seminary, later transferring to Yale Theological School. His father was bitterly disappointed, his mother triumphant.

As Noyes's religious convictions grew stronger, he began to look at his parents' marriage with an increasingly jaundiced eye. He viewed his father as a drunkard and an unbeliever, and his mother as weak and sinful for having yielded to such a degrading marriage. Increasingly dubious of the possibility of sustained happiness between a man and a woman, he entered into a series of intense friendships with other men. He spoke of Chauncey Dutton as going "hand in hand with me into the 'dark valley' of [religious] conviction," and that his and Dutton's "hearts were knit together with a love 'passing the love of women.'"[24] Noyes envisioned his winning of male converts in overtly sexual terms. Of one man he said, "He followed me home from the meeting, as he afterwards said, to give me battle. The Lord gave me wisdom and power, and for the first time he was stripped naked and perfectly confounded."[25] He shared an especially intimate relationship with David Harrison of Meriden, Connecticut. Harrison, a married man with children, left his family and for six weeks lived with Noyes in a hotel in New Haven. "*[H]e* proposed," avowed Noyes, "without any suggestion from me, to leave his family and go out with me. . . ."[26] But Noyes later described himself as the aggressor in the relationship, recalling that he had said to Harrison, "I believe it is the will of God that we should have a season of undisturbed communion with each other. . . . If you will take board with me at the Temperance House, I will pay your bill."[27] The ménage raised eyebrows, and Noyes recorded that the two men were

> in much outward contempt, but in much inward contentment, somewhat more than six weeks. . . . We perceived much excitement and distress among many who beheld us in these strange circumstances; and especially among Harrison's friends and neighbors in Meriden. Many things were said and done to seduce or frighten us from what we knew to be the will of God.[28]

The will of God would lead Noyes on a path that set him at odds with the religious establishment he had once hoped to join. He completed his religious studies and received a license to preach from the Yale Theological School, but that license was rescinded when in 1834 he publicly announced his adherence to the doctrine of perfectionism: the belief that he was radically perfect and therefore incapable of committing any sin. Noyes believed that God places a higher value on inward attitude than on outward actions, and that although everyone is capable of some improvement, it was possible to reach a stage of perfection in which anything one did would be acceptable to God, as long as one's motivations were correct. In language that echoes the erotically charged ecstasy of St. Teresa of Avila, Noyes wrote of the genesis of his religious beliefs:

> The thought I have thus sketched was like a barbed arrow in my heart. Every time I handled it, it entered deeper. It brought me into an agony of conviction, from which I knew there was no escape except by the abandonment once for all of the whole body of sin.

That conviction led to a cleansing epiphany. One night as he lay in bed he felt himself penetrated by a divine presence which filled him, withdrew, filled him, and withdrew.

Three times in quick succession a stream of eternal love gushed through my heart, and rolled back again to its source. "Joy unspeakable and full of glory" filled my soul. . . . I knew that my heart was clean, and that the Father and the Son had come and made it their abode.[29]

One result of this cleansing of the heart was a reformulation of the concept of sin, particularly sins involving sexuality. "I then came to the conclusion in which I have since stood," Noyes explained,

viz., that the outward act of sexual connection is as innocent and comely as any other act, or that if there is any difference in the character of outward acts, that this is the most noble and comely of all. . . . God tells me that he does not care so much what I do as how I do it. . . .[30]

He is speaking here primarily of nonmarital heterosexual sex, but the radical implications of his teaching should be clear. By suggesting that nonprocreative sexual intercourse can be considered innocent and comely, Noyes was striking at the most basic tenet of the Christian sexual theology of the period: that the pleasure of sexuality is justifiable *only* in the context of intentional procreation. Looking back on the early days of his preaching, Noyes admitted that some of his early followers perhaps took his message of sexual freedom a bit too far. But by forbidding most sexual acts, he maintained,

the church and the world have swung far beyond the center to the right. Perfectionism took away the restraining force, and some swung far beyond the center to the left. In this case, the church and the world are the cause, for they placed men in a position of unnatural restraint.[31]

Noyes's first convert was Abigail Merwin, a woman eight years his senior, with whom Noyes entered into a type of spiritual (and, according to Noyes, sexless) union. "I was conscious of no feelings toward her but those of calm brotherly love," Noyes wrote. "The idea of marriage never entered my thoughts. Indeed, it had been my intention to lead a single life, and this intention was not disturbed by my acquaintance with her." But when Merwin abandoned the perfectionist movement and married another man, Noyes denounced her infidelity. "I saw her, standing, as it were, on the pinnacle of the universe, in the glory of an angel; but a voice from which I could not turn away, pronounced her title—'*Satan transformed into an angel of light*.'"[32] Like his mother, Abigail Merwin had betrayed his devotion and degraded herself in the arms of another man.

In 1836 Noyes established a Bible school in Putney, Vermont, and began spreading the doctrine of perfectionism. The movement was impoverished, and he welcomed the generous monetary contributions of Harriet A. Holton, a fairly wealthy spinster living in Westminster, Vermont, who wrote to him expressing her belief in the wisdom of his teachings. In Holton, Noyes saw a way out of his straightened financial circumstances, and in 1838 he wrote her a letter proposing marriage. In the "open marriage" arrangement he described in his proposal can be seen the outlines of the unorthodox sexual arrangements on which the Oneida Community would be founded:

> We can enter into no engagements with each other which shall limit the range of our affections as they are limited in matrimonial engagements by the fashion of this world. I desire and expect my yoke-fellow will love all who love God, whether man or woman, with a warmth and strength of affection which is unknown to earthly lovers, and as free as if she stood in no particular connection with me. In fact the object of my connection with her will not be to monopolize and enslave her heart or my own, but to enlarge and establish both in the free fellowship of God's universal family.[33]

Holton apparently believed that the marriage was to be sexless, but before the wedding ceremony Noyes (himself still a virgin) made it clear he expected her to share his bed, and she agreed to the stipulation.

Noyes founded a perfectionist religious colony in Putney in 1841, but when the surrounding community rose up against them because of their unorthodox sexual practices, he transferred his followers to the new Oneida Community, in Madison and Lennox Counties, New York. Between 1848 and 1879, the community would grow to over 200 members, thrive and then decline, eventually becoming a private corporation best known today for its stainless flatware. Noyes's sexual theology remained the central organizing principle for the community throughout its thirty-year history.

For Noyes, God was essentially hermaphroditic: God the Father embodied the male principle, while God the Son (Christ) embodied the female. The Father filled the Son with saving grace, and the Son in turned entered and filled receptive Mankind. Noyes saw no distinction between *eros* and *agape*—all love was sexual, all love was pure, and the numinous essence that flowed through the universe, connecting the material and spiritual worlds, was male semen. It was semen from God the Father entering into the body of a receptive Adam which brought about the creation of mankind:

> When the vital fluid from God entered into combination with Adam's body, that fluid took the *form* of that body. . . . If it had been instantly withdrawn, before a permanent union of it with matter was formed, it would doubtless have remained an incohesive fluid—an undistinguished part of the whole spirit of life. But as soon as it entered into combination with the dust-formed body, it received the shape and cohesiveness of that body—became partially indurated or congealed; so that it ever afterward retained a definite shape, and of course an identity separate from that of the universal spirit of life.[34]

Adam's willingness to be penetrated by God, to take in and capture God's fluid essence, allowed his dust-formed body to be animated and made human. Noyes almost implies that Adam's retention of the God-fluid was an aggressive act, the dust striving to become the deity by preventing God from withdrawing. Noyes sought a similar impregnation for himself: "If I have unfeigned, simple faith, he can fertilize me; the pollen of his Spirit can make me fruitful; but he will not give it to me except as I turn my face toward him and open myself to him."[35]

Noyes utilized this elaborate sexual theology to justify his doctrine of complex marriage. In the Oneida Community all special attachments were discouraged, and all postpubescent males and females were in theory "married" to all others. The doctrine of perfectionism embraced what Noyes called "Biblical Communism"—a perfect sharing which excluded monogamous love. "When the will of God is done on earth, as it is in heaven," he wrote, *there will be no marriage.* The marriage supper of the Lamb is a feast at which *every dish is free to every guest.* Exclusiveness, jealousy, quarreling, have no place there. In a holy community, there is no more reason why sexual intercourse should be restrained by law, than why eating and drinking should be—and there is as little occasion for shame in the one case as in the other."[36]

Members of the Oneida Community were expected to be open to a sexual "brotherhood" (despite the masculine terminology, ostensibly heterosexual in nature) in which individual partiality was set aside in the interest of "fellowship."

The young were expected to join in at an early age. The sexual initiation of adolescent males was the responsibility of the older, postmenopausal women in the community, while Noyes reserved to himself the right to deflower any young girl shortly after the onset of menstruation. All sexual contact among members of the community was in theory consensual, and most arrangements were made through a third party, usually an elder of the community. All requests for sexual intimacy were initiated by the male. A man interested in sexual intercourse would indicate to an elder the object of his desire. The elder would then pass along the information. If the object of desire was uninterested, the elder would return with the disappointing news. This formality was instigated to reduce the severity of bruised egos among members of the extended family, but it also facilitated coercion. If the elders believed a particular connection would be beneficial, or that refusal was based on a principle of unacceptable exclusivity, persuasion could be brought to bear on the reluctant participant.

To guard against the complication of unwanted pregnancies, Noyes developed a technique which he called "male continence"—a practice whereby the man would withdraw from intercourse not immediately prior to ejaculation (coitus interruptus) but before reaching the point where sexual climax was inevitable (coitus reservatus). Only when a pregnancy was specifically desired (that is, authorized by a committee of elders) would sexual intercourse be allowed to proceed. Noyes described standard nonprocreative heterosexual intercourse as a form of inconvenient masturbation for the man, and in an analogy which reveals something of his own complex sexual psychology, he asserted that "after marriage it is as foolish and cruel to expend one's seed on a wife merely for the sake of getting rid of it, as it would be to fire a gun at one's best friend merely for the sake of unloading it."[37]

The goal of the doctrine of male continence was to provide women with multiple orgasms from a variety of partners, without the fear of pregnancy. Under optimal circumstances, men would never experience the depletion of orgasm. At first blush, this arrangement would seem to be a boon to women (particularly during a time when death in childbirth was an all-too-common occurrence); it was in fact deeply misogynous, given the theological framework on which it was hung. Noyes identified divinity with the vital fluid exchanged during intercourse. God the Father filled Christ, who in turn filled Adam—the prototype of man. Each orgasm a person experienced depleted him or her of this vital fluid, draining the human soul of its divinity. Under the practice of male continence, men in the Oneida Community strove to withhold their vital fluid from the women, while coaxing the women to experience multiple orgasms—multiple losses of divine grace. Noyes and his male followers showed their spiritual superiority over women by blocking the flow of divinity, by retaining within themselves the gift handed down from Adam.

Taking the doctrine to its ultimate conclusion, there was only one way in which a male in the Oneida Community could experience ejaculation without a net loss of grace: through a homosexual encounter. By sharing homosexual sex, by being alternately the inserter and then the receptor, two men could create a closed spiritual ecosystem where spermatic grace was lost but then immediately regained in a repeatable cycle. The two men could reenact the transfer of divinity from God to Adam and yet end with a spiritual stasis, with neither of them depleted.

If homosexual activity was a regular or occasional practice at Oneida, it was not recorded in the many publications issued by the community to spread their peculiar gospel. This silence is not surprising, considering the public hostility aroused by the theories that *were* published during Noyes's lifetime. "Mr. Noyes . . ." one critic charged,

> has descended so low and unblushingly published sentiments so sensual and debasing in their character and tendency, and in some instances used language so very obscene and vulgar that it is extremely difficult and almost impossible to present the subject in a just light, without transgressing the common rules of propriety.[38]

Although no published evidence has yet appeared that openly homosexual men lived in the Oneida Community, it should be noted that some of the men definitely did *not* take part in the system of complex marriage. In 1937 Pierrepont Noyes published a memoir titled *My Father's House: An Oneida Boyhood,* in which he recalled that one of the men chosen to take care of rearing the children in the Children's House was believed to be celibate, and that there were other men like him. These men present something of a puzzlement, since Noyes developed his elaborate program of complex marriage in order to interweave his "family" into a closely knit social unit. That some men chose to live in the community but apparently not take part in its central organizational practice inevitably raises questions about their reasons for following Noyes in the first place.

Noyes based his theology on explicitly homoerotic images and on a belief in the numinous power of semen. By creating a community where everyone—and no one—was married and where sexual desire was encouraged to flow unimpeded, Noyes demonstrated the alluring possibility of an alternative lifestyle built on a new understanding of sex and salvation. The Oneida Community was said to vibrate with raw sexual energy while still clothing itself in a dignified veil of Christian righteousness. Its paradoxical call to a type of spiritual carnality based on a theology of God-Man sexual couplings made it an intriguing alternative to more traditional Christian or utopian communities.

Men and women came to the Shakers, the Mormons, and the Oneida perfectionists along many different paths, seeking out these utopian communities for reasons as varied and as complex as the individuals themselves. But to focus on one motivation among many, what might these communities have offered to deeply spiritual men who found themselves emotionally and erotically drawn to other men?

The Shaker commitment to celibacy effectively removed a man from community pressure to enter into a sexual relationship with a woman, and far from being a sacrifice, Shaker literature promised him that with the renunciation of his sexuality would come joy. For a man struggling to *understand*—let alone overcome—homosexual desire, it would indeed be a gift to be simple and free. Moreover, the Shakers offered him all the trappings of male privilege—the domestic support of women, the financial wherewithal to pursue his chosen craft, the opportunity to mentor children, the respect of a close, loving community—without the concomitant sexual expectations which would come with being a husband. The Shaker communities were the American Protestant counterparts of the Catholic monasteries of Europe, and no doubt attracted men for many of the same reasons.

For a man who found himself unable to integrate either homosexual activity or celibacy into his life, a man fearful of losing control of his unlawful desires, the Mormons offered a reassuring moral straitjacket. The doctrine of celestial marriage linking a man and a woman for eternity, and the pervasive theological emphasis on marriage and procreation, provided an effective means of forcing a troublesome libido into strictly regulated channels. Paradoxically, even plural marriage could be considered an attractive escape, since it rejected the scrutiny and emotional demands of a dyadic relationship in favor of a more diffuse family life. Sexual relations were forbidden during pregnancy, menstruation, or lactation, so Mormon theology provided convenient excused absences from the marital bed. Finally, the expectation of extensive missionary travel promised a man time away from his nuclear family, in the intimate company of another man who might perhaps be struggling with the same weakness.

The Oneida Perfectionists offered the most attractive alternative of the three. John Humphrey Noyes centered his theology on the saving grace of semen. Beginning with the image of God penetrating and infusing his divine essence into a receptive Adam, Noyes described a universe suffused with erotic energy—a vital fluid which men were encouraged to withhold from women. He created a community that extracted both the romance and the obligation from heterosexual coupling and replaced them with a system as impersonal as the postal service. Men were in complete control of all sex acts: they initiated them, dictated the sexual position to be used, and withdrew at will. The Oneida Community was in theory heterosexual, yet it represented a rejection of the traditional male-female dyad and the exultation of a male-centered sexual theology.

It is unlikely that any man would have entered any of these three communities for the conscious purpose of seeking homosexual contacts. None of the three preached or in any way overtly sanctioned same-sex encounters. All three were religious communities whose sexual practices were based on strict scriptural interpretation. Yet all three also offered sanctuary from the enormous pressure exerted by small communities who expected all of their men to follow the traditional path of courtship, marriage, and fatherhood. To become a Shaker, Mormon, or Perfectionist was in some ways to embrace exile, to leap from the oppressive familiar to the despised new. Particularly in their formative years, these communities faced contempt, ridicule, and at times violent oppression. It was a radical act to join any of them, and the result for many converts was a total rejection by their birth families. That rejection, too, was part of the lure and part of the bond, especially for men who since adolescence had felt themselves to be misfits and outcasts. The Shakers, the Mormons, and the Perfectionists offered in a paradoxical way both an escape from homosexual desire and the tantalizing promise of fulfilling it—if only on a sublimated level. No other Judeo-Christian faith offered what these religious communities explicitly promised: spirituality and sexuality intermingled in ways as complex and inscrutable as the human psyche.

Chapter 10

Gender Anarchy
As a Revolutionary Threat

Oh! were there but some Island vast and wide,
Where Nature's Drest in all her choicest Pride . . .
There with a Score of Choice Selected Friends,
Who know no private Interests nor Ends,
We'd Live, and could we Procreate like Trees,
And without Womans Aid—
Promote and Propogate our Species. . . .
Each day our Thoughts should new Diversion find,
But never, never think on Woman-kind.

Richard Ames

In the late afternoon of December 16, 1773, in the parlor of Boston printer Benjamin Edes, a group of men gathered to put on costumes. The parlor door was closed to provide the men with privacy, and Edes's son Peter was assigned the task of mixing bowls of rum punch in an adjacent room. Periodically the door would open, the elder Edes would slip out quickly to fetch more punch for his friends, then close the door behind him so his son could not watch the goings-on. Across town at the same time, fifteen-year-old Joseph Levering held high a whale oil lamp in a darkened carpenter's shop while a dozen men slipped into shawls, blankets, and cast-off dresses, wrapped scarves around their hair, and painted their faces with a mixture of red ocher, lampblack, and axle grease. And in still another part of Boston, schoolboy Benjamin Russell secretly peered into the window of his family woodshed and watched his father and another man applying burnt cork to each other's cheeks. The two men laughed uproariously as they blackened their faces and donned their outfits.

At a few minutes before six o'clock the doors of Old South Meeting House burst open and a defiant mob poured out into the streets. There they encountered the disguised men. "They say the actors were *Indians* from *Narragansett,*" wrote John Andrews.

> Whether they were or not, to a transient observer they appear'd as *such,* being cloath'd in Blankets with the heads muffled, and copper color'd countenances, being each arm'd with a hatchet or axe, and pair of pistols, nor was their *dialect* different from which I conceive these geniuses to *speak,* as their jargon was unintelligible to all but themselves.[1]

The "Indians" were predominately young men. Of those who could later be identified, only seven were older than forty, sixteen were in their thirties, and thirty-eight were in their twenties. At least fifteen were teenaged apprentices.[2] "It was proposed that young men, not much known in town and not liable to be easily recognized should lead the business," recalled Joshua Wyeth, explaining that "most of the persons selected for the occasion were apprentices and journeymen, as was the case with myself, living with tory masters."[3]

The crowd slowly swelled until they reached Griffin's Wharf, and there in an orderly fashion and in near-total silence, they split into three groups, boarded three of the ships at anchor in the shallow waters, and proceeded to remove chests of tea from the holds. Each chest was smashed open and its contents dumped overboard. The "Indians" were careful of the other cargo, and nothing else on the three ships was damaged except for one padlock, which was later replaced. When the tea had been dumped, the men withdrew as silently as they had arrived. As they marched through the streets of Boston they passed a home where British Admiral John Montagu happened to be spending the night. The admiral pushed open a window and called to them, "Well, boys, you've had a fine, pleasant evening for your Indian caper, haven't you? But mind, you've got to pay the fiddler yet!" One of the men called back in a equally jocular and defiant tone, "Oh, never mind, Squire. Just come out here, if you please, and we'll settle the bill in two minutes."[4]

The Boston Tea Party—as the "Indian caper" came to be known— was not the spontaneous act of an irate mob. It was a meticulously planned response to the newly imposed British tax on tea. Three days earlier, in a secret session held at Faneuil Hall, the Committees of

Correspondence had mapped out the assault: three boarding parties dressed as Indians to remove the tea before the consigners could pay the new tax and pass it along to the public. But why the disguise as Indians? A disguise of some sort was necessary, of course, because the actions they were undertaking were illegal. It was important that the party leaders not be identifiable and therefore subject to arrest by the British colonial government. Yet in adopting an Indian identity no one was trying to make the authorities believe that Narragansett Indians had actually invaded the city of Boston to protest the drinking of tea. The costumes were imperfect representations, meant to fool nobody. No contemporary source mentions the wearing of feathers or war paint of any kind. While some men used red ocher on their faces, most used lampblack, soot, or burnt cork, which darkened their skin but did not make them appear to be red men. In their assortment of rags, shawls, and old dresses, with their faces daubed with color, they looked more like slatternly crones than Indian warriors.

The disguise provided the participants with a sense of license. The masquerade freed them from their inhibitions and allowed them to engage in activities very foreign to their normal conduct. The atmosphere was festive with camaraderie and lightened by rum, but this was not a drunken brawl. The young men who carried out the Boston Tea Party were consciously participating in a symbolic action. The action was carefully planned and meticulously executed to send an unambiguous message to the colonial government and to Parliament back in London. The disguise was part of that message. Although the citizens of Boston did not live in fear of Indian raids, the settlers on the periphery of the colonies were still subject to periodic attacks, and the idea of rampaging Indians could invoke real terror. This context of unrestrained savagery breaking in on a "civilized" settlement was being referenced by the protesters. The Indian-as-symbol represented the outsider, the not-Briton, the powerless one, and by appropriating his identity the participants were threatening to embrace his outsider status. That they were also vaguely feminine in appearance added an extra touch of the bizarre. (The blackened faces might also have been an allusion to another suppressed group—African Americans—but it is more likely the men were drawing on an older English protest convention which conjured up dark demons and subterranean imps.) The participants in the Boston Tea Party were giving the authorities a vision of a world that might come about if the rights of the colonists were not respected, a world in which the dispossessed would rise up and take control. This was political street theater, and the "actors" (as observer John Andrews called them) were costumed as gender-bending Indians. Admiral Montagu might dismiss the action as an "Indian caper," but in their calm defiance the participants were sending a deadly serious message about what America might become.

The gathering at the Old South Meeting House had ended with someone shouting out, "Boston Harbor a teapot tonight."[5] The event only later became known as "the Boston Tea Party," but the image of brewing tea was present from the start. Tea parties in colonial Boston were dignified social events with strong gender associations. Women brewed and poured tea. Indians were rarely found in polite parlors. The Boston Tea Party drew its satiric snap from the incongruous images of cross-dressing and misrule. That Indians and women had seized the harbor was the joke. It was also the threat.

Tradition holds that when Lord Cornwallis surrendered to General Washington at Yorktown British fifers played the tune "The World Turned Upside Down." The story may be apocryphal, but the song goes to the heart of a recurrent theme in the protest rituals of the American Revolution:

> If buttercups buzz'd after the bee,
> If boats were on land, churches on sea,
> If ponies rode men and if grass ate the cows,
> And cats should be chased into holes by the mouse,
> If the mamas sold their babies
> To the gypsies for half a crown;
> If summer were spring and the other way round,
> Then all the world would be upside down.

If the British troops saw in the victory of the rag-tag rebels a reversal of the natural order of things, that was exactly the world that the Americans had threatened to create. Although it is ultimately futile to try to reduce to one overarching theme an event as intricate and contradictory as the American Revolution, one recurring motif may be identified which is of interest to the current study and which speaks directly to this view of the world turned upside down. The twin threats of gender anarchy and the proliferation of nonprocreative sexuality were employed as powerful tropes by leaders of the Revolu-

tion. Understanding this aspect of the break with Britain will help illuminate the reasons why male-male sexuality could be accepted
with such equanimity in the early years of America's history.

To appreciate the impact of the threat of gender anarchy in America one must first understand the power of the image of the world
turned right side up. Susan E. Klepp begins her analysis of women
and fertility in colonial America by quoting Poor Richard:

A Ship under sail and a big-bellied Woman,
Are the handsomest two things that can be seen in common.[6]

Klepp points to the discourse of pregnancy—teeming, flourishing,
breeding, fruitful, prolific, lusty, big with child, gone with child, great
with child, big bellied—to demonstrate an attitude toward procreative sexuality that was dominant in the early years of the eighteenth
century, but which gradually changed with the new Republic. "American women," Klepp writes, "adapted a revolutionary rhetoric of independence, self-control, sensibility, contractual equity, and numeri-
cal reasoning to their procreative physicality, recasting and reshaping
their bodily images between 1760 and 1820 to de-emphasize bellies
and to stress head and heart."[7] Klepp's primary interest is in the attitude of American women toward pregnancy, yet it is clear that the
particular paean to fruitfulness that she quotes originated not with
women but with a man. Few colonial women facing the dangers of
childbirth would rejoice in the image of themselves as lusty, breeding, and big bellied. These are male images of contentment—the ripe
harvest, the full barn, the fecund wife bringing forth many strong
sons.

This was the way life was supposed to be. This was how far America had come from the hard-scrabble early days. This was the pros-
perity that Britain was trying to control and dominate. The protest
movement against British interference very consciously selected as
one of its major themes the threat of sterility. America's golden harvest could be blighted by the cold greed of Parliament. It was both a
warning to John Bull not to exploit his colonies and an alarm to colonists who might become complaisant with their own precarious pros-
perity. Deep in the background also lurked the misogynist dream of
an all-male fecundity, the vision of Euripides and John Milton and
Richard Ames and the young Thomas Jefferson (and even "Ossian")

of a world in which men need not rely at all on big-bellied women to bring forth strong sons. The men knew they could survive on their own if they had to, because they had done it all before. It was not a future they welcomed, but it was a threat they were prepared to carry out.

If America was not permitted to follow the "normal" flow of civilized development, the protesters warned, it could just as easily take a different—*unnatural*—course. The choice was up to Britain. This conviction that only the heteronormative family structure stood between peaceful civilization and a return to unregulated discord impressed itself so deeply on the American psyche that as late as 1857 William Alcott could write that marriage "is the golden chain that binds society together. Remove it, and you set the world ajar, if you do not drive it back to its original chaos."[8] Christopher Newfield has written persuasively about the simultaneous emergence in the nineteenth century of the concept of the pathologized homosexual and the study of the psychology of crowds—both representative of "psychic structures that threaten collective order."[9] The American colonists in the eighteenth century were raising just this spectre of uncontrolled, nonprocreative chaos when they warned that the colonies might become as a whole what they were still at their margins: male-dominated regions unfit for the nurturing of families.

This was no idle threat. The gender balance of the colonies was precarious, and the farther west one traveled the more one entered a predominately masculine realm. Life on the frontier was a daily challenge, but it was a challenge being daily met by men who had learned to do without the niceties of civilization. The Revolution's leaders shared an innate sense of their own male privilege; women were highly desirable but ultimately unnecessary for the winning of a continent. Women and children were the goal of the struggle, the reward for beating back the wilderness, but they were not the agents of change. It was men who controlled the country's fate, men who had shown that they could sustain a society in the absence of women, if that was required. Even the manifestly heterosexual, profoundly married John Adams thought in terms of masculine parturition. In June 1776, as the (all-male) debates in Philadelphia reached a climax, he wrote to his wife Abigail, "These throes will usher in the birth of a fine boy."[10] No fecund women required.

The participants in the Revolution strongly desired that the world be turned right side up. The majority of them wanted to tend their farms, expand their businesses, marry their sweethearts, and produce many children. They wanted, in short, to replicate the family-centered stability of European village life. They also wanted to move away from a world in which the gender balance was tilted, with too few marriageable women, a world in which young men engaged in unseemly practices because the usual progress of a sexual life was effectively closed to them. If the march of progress was hindered by Parliamentary interference, they predicted the return of raw frontier life. To make their point they invoked the nightmare of a world turned upside down, a world in which men played the part of women, in which Indians asserted control over white property, in which sexually immature boys rioted in the night. This theme played itself out again and again in the streets of Revolutionary America.

One of the most striking aspects of the disturbances leading up to the American Revolution is the carefully controlled use of mob action. Unlike the unruly masses who looted and sacked Paris during the Reign of Terror, American crowds for the most part focused their anger on judiciously chosen structures and institutions. Collateral damage to surrounding buildings was small, and serious injury or death was almost unknown. A broadside published in Philadelphia demonstrates the careful choreography of public demonstrations even up to the end of the war. The broadside called for a celebration of the victory at Yorktown but sought to channel popular response into well-defined parameters: "[T]hose citizens, who choose to ILLUMINATE on the GLORIOUS OCCASION, will do it this evening at Six, and extinguish the lights at Nine o'clock. Decorum and harmony are earnestly recommended to every Citizen and a general discountenance to the least appearance of riot."[11]

Revolutionary leaders were able to focus mass action—even crowd violence—because they harnessed what Robert B. Shoemaker (writing of the original English traditions) has called "the ritualized inversionary disorder embedded in traditional holiday celebrations."[12] Inversion—the world turned upside down—had its roots in the festivals of misrule prevalent in medieval times, but by the eighteenth century inversion had become such a commonplace of European culture in both of its aspects (celebration and social protest) that it is impossible to gauge motivation behind the various modes of agitation employed by the colonists. To some extent their message was pointed and specific to the cause at hand, but it was also inextricably mixed with folk traditions which could be invoked on an unconscious—though no less powerful—level. Two of those modes of celebration/protest are of particular interest to the current study: male-to-female cross-dressing and the use of preadolescent boys as surrogate agents of social unrest.

From at least the time of Henry VIII, English festivals featured cross-dressing males as a vivid symbol of inversionary misrule. In the northern counties a grotesque female named Bessy appeared on the first Monday after Epiphany. Always a man dressed as a woman, Bessy would cavort in the company of a fur-clad Fool while exhorting spectators to give her small gifts of money. In other locales, May festivities each spring featured the figures of the outlaw Robin Hood and his mate Maid Marian. Maid Marian was sometimes played by a woman in some of the processions, but she was always played by a cross-dressing man in the accompanying Morris Dances.[13] In Wales the men who took part in the analogous *ceffyl pren* "blackened their faces and wore women's garb."[14] All of these festivals drew on traditional seasonal celebrations in which the structures of authority would be turned upside down. The celebrations served as an escape valve for social discontent, but the temporary misrule of the powerless merely reenforced the status quo once the ribbons and foolscaps had been packed away for another season. Cross-dressing was a recurrent manifestation of this topsy-turvy world, sometimes featuring women who dressed as men, but always men dressing as women.

With the abolition of the ecclesiastical courts in the sixteenth century, England lost one established method of enforcing community standards of morality. In response, the common people (especially in the rural areas) revived ancient shaming rituals such as the skimmington (or riding) and the charivari, with its accompanying rough music. In its purest version the gendered aspects of the skimmington ritual were foremost. The men of a village would assemble in front of the house of a woman with a reputation for being a henpecking scold. "[T]he principal group in the Skimmington was the stuffed figure of a man placed on horseback with a man in woman's clothes riding behind him and beating the figure about the head with a wooden ladel."[15] One goal of the skimmington was to humiliate the husband for not controlling his wife, but physical violence was sometimes also directed against the woman, usually in the form of dunking in a pond, river, or privy. By the early seventeenth century in England, the skimmington had broken away from its original purpose as a village ritual and had taken on wider, more political, more confrontational aspects. During the riots protesting the enclosure of royal forests in Dorset, Wiltshire, and Gloucestershire a leader named John Williams, described as "one of those strange popular leaders who emerged in times of crisis and who captured the public imagination by their feats of daring and their defiance of authority," dressed in women's clothing and took on the name Lady Skimmington.[16]

Williams was not the first or the last of the cross-dressing popular heroes. From as early as the fifteenth century, men dressed themselves as women and claimed to be fairies—evanescent beings who appeared at night and fled with the morning dew. During Jack Cade's Rebellion (dramatized by Shakespeare in *Henry VI*), farmers who called themselves "servants of the Queen of the Fairies" raided the game in the park of the Duke of Buckingham. In 1531 supporters of Catherine of Aragon—many of them men dressed as women—tried to kidnap Anne Boleyn. In 1629 male weavers dressed as women engaged in a grain riot in Essex. (In a foreshadowing of the Boston Tea Party they sacked a ship believed to be exporting grain to the Netherlands.) In 1718 in Cambridge a mob of students led by "a virago, or man in woman's habit" attacked a Dissenting meetinghouse. In 1736 in Edinburgh men dressed as women and led by "Madge Wildfire" rioted to protest exorbitant taxes. In the 1760s in Ireland the Whiteboys, dressed in frocks and claiming to be fairies, fought for justice for the poor under the leadership of Sieve Oultagh, or "Ghostly Sally." (The Whiteboys would later find their counterpart in America in the Molly Maguires.) Protests against the Industrial Revolution led to the smashing of Lancashire looms by "General Ludd's Wives"— two men dressed as women. In 1839 the so-called Rebecca Riots erupted when toll gates were constructed on some traditionally public roads in Wales. "Almost as soon as they had been erected," George Rudé writes, "two of the gates were destroyed at night by men with blackened faces, several of whom dressed in women's clothes."[17] The protests were led by a mysterious cross-dressing figure described as "a man with a drawn sword" riding "a splendid horse," speaking "excellent English like an Englishman."[18] Though several Welsh patriots were suspected, the identity of the man who called himself only "Rebecca" has never been established.[19]

Just as cross-dressing Britons, Scots, Irishmen, and Welshmen destroyed fences, toll gates, and machinery, tenant farmers in the early nineteenth century rose up against their landlords in America's own Hudson River Valley—many of the men wearing calico dresses. When the Dutch West India Company controlled the lands along the Hudson it granted patroonships to a few powerful men as a means of encouraging colonization, and the English who succeeded them retained this system of feudal land ownership. In 1766 tenant farmers rose up in armed revolt, but they were brutally suppressed by the king's soldiers. The patroons did not shrink from placing the conflict in a specifically gendered context. To them, this was a struggle to see whose manhood would prevail. In Dutchess County a leader of the tenant uprising was sentenced to the traditional punishment for a traitor: "to be hung, cut down, and have his severed genitals and extracted intestines burnt before his eyes. . . ."[20]

After the Revolutionary War, many of the tenant farmers hoped that the vast patroonships would be broken up into smaller parcels, but the landlords who supported the war not only retained their own lands but also acquired the holdings of their defeated Tory neighbors. In the 1840s the tenants once again rebelled against the landowners, and this time they chose to disguise themselves as "calico Indians," blending the costume of the Boston Tea Party with that of the traditional English cross-dressing protester. "No two costumes were alike in color, style, or decoration," writes Henry Christman, "and their arms were makeshift and varied. . . . Some of the chiefs of the tribes were distinguishable by long dresses like women's nightgowns."[21] To further the gender confusion, the rebels chose the tin horn as their means of long-distance communication among members of the group. The tin horn traditionally was used by women to signal that a meal was ready. A local newspaper complained about this usurpation of the women's instrument: "If the housewife should be so indiscreet as to use this method of calling laborers from the fields at noon, the Anti-Rent leaguers come in a crowd and eat up the dinner prepared for her family."[22]

Why this appropriation by white men of the persona of Indians and women? On a practical level, these represented disguises that could be readily assembled from relatively inexpensive materials found in most households—though the amount of material required to make a dress was not insignificant. It is important to note, however, that few men who resorted to these disguises were making a serious effort to pass as either an Indian or a woman; they were not attempting to fool the authorities into thinking that the blame lay elsewhere. Yet if the point of the disguise was merely to obscure one's identity and thereby avoid detection and punishment, there were easier ways of accomplishing that end. Clearly the repeated and specific appropriation of the Indian or female identity held some deeper significance.

The practice served as an unmistakable threat of a particular kind of social chaos. The oppressors were again being given a foretaste of the world turned upside down, a vision of a degenerate society in which the powerless have grabbed control—but not just any powerless group. It was not that oppressed men were rising up against their oppressors, but instead that the very structures of white patriarchal power were being shaken to their foundations. The sometimes festive air that accompanied many of these disturbances was fueled by the absurdity of the notion that Indians or women might ever actually possess power. Invoked also was the outrageous image of the cross-dressing London molly, the flagrant sodomite reveling in his effeminacy. Here was another object of ridicule and disdain. In this the heterosexual white male protesters shared certain values with the oppressors they were protesting. On the surface this type of gender-bending and racial appropriation might appear as social criticism, but in actuality it was deeply conservative—a way of maintaining order and stability by clarifying the society's established power hierarchies. The conscious *reversal* of a social structure is one way of clearly defining what that social structure truly is.[23] White heterosexual men who dressed as Indians or women subverted the dominant paradigm, but only to reappropriate it for themselves, since they could easily throw off their feigned impotence and assume their "proper" role. The message was clear: transfer power to us, or suffer the consequence of having this country degenerate into gender and racial chaos.

This carefully regulated vision of chaos was almost always accompanied by a cacophony of noise known as a charivari, a din of "rough music" performed on horns, whistles, pots and pans, and the like. The charivari originated as a public demonstration of a community's disapproval of an inappropriate marriage. It was usually employed to protest a union in which there was a vast difference in ages between the spouses, or in cases where the community felt a widow or widower was remarrying too soon. Although the atmosphere of a charivari was frequently playful, the social message underlying it was serious and the threat of potential violence was real. The charivari, despite its boisterous buffoonery, was also a basically conservative ritual. It sought to impose generally accepted community standards on errant members of society.

By the mid-nineteenth century the charivari in America had evolved into the shivaree, a ceremony almost exclusively associated with a wedding. In the process it became institutionalized, an expected part of the nuptial proceedings, like the wedding banquet or the tossing of the bouquet. Family members and guests would attempt to disrupt the wedding night by descending on the newlywed couple's house banging on pots and pans and playing discordantly on musical instruments. Sometimes the bride and/or the groom would be "kidnapped" or dunked in a river or horse trough.[24] The vestiges of the seventeenth-century charivari could still be seen, but the political significance had been removed and the sexual message turned on its head. Here the community was protesting not an inappropriate marriage, but marriage itself—the fact that the bride and groom were (presumably) about to experience sexual intercourse for the first time. The community was on some level protesting this loss of innocence. The shivaree reflected America's continuing uneasiness with sexuality, even sexuality within the context of marriage. Participants were making a mock attempt to postpone what they presumably should have been encouraging: the formation of another family unit to expand and consolidate the community. Submerged deep within the institution of the shivaree was the acknowledgment that the ongoing process of civilizing was tinged with regret for the loss of a wild, unregulated youth.

The skimmington and the charivari were not the only modes of colonial protest that had strong overtones of gender and sexuality. Little attention has been given to the fact that prepubescent and adolescent boys were deliberately employed as agents provocateurs in the years leading up to the rupture with Britain. Many of the Stamp Act rioters in Boston were "Boys and Children," and when a crowd attacked the home of Thomas Hutchinson, the scapegoat for the colony's anger, the assailants were described as "a number of boys from 14 to sixteen

Years of age, som mere Children which did a great deal of damage."[25] In New York the Stamp Act was protested by "a great number of boys carrying Torches & a scaffold," and in the succeeding weeks hundreds of boys "frequently tramped the streets at night shouting 'Liberty and No Stamps!'"[26] By 1769 boys were regularly employed to harass merchants who failed to comply with the nonimportation embargo. Boys were even viewed as the vanguard of the Continental Army. A song published in New York in 1776 gleefully boasted, "Our Children rout your Armies, our Boats destroy your Fleet."[27]

The use of boys was a deliberate policy followed by the Revolutionary leaders, but the reasons for the policy are somewhat complex. Certainly one motive was to create a public disturbance and deliver a political message without provoking a strong response from the colonial government. When Massachusetts Governor Francis Bernard dismissed the riots as "boyish sport" he was reacting just as the leaders hoped. Here, too, we see the ritual use of feigned impotence to cloak real power. Just as protesters dressed as women to tear down fences and harass cruel landlords, the American Revolution used boys for the very fact of their not-yet-male-ness. It was a way of challenging British authority while avoiding the adult male role of political adversary. The adolescent (and in many cases preadolescent) boys acted out an oedipal drama in which Britain—the abusive parent—was mocked and challenged by its impotent children. In this way Britain was shamed and taunted, while the colonists did not have to face up to the (adult) diplomatic consequences. "Boyish sport" need not bring down the wrath of the British government.

The leaders of the Revolution were able to use boys in this strategic fashion because of the long tradition of boy protesters in English culture. The inversionary elements of misrule expressed in cross-dressing also had their expression in the temporary empowerment of young boys. Up until the sixteenth century in Britain many parishes, monasteries, and scholastic establishments observed the annual selection of a Boy Bishop. Elected on St. Nicholas's Day (December 6), the boy would preside at all of the Christmas festivities for the season. Dressed in pontifical vestments and accompanied by young companions dressed as priests, he led processions around the parish acting as a surrogate bishop, even in some locations wielding episcopal powers. The boy would serve until December 28, the Feast of the Slaughter of the Holy Innocents. The practice brought together several tenets of the Christian faith: the god-child, the sacrificial lamb, the last made first. It also, of course, harkened back to midwinter inversionary celebrations of misrule, with the powerless boy suddenly (though temporarily) becoming the font of power. The custom was abolished by Henry VIII, restored briefly under Mary, and then abolished again by Elizabeth, though it continued in isolated Catholic strongholds. Because it was so vigorously suppressed by the Crown, the celebration took on an added aura of challenge to established authority.

In colonial America (especially in Boston and New York) the Boy Bishop festival was fused with Guy Fawkes Day to produce Pope's Day. Ostensibly an expression of anti-Catholicism, Pope's Day celebrations drew on a long tradition of autumn festivals: harvest/fertility rites, the Celtic Samhain, the Christian All Souls' Day, and Halloween, as well as the actual anniversary of the Gunpowder Plot to blow up Parliament (November 5). Puritan New England banned all holidays (including Christmas, New Year's, Easter, and May Day) since such celebrations smacked of paganism or (worse) popery. The anti-Catholic Pope's Day alone received official sanction, and into it the populace poured all their hunger for festivity.

In Boston, Pope's Day was marked by two parades, one originating in the South End and one in the North End. Whereas in England effigies of Guy Fawkes (called "guys") were paraded through the streets and then burned, in Boston effigies of the pope were borne on elaborately decorated "pope carts" drawn by young apprentices. Neighborhood rivalry led to annual competitions to see who could create the most impressive cart, and banners which read "North end forever" and "South end forever" were as much a part of the pope cart design as any antipapal sentiments. The crowds took great pride in their neighborhood's own effigy. In an inversion of an inversion, a parade originally designed to mock the real pope and his papal processions became a manifestation of local pride, with the pope's effigy a type of beloved mascot. This rivalry perhaps inevitably led to violence, with each neighborhood trying to destroy the other's cart. Fistfights and stone throwing became increasingly bloody, and in 1764 a boy was run over by one of the carts and killed. "The insurrectionary potential in this rowdy holiday was evident," writes Peter Shaw.

Its threats to peace officers, together with a certain wantonness of symbolism, breathed defiance of authority in general. In substituting the pope for Guy Fawkes, moreover, Americans had put their own anti-Catholic concerns ahead of the holiday's concern with treason against the king.[28]

Eventually even anti-Catholic concerns were given short shrift. If the pope replaced Guy Fawkes as the center of the celebration, and if the effigy of the pope was being treated as a beloved mascot, the symbolism of the event was hopelessly muddled far beyond anyone's ability to sort it out.

The Pope's Day parades were dominated by little boys and adolescents. The cart and effigies were created by apprentices, and were followed through the streets by a parade of "devil's imps," boys with blackened faces wearing jester's caps. The boys harkened back to a standard feature of British parades: a contingent of chimney sweeps. The sweeps, or "climbing boys," were ambiguous figures in eighteenth-century culture. In crowded cities where a small chimney fire could lead to a major conflagration, their work was vital to the survival of the community. The popular view of the chimney sweeps was tinged with romanticism, since they seemed to be children who never grew up. Because the job entailed climbing into and around narrow flues, it could be done only by small boys. With the onset of puberty and its resulting growth spurt, the chimney sweep was forced to find a new way of making a living. Nearly indistinguishable from one another with their blackened faces and tattered clothes, the sweeps took on the aura of the *puer eternis,* the eternal child. Yet as much as they romanticized the boys, people realized that a chimney sweep's life was brutal and often short. Most were abandoned orphans unable to survive in any other way. Many fell to their deaths, were suffocated in collapsed passages, or contracted various lung diseases. Those who survived through puberty often contracted scrotal cancer. Their presence in parades therefore evoked a variety of responses: affectionate gratitude for the heroes of the hearth, parental-like pride in their strutting display, and deep guilt at the realization that these boys were being sacrificed for the good of the community.[29]

Few of the boys with blackened faces who accompanied the pope cart were actually chimney sweeps themselves, but they drew for their symbolism on this well-established tradition. The tradition had at its heart the idea of impotence: physical immaturity (since climbing boys were of necessity very small children) and actual sexual impotence (since they were preadolescent and eventually subject to scrotal cancer). In the topsy-turvy world of misrule, these sexually immature urchins could for a brief interval strut the public streets like rakish studs. The Pope's Day boys were raucous and unruly, but the celebration itself was a well-established ritual. When the time arrived to shake up the colonial authorities, the revolutionary leaders could turn to this antiestablishment, antiauthoritarian holiday as a model for social protest. The boys who took to the streets to agitate against the Stamp Act merely employed the conventions of the Pope's Day celebrations to put across a different message.

On February 22, 1770, a group of "many hundreds" of boys picketed the shop of Theophilus Lilly, a Boston merchant who refused to acknowledge the nonimportation boycott. The boys were confronted by Ebenezer Richardson, a customs informer, who in turn became the target of the mob. Richardson retreated to his home, and when the boys began to break in, he fired his rifle into the crowd, killing eleven-year-old Christopher Seider. Seider was given a grand ceremonial funeral. School was adjourned for the day, and a procession of 500 boys marching two by two, followed by more than 2,000 adults, wound its way from the Liberty Tree to the place of burial. It was one of the largest funerals ever witnessed in colonial Boston.[30]

Revolutionary leaders seized upon Christopher Seider's death for its symbolic value. Poet Phillis Wheatley called him "the first martyr for the cause." He was the perfect embodiment of one of the most popular themes: Britain as an unnatural parent murdering her children in the streets. But the eleven-year-old's *presence* at the riot was as symbolically important as was his death. In using boys to carry the revolution to the streets, the leaders were warning the British government of what America was prepared to become if Parliament continued to treat the colonies as immature children (or powerless women). To make sure that the message was understood, the leaders of the revolution evoked gendered images of civil discontent which were deeply ingrained in British culture. Only when the threat of permanent inversionary misrule was ignored did America finally bring forth the Minutemen—men, not boys—to fight in earnest.

Chapter 11

Male Intimacy at the Fringes

The innkeeper wanted to put me into the same bed with a Swedish merchant whom I fell in with on the way, but I succeeded in getting a single blanket to lie on the floor.

Augustus John Foster

Along the [Davy] Crockett frontier male sexuality was violent, non-reproductive, usually non-genital and frequently homosexual.

Carroll Smith-Rosenberg

The American Revolution was fought to secure domestic tranquility. For many men this meant a safe space where they could raise a family and earn a decent living. The ideal of America in the early years was centered on the small farm, or the shop with a home above, where a man could gather his wife and children to his side. But this ideal was not the reality on the frontier or on the isolated trails through the forests that linked one community with another. In a society in which women were chained to the hearth, the rowdy, entrepreneurial, ragged edges of the country were the undisputed domain of men.

Carroll Smith-Rosenberg characterizes this rambunctious sexuality as "violent . . . and frequently homosexual," but one wonders how much of the perceived violence was actual and how much was merely rough sexual play which allowed both men to maintain their masculine self-image.[1] Smith-Rosenberg uses Davy Crockett's mythical persona as her exemplar, and certainly in the most explicit of her examples the sexual violence is tempered by an element of playfulness, and perhaps even consent. Crockett recalls a struggle with a stagecoach driver:

Says I, take care how I lite on you, upon that I jumped right down upon the driver and he tore my trowsers right off me. I was driven almost distracted and should have been used up, but luckily there was a poker in the fire which I thrust down his throat, and by that means mastered him. Says he, stranger you are the yellow flower of the forest. If you are ever up for Congress I'll come all the way to Duck river . . . for you.[2]

The coach driver, after denuding Crockett, is "mastered" by having Crockett's hot poker shoved down his throat. As Smith-Rosenberg notes, this is in actuality a type of literary pornography, published in the early nineteenth century in Nashville, Boston, New York, Philadelphia, and Baltimore, and eagerly consumed by a young, male, urban audience. "The Davey Crockett myths," writes Smith-Rosenberg, "flourished during the same years that fear of youthful masturbation reached its apex—the 1830s through the 1850s," and the link between the national obsession with masturbation and the evident popularity of frontier tales is intriguing.[3] In the episode quoted above, one of the most striking features is the mutuality of the encounter. The struggle is certainly violent, but after being penetrated by Crockett's hot poker the stage driver genially compliments the frontiersman and promises to vote for him if he ever runs for Congress. (In the process the driver of course reasserts his maleness, since only a free white male possessed the privilege of suffrage.) Yes, this is in one sense a scene of very violent rape, but it is cartoon violence and a rape with a certain element of grudging consent and no hard feelings afterward.

What type of sexuality is being described for these young male readers? Penetration *per os* places the inserter in a very vulnerable position and requires an element of participation on the part of the receiver (though in true rape the "consent" is obtained by coercion, through the threat of greater bodily harm). The sexual dynamics here are ambiguous, since the receiver has the power to cause both ecstatic pleasure and excruciating pain. Mutuality (or at least temporary consent) is a basic requirement, and such mutuality would be necessary to permit male-male sexuality to flourish in a frontier setting, particularly if (as Kinsey reported in his survey of cowboys and ranchers) there was an absence of gender role-playing. It is therefore interesting to note that in her study Smith-Rosenberg discovered that allusions to "buggery, *vagina dentata* exhibition and male homosexuality occur in virtually every Crockett almanac."[4] Did the fiction reflect the reality, or was the reality aided by the fiction? Did some young men from Boston head toward the open spaces of the West because they had been primed with visions of intense male-male sexual encounters? Theodore Winthrop's breathless paean to the "Adonis of the copper-skins" suggests that they did.

The gender disparity and enforced male-male intimacy of these liminal spaces is the subject of frequent comment in the journals and memoirs of European visitors. Rare is the traveler who does not speak with disdain of the American custom of having complete strangers share beds in wayside inns or rented lodgings. David Montagu Erskine wrote to his father in 1799 of the living arrangements he and his companions encountered among the transient inhabitants of Washington, DC.

> Each of us have a bed room to ourselves, if we chuse, but people in this country seem to think so lightly of such an indispensable comfort as I consider it, that I believe there are but three of us, who have rooms to ourselves.[5]

Edward Thornton, secretary to the new British minister to the United States, wrote to his former employer in 1792,

> Mr. Hammond's rank may possibly secure him from some of the inconveniences, which others, rendered fastidious by the style of travelling in England, are loud in their complaints of, such as . . . fellow lodgers in the same room and not infrequently in the same bed.[6]

Hammond's successor, Augustus John Foster, was equally appalled by what he encountered in America's inns: "[T]he Accomodations are infamous. at one Place the Host carried off the upper Part of a Bed for himself & proposed to me & another person that we should sleep together on the under Part."[7]

That European visitors were uncomfortable with the idea of sharing a bed with a strange man is well documented. What is less clear is the reason for their discomfort. All write as though the "infamy" of the situation would be clear to the reader, but they do not specify whether the problem is a general objection to the invasion of personal space or if there is a specifically sexual aspect to their discomfort.

When two strangers climbed into a bed together in early America, did either or both of them regard it as a potentially sexual situation? An answer may be gleaned from the diary of Lt. John Le Couteur.

Le Couteur, a British army officer from the Isle of Jersey, traveled through New York in 1816 accompanied by Captain George Thew Burke. Despite the recently ended War of 1812, the two Englishmen found the Americans they encountered to be "familiar & gruff but civil, if used good humouredly." Le Couteur and Burke arrived at an inn one day after dinner had been served and cleared, and they were hard-pressed to convince the hostess to bring out more food. "But this was not the last grievance," Le Couteur recorded in his diary.

> There was only one spare bed, a small one, which of course I in-sisted Burke should take. The Yankee Landlord wished me to take half of it as a matter of course but I said: "we Britishers were *particular* on that *pint*." "Then," said mine host, "I guess if you don't *chuse* to take half a bed with some one, you'll jist sleep in a cheer [chair] or by the kitchen fire." "Well, landlord," I said, "since I may chuse," looking at some dozen Men in the room. . . .'"[8]

Here about nineteen or twenty words have been obliterated in the diary.[9] Whether the passage was censored by Le Couteur himself or by a later owner is unknown, but from the context it is clear that the excised words must have said something about the idea of two men sharing a bed, and the fact that they were censored strongly hints that the reference was sexual. Whatever Le Couteur's frank comment was, it shocked the landlord. The diary picks up with the words, ". . . this I said in such a business like way, that mine host looked aghast and the Yankees burst into a roar of laughter: —'Well, I'm blowed, Landlord, if the Britisher aint done ye. . . .'" And then another twenty-five words of the diary have been obliterated. Le Couteur, after sur-veying the dozen or so men presented to him as potential bed part-ners, perhaps turned to the landlord and said something along the lines of "Since you are by far the most handsome man in the room, I choose you."

Even with half the narrative censored, the incident tells us much about the sexual tension inherent in the practice of sharing beds. First, Le Couteur confirms that on the *pint* of bed sharing the British were more squeamish than the Americans. His presumably flirtatious comment to the landlord suggests an awareness of the sexual overtones inherent in the custom. His frankness about the matter leaves the landlord "aghast"—a reaction suggesting that the lieutenant has said something outrageous and unexpected, something which should have remained unsaid. The other guests in the inn burst into a roar of laughter, immediately understanding the implications of Le Couteur's comment and heartily appreciating the embarrassment he has caused the landlord. All of which suggests that, while they had adjusted to the forced intimacy of life on the road, the other guests in the inn were not unaware of its underlying sexual implications. They as Americans had made an accommodation to the practice, but they were fully aware that from an outsider's perspective the arrangement was still rather dubious.

This point is driven home by a second incident recorded by Le Couteur.

> At another place I was sleeping in a smallish bed, in a long common bedroom, when I was waked by a great naked leg, coming into my bed. "What the Devil do you mean, my friend, this is not your bed!" "Oh, guess I didn't know—the help told me to get in here." "Leave the Britisher alone!", called another hospitable Yankee, "and come into bed here, don't be waking us all with your *noise*."[10]

The unidentified voice in the night recognized that the Britisher had not yet managed to desexualize the experience of sharing a bed with another man, and offered half of his own blanket as a way of restoring the peace.

Having a strange man as a bed partner was a fact of life for men who traveled through the liminal spaces of early America, but while acknowledging that the practice was common, we should not assume that it therefore was stripped of all sexual piquancy for the men who found themselves in close physical proximity to another undressed male. A "great naked leg" entering one's bed would be difficult to ignore. If the stranger was drunk, dirty, or physically unattractive by most people's standards, sharing the bed would have been unpleasant but perhaps unavoidable. But if the bed partner was handsome and personable, the physical intimacy may well have invoked a more complex response. As E. Anthony Rotundo has observed,

Many middle-class men grew up in large families where children, of necessity, shared a bed. Boys were the natural choice as bed partners for other boys, so the habit of sleeping with one or more brothers developed early in life and continued throughout childhood. . . . [E]xperience earlier in life may have given the act of sleeping together—for some men in some circumstances— an aura of warmth and intimacy. After all, there were males who had grown up spending the night with brothers who were also their dearest friends, and this experience could add a deeper meaning to the act of sharing a bed with another male.[11]

Rotundo points to the contrast in the popular literature of the nineteenth century between the cozy warmth of home and the cold cruelty of the outside world. It was a contrast meant primarily to remind young men of their obligations to parents and siblings, yet the symbolism really did reflect the harsh facts of life on the road in early America. For a traveler cold and far from home, the body heat of a friendly stranger might be welcomed as a pleasant sanctuary. "Once we recognize that this possibility of intimacy in bed could exist in an era when men slept together as a casual occurrence," Rotundo continues,

then we can see the spectrum of meanings that attached to the act of sharing a bed. . . . In a society that had no clear concept of homosexuality, young men did not need to draw a line between right and wrong forms of contact, except perhaps at genital play.[12]

It is the contention of the current study that the dividing line between "right and wrong forms of contact" was rarely as unambiguous as the legislators and preachers wished it to be.

We have seen that for the majority of the American colonists the Christian Bible played a clearly secondary role in their development of a sense of morality. Particularly in the years immediately before, during, and after the Revolution, Enlightenment principles of rationality and scientific proof played a much stronger role than received religious dogma, and an appeal to natural law (however fungible the concept) had much more force than an invocation of holy writ. Bible stories rarely appeared in school texts, and conduct manuals stressed the utilitarian value of the Golden Rule rather than the proscriptions of the Ten Commandments. For the uneducated populace, religious hegemony of any kind smacked of popish domination; the individual conscience was the proper compass for an American, and to follow the dictates of one's own conscience was to demonstrate emotional maturity.

Social control in early America was always weakest at the margins. In the absence of large numbers of women and children a certain pragmatism was called for—and Americans were nothing if not pragmatic. Many men who might not otherwise have engaged in same-sex activity acceded to what Vincent Bertolini has called "the pull of the transgressive-practical."[13] The development of America from a few weak settlements to a world power was a delicate dance of sexuality and accommodation. The gender disparity that was a feature of colonization patterns led to an unavoidable adjustment in expectations about sexual conduct. Rather than impose celibacy on male-dominated communities, Americans allowed for a level of homosexual interaction, insisting only on discretion, mutuality, and a respect for the traditional male gender role. This laissez-faire attitude toward male-male sexuality in isolated regions persisted at least into the mid-twentieth century.

As the country grew and communities formed and consolidated, sexual restraint became the mark of social attainment. Progress was measured by how strictly the heterosexual paradigm could be imposed, and with the rise of the cult of true womanhood, even heterosexuality was replaced by an ideal of chaste, intellectual unions. It is no coincidence that African Americans and indigent immigrants were traditionally pictured as being sexually voracious. The stereotype of the lustful Negro buck or the blowsy Irish barmaid were necessary props to the mythology of American progress. Even the "underclasses" at times measured their own social achievement by how far they had removed themselves from the libidinous stereotype of their ethnicity.

Most Americans (whether they were conscious of it or not) embraced a Filmerian view of society. "Civilization" was replicated in the structure of the family. Civilization was created *out of* the structure of the family, accreted like a growing coral reef, with each new family unit reaching out and progressively imposing a more secure order on the anarchic wilderness. Without husbands, wives, and children there was nothing—only savageness and the forest primeval. Yet Americans always had mixed feelings about the civilizing process. Many immigrants came to this country to escape the ossified social structures of their homelands. To black slaves, the growth of white communities meant a tightening of the shackles that held them in bondage. To Native Americans, encroaching farmlands and ranches meant the death of their way of life. Among even the most jingoistic of white Americans, an enthusiasm for progress was tinged with regret for a paradise lost.

Hence we have America's romanticized infatuation with the rebel, the outcast, the lonely (unmarried) individual living on the margins of society. America in its formative years provided a convenient outlet for men who could not see themselves in the role of husband/father, men who fled the patriarchal straitjacket. Frederick Jackson Turner's classic frontier thesis was largely demolished by twentieth-century scholarship, but perhaps it needs to be resurrected in part in order to understand the history of American male sexuality.[14] America's frontiers *did* provide an escape from the encroaching pressures of family life for men who were not yet ready to become part of the accretive process of domesticity. Most of these men were not "homosexual" in our current understanding of that term, but they helped create communities that allowed for an alternative sexuality based on availability of partners rather than gender. When Secretary of the Treasury Albert Gallatin told British Minister Augustus John Foster that "the Grecian Vice" was common among the backwoodsmen of America, he was not fulminating against an abomination that threatened the foundations of the Republic. Rather, he harkened back to the classical roots of the phenomenon and dismissed it as an unfortunate (and temporary) bad habit. Like the gay men who were urban pioneers in New York and San Francisco during the 1970s, these backwoodsmen pushed into areas unsafe for families and laid down the foundations upon which "civilization" (i.e., a white, middle-class lifestyle) could be constructed in the region.

Some of these men settled down to become part of the growing process; others moved on to newer regions where sexual roles were still fluid. The tenor of the times mandated silence, so surviving documentation is slim. How did these men think about themselves? Any attempt to track the development of a "homosexual identity" during the early years of American history presents a daunting challenge—

for the time being. Unless scholarship can uncover a cache of diaries, essays, or love letters yet unknown to researchers, we can only guess about some of the emotional specifics of these relationships. Life at sea and "among the backwoodsmen" certainly included male-male sexuality, but most men did not write home about it. In the absence of long introspective analytical accounts, researchers must rely on a type of historical triangulation to pinpoint homosexual desire. Although this careful cartography can yield unassailable proof that male-male sexual *activity* was present during the period, it unfortunately only hints at how these men *felt* about their sexual natures.

In looking at the lives of men who chose to move into the margins of American society, we uncover a broad range of responses to same-sex activity. Although so far there are only tantalizing hints that significant numbers of these men constructed a self-identity around their sexual behavior, it does seem incorrect to claim that homosexuality is merely a social construct invented by medical and judicial authorities sometime in the late nineteenth century. Clearly some men in the eighteenth and early nineteenth centuries realized the difference in their own sexual response. Perhaps most of them aspired to a life that conformed to the heterosexual norm, since society provided them with few approved alternatives. For those who rejected the norm— and those who attempted but failed to conform to it—life was necessarily a challenge. The ample evidence demonstrates that men formed profound emotional bonds during this period of American history. Those emotional bonds necessarily raised issues of sexual conduct for these men, but a fuller understanding of their options for happiness awaits further historical research.

Notes

The following are abbreviations used for manuscript collections in this notes section.

HL	Huntington Library, San Marino, California
HSP	Historical Society of Pennsylvania
LC	Library of Congress
MHS	Missouri Historical Society
NYHS	New-York Historical Society
OCHS	Oneida County (NY) Historical Society
SotC	Society of the Cincinnati, Washington, DC
USMA	United States Military Academy, West Point
YBL	Yale University, Beinecke Library

Preface

1. The sweepingly named *Sex and Sexuality in Early America* (New York: New York University Press, 1998) devotes only two of its 341 pages to homosexuality. A recent issue of the *William and Mary Quarterly* (vol. 60, no. 1), which was published after most of the current text had been written, includes several articles and brief notes that are a significant contribution to the discussion of homosexuality in early America.

2. Albert Dodd, Diary, Yale University Library, quoted in David Deitchur, *Dear Friends: American Photographs of Men Together, 1840-1918* (New York: Harry N. Abrams, 2001), p. 62, and Jonathan Ned Katz, *Love Stories: Sex Between Men Before Stonewall* (Chicago: University of Chicago Press, 2001), p. 29.

3. For a detailed discussion of homoerotic epistolary traditions in Germany, see Simon Richter, "The Ins and Outs of Intimacy: Gender, Epistolary Culture, and the Public Sphere," *The German Quarterly,* 69, no. 2 (Spring 1996), pp. 111-124.

4. Gregory D. Massey, *John Laurens and the American Revolution* (Columbia: University of South Carolina Press, 2000), pp. 4, 40.

5. Ibid., p. 79.

6. Ibid., p. 81.

7. For the fuller form of the quotation see *Gay American History: Lesbian and Gay Men in the U.S.A., a Documentary,* edited by Jonathan Katz (New York: Thomas Y. Crowell, 1976), p. 453.

8. Massey, *John Laurens and the American Revolution,* p. 81.

9. Ibid., p. 159.

10. Ibid., p. 81.

11. Ibid., pp. 167-168.

12. Ibid., p. 169.

13. Quoted in *Gay American History,* notes, p. 645.

14. Alfred Kinsey, Wardell B. Pomeroy, and Clyde E. Martin, *Sexual Behavior in the Human Male* (Philadelphia: W.B. Saunders, 1948), pp. 650, 651.

15. "Historical United States Census Data Browser," made available on the Internet at fisher.lib.virginia.edu/collections/stats/histcensus by the Inter-University Consortium for Political and Social Research, Ann Arbor, MI.

16. Christopher Nealon, *Foundlings: Lesbian and Gay Historical Emotion Before Stonewall* (Durham, NC: Duke University Press, 2001), p. 122.

17. Michel Foucault, *The History of Sexuality* (New York: Pantheon Books, 1978-1986), p. 101. For those suggesting a revision or refinement of Foucault's theories, see David M. Halperin, "Forgetting Foucault: Acts, Identities, and the History of Sexuality," *Representations,* no. 63 (Summer 1998), pp. 93-120; Graham Robb, "Bosom Buddies," *New York Times Book Review* (June 3, 2001), p. 18; and, especially, Tasmin Spargo, *Foucalt and Queer Theory* (Cambridge, UK: Icon Books, 1999) and the writings of Richard Godbeer and Regina Kunzel.

18. Kinsey et al., *Sexual Behavior in the Human Male,* p. 638.

Chapter 1

1. August John Foster, Diary, 1806, Augustus John Foster Papers, LC, p. 12.

2. William Bradford, *Of Plymouth Plantation, 1620-1647* (New York: Alfred A. Knopf, 1982), p. 321.

3. Ibid., p. 322.

4. Richard Godbeer, "'The Cry of Sodom': Discourse, Intercourse, and Desire in Colonial New England," *William and Mary Quarterly,* Third Series, 52, no. 2 (April 1995), p. 262.

5. James Adair, *The History of the American Indians, Particularly Those Nations Adjoining to the Mississippi, East and West Florida, Georgia, South and North Carolina, and Virginia* (New York: Johnson Reprint Corp., 1968), p. 163.

6. D.A. Coward, "Attitudes to Homosexuality in Eighteenth-Century France," *Journal of European Studies,* 10, no. 40 (December 1980), p. 241.

7. Benjamin Rush, *Medical Inquiries and Observations Upon the Diseases of the Mind* (Philadelphia: Kimber & Richardson, 1812), p. 353.

8. James Tongue, *An Inaugural Dissertation Upon the Three Following Subjects: An Attempt to Prove, That the Lues Venerea was Not Introduced into Europe from America. . . .* (Philadelphia: Printed by the Author, 1801), p. 39.

9. William Robertson, *The History of America* (London: Printed by A. Strahan, 1803), vol. 11, p. 65.

10. Corneille de Pauw, *Recherches Philosophiques sur les Americains, ou Memoires Interessants Pour Servir A l'Histoire de l'Espece Humaine* (London: 1770), pp. 19-20; *A General History of the Americans: Of Their Customs, Manners, and Colours,* selected by Daniel Webb (Rochdale [Eng.]: Printed by and for T. Wood, 1806), pp. 2, 46-47.

11. Quoted in Robert F. Berkhofer Jr., *The White Man's Indian: Images of the American Indian from Columbus to the Present* (New York: Alfred A. Knopf, 1978), p. 42.

12. Ibid., p. 8.

13. Crèvecoeur, Michel Guillaume (Saint John de), *Journey into Northern Pennsylvania and the State of New York* (Ann Arbor: University of Michigan Press, 1964), p. 53.

14. Samuel Williams, *The Natural and Civil History of Vermont* (Walpole, Newhampshire: Printed by Isaiah Thomas and David Carlisle, 1794), vol. 1, p. 224.

15. *Journals of the Lewis & Clark Expedition,* edited by Gary E. Moulton (Lincoln: University of Nebraska Press, 1983-2001), vol. 3, p. 260.

16. *Letters of the Lewis and Clark Expedition: With Related Documents, 1783-1854,* 2nd ed., edited by Donald Jackson (Urbana: University of Illinois Press, 1978), vol. 2, p. 531.

17. Robert Fulton and Steven W. Anderson, "The Amerindian 'Man-Woman': Gender, Criminality, and Cultural Continuity," *Current Anthropology,* 33, no. 5 (December 1992), p. 603.

18. Charles Callender and Lee M. Kochems, "The North American Berdache," *Current Anthropology,* 24, no. 4 (August-October 1983), p. 447. For the most extensive discussion of the berdache tradition see Walter L. Williams, *The Spirit and the Flesh: Sexual Diversity in American Indian Culture* (Boston: Beacon Press, 1986).

19. For a detailed discussion of the various roles of the berdaches and how they were viewed, see Richard C. Trexler, *Sex and Conquest: Gendered Violence, Political Order, and the European Conquest of the Americas* (Ithaca, NY: Cornell University Press, 1995), pp. 64-140.

20. Quoted in Fulton and Anderson, "The Amerindian 'Man-Woman'," p. 606.

21. Quoted in Callender and Kochems, "The North American Berdache," p. 453.

22. Will Roscoe, *The Zuni Man-Woman* (Albuquerque: University of New Mexico Press, 1991).

23. Kathleen M. Brown, *Good Wives, Nasty Wenches, and Anxious Patriarchs: Gender, Race, and Power in Colonial Virginia* (Chapel Hill: University of North Carolina Press, 1996), p. 2.

24. For a more detailed and cogent discussion of the ramifications of Filmerian and Lockean views of colonial society, see Mary Beth Norton, *Founding Mothers & Fathers: Gendered Power and the Forming of American Society* (New York: Vintage Books, 1997). Locke's views of societal/familial structures could at times be close to those of Filmer. See Elizabeth Barnes, "Affecting Relations, Pedagogy, Patriarchy, and the Politics of Sympathy," *American Literary History,* 8, no. 4 (Winter 1996), p. 598.

25. William Strachey, *For the Colony in Virginea Britannia, Lavves Diuine, Morall, and Martiall, &c* (London: for Walter Burre, 1612), p. 5.

26. Norton, *Founding Mothers & Fathers,* p. 18.

27. Winthrop D. Jordan, *White Over Black: American Attitudes Toward the Negro, 1550-1812* (New York: Norton, 1968), p. 78.

28. For differing interpretations of the Davis case, see Brown, *Good Wives, Nasty Wenches, and Anxious Patriarchs,* p. 195; Thomas N. Ingersoll, *Mammon and Manon in Early New Orleans: The First Slave Society in the Deep South, 1718-1819* (Knoxville: University of Tennessee Press, 1999), pp. 459-460, note 79; Jordon, *White Over Black,* p. 78.

29. Jordon, *White Over Black,* p. 78, note 79.

30. [Virginia] *Statutes at Large: Being a Collection of All the First Session of the Legislature, in the Year 1619* (New York: Bartow, 1823), p. 286. "Be it therefore enacted by this present Grand Assembly, That the masters of the severall familys within the collony shall be responsible for all the publique duties, tithes and charges, due from all persons in their familys. And shall detaine and keep in their hands and custody the cropps and shares of all ffreemen within their familys vntil satisfaction be made of all such publique duties, tithes and charges, And it shall be understood where they make a joynt cropp, that he which hath the comand shall be adjudged the master of the family. Laws of Virginia, Act VI, October, 1644—19th Charles 1st."

31. On settlement patterns around the Chesapeake and the isolation of neighbors, see Norton, *Founding Mothers & Fathers*, p. 80; Brown, *Good Wives, Nasty Wenches and Anxious Patriarchs*, p. 265.

32. Colin L. Talley, "Gender and Male Same-Sex Erotic Behavior in British North America in the Seventeenth Century," *Journal of the History of Sexuality*, 6, no. 3 (1996), p. 407.

33. Arthur W. Calhoun, *A Social History of the American Family, I: Colonial Period* (Cleveland: Arthur H. Clark Co., 1917), p. 52.

34. *The Key* (Fredericktown, MD), 1, no. 14 (April 14, 1798), p. 106.

35. Vincent J. Bertolini, "The Erotics of Sentimental Bachelorhood in the 1850s," *American Literature*, 68, no. 4 (December 1996), p. 708.

36. *The Old Bachelor*, [by William Wirt et al.] (Richmond, VA: Printed at the Enquirer Press, for Thomas Ritchie and Fielding Lucas, 1814), p. 6.

37. Mark E. Kann, *On the Man Question: Gender and Civic Virtue in America* (Philadelphia: Temple University Press, 1991), p. 201.

38. Alfred Kinsey, Wardell B. Pomeroy, and Clyde E. Martin, *Sexual Behavior in the Human Male* (Philadelphia: W.B. Saunders, 1948), pp. 457-459.

39. Kenneth A. Lockridge, "Colonial Self-Fashioning: Paradoxes and Pathologies in the Construction of Genteel Identity in Eighteenth-Century America," in *Through a Glass Darkly: Reflections on Personal Identity in Early America*, edited by Ronald Hoffman, Mechal Sobel, and Fredrika J. Teute (Chapel Hill: University of North Carolina Press, 1997), pp. 323-324.

40. Ibid., pp. 320-321.

41. Anya Jabour, "Male Friendship and Masculinity in the Early National South: William Wirt and His Friends," *Journal of the Early Republic*, 20 (Spring 2000), pp. 83-111.

42. Oral history interviews conducted by the present author for the Gay Bears Oral History Project. Recordings and transcripts available through The University Archives, University of California, Berkeley.

43. Quoted in Jabour, "Male Friendship and Masculinity in the Early National South," p. 88.

44. Ibid., p. 91.

45. Ibid., pp. 93-101.

46. E. Anthony Rotundo, "Romantic Friendship: Male Intimacy and Middle Class Youth in the Northern United States, 1800-1900," *Journal of Social History*, 23 (Fall 1989), pp. 1-25.

47. Quoted in Barbara G. Carson, *Ambitious Appetites: Dining, Behavior, and Patterns of Consumption in Federal Washington* (Washington, DC: The American Institute of Architects Press, 1990), p. 85.

48. Quoted in Jabour, "Male Friendship and Masculinity in the Early National South," p. 102.

49. Ibid., p. 104.

50. Ibid., p. 93.

51. Ibid., pp. 89, 91.

52. Kinsey et al., *Sexual Behavior in the Human Male*, p. 651.

53. John P. Kennedy, *Memoirs of the Life of William Wirt, Attorney-General of the United States* (Philadelphia: Blanchard and Lea, 1854), vol. 1, pp. 66-67.

54. Kenneth A. Lockridge, *On the Sources of Patriarchal Rage: The Commonplace Books of William Byrd and Thomas Jefferson and the Gendering of Power in the Eighteenth Century* (New York: New York University Press, 1992), p. 54.

55. Ibid., p. 68.

56. K.J.H. Berland, "William Byrd's Sexual Lexicography," *Eighteenth Century Life*, 23, n.s., no. 1 (February 1999), pp. 4-8.

57. Cynthia Koch, "The Virtuous Curriculum: Schoolbooks and American Culture, 1785-1830," doctoral dissertation, University of Pennsylvania, 1991, p. 98.

58. Ibid., p. 309.

59. J.S. Thompson to William Wirt, January 22, 1825, William Wirt Papers, LC, quoted in Anya Jabour, "Masculinity and Adolescence in Antebellum America: Robert Wirt at West Point, 1820-1821," *Journal of Family History,* 23, no. 4 (October 1998), p. 403.

60. *A Short Introduction to the Latin Tongue, 1709.* Reprint. (Menston, Eng.: The Scolar Press, 1971), p. 41. For this insight I am indebted to my colleague Lawrence Cohen at the University of California, Berkeley.

61. Marcus Tullius Cicero, *Cicero's Epistles to Atticus,* translated by William Guthrie (London: T. Waller, 1752), vol. 1, p. ii-iii.

62. Koch, "The Virtuous Curriculum," p. 498.

Chapter 2

1. Simon Richter, "Winckelmann's Progeny: Homosocial Networking in the Eighteenth Century," in *Outing Goethe & His Age,* edited by Alice A. Kuzniar (Stanford, CA: Stanford University Press, 1996), pp. 33-34.

2. James D. Steakley, "Sodomy in Enlightenment Prussia: From Execution to Suicide," in *The Pursuit of Sodomy: Male Homosexuality in Renaissance and Enlightenment Europe,* edited by Kent Gerard and Gert Hekma (Binghamton, NY: Harrington Park Press, 1989), p. 170.

3. Ibid., p. 169.

4. Ibid., p. 170.

5. Jasper Ridley, *The Freemasons* (London: Robinson, 2000), p. 60.

6. Mirabeau, Honoré-Gabriel de Riquetti, comte de, *The Secret History of the Court of Berlin: or The Character of the King of Prussia, His Ministers, Mistresses, Generals, Courtiers, Favourites, and the Royal Family of Prussia* (London: H. S. Nichols, 1895), vol. 2, pp. 48-49.

7. Christian Graf von Krockow, *Die preußischen Brüder: Prinz Heinrich und Friedrich der Große: ein Doppelportrait* (Stuttgart: Deutsche Verlags-Anstalt, 1996), p. 178.

8. Ibid., pp. 144-145.

9. Steakley, "Sodomy in Enlightenment Prussia," p. 17.

10. von Krockow, *Die preußischen Brüder,* pp. 187-193.

11. "Zur Seelenkrankheitskunde," *Magazin zur Erfahrungsseelenkunde,* no. 8 (1791), p. 9, quoted in Steakley, "Sodomy in Enlightenment Prussia," pp. 171-172.

12. Richter, "Winckelmann's Progeny," p. 38.

13. For a discussion of the effect of the Napoleonic invasions on Germanic views of masculinity, see Karen Hagemann, "Of 'Manly Valor' and 'German Honor': Nation, War, and Masculinity in the Age of the Prussian Uprising Against Napoleon," *Central European History,* 30, no. 2 (June 1997), pp. 187-220.

14. Anthony Copley, *Sexual Moralities in France, 1780-1980: New Ideas on the Family, Divorce, and Homosexuality: An Essay on Moral Change* (London: Routledge, 1989), p. 19.

15. Jeffrey Merrick, "Sodomitical Scandals and Subcultures in the 1720s," *Men and Masculinities,* 1, no. 4 (April 1999), p. 378.

16. Copley, *Sexual Moralities in France, 1780-1980,* pp. 19-20.

17. Claude Courouve, *Les Assemblées de la Manchette: Documents sur l'Amour Masculin au XVIIIe Siècle* (Paris: Courouve, 1987), p. 17. ["J'ai été raccroché par un particulier qui avait son vit à la main, et m'a demands si je bandais et s'approchant de moi a voulu mettre sa main dans ma culotte. Lui ayant di qu'il ne fallait pas s'exposer dans cet endroit, il m'a demandé si j'avais une chambre, où nous puissions aller nous branler le vit ou nous enculer. Il m'a encore dit qu'il y avait plus de 20 ans qu'il se melait de la bardacherie, et qu'il connaissait quantité de laquais avec lesquels il se divertissait for souvent, se branlant le vit ou s'enculant suivant qu'ils le voulaient."]

18. Courouve, *Les Assemblées de la Manchette,* p. 25. ["Etant dans le cabaret, it m'a fait entrer dans un et dont il m'a fait fermer la porte et s'est mis tout à découvert, me demandant si j'était en humeur; il s'est jeté sur moi voulant mettre sa main dans ma culotte; il s'est montré à moi tout à découvert par devant et j'ai aperçu qu'il y était rasé; je lui ai demandé pourquoi il était rasé dans cet endroit; il m'a dit que c'était à cause qu'on disait qu'il était châtré parce que la nature a été très ingrate pour lui de ce côté-la. Je lui ai dit: 'Allons-nous en plutôt chez vous, nous ne sommes pas bien ici'—et cela dans le dessein de le faire arrêter—Il m'a demands à voir mon derrière, je lui ai dit: 'Vous en verrez assez quand nous serons chez vous'; il m'a dit que nous ne pouvions point aller chez lui parce qu'il était marié, il m'a demandé à venir plutôt chez moi. Je lui ai dit que j'avais un camarade, il m'a dit: 'Vous irez voir devant si votre camarade y est, et vous resterez dans la rue pour me le dire.' Il m'a proposé de consommer l'action avec lui, et qu'il serait le patient, qu'il aimait fort cela, et que cela le mettait en humeur pour être ensuite l'agent."]

19. D.A. Coward, "Attitudes to Homosexuality in Eighteenth-Century France," *Journal of European Studies,* 10, no. 40 (December 1980), p. 235.

20. Jeffrey Merrick, "Sodomitical Inclinations in Early Eighteenth-Century Paris," *Eighteenth-Century Studies,* 30, no. 3 (1997), pp. 289-295.

21. Courouve, *Les Assemblées de la Manchette,* p. 11. ["La loi ne prévoyant pas ce délit."]

22. Courouve, *Les Assemblées de la Manchette,* p. 8. ["Ce qui n'offense pas la societé n'est pas du ressort de sa justice."]

23. Coward, "Attitudes to Homosexuality in Eighteenth-Century France," p. 239.

24. Michel Rey, "Parisian Homosexuals Create a Lifestyle, 1700-1750: The Police Archives," in *Unauthorized Sexual Behavior During the Enlightenment,* edited by Robert P. Maccubbin (a special issue of *Eighteenth Century Life,* 9, n.s., no. 3 [May 1985]), p. 186.
25. Ibid., p. 186.
26. Ibid., p. 187.
27. Courouve, *Les Assemblées de la manchette,* p. 29.
28. Coward, "Attitudes to Homosexuality in Eighteenth-Century France," p. 244.
29. Michel Delon, "The Priest, the Philosopher, and Homosexuality in Enlightenment France," in *Unauthorized Sexual Behavior During the Enlightenment,* edited by Robert P. Maccubbin (a special issue of *Eighteenth Century Life,* 9, n.s., no. 3 [May 1985]), p. 124.
30. Louis Crompton, "Homophobia in Georgian England," in *Among Men, Among Women: Sociological and Historical Recognition of Homosocial Arrangements,* edited by Mattias Duyves et al. (Amsterdam: Sociologisch Instituut, 1983), p. 236.
31. *Fleta,* edited with a translation by H.G. Richardson and G.O. Sayles (London: Bernard Quaritch for the Selden Society, 1955), vol. 2, p. 90.
32. Quoted in Retha M. Warnicke, "Sexual Heresy at the Court of Henry VIII," *The Historical Journal,* 20, no. 2 (June 1987), p. 250.
33. Quoted in Rictor Norton, *Mother Clap's Molly House: The Gay Subculture in England 1700-1830* (London: GMP Publishers, 1992), pp. 15-16.
34. Netta Murray Goldsmith, *The Worst of Crimes: Homosexuality and the Law in Eighteenth-Century London* (Aldershot: Ashgate, 1998), p. 6.
35. Quoted in Arno Karlen, *Sexuality and Homosexuality: A New View* (New York: Norton, 1971), pp. 140-141.
36. Quoted in Richard Davenport-Hines, *Sex, Death and Punishment: Attitudes to Sex and Sexuality in Britain Since the Renaissance* (London: Collins, 1990), p. 92.
37. Quoted in Norton, *Mother Clap's Molly House,* p. 67.
38. Ibid., p. 44.
39. Dennis Rubini, "Sexuality and Augustan England: Sodomy, Politics, Elite Circles and Society," in *The Pursuit of Sodomy: Male Homosexuality in Renaissance and Enlightenment Europe,* edited by Kent Gerard and Gert Hekma (Binghamton, NY: Harrington Park Press, 1989), p. 358.
40. Ibid., p. 351.
41. Norton, *Mother Clap's Molly House,* p. 52.
42. Quoted in Norton, *Mother Clap's Molly House,* p. 55.
43. Herman Melville, *Redburn: His First Voyage, Being the Sailor-Boy Confessions and Reminiscences of the Son-of-a-Gentleman, in the Merchant Service* (London: Penguin Books, 1986), p. 309.
44. Ibid., p. 310.
45. Quoted in Norton, *Mother Clap's Molly House,* pp. 189-190.
46. Ibid., p. 189.
47. Raymond Stephanson, "'Epicoene Friendship': Understanding Male Friendship in the Early Eighteenth Century, with Some Speculations About Pope," *The Eighteenth Century,* 38, no. 2 (1997), p. 152.

48. Randolph Trumbach, "Sex, Gender, and Sexual Identity in Modern Culture: Male Sodomy and Female Prostitution in Enlightenment London," *Journal of the History of Sexuality*, 2, no. 2 (1991), p. 188.

49. Davenport-Hines, *Sex, Death and Punishment*, p. 63.

50. Polly Morris, "Sodomy and Male Honor: The Case of Somerset, 1740-1850," in *The Pursuit of Sodomy: Male Homosexuality in Renaissance and Enlightenment Europe,* edited by Kent Gerard and Gert Hekma (Binghamton, NY: Harrington Park Press, 1989), p. 399.

51. *Passionate Encounters in a Time of Sensibility,* edited by Maximillian E. Novak and Anne Mellor (Newark: University of Delaware Press, 2000), p. 11.

52. For a brief discussion of the sexual allure of the exotic Other as an expression of sensibility, see Julie Ellison, "The Gender of Transparency: Masculinity and the Conduct of Life," *American Literary History*, 4, no. 4 (Winter 1992), note 14, pp. 603-604. Ellison focuses on transgressive desire between white men and women of color, but her "erotic aliens" might just as likely have been male.

53. George E. Haggerty, "'What Is This Secret Sin?': Sexuality and Secrecy in the Writings of Horace Walpole," in *Passionate Encounters in a Time of Sensibility,* pp. 127-149.

54. Quoted in Miles Ogborn, "Locating the Macaroni: Luxury, Sexuality and Vision in Vauxhall Gardens," *Textual Practice*, 11, no. 3 (1997), p. 449.

55. Ibid., p. 457.

56. Ibid., p. 449.

57. Ibid.

58. Ibid., p. 450.

59. J.A. Leo Lemay, "The American Origins of 'Yankee Doodle,'" *William and Mary Quarterly*, Third Series, 33, no. 3 (July 1976), pp. 444-445.

60. Quoted in Amanda Foreman, *Georgiana, Duchess of Devonshire* (New York: Random House, 1998), p. 56.

61. Quoted in Richard Davenport-Hines, *Sex, Death and Punishment*, p. 65.

62. Davenport-Hines, *Sex, Death and Punishment*, p. 64.

63. Ibid., p. 85.

64. *The Oxford English Dictionary*, 2nd ed. (Oxford: Clarendon Press, 1989), vol. 6, p. 409.

65. Melville, *Redburn*, p. 298.

Chapter 3

1. Robert Middlekauff, "Why Men Fought in the American Revolution," *The Huntington Library Quarterly*, 43, no. 2 (Spring 1980), p. 136.

2. Joseph Gardner Andrews, *A Surgeon's Mate at Fort Defiance: The Journal of Joseph Gardner Andrews for the Year 1795,* edited by Richard C. Knopf (Columbus: Ohio Historical Society, 1957), p. 75.

3. Ibid., p. 86.

4. Journals and Diaries, Fort Bellefontaine, Order Book, 21 September 1808 [manuscript], MHS.

5. James E. Valle, *Rocks & Shoals: Naval Discipline in the Age of Fighting Sail* (Annapolis, MD: Naval Institute Press, 1996), pp. 12-13.

6. Charles Rockwell, *Sketches of Foreign Travel and Life at Sea: Including a Cruise on Board a Man-of-War* (Boston: Tappan and Dennet, 1842), vol. 2, p. 413.

7. Valle, *Rocks & Shoals,* p. 203; *The Oxford English Dictionary,* 2nd ed. (Oxford: Clarendon Press, 1989), vol. 9, p. 1005.

8. Harold D. Langley, *Social Reform in the United States Navy, 1798-1862* (Urbana: University of Illinois Press, 1967), pp. 221-222.

9. George Washington to the Continental Congress, September 24, 1776, George Washington Papers, LC.

10. John S. Hare, "Military Punishments in the War of 1812," *The Journal of the American Military History Institute,* 4, no. 4 (Winter 1940), p. 234.

11. John Le Couteur, *Merry Hearts Make Light Days: The War of 1812, Journal of Lieutenant John Le Couteur, 104th Foot,* edited by Donald E. Graves (Ottawa: Carleton University Press, 1993), p. 80.

12. Andrews, *A Surgeon's Mate at Fort Defiance,* p. 16.

13. Michel Foucault, *Discipline and Punish: The Birth of the Prison* (New York: Vintage Books, 1995), pp. 8, 14.

14. Orderly Book of the Corps of Artillerists and Engineers, Commenced at West Point Jan'y lst 1798, no. 4, 27 January 1799 [manuscript], USMA.

15. Hugh F. Rankin, *Francis Marion: The Swamp Fox* (New York: Crowell, 1973), p. 21.

16. Quoted in Robert Harry Berlin, "The Administration of Military Justice in the Continental Army During the American Revolution, 1775-1783," doctoral dissertation, University of California, Santa Barbara, 1976, p. 202.

17. For a fuller discussion of this practice, see James Grantham Turner, *Libertines and Radicals in Early Modern London: Sexuality, Politics and Literary Culture, 1630-1685* (Cambridge: Cambridge University Press, 2002), pp. 32-37; Violet Alford, "Rough Music or Charivari," *Folklore,* 70 (December 1959), pp. 505-518.

18. Langley, *Social Reform in the United States Navy,* p. 140.

19. Richard Henry Dana, *Two Years Before the Mast: A Personal Narrative of Life at Sea* (New York: Penguin Books, 1981), p. 155.

20. Ibid., pp. 469-470.

21. Quoted in Langley, *Social Reform in the United States Navy,* pp. 159-160.

22. Quoted in *Shipboard Life and Organisation, 1731-1815,* edited by Brian Lavery (Aldershot: Ashgate, 1998), p. 436.

23. Karen Halttunen, "Humanitarianism and the Pornography of Pain in Anglo-American Culture," *The American Historical Review,* 100, no. 2 (April 1995), p. 325.

24. Herman Melville, *White-Jacket, or the World in a Man-of-War* (Oxford: Oxford University Press, 1990), p. 139.

25. Iain McCalman, "Unrespectable Radicalism: Infidels and Pornography in Early Nineteenth-Century London," *Past and Present,* no. 104 (August 1984), p. 90.

26. Charles R. Anderson, "A Reply to Herman Melville's White-Jacket by Rear-Admiral Thomas O. Selfridge, Sr.," *American Literature,* 7, no. 2 (May 1935), p. 138 (notes).

27. Quoted in Myra C. Glenn, "The Naval Reform Campaign Against Flogging: A Case Study in Changing Attitudes Toward Corporal Punishment, 1830-1850," *American Quarterly,* 35, no. 4 (Autumn 1983), p. 415.

28. Glenn, "The Naval Reform Campaign Against Flogging," p. 413.

29. Quoted in Langley, *Social Reform in the United States Navy,* p. 183.
30. General Orders, March 3, 1778, George Washington Papers, 1741-1799, LC.
31. General Orders, March 14, 1778, George Washington Papers, 1741-1799, LC.
32. *Summer Soldiers: A Survey & Index of Revolutionary War Courts-Martial,* edited by James C. Neagles (Salt Lake City: Ancestry Incorporated, 1986).
33. *Numbered Record Books, Microfilm Series M853,* roll 9, vol. 58 (13 March 1782-12 May 1782), National Archives, Washington, DC.
34. Journals and Diaries, Fort Bellefontaine, June 13, 1809, MHS.
35. Journals and Diaries, Fort Bellefontaine, July 4, 1809, MHS.
36. Norman W. Caldwell, "The Enlisted Soldier at the Frontier Post, 1790-1814," *Mid-America: An Historical Review,* 37, no. 4 (October 1955), pp. 200-201.
37. Anthony Wayne, General Orders, vol. 7, May 6, 1795, and May 10, 1795, USMA.
38. Anthony Wayne, General Orders, vol. 1, November 17, 1792, USMA.
39. Anthony Wayne, General Orders, vol. 1, October 18, 1792, USMA.
40. Anthony Wayne, General Orders, vol. 7, August 22, 1795, USMA.
41. Anthony Wayne, General Orders, vol. 1, November 15, 1792, USMA.
42. Anthony Wayne, General Orders, vol. 9, April 14, 1795, USMA.
43. Anthony Wayne, General Orders, vol. 3, June 6, 1793, USMA.
44. Anthony Wayne, General Orders, vol. 4, September 10, 1793, USMA.
45. B.R. Burg, *An American Seafarer in the Age of Sail: The Erotic Diaries of Philip C. Van Buskirk, 1851-1870* (New Haven, CT: Yale University Press, 1994), pp. 74, 186.
46. *Fleta,* edited with a translation by H.G. Richardson and G.O. Sayles (London: Bernard Quaritch, 1955), vol. 2, p. 90.
47. Valle, *Rocks & Shoals,* pp. 328, 327.
48. Quoted in Valle, *Rocks & Shoals,* p. 166.
49. Ibid., p. 167.
50. Quoted in Valle, *Rocks & Shoals,* p. 168.
51. Valle, *Rocks & Shoals,* pp. 169-170.
52. Quoted in Valle, *Rocks & Shoals,* pp. 170-171.
53. Valle, *Rocks & Shoals,* pp. 172-173.
54. Ibid., pp. 173-174.
55. Ibid., p. 166.
56. Langley, *Social Reform in the United States Navy,* p. 172.
57. Valle, *Rocks & Shoals,* p. 174.
58. Melville, *White-Jacket,* p. 379.
59. Burg, *An American Seafarer in the Age of Sail,* p. xi.
60. Ibid., p. 26.
61. Ibid., p. 75.
62. Ibid., p. 79.
63. Ibid., p. 81.
64. Ibid., p. 93.
65. "The Jolly Young Waterman" [song sheet] [New York: H. De Marsan, 1860], America Singing: Nineteenth-Century Song Sheets Collection, Library of Congress.

66. Herman Melville, *Redburn: His First Voyage, Being the Sailor-Boy Confessions and Reminiscences of the Son-of-a-Gentleman, in the Merchant Service* (London: Penguin Books, 1986), p. 294.

67. Ibid., p. 295.

68. "Harry Bluff" [song sheet] (New York: H. De Marsan, n.d.), America Singing: Nineteenth-Century Song Sheets Collection, Library of Congress.

69. "The Female Sailor" [song sheet] (Boston: L. Deming, n.d.), America Singing: Nineteenth-Century Song Sheets Collection, Library of Congress.

70. "The Handsome Cabin Boy" [song sheet] (New York: H. De Marsan, n.d.), America Singing: Nineteenth-Century Song Sheets Collection, Library of Congress.

71. Ward Stafford, *Important to Seamen,* quoted in Roald Kverndal, *Seamen's Missions: Their Origin and Early Growth, a Contribution to the History of the Church Maritime* (Pasadena, CA: William Carey Library, 1986), pp. 622-623.

72. William M. Wood, "Practical Reflections Upon the Grog Ration," in Wood's *Shoulder to the Wheel of Progress* (Buffalo: Derby, Orton and Mulligan, 1853), pp. 135-136.

Chapter 4

1. Quoted in Rudolf Cronau, *The Army of the American Revolution and Its Organizer* (New York: Rudolf Cronau, 1923), pp. 106-107.

2. John McAuley Palmer, *General von Steuben* (New Haven, CT: Yale University Press, 1937), p. 50.

3. Friedrich Wilhelm von Steuben, undated autobiographical fragment, Steuben Papers, NYHS.

4. Palmer, *General von Steuben,* p. 92.

5. Ibid., p. 126.

6. Quoted in *Gay American History: Lesbian and Gay Men in the U.S.A., a Documentary* [edited] by Jonathan Katz (New York: Thomas Y. Crowell, 1976), pp. 453-454.

7. *Gay American History,* notes, p. 645.

8. Quoted in *Gay American History,* pp. 455-456.

9. Frederick William von Steuben, *Baron von Steuben's Revolutionary War Drill Manual: A Facsimile Reprint of the 1794 Edition* (New York: Dover Publications, 1985), pp. 22-25.

10. Palmer, *General von Steuben,* pp. 147-148.

11. Benjamin Walker to Baron von Steuben, February 18, 1780, Steuben Papers, NYHS.

12. Benjamin Walker to Baron von Steuben, February 24, 1780, Steuben Papers, NYHS.

13. Benjamin Walker to Baron von Steuben, March 10, 1780, Steuben Papers, NYHS.

14. Lloyd Beall to Henry Burdick, November 14, 1807, Henry Burdick Papers, USMA.

15. Phillips to Commanding Officer of the American Troops, April 26, 1781, Steuben Papers, NYHS.

16. Quoted in Palmer, *General von Steuben,* p. 266.

17. Benjamin Walker to Baron von Steuben, March, 10, l780, Steuben Papers, NYHS.

18. Benjamin Walker to Baron von Steuben, February 2, 1780, Steuben Papers, NYHS.

19. Palmer, *General von Steuben,* p. 324.

20. Quoted in Palmer, *General von Steuben,* p. 206.

21. The Historical Society pf Pennsylvania (HSP), Richard Peters Papers, v. 9, p. 25, Friedrich von Steuben to Richard Peters, June 12, 1779.

22. Benjamin Walker to Baron von Steuben, January 23, 1783, Steuben Papers, NYHS.

23. Ibid.

24. Benjamin Walker to Baron von Steuben, February 19, 1783, Steuben Papers, NYHS.

25. The Historical Society of Pennsylvania (HSP), Dreer Collection, Revolutionary Generals, Friedrich von Steuben to Benjamin Walker, December 27, 1782. ["Cette Chienne de correspondence ministeriale m'a coute infiniment des peines. Vous savez que je suis sans assistance, meme pour ma correspondence Angloise. Que ferai-je mon ami, si je doit faire encore une Compagne. je ne croie pas que Popham a envie de me rejoindre du moins j'e n'ai pas une ligne de Lui, ou trouvais-je un W_____ mais je ne doit pas Vous rendre trop vaine. Mais serieusement—ou trouverai-je un homme qui peut conduire ma correspondence. Voyez un peu si Vous pouvez me proposses un bon sujet—Vous savez cequil me faut. je comte toujours sur mon North, Vous savez cependant que sa force ne consiste pas dans sa plume. Vous savez aussi quil est aussi paresseur quil est aimable."]

26. The Historical Society of Pennsylvania (HSP), Simon Gratz Collection (#250), Case 8, Box 14, William North to Benjamin Walker, March 9, 1784.

27. The Historical Society of Pennsylvania (HSP), Simon Gratz Collection (#250), Case 4, Box 22, William North to Benjamin Walker, February 16, 1783.

28. The Historical Society of Pennsylvania (HSP), Simon Gratz Collection (#250), Case 2, Box 1, William North to Benjamin Walker, September 28, [no year].

29. The Historical Society of Pennsylvania (HSP), Simon Gratz Collection (#250), Case 4, Box 13, William North to Benjamin Walker, Sunday, June 13, [no year]; for a discussion of the term *bougre* as a homosexual slur see D.A. Coward, "Attitudes to Homosexuality in Eighteenth-Century France," *Journal of European Studies,* 10, no. 40 (December 1980), pp. 239-240, and Nancy Shoemaker, "An Alliance Between Men: Gender Metaphors in Eighteenth-Century American Indian Diplomacy East of the Mississippi," *Ethnohistory,* 46, no. 2 (Spring 1999), pp. 248, 249.

30. Quoted in Palmer, *General von Steuben,* p. 335.

31. Ibid., p. 361.

32. Ibid., p. 345.

33. Baron von Steuben to William North, Von Steuben Correspondence, nos. 1321 and 71.42, SotC; ["Goodbye my dear and tender friend, I am to my last breath your truly loving and sincere friend"].

34. The Historical Society of Pennsylvania (HSP), Simon Gratz Collection (#250), Alphabetical Series, William North to Benjamin Walker, May 30, 1788.

35. The Historical Society of Pennsylvania (HSP), Simon Gratz Collection (#250), Case 2, Box 1, William North to Benjamin Walker, September 28, 17[83].

36. Baron von Steuben to William North, February 17, 1790, YBL.

37. Quoted in Palmer, *General von Steuben,* p. 393.

38. Ibid., p. 403.

39. Ibid., p. 403.

40. Baron von Steuben, Last Will and Testament, February 12, 1794, Steuben Papers, NYHS.

41. Ibid.

42. William North to Baron von Steuben, January 8, 1789, Steuben Papers, NYHS.

43. The Historical Society of Pennsylvania (HSP), Simon Gratz Collection (#250), Case 4, Box 13, William North to Benjamin Walker, November 23, 1788.

44. The Historical Society of Pennsylvania (HSP), Simon Gratz Collection (#250), Case 4, Box 13, William North to Benjamin Walker, November 16, 1788.

45. The Historical Society of Pennsylvania (HSP), Simon Gratz Collection (#250), Case 2, Box 1, William North to Benjamin Walker, September 18, 1800.

46. The Historical Society of Pennsylvania (HSP), Simon Gratz Collection (#250), Case 4, Box 13, William North to Benjamin Walker, November [no day] 1792.

47. *Correspondence of the Van Cortlandt Family of Cortlandt Manor,* compiled and edited by Jacob Judd (Tarrytown, NY: Sleepy Hollow Restorations, 1977), vol. 2, pp. 489-490.

48. The Historical Society of Pennsylvania (HSP), Simon Gratz Collection (#250), Case 4, Box 13, William North to Benjamin Walker, November 11, 1811.

49. The Historical Society of Pennsylvania (HSP), Simon Gratz Collection (#250), Case 4, Box 13, William North to Benjamin Walker, June 11, 1813.

50. The Historical Society of Pennsylvania (HSP), Simon Gratz Collection (#250), Case 4, Box 13, William North to Benjamin Walker, August 9, 1815.

51. The Historical Society of Pennsylvania (HSP), Simon Gratz Collection (#250), Case 4, Box 13, William North to Benjamin Walker, July 2, 1817.

52. The Historical Society of Pennsylvania (HSP), Simon Gratz Collection (#250), Case 4, Box 13, William North to Benjamin Walker, September 15, 1817.

53. The Historical Society of Pennsylvania (HSP), Simon Gratz Collection (#250), Case 4, Box 13, William North to Benjamin Walker, October 4, 1817.

54. Holograph will of Benjamin Walker, OCHS.

Chapter 5

1. Chastellux, François Jean, marquis de. *Travels in North America in the Years 1780, 1781 and 1782,* a revised translation with introduction and notes by Howard C. Rice Jr. (Chapel Hill: University of North Carolina Press, 1963), vol. 2, p. 392.

2. Jack McLaughlin, "Jefferson, Poe, and Ossian," *Eighteenth-Century Studies,* 26, no. 4 (Summer 1993), p. 629.

3. James Macpherson, *The Poems of Ossian, &c* (Edinburgh: James Ballantyne, 1805), vol. 1, pp. 183-184.

4. Ibid., vol. 1, pp. 79-81.

5. Eve Kosofsky Sedgwick, *Between Men: English Literature and Male Homosocial Desire* (New York: Columbia University Press, 1985), pp. 21-27.

6. Macpherson, *The Poems of Ossian,* vol. 2, p. 469.

7. Dafydd Moore, "Heroic Incoherence in James Macpherson's *The Poems of Ossian,*" *Eighteenth-Century Studies,* 34, no. 1 (2000), p. 44.

8. *Catalogue of the Library of Thomas Jefferson,* compiled with annotations by E. Millicent Sowerby (Washington, DC: The Library of Congress, 1955), vol. 4, p. 456.

9. Tobias Smollett, *The Adventures of Roderick Random* (Oxford: Oxford University Press, 1979), pp. 194-195.

10. Ibid., p. 195.

11. Ibid., p. 198.

12. Ibid., p. 199.

13. Ibid., p. 309.

14. Ibid., p. 310.

15. George K. Smart, "Private Libraries in Colonial Virginia," *American Literature,* 10, no. 1 (March 1938), p. 31.

16. "Books in Williamsburg," *William and Mary College Quarterly Historical Magazine,* 15, no. 2 (October 1906), p. 112.

17. James Napier, "Some Book Sales in Dumfries, Virginia, 1794-1796," *William and Mary Quarterly,* Third Series, 10, no. 3 (July 1953), p. 444.

18. Holograph will of Benjamin Walker, OCHS.

19. Clare A. Lyons, "Mapping an Atlantic Sexual Culture: Homoeroticism in Eighteenth-Century Philadelphia," *William and Mary Quarterly,* Third Series, 60, no. 1 (January 2003), p. 128.

20. Robert H. MacDonald, "The Frightful Consequences of Onanism: Notes on the History of a Delusion," *Journal of the History of Ideas,* 28, no. 3 (July-September 1967), pp. 423-426.

21. *Onania, or, The Heinous Sin of Self-Pollution: And All Its Frightful Consequences, in Both Sexes, Consider'd* (London: J. Isted, 1730), supplement, pp. 76-77.

22. Ibid., p. 2.

23. Bradley Chapin, "Felony Law Reform in the Early Republic," *Pennsylvania Magazine of History and Biography,* 113, no. 2 (April 1989), p. 171.

24. William Waller Hening, *The New Virginia Justice: Comprising the Office and Authority of Justice of the Peace, in the Commonwealth of Virginia* (Richmond: Printed by T. Nicolson, 1795), pp. 93-94.

25. "Laws of Virginia, October 1792," in *The Statutes at Large of Virginia,* [compiled] by Samuel Shepherd (Richmond: Samuel Shepherd, 1835), p. 113.

26. Jefferson's library included copies of *Domestic Medicine* by William Buchan (London: 1786), *Observations sur l'Usage des Végétaux Exotiques . . . dans les Maladies Vénériennes* by Jacques Dupau (Paris: 1782), *A Treatise on the Venereal Disease* by John Hunter (London: 1786), *Nouvelles Observations sur les Effets du Rob Anti-syphilitique* by Denys Laffecteur (Paris: 1781), and *A Discourse Concerning Gleets* by Daniel Turner (London: 1729). As has been discussed, Jefferson's copy of *Onania* contained titillating case studies, but no explicit references to homosexuality.

27. Jean Astruc, *Traité des Maladies Vénériennes* (Paris: Guillaume Cavelier, 1740), vol. 2, p. 473.

28. Ibid., pp. 455-456. ["On a honte, il est vrai, de rebattre tant de fois de si vilaines choses; mais, dans un Ouvrage comme celui-ci, on ne pouvoit se dispenser de rapporter une cause des Maladies Vénériennes, qui, à la confusion & à l'opprobre du genre humain, ne se trouve que trop véritable & trop fréquente. L'intérêt même des bonne mœurs sembloit éxiger qu'on la rappallât souvent; afin d'epouvanter ceux qui osent s'abandonner à un pareil débordement, & que, s'ils sont insensibles à la vois de la Nature deshonorée, & incapables d'être arrêtés par la terreur des jugemens de Dieu, ils le soient du-moins par la crainte des Maladies qui suivent leurs actions criminelles."]

29. Nikolai Deflef Falck, *A Treatise on the Venereal Disease* (London: The Author, 1772), pp. 94-95.

30. Ibid., p. 95.

31. William Buchan, *Observations Concerning the Prevention and Cure of the Venereal Disease* (London: Printed for T. Chapman, 1796), pp. 28-29.

32. John Marten, *A Treatise of All the Degrees and Symptoms of the Venereal Disease, in Both Sexes,* 6th ed., corrected and enlarged. (London: Printed by and sold by S. Crouch, etc., 1708), pp. 68-69.

33. My survey included works by Gideon de Angelis, Benjamin Bell, Francis Bertody, William Buchan, Richard Carmichael, Thomas Copeland, Jean Jacques Giraud, William M. Hand, John Hunter, Horatio Jameson, Samuel Lee, José Masdevall, Andrew Mathias, Felix Ouvière, William Hayne Simers, Cosmo Stevenson, Frantz Swediaur, Alexander Thomson, James Tongue, and Henry Wilkins.

34. Frantz Swediaur, *A Complete Treatise on the Symptoms, Effects, Nature and Treatment of Syphilis* (Philadelphia: Thomas Dobson, William Fry, 1815), pp. 239-240.

35. Thomas Copeland, *Observations on Some of the Principle Diseases of the Rectum and Anus* (Philadelphia: A. Finley; Fry and Kammerer, 1811), p. 43.

36. Cosmo Gordon Stevenson, *Observations on the Disease of Gonorrhœa* (Philadelphia: Printed for the Author by A. and G. Way, 1803), pp. 33, 48.

37. Frederick Hollick, *A Popular Treatise on Venereal Diseases in All Their Forms* (New York: T.W. Strong, 1852), p. 135.

38. Ibid., pp. 136-137.

39. Ibid., pp. 291-292.

40. Ibid., p. 293.

41. Ibid., pp. 294-295.

42. William Hayne Simers, *Medical Advice* (New York: s.n., 1805), title page.

43. James Tongue, *An Inaugural Dissertation, Upon the Three Following Subjects . . .* (Philadelphia: Printed by the Author, 1801), p. 40.

44. Swediaur, *A Complete Treatise on the Symptoms,* p. 7.

45. Felix Pascalis, *Observations and Practical Remarks on the Nature, Progress and Operation of the Venereal Disease* [New York?: 1811?], p. 7.

46. Charles E. Rosenberg, "Sexuality, Class and Role in 19th-Century America," *American Quarterly,* 25, no. 2 (May 1973), p. 141.

Chapter 6

1. *A Treatise on the Gonorrhoea,* by a Surgeon of Norfolk, Virginia (Norfolk: Printed by John M'Lean, 1787), p. 15.

2. Charles Clifton, "Rereading Voices from the Past: Images of Homo-Eroticism in the Slave Narrative," in *The Greatest Taboo: Homosexuality in Black Communities,* edited by Delroy Constantine-Simms (Los Angeles: Alyson Books, 2001), pp. 343-361.

3. Kristin Hoganson, "Garrisonian Abolitionists and the Rhetoric of Gender, 1850-1860," *American Quarterly,* 45, no. 4 (December 1993), p. 566.

4. Harriet Beecher Stowe, *Uncle Tom's Cabin: or, Life Among the Lowly* (Cambridge, MA: Belknap Press of Harvard University Press, 1962), p. 158.

5. Ibid., p. 230.

6. Ibid., p. 236.

7. Ibid., pp. 156-157.

8. Ibid., p. 169.

9. Ibid., p. 171.

10. Ibid.

11. Ibid., p. 226.

12. Ibid., p. 190.

13. Ibid., p. 228.

14. Ibid., pp. 340-341.

15. Leon Litwack, *Been in the Storm So Long: The Aftermath of Slavery* (New York: Knopf, 1979), p. 40.

16. Harriet A. Jacobs, *Incidents in the Life of a Slave Girl, Written by Herself* (Cambridge, MA: Harvard University Press, 2000), p. 192.

17. Ibid.

18. Kirsten Fischer, *Suspect Relations: Sex, Race, and Resistance in Colonial North Carolina* (Ithaca, NY: Cornell University Press, 2002), p. 147.

19. Gary D. Engle, *This Grotesque Essence: Plays from the American Minstrel Stage* (Baton Rouge: Louisiana State University Press, 1978), p. xv.

20. For an extended discussion of this change see Robert C. Toll, *Blacking Up: The Minstrel Show in Nineteenth-Century America* (New York: Oxford University Press, 1974).

21. Engle, *This Grotesque Essence,* p. xxiii.

22. Eric Lott, *Love and Theft: Blackfaced Minstrelsy and the American Working Class* (New York: Oxford University Press, 1993), pp. 164-165, emphasis added.

23. Eric Lott, "Love and Theft: the Racial Unconscious of Blackface Minstrelsy," *Representations,* no. 39 (Summer 1992), p. 25.

24. Walt Whitman, "The Old Bowery, a Reminiscence of New York Plays and Acting Fifty Years Ago" in *Prose Works 1892,* edited by Floyd Stovall (New York: New York University Press, 1964), vol. 2, p. 595.

25. Eric Lott, *Love and Theft,* p. 162.

26. Ibid.

27. *Christy's Ram's Horn Nigga Songster* (New York: Marsh, n.d.), quoted in Alexander Saxton, "Blackface Minstrelsy and Jacksonian Ideology," *American Quar-*

terly, 27, no. 1 (March 1975), pp. 11-12; for the opening lines (which do not appear in Saxton) see Eric Lott, *Love and Theft,* p. 164.

28. Saxton, "Blackface Minstrelsy and Jacksonian Ideology," p. 12.

29. Eric Lott, "'The Seeming Counterfeit': Racial Politics and Early Blackface Minstrelsy," *American Quarterly,* 43, no. 2 (June 1991), p. 234.

30. Robert C. Toll, *Blacking Up,* p. 49.

31. Davy Crockett, "Speech of Colonel Crockett in Congress," in *Davy Crockett's Almanack of Wild Sports in the West,* 1, no. 3 (1837), p. 40.

32. Thomas J. Gilfoyle, *City of Eros: New York City, Prostitution, and the Commercialization of Sex, 1790-1920* (New York: Norton, 1992), pp. 136-137. See also Jonathan Ned Katz, *Love Stories: Sex Between Men Before Homosexuality* (Chicago: University of Chicago Press, 2001), pp. 80-87.

33. *People vs. Lewis Humphrey,* filed June 9, 1803, box 14 (New York City) District Attorney's Indictment Papers, quoted in Shane White, "'We Dwell in Safety and Pursue Our Honest Callings': Free Blacks in New York City, 1783-1810," *The Journal of American History,* 75, no. 2 (September 1988), p. 468.

34. Jack D. L. Holmes, "Do It! Don't Do It!: Spanish Laws on Sex and Marriage," in *Louisiana's Legal Heritage,* edited by Edward F. Haas (Pensacola, FL: Published for the Louisiana State Museum by the Perdido Bay Press, 1983), pp. 20-21.

35. Eugene Smith, "Edward Livingston, and the Louisiana Codes," *Columbia Law Review,* 2 (1902), p. 31.

36. Edward Livingston, *A System of Penal Law, for the State of Louisiana* (Philadelphia: James Kay, Jun. & Brother, 1833), p. 17.

37. Ibid., p. 418.

38. Thomas Jefferson to Edward Livingston, March 25, 1825, Thomas Jefferson Papers, LC.

Chapter 7

1. Edward Channing, *The Jeffersonian System* (New York: Harper, 1906), p. 178; Richard Beale Davis, "Introduction" in Augustus John Foster, *Jeffersonian America* (San Marino, CA: Huntington Library, 1954), p. xi; Marshall Smelser, *The Democratic Republic 1801-1815* (New York: Harper Row, 1968), p. 201; Nathan Schachner, *Aaron Burr: A Biography* (New York: Frederick A. Stokes, 1937), p. 285.

2. Quoted in William H. Masterson, *Tories and Democrats: British Diplomats in Pre-Jacksonian America* (College Station, TX: Texas A & M University Press, 1985), p. 73.

3. Masterson, *Tories and Democrats,* p. 75.

4. Dumas Malone, *Jefferson the President, First Term, 1801-1805* (Boston: Little, Brown, 1970), p. 378.

5. Augustus John Foster, *Jeffersonian America,* p. 10.

6. Margaret Bayard Smith, *Forty Years of Washington Society* (London: Fisher Unwin, 1906), pp. 45-46.

7. Malone, *Jefferson the President,* p. 382.

8. Malcolm Lester, *Anthony Merry Redivivus: A Reappraisal of the British Minister to the United States, 1803-6* (Charlottesville: University Press of Virginia, 1978), p. 21.

9. Augustus John Foster to Lady Elizabeth Foster, August 30, 1806, Augustus John Foster Papers, container 2, LC.

10. Lester, *Anthony Merry Redivivus,* p. 123.

11. A. J. Foster to E. Foster, December 30, 1804, Augustus John Foster Papers, container 2, LC.

12. Masterson, *Tories and Democrats,* pp. 153, 162.

13. Ibid., p. 160.

14. Amanda Foreman, *Georgiana, Duchess of Devonshire* (New York: Random House, 1998), p. xvi.

15. Ibid., p. 97.

16. A. J. Foster to E. Foster, December 31, 1805-1 January 1806, Augustus John Foster Papers, LC. (This letter is misfiled in the LC collection, due to a discrepancy in dating.)

17. A. J. Foster to E. Foster, June 2, 1805, Augustus John Foster Papers, container 2, LC.

18. A. J. Foster to E. Foster, August 30, 1806, Augustus John Foster Papers, container 2, LC.

19. Augustus John Foster, Notes on the United States of America, notebook [1] [manuscript], pp. 34-35, HL. [NB: Foster created two manuscript copies of this work, one which is now owned by the Library of Congress, and one now owned by the Huntington Library. The texts differ slightly, at times in important ways.]

20. Ibid., p. 36.

21. A. J. Foster to E. Foster, April 24, 1805, Augustus John Foster Papers, container 2, LC.

22. A. J. Foster to E. Foster, July 30-August 4, 1805, Augustus John Foster Papers, container 2, LC.

23. A. J. Foster to E. Foster, February 15, 1805, Augustus John Foster Papers, container 2, LC.

24. A. J. Foster to E. Foster, October 28, 1806, Augustus John Foster Papers, container 2, LC.

25. Foster, Notes on the United States, notebook [1], pp. 38-39.

26. A. J. Foster to E. Foster, October 5, 1804, Augustus John Foster Papers, LC.

27. A. J. Foster to E. Foster, October 5, 1807, Augustus John Foster Papers, container 3, LC.

28. A. J. Foster to E. Foster, April 25, 1807, Augustus John Foster Papers, container 3, LC.

29. A. J. Foster to E. Foster, December 31, 1805-January 1, 1806, Augustus John Foster Papers, LC. (This letter is misfiled in the LC collection due to a discrepancy in dating.)

30. Edward W. Said, *Orientalism* (New York: Pantheon Books, 1978), p. 8.

31. *Exoticism in the Enlightenment,* edited by G.S. Rousseau and Roy Porter (Manchester: Manchester University Press, 1990), p. 4.

32. Roger Austin, *Genteel Pagan: The Double Life of Charles Warren Stoddard* (Amherst: University of Massachusetts Press, 1991), p. 51.

33. Theodore Winthrop, *John Brent* (Boston: Ticknor and Fields, 1862), p. 38.

34. Leslie A. Fiedler, *Love and Death in the American Novel* (Normal, IL: Dalkey Archive Press, 1997), p. 192.

35. John W. Hallock, *The American Byron: Homosexuality and the Fall of Fitz-Greene Halleck* (Madison: University of Wisconsin Press, 2000), pp. 38-39.

36. Roy Porter, "The Exotic As Erotic: Captain Cook at Tahiti," in *Exoticism in the Enlightenment,* p. 118.

37. August John Foster, Notes on the United States of America, notebook [2] [manuscript], pp. 58-59, LC. [NB: Foster created two manuscript copies of this work, one which is now owned by the Library of Congress, and one now owned by the Huntington Library. The texts differ slightly, at times in important ways.]

38. Ibid., p. 61.

39. Foster, *Jeffersonian America,* pp. 34-35.

40. George Catlin, *Letters and Notes on the Manners, Customs, and Conditions of the North American Indians* (New York: Dover Publications, 1973), vol. 2, pp. 214-215.

41. Walter L. Williams, *The Spirit and the Flesh: Sexual Diversity in American Indian Culture* (Boston: Beacon Press, 1986), pp. 107-108. In a note Williams credits Paul Voorhis and Raymond DeMallie for establishing that the sentence is not in the Sac and Fox nor Dakota language.

42. Catlin, *Letters and Notes,* p. 215.

43. A. J. Foster to E. Foster, December 27, 1805, Augustus John Foster Papers, container 2, LC.

44. Foster, Notes on the United States, pp. 64-65, LC.

45. Ibid., p. 65.

46. Ibid., p. 71.

47. A. J. Foster to E. Foster, March 10, 1806, Augustus John Foster Papers, container 2, LC.

48. Foster, Notes on the United States, pp. 68-69, LC.

49. Ibid., p. 69.

50. A. J. Foster to E. Foster, March 27, 1806, Augustus John Foster Papers, container 2, LC.

51. A. J. Foster to E. Foster, February 1, 1806, Augustus John Foster Papers, container 2, LC.

52. A. J. Foster to E. Foster, March 25, 1806, Augustus John Foster Papers, container 2, LC.

53. Ibid. [I am indebted to Massimiliano Carocci for his help in translating Foster's poor Italian.]

54. A. J. Foster to E. Foster, July 20, 1806, Augustus John Foster Papers, container 2, LC.

55. A. J. Foster to E. Foster, January 2, 1812, Augustus John Foster Papers, container 3, LC.

56. Quoted in Masterson, *Tories and Democrats,* p. 166.

57. *The Dictionary of National Biography,* edited by Sir Leslie Stephen and Sir Sidney Lee (London: Oxford University Press, 1949-1950), p. 492.

58. A. J. Foster to E. Foster, March 10, 1806, Augustus John Foster Papers, container 2, LC.

59. Gamaliel Bradford, *Damaged Souls* (Boston: Houghton Mifflin, 1923), pp. 153-154.

60. Thomas P. Cope, *Philadelphia Merchant: The Diary of Thomas P. Cope, 1800-1851*, edited by Eliza Cope Harrison (South Bend, IN: Gateway Editions, 1978), p. 259.

61. Daniel Mallory, *Short Stories and Reminiscences of the Last Fifty Years* (New York: D. Mallory; Philadelphia: Carey & Hart, 1842), pp. 111-122.

62. Quoted in William Cabell Bruce, *John Randolph of Roanoke, 1773-1833* (New York: G.P. Putnam's Sons, 1922), vol. 2, pp. 605-606.

63. Ibid., vol. 1, p. 324.

64. Ibid., vol. 2, p. 600.

65. Quoted in Malone, *Jefferson the President*, p. 444.

66. Hugh A. Garland, *The Life of John Randolph of Roanoke* (New York: Greenwood Press, 1969), p. 11.

67. Quoted in Garland, *The Life of John Randolph of Roanoke*, p. 11.

68. Bruce, *John Randolph of Roanoke, 1773-1833*, vol. 2, p. 350.

69. Quoted in Bruce, *John Randolph of Roanoke, 1773-1833*, vol. 2, p. 499.

70. Quoted in Garland, *The Life of John Randolph of Roanoke*, p. 344.

71. John Randolph, *Collected Letters of John Randolph of Roanoke to Dr. John Brockenbrough, 1812-1833*, edited by Kenneth Shorey (New Brunswick, NJ: Transaction Book, 1988), p. 22.

72. Quoted in Bruce, *John Randolph of Roanoke, 1773-1833*, vol. 1, p. 127.

73. Ibid., vol. 1, p. 135.

74. Ibid., vol. 2, p. 546.

75. Bruce, *John Randolph of Roanoke, 1773-1833*, vol. 2, pp. 592-593.

76. William Ewart Stokes, "Randolph of Roanoke: A Virginia Portrait, the Early Career of John Randolph of Roanoke, 1773-1805," doctoral dissertation, University of Virginia, 1955.

77. Quoted in Bruce, *John Randolph of Roanoke, 1773-1833*, vol. 2, pp. 417-419.

78. Ibid., vol. II, p. 315.

79. Bruce, *John Randolph of Roanoke, 1773-1833*, vol. 2, p. 344.

80. Quoted in Robert Dawidoff, *The Education of John Randolph* (New York: Norton, 1979), p. 53.

81. *Collected Letters of John Randolph of Roanoke*, p. 68.

82. Quoted in Dawidoff, *The Education of John Randolph*, p. 30.

83. Ibid., p. 273.

84. Elijah H. Mills, as quoted in Bruce, *John Randolph of Roanoke, 1773-1833*, vol. 2, pp. 409-410.

85. Bruce, *John Randolph of Roanoke, 1773-1833*, vol. 2, p. 365.

86. Quoted in Bruce, *John Randolph of Roanoke, 1773-1833*, vol. 2, pp. 320-321.

87. Quoted in Dawidoff, *The Education of John Randolph*, p. 63.

88. Stokes, "Randolph of Roanoke," pp. 297-298.

89. Bruce, *John Randolph of Roanoke, 1773-1833*, vol. 2, p. 319.

90. Robert Dawidoff, "Randolph, John," in *American National Biography*, general editors, John A. Garraty, Mark C. Carnes (New York: Oxford University Press, 1999), vol. 18, p. 131.

91. Stephen E. Ambrose, *Undaunted Courage: Meriwether Lewis, Thomas Jefferson, and the Opening of the American West* (New York: Touchstone, 1997), p. 65.

92. Michael Durey, *"With the Hammer of Truth": James Thomson Callender and America's Early National Heroes* (Charlottesville: University Press of Virginia, 1990), p. 154.

93. Ibid., p. 146.

94. Richmond (Va.) *Recorder,* vol. 1, no. 47 (May 26, 1802).

95. Kim Tousley Phillips, *William Duane, Radical Journalist in the Age of Jefferson* (New York: Garland Publishing, 1989), p. 29.

96. Richmond (Va.) *Recorder,* vol. 2, no. 71 (November 10, 1802).

97. Quoted in Martin Duberman, "'Writhing Bedfellows': Two Young Men from Antebellum South Carolina's Ruling Elite Share 'Extravagant Delight,'" *Journal of Homosexuality,* 6, no. 12 (Fall/Winter 1980/81), p. 87.

98. Richmond (Va.) *Recorder,* vol. 2, no. 72 (November 17, 1802).

99. Richmond (Va.) *Examiner,* vol. 3, no. 463 (July 6, 1803).

Chapter 8

1. Benjamin Rush, *Medical Inquiries and Observations, Upon the Diseases of the Mind* (Philadelphia: Kimber & Richardson, 1812), p. 351.

2. Ibid., p. 355.

3. Sam Bass Warner Jr., *The Private City: Philadelphia in Three Periods of Its Growth* (Philadelphia: University of Pennsylvania Press, 1987), p. 19.

4. Clare Anna Lyons, "Sex Among the 'Rabble': Gender Transitions in the Age of Revolution, Philadelphia, 1750-1830," doctoral dissertation, Yale University, 1996, p. 181.

5. Ibid., p. 413.

6. Ibid., pp. 187-188.

7. Ibid., p. 19.

8. Quoted in Peter Thompson, "A Social History of Philadelphia's Taverns, 1683-1800," doctoral dissertation, University of Pennsylvania, 1989, p. 78.

9. Geoffrey May, *Social Control of Sex Expression* (New York: William Morrow, 1931), p. 247.

10. Quoted in Henry Sprogle, *The Philadelphia Police, Past and Present* (Philadelphia: [s.n.], 1887), pp. 31-33.

11. For a general discussion of drinking culture in early America, with references to Philadelphia, see W. J. Rorabaugh, *The Alcoholic Republic: An American Tradition* (New York: Oxford University Press, 1979). For a discussion of the practice of giving toasts as a political statement, see Richard J. Hooker, "The American Revolution Seen Through a Wine Glass," *William and Mary Quarterly,* Third Series, 11, no. 1 (January 1954), pp. 52-77.

12. *Pennsylvania Gazette,* August 8, 1787.

13. John F. Wallace Collection, "Ancient Records," December 4, 1704, HSP, quoted in Stephen J. Rosswurm, "Arms, Culture and Class: The Philadelphia Militia and the 'Lower Orders' in the American Revolution," doctoral dissertation, University of Pennsylvania, 1975, p. 52.

14. Thompson, "A Social History of Philadelphia's Taverns, 1683-1800," p. 114; see also John Fanning Watson, *Annals of Philadelphia and Pennsylvania in the Olden Time* (Philadelphia: E. Thomas, 1857), p. 307.

15. Gottlieb Mittelberger, *Gottlieb Mittelberger's Journey to Pennsylvania in the Year 1750,* translated by Carl Theo Eben (Philadelphia: John Joseph McVey, 1898), p. 63.

16. Warner, *The Private City,* pp. 16-19.

17. Quoted in Sprogle, *The Philadelphia Police, Past and Present,* p. 42.

18. G.S. Rowe and Billy G. Smith, "Prisoners: The Prisoners for Trial Docket and the Vagrancy Docket," in *Life in Early Philadelphia: Documents from the Revolutionary and Early National Periods,* edited by Billy G. Smith (University Park, PA: Pennsylvania State University Press, 1995), p. 59; see also Michael Meranze, *Laboratories of Virtue: Punishment, Revolution, and Authority in Philadelphia, 1760-1835* (Chapel Hill: University of North Carolina Press, 1996), p. 83.

19. Lyons, "Sex Among the 'Rabble,'" p. 188.

20. Rowe and Smith, "Prisoners," p. 78.

21. Allen Steinberg, *The Transformation of Criminal Justice, Philadelphia, 1800-1880* (Chapel Hill: University of North Carolina Press, 1989), p. 124.

22. Leslie C. Patrick Stamp, "The Prison Sentence Docket for 1795: Inmates at the Nation's First State Penitentiary," *Pennsylvania History,* 60 (1993), p. 366.

23. Meranze, *Laboratories of Virtue,* pp. 21, 78-79.

24. William Bradford, *An Enquiry How Far the Punishment of Death is Necessary in Pennsylvania* (Philadelphia: Printed by T. Dobson, 1793), pp. 20-21.

25. Ibid., p. 21.

26. Elizabeth Drinker, *Extracts from the Journal of Elizabeth Drinker, from 1759 to 1807, A.D.,* edited by Henry D. Biddle (Philadelphia: Lippincott, 1889), p. 264.

27. Ibid., p. 266.

28. Ibid., pp. 297-298.

29. Ibid., p. 297.

30. Alexander Hamilton, *The History of the Ancient and Honorable Tuesday Club,* edited by Robert Micklus (Chapel Hill: University of North Carolina Press, 1990), vol. 1, p. xvii.

31. Quoted in Elaine G. Breslaw, "Wit, Whimsy, and Politics: The Uses of Satire by the Tuesday Club of Annapolis, 1744-1756," *William and Mary Quarterly,* Third Series, 32, no. 2 (April 1975), p. 299.

32. For a fuller discussion of these parallels see Breslaw, "Wit, Whimsy, and Politics," pp. 300-302.

33. Hamilton, *History,* vol. 1, p. 150.

34. Ibid., p. 190.

35. Quoted in Hamilton, *History,* vol. 1, p. lxxxiv.

36. Paul Goodman, *Toward a Christian Republic: Antimasonry and the Great Transition in New England, 1826-1836* (New York: Oxford University Press, 1988), pp. 3-4.

37. Steven C. Bullock, *Revolutionary Brotherhood: Freemasonry and the Transformation of the American Social Order, 1730-1840* (Chapel Hill: University of North Carolina Press, 1996), p. 4.

38. Mark C. Carnes, *Secret Ritual and Manhood in Victorian America* (New Haven, CT: Yale University Press, 1989), p. 120.

39. Thaddeus Mason Harris, *A Discourse, Delivered at Bridgewater November 3, 1797: At the Request of the Members of Fellowship Lodge* (Boston: Printed by Samuel Hall, 1797), p. 8.

40. William Bentley, *A Discourse, Delivered in Roxbury, October 12, 5796* [sic]: *Before the Grand Lodge of Free and Accepted Masons in the Commonwealth of Massachusetts* (Boston: William Spotswood, 1796), pp. 8, 11.

41. Ibid., p. 16.

42. Ronald P. Formisano, with Kathleen Smith Kutolowski, "Antimasonry and Masonry: The Genesis of Protest, 1826-1827," *American Quarterly,* 29, no. 2 (Summer 1977), p. 143.

43. Paul Goodman, *Toward a Christian Republic,* p. 83.

44. Illustration reproduced in Bullock, *Revolutionary Brotherhood,* p. 27.

45. Quoted in Bullock, *Revolutionary Brotherhood,* p. 80.

46. Ibid.

47. For an extended discussion of this newspaper entry, see Thomas A. Foster, "Antimasonic Satire, Sodomy, and Eighteenth-Century Masculinity in the Boston Evening-Post," *William and Mary Quarterly,* Third Series, 60, no. 1 (January 2003), pp. 171-184.

48. *Boston Evening-Post,* January 7, 1751, with minor correction to the last line, mistranscribed in Foster.

49. Sean Wilentz, *Chants Democratic: New York City & the Rise of the American Working Class, 1788-1850* (New York: Oxford University Press, 1986), p. 88.

50. Goodman, *Toward a Christian Republic,* pp. 24, 54, 59, 83-85; David Brion Davis, "Some Themes of Counter-Subversion: An Analysis of Anti-Masonic, Anti-Catholic, and Anti-Mormon Literature," *The Mississippi Valley Historical Review,* 47, no. 2 (September 1960), p. 222.

51. For discussion of the gender implications of Masonic membership, see Goodman, *Toward a Christian Republic,* pp. 16-17, 80-102.

Chapter 9

1. Quoted in Rosabeth Moss Kanter, "Commitment and Social Organization: A Study of Commitment Mechanisms in Utopian Communities," *American Sociological Review,* 33, no. 4 (August 1968), p. 515.

2. Ibid., p. 508.

3. Louis J. Kern, *An Ordered Love: Sex Roles and Sexuality in Victorian Utopias, the Shakers, the Mormons, and the Oneida Community* (Chapel Hill: University of North Carolina Press, 1981), p. 132.

4. Abigail Alcott, Diary, July 2, 1843, quoted in Richard Francis, "Circumstances and Salvation: The Ideology of the Fruitlands Utopia," *American Quarterly,* 25, no. 2 (May 1973), p. 224.

5. Kern, *An Ordered Love,* pp. 83-84.

6. Ibid., pp. 81-82.

7. Diane Sasson, *The Shaker Spiritual Narrative* (Knoxville: University of Tennessee Press, 1983), pp. 36-37.

8. Quoted in Sasson, *The Shaker Spiritual Narrative,* pp. 48-49.

9. Kern, *An Ordered Love,* p. 89.

10. Ibid., p. 94.

11. Quoted in Stephen J. Stein, *The Shaker Experience in America: A History of the United Society of Believers* (New Haven, CT: Yale University Press, 1992), p. 155.

12. Ibid.

13. Kern, *An Ordered Love*, p. 100.

14. Lawrence Foster, *Religion and Sexuality: Three American Communal Experiments of the Nineteenth Century* (New York: Oxford University Press, 1981), p. 56.

15. Kern, *An Ordered Love*, p. 104.

16. Wilford Woodruff, *Wilford Woodruff's Journal, 1833-1898: A Typescript*, edited by Scott G. Kenney (Midvale, UT: Signature Books, 1983), vol. 2, p. 227.

17. Quoted in D. Michael Quinn, *Same-Sex Dynamics Among Nineteenth-Century Americans: A Mormon Example* (Urbana: University of Illinois Press, 1996), p. 136.

18. Ibid.

19. *The Wasp* (Nauvoo, Illinois), July 27, 1849 ("Extra").

20. Ibid.

21. *The Words of Joseph Smith: The Contemporary Accounts of the Nauvoo Discourses of the Prophet Joseph,* compiled and edited by Andrew F. Ehat and Lyndon W. Cook (Provo, UT: Religious Studies Center, Brigham Young University, 1980), p. 156.

22. For a fuller description of modern interpretations of the story of Sodom, see John Boswell, *Christianity, Social Tolerance and Homosexuality: Gay People in Western Europe from the Beginning of the Christian Era to the Fourteenth Century* (Chicago: University of Chicago Press, 1980), pp. 92-98.

23. Kern, *An Ordered Love*, p. 209.

24. John H. Noyes, *Confessions of John H. Noyes, Part I, Confession of Religious Experience, Including a History of Modern Perfectionism* (Oneida Reserve: Leonard & Company Printers, 1849), pp. 16, 11.

25. *Religious Experience of John Humphrey Noyes, Founder of the Oneida Community,* compiled and edited by George Wallingford Noyes (New York: Macmillan, 1923), p. 190.

26. Noyes, *Confessions*, p. 66.

27. Ibid., p. 67.

28. Ibid.

29. *Religious Experience*, pp. 103, 110.

30. Quoted in Foster, *Religion and Sexuality*, pp. 79-80.

31. Foster, *Religion and Sexuality*, p. 88.

32. Noyes, *Confessions*, p. 42.

33. Quoted in Kern, *An Ordered Love*, p. 215.

34. John Humphrey Noyes, *The Berean: A Manual for the Help of Those Who Seek the Faith of the Primitive Church* (Putney, VT: Published at the Office of the Spiritual Magazine, 1847), pp. 57-58.

35. John Humphrey Noyes, *Home-talks* (Oneida: Published by the Community, 1875), p. 165.

36. Quoted in Spencer C. Olin Jr., "The Oneida Community and the Instability of Charismatic Authority," *The Journal of American History*, 67, no. 2 (Sept. 1980), p. 291.

37. Foster, *Religion and Sexuality*, p. 94.

38. Quoted in Kern, *An Ordered Love*, p. 55.

Chapter 10

1. Quoted in Wesley S. Griswold, *The Night the Revolution Began: The Boston Tea Party, 1773* (Brattleboro, VT: Stephen Greene Press, 1972), pp. 93, 95.
2. Ibid., p. 96.
3. Quoted in Alfred F. Young, *The Shoemaker and the Tea Party: Memory and the American Revolution* (Boston: Beacon Press, 1999), p. 43.
4. Quoted in Griswold, *The Night the Revolution Began,* pp. 105-106.
5. Griswold, *The Night the Revolution Began,* p. 92.
6. Susan E. Klepp, "Revolutionary Bodies: Women and the Fertility Transition in the Mid-Atlantic Region, 1760-1820," *The Journal of American History,* 85, no. 3 (December 1998), p. 910.
7. Ibid., p. 911.
8. Quoted in Vincent J. Bertolini, "Fireside Chastity: The Erotics of Sentimental Bachelorhood in the 1850s," *American Literature,* 68, no. 4 (December 1996), p. 715.
9. Christopher Newfield, *The Emerson Effect: Individualism and Submission in America* (Chicago: University of Chicago Press, 1996), p. 93.
10. John Adams, *Familiar Letters of John Adams and His Wife Abigail Adams, During the Revolution* (New York: Hurd and Houghton, 1876), p. 185.
11. Quoted in David Waldstreicher, "Rites of Rebellion, Rites of Assent: Celebrations, Print Culture, and the Origins of American Nationalism," *The Journal of American History,* 82, no. 1 (June 1995), p. 55.
12. Robert B. Shoemaker, "The London 'Mob' in the Early Eighteenth Century," *Journal of British Studies,* 26, no. 3 (July 1987), p. 290.
13. Natalie Zemon Davis, "Women on Top: Symbolic Sexual Inversion and Political Disorder in Early Modern Europe," in *The Reversible World: Symbolic Inversion in Art and Society,* edited by Barbara A. Babcock (Ithaca, NY: Cornell University Press, 1978), pp. 165-166.
14. Ibid., pp. 167-168.
15. *Wiltshire Archaeological and Natural History Magazine,* 50, no. 179 (1943), pp. 279, 363.
16. D.G.C. Allan, "The Rising in the West, 1628-1631," *The Economic History Review,* New Series, 5, no. 1 (1952), pp. 76-77.
17. George F. E. Rudé, *The Crowd in History: A Study of Popular Disturbances in France and England, 1730-1848* (London: Lawrence and Wishart, 1981), p. 157.
18. Ibid., p. 162.
19. For the most extensive discussion, see Davis, "Women on Top," pp. 177-182.
20. Staughton Lynd, *Anti-Federalism in Dutchess County, New York: A Study of Democracy and Class Conflict in the Revolutionary Era* (Chicago: Loyola University Press, 1962), pp. 37-38.
21. Henry Christman, *Tin Horns and Calico: A Decisive Episode in the Emergence of Democracy* (New York: Henry Holt, 1945), p. 75.
22. Quoted in Christman, *Tin Horns and Calico,* p. 81.
23. Davis, "Women on Top," pp. 152-153.
24. Loretta T. Johnson, "Charivari/Shivaree: A European Folk Ritual on the American Plains," *Journal of Interdisciplinary History,* 20, no. 3 (Winter 1990), pp. 371-387.

25. Quoted in Peter Shaw, *American Patriots and the Rituals of the Revolution* (Cambridge, MA: Harvard University Press, 1981), p. 191.

26. Ibid.

27. Quoted in David Waldstreicher, "Rites of Rebellion, Rites of Assent," p. 55.

28. Shaw, *American Patriots and the Rituals of Revolution*, p. 18.

29. For an extensive discussion of chimney sweeps in New York City, see Paul A. Gilje and Howard B. Rock, "'Sweep O! Sweep O!': African-American Chimney Sweeps and Citizenship in the New Nation," *William and Mary Quarterly*, Third Series, 51, no. 3 (July 1994), pp. 507-538. Most chimney sweeps in Boston were white.

30. Shaw, *American Patriots and the Rituals of the Revolution*, pp. 193-194; Alfred F. Young, "George Robert Twelves Hewes (1742-1840): A Boston Shoemaker and the Memory of the American Revolution," *William and Mary Quarterly*, Third Series, 38, no. 4 (October 1981), p. 586; Kirstin Wilcox, "The Body into Print: Marketing Phillis Wheatley," *American Literature*, 71, no. 1 (March 1999), pp. 19-21.

Chapter 11

1. Carroll Smith-Rosenberg, "Davey Crockett As Trickster: Pornography, Liminality and Symbolic Inversion in Victorian America," *Journal of Contemporary History*, 17, no. 2 (April 1982), p. 344.

2. Ibid.

3. Ibid., p. 331.

4. Ibid., p. 350.

5. Quoted in Patricia Holbert Menk, "D. M. Erskine: Letters from America, 1798-1799," *William and Mary Quarterly*, Third Series, 6, no. 2 (April 1949), p. 270.

6. Quoted in S.W. Jackman, "A Young Englishman Reports on the New Nation: Edward Thornton to James Bland Burges, 1791-1793," *William and Mary Quarterly*, Third Series, 18, no. 1 (January 1961), p. 115.

7. Quoted in Marilyn Kay Parr, "Augustus John Foster and the 'Washington Wilderness': Personal Letters of a British Diplomat," doctoral dissertation, George Washington University, 1987, p. 147.

8. John Le Couteur, *Merry Hearts Make Light Days: The War of 1812 Journal of Lieutenant John Le Couteur, 104th Foot*, edited by Donald E. Graves (Ottawa: Carleton University Press, 1993), p. 250, and footnote 2, p. 259.

9. I am indebted to Rebecca Dawkins of the Jersey Archive, St. Helier, Isle of Jersey, for examining the original of this manuscript to ascertain that the writing has indeed been obscured to the point that it cannot be read. Personal letter, August 8, 2000.

10. Le Couteur, *Merry Hearts Make Light Days*, p. 250.

11. E. Anthony Rotundo, "Romantic Friendship: Male Intimacy and Middle-Class Youth in the Northern United States, 1800-1900," *Journal of Social History*, 23, no. 1 (Fall 1989), pp. 10-11.

12. Ibid., p. 12.

13. Vincent J. Bertolini, "The Erotics of Sentimental Bachelorhood in the 1850s," *American Literature*, 68, no. 4 (December 1996), p. 716.

14. Frederick Jackson Turner, *The Significance of the Frontier in American History* (Madison: State Historical Society of Wisconsin, 1894).

Bibliography

Manuscript Collections Consulted

Henry Burdick Papers, United States Military Academy Archives
Dreer Collection, Historical Society of Pennsylvania
Augustus John Foster, Notes on the United States of America, Huntington Library
Augustus John Foster, Notes on the United States of America, Library of Congress
Augustus John Foster Papers, Library of Congress
Simon Gratz Collection, Historical Society of Pennsylvania
Thomas Jefferson Papers, Library of Congress
Journals and Diaries, Fort Bellefontaine, Order Book, Missouri Historical Society
Numbered Record Books, Microfilm Series M853, roll 9, vol. 58 (13 March 1782-12 May 1782), National Archives, Washington, DC
Orderly Book of the Corps of Artillerists and Engineers, Commenced at West Point Jan'y lst 1798, United States Military Academy Archives
Friedrich Wilhelm von Steuben Papers, Beinecke Library, Yale University
Friedrich Wilhelm von Steuben Papers, New-York Historical Society
Friedrich Wilhelm von Steuben Papers, Society of the Cincinnati, Washington, DC
Benjamin Walker Papers, Oneida County (NY) Historical Society
George Washington Papers, Library of Congress
Anthony Wayne, General Orders, United States Military Academy Archives

Books and Articles

Adair, James (1968). *The History of the American Indians, Particularly Those Nations Adjoining to the Mississippi, East and West Florida, Georgia, South and North Carolina, and Virginia.* New York: Johnson Reprint Corp.

Adams, John (1876). *Familiar Letters of John Adams and His Wife Abigail Adams, During the Revolution.* New York: Hurd and Houghton.

Alford, Violet (1959). "Rough Music or Charivari." *Folklore,* 70 (December), 505-518.

Allan, D.G.C. (1952). "The Rising in the West, 1628-1631." *The Economic History Review,* New Series, 5(1), 76-85.

Ambrose, Stephen E. (1997). *Undaunted Courage: Meriwether Lewis, Thomas Jefferson, and the Opening of the American West.* New York: Touchstone.

Anderson, Charles R. (1935). "A Reply to Herman Melville's White-Jacket by Rear-Admiral Thomas O. Selfridge, Sr." *American Literature,* 7(2) (May), 123-144.

Andrews, Joseph Gardner (1957). *A Surgeon's Mate at Fort Defiance: The Journal of Joseph Gardner Andrews for the Year 1795,* edited by Richard C. Knopf. Columbus: Ohio Historical Society.

Astruc, Jean (1740). *Traité des Maladies Vénériennes.* Paris: Guillaume Cavelier.

Austin, Roger (1991). *Genteel Pagan: The Double Life of Charles Warren Stoddard.* Amherst: University of Massachusetts Press.

Barnes, Elizabeth (1996). "Affecting Relations, Pedagogy, Patriarchy, and the Politics of Sympathy." *American Literary History,* 8(4) (Winter), 597-614.

Bentley, William (1796). *A Discourse, Delivered in Roxbury, October 12, 5796* [sic]: *Before the Grand Lodge of Free and Accepted Masons in the Commonwealth of Massachusetts.* Boston: William Spotswood.

Berkhofer, Robert F. (1978). *The White Man's Indian: Images of the American Indian from Columbus to the Present.* New York: Alfred A. Knopf.

Berland, K.J.H. (1999). "William Byrd's Sexual Lexicography." *Eighteenth Century Life,* n.s. 23(1) (February), 1-11.

Berlin, Robert Harry (1976). The Administration of Military Justice in the Continental Army During the American Revolution, 1775-1783, doctoral dissertation, University of California, Santa Barbara.

Bertolini, Vincent J. (1996). "Fireside Chastity: The Erotics of Sentimental Bachelorhood in the 1850s," *American Literature,* 68(4) (December), 707-737.

"Books in Williamsburg" (1906). *William and Mary College Quarterly Historical Magazine,* 15(2) (October), 100-113.

Boswell, John (1980). *Christianity, Social Tolerance and Homosexuality: Gay People in Western Europe from the Beginning of the Christian Era to the Fourteenth Century.* Chicago: University of Chicago Press.

Bradford, Gamaliel (1923). *Damaged Souls.* Boston: Houghton Mifflin.

Bradford, William (1793). *An Enquiry How Far the Punishment of Death is Necessary in Pennsylvania.* Philadelphia: Printed by T. Dobson.

Bradford, William (1982). *Of Plymouth Plantation, 1620-1647.* New York: Alfred A. Knopf.

Breslaw, Elaine G. (1975). "Wit, Whimsy, and Politics: The Uses of Satire by the Tuesday Club of Annapolis, 1744-1756." *William and Mary Quarterly,* Third Series, 32(2) (April), 295-306.

Brown, Kathleen M. (1996). *Good Wives, Nasty Wenches, and Anxious Patriarchs: Gender, Race, and Power in Colonial Virginia.* Chapel Hill: University of North Carolina Press.

Bruce, William Cabell (1922). *John Randolph of Roanoke, 1773-1833.* New York: G.P. Putnam's Sons.

Buchan, William (1796). *Observations Concerning the Prevention and Cure of the Venereal Disease.* London: Printed for T. Chapman.

Bullock, Steven C. (1996). *Revolutionary Brotherhood: Freemasonry and the Transformation of the American Social Order, 1730-1840.* Chapel Hill: University of North Carolina Press.

Burg, B.R. (1994). *An American Seafarer in the Age of Sail: The Erotic Diaries of Philip C. Van Buskirk, 1851-1870.* New Haven, CT: Yale University Press.

Caldwell, Norman W. (1955). "The Enlisted Soldier at the Frontier Post, 1790-1814." *Mid-America: An Historical Review,* 37(4) (October), 195-204.

Calhoun, Arthur W. (1917). *A Social History of the American Family,* I: *Colonial Period.* Cleveland: Arthur H. Clark Co.

Callendar, Charles and Lee M. Kochems (1983). "The North American Berdache." *Current Anthropology,* 24(4) (August-October), 443-470.

Carnes, Mark C. (1989). *Secret Ritual and Manhood in Victorian America.* New Haven, CT: Yale University Press.

Carson, Barbara G. (1990). *Ambitious Appetites: Dining, Behavior, and Patterns of Consumption in Federal Washington.* Washington, DC: The American Institute of Architects Press.

Catalogue of the Library of Thomas Jefferson (1955). Compiled with annotations by E. Millicent Sowerby. Washington, DC: The Library of Congress.

Catlin, George (1973). *Letters and Notes on the Manners, Customs, and Conditions of the North American Indians.* New York: Dover Publications.

Channing, Edward (1906). *The Jeffersonian System.* New York: Harper.

Chapin, Bradley (1989). "Felony Law Reform in the Early Republic." *Pennsylvania Magazine of History and Biography,* 113(2) (April), 163-183.

Chastellux, François Jean, marquis de (1963). *Travels in North America in the Years 1780, 1781 and 1782,* a revised translation with introduction and notes by Howard C. Rice Jr. Chapel Hill: University of North Carolina Press.

Christman, Henry (1945). *Tin Horns and Calico: A Decisive Episode in the Emergence of Democracy.* New York: Henry Holt.

Cicero, Marcus Tullius (1752). *Cicero's Epistles to Atticus,* translated by William Guthrie. London: T. Waller.

Clifton, Charles (2001). "Rereading Voices from the Past: Images of Homo-Eroticism in the Slave Narrative." In *The Greatest Taboo: Homosexuality in Black Communities* (pp. 40-49), edited by Delroy Constantine-Simms. Los Angeles: Alyson Books.

Cope, Thomas P. (1978). *Philadelphia Merchant: The Diary of Thomas P. Cope, 1800-1851,* edited by Eliza Cope Harrison. South Bend, IN: Gateway Editions.

Copeland, Thomas (1811). *Observations on Some of the Principle Diseases of the Rectum and Anus.* Philadelphia: A. Finley; Fry and Kammerer.

Copley, Anthony (1989). *Sexual Moralities in France, 1780-1980: New Ideas on the Family, Divorce, and Homosexuality: An Essay on Moral Change.* London: Routledge.

Correspondence of the Van Cortlandt Family of Cortlandt Manor (1977). Compiled and edited by Jacob Judd. Tarrytown, NY: Sleepy Hollow Restorations.

Courouve, Claude (1987). *Les Assemblées de la Manchette: Documents sur l'Amour Masculin au XVIIIe Siècle.* Paris: Courouve.

Coward, D. A. (1980). "Attitudes to Homosexuality in Eighteenth-Century France." *Journal of European Studies,* 10(40) (December), 231-255.

Crèvecoeur, Michel Guillaume (Saint John de) (1964). *Journey into Northern Pennsylvania and the State of New York.* Ann Arbor: University of Michigan Press.

Crockett, Davy (1838-1853). *Davy Crockett's Almanac.* Philadelphia.

Crompton, Louis (1983). "Homophobia in Georgian England." In *Among Men, Among Women: Sociological and Historical Recognition of Homosocial Arrangements* (pp. 235-244), edited by Mattias Duyves et al. Amsterdam: Sociologisch Instituut.

Cronau, Rudolf (1923). *The Army of the American Revolution and Its Organizer.* New York: Rudolf Cronau.

Dana, Richard Henry (1981). *Two Years Before the Mast: A Personal Narrative of Life at Sea.* New York: Penguin Books.

Davenport-Hines, Richard (1990). *Sex, Death and Punishment: Attitudes to Sex and Sexuality in Britain Since the Renaissance.* London: Collins.

Davis, David Brion (1960). "Some Themes of Counter-Subversion: An Analysis of Anti-Masonic, Anti-Catholic, and Anti-Mormon Literature." *The Mississippi Valley Historical Review,* 47(2) (September), 205-224.

Davis, Natalie Zemon (1978). "Women on Top: Symbolic Sexual Inversion and Political Disorder in Early Modern Europe." In *The Reversible World: Symbolic Inversion in Art and Society* (pp. 147-190), edited by Barbara A. Babcock. Ithaca, NY: Cornell University Press.

Dawidoff, Robert (1979). *The Education of John Randolph.* New York: Norton.

Dawidoff, Robert (1999). "Randolph, John," in *American National Biography* (Vol. 18, pp. 129-131), general editors, John A. Garraty, Mark C. Carnes. New York: Oxford University Press.

Deitchur, David (2001). *Dear Friends: American Photographs of Men Together, 1840-1918.* New York: Harry N. Abrams.

Delon, Michel (1985). "The Priest, the Philosopher, and Homosexuality in Enlightenment France." In *Unauthorized Sexual Behavior During the Enlightenment,* edited by Robert P. Maccubbin, a special issue of *Eighteenth Century Life,* n.s., 9(3) (May), 122-131.

The Dictionary of National Biography (1949-1950). Edited by Sir Leslie Stephen and Sir Sidney Lee. London: Oxford University Press.

Drinker, Elizabeth (1889). *Extracts from the Journal of Elizabeth Drinker, from 1759 to 1807, A.D.,* edited by Henry D. Biddle. Philadelphia: Lippincott.

Duberman, Martin (1980-1981). "'Writhing Bedfellows': Two Young Men from Antebellum South Carolina's Ruling Elite Share 'Extravagant Delight.'" *Journal of Homosexuality,* 6(12) (Fall/Winter), 85-101.

Durey, Michael (1990). *"With the Hammer of Truth": James Thomson Callender and America's Early National Heroes.* Charlottesville: University Press of Virginia.

Ellison, Julie (1992). "The Gender of Transparency: Masculinity and the Conduct of Life." *American Literary History,* 4(4) (Winter), 584-606.

Engle, Gary D. (1978). *This Grotesque Essence: Plays from the American Minstrel Stage.* Baton Rouge: Louisiana State University Press.

Falck, Nikolai Deflef (1772). *A Treatise on the Venereal Disease.* London: The Author.

"The Female Sailor" [song sheet]. [Boston: L. Deming, n.d.], in *America Singing: Nineteenth-Century Song Sheets Collection,* Library of Congress.

Fiedler, Leslie A. (1997). *Love and Death in the American Novel.* Normal, IL: Dalkey Archive Press.

Fischer, Kirsten (2002). *Suspect Relations: Sex, Race, and Resistance in Colonial North Carolina.* Ithaca, NY: Cornell University Press.

Fleta (1955). Edited with a translation by H.G. Richardson and G.O. Sayles. London: Bernard Quaritch for the Selden Society.

Foreman, Amanda (1998). *Georgiana, Duchess of Devonshire.* New York: Random House.

Formisano, Ronald P. with Kathleen Smith Kutolowski (1977). "Antimasonry and Masonry: The Genesis of Protest, 1826-1827." *American Quarterly,* 29(2) (Summer), 139-165.

Foster, Augustus John (1954). *Jeffersonian America.* San Marino, CA: Huntington Library.

Foster, Lawrence (1981). *Religion and Sexuality: Three American Communal Experiments of the Nineteenth Century.* New York: Oxford University Press.

Foster, Thomas A. (2003). "Antimasonic Satire, Sodomy, and Eighteenth-Century Masculinity in the Boston Evening-Post." *William and Mary Quarterly,* 60(1) (January), 171-184.

Foucault, Michel (1978-1986). *The History of Sexuality.* New York: Pantheon Books.

Foucault, Michel (1995). *Discipline and Punish: The Birth of the Prison.* New York: Vintage Books.

Francis, Richard (1973). "Circumstances and Salvation: The Ideology of the Fruitlands Utopia." *American Quarterly,* 25(2) (May), 202-234.

Fulton, Robert and Steven W. Anderson (1992). "The Amerindian 'Man-Woman': Gender, Liminality, and Cultural Continuity." *Current Anthropology,* 33(5) (December), 603-610.

Garland, Hugh A. (1969). *The Life of John Randolph of Roanoke.* New York: Greenwood Press.

A General History of the Americans: Of Their Customs, Manners, and Colours (1806). Selected by Daniel Webb. Rochdale, [Eng.], Printed by and for T. Wood.

Gilfoyle, Thomas J. (1992). *City of Eros: New York City, Prostitution, and the Commercialization of Sex, 1790-1920.* New York: Norton.

Gilje, Paul A. and Howard B. Rock (1994). "'Sweep O! Sweep O!': African-American Chimney Sweeps and Citizenship in the New Nation." *William and Mary Quarterly,* Third Series, 51(3) (July), 507-538.

Glenn, Myra C. (1983). "The Naval Reform Campaign Against Flogging: A Case Study in Changing Attitudes Toward Corporal Punishment, 1830-1850." *American Quarterly,* 35(4) (Autumn), 408-425.

Godbeer, Richard (1995). "'The Cry of Sodom': Discourse, Intercourse, and Desire in Colonial New England." *William and Mary Quarterly,* Third Series, 52(2) (April), 259-286.

Goldsmith, Netta Murray (1998). *The Worst of Crimes: Homosexuality and the Law in Eighteenth-Century London.* Aldershot: Ashgate.

Goodman, Paul (1988). *Toward a Christian Republic: Antimasonry and the Great Transition in New England, 1826-1836.* New York: Oxford University Press.

Griswold, Wesley S. (1972). *The Night the Revolution Began: The Boston Tea Party, 1773.* Brattleboro, VT : Stephen Greene Press.

Hagemann, Karen (1997). "Of 'Manly Valor' and 'German Honor': Nation, War, and Masculinity in the Age of the Prussian Uprising Against Napoleon." *Central European History,* 30(2) (June), 187-220.

Haggerty, George E. (2000). "'What Is This Secret Sin?': Sexuality and Secrecy in the Writings of Horace Walpole." In *Passionate Encounters in a Time of Sensibility* (pp. 127-149), edited by Maximillian E. Novak and Anne Mellor. Newark: University of Delaware Press.

Hallock, John W. (2000). *The American Byron: Homosexuality and the Fall of Fitz-Greene Halleck.* Madison: University of Wisconsin Press.

Halperin, David M. (1998). "Forgetting Foucault: Acts, Identities, and the History of Sexuality." *Representations,* 63 (Summer), 93-120.

Halttunen, Karen (1995). "Humanitarianism and the Pornography of Pain in Anglo-American Culture." *The American Historical Review,* 100(2) (April), 303-334.

Hamilton, Alexander (1990). *The History of the Ancient and Honorable Tuesday Club,* edited by Robert Micklus. Chapel Hill: University of North Carolina Press.

"The Handsome Cabin Boy" [song sheet]. [New York: H. De Marsan, n.d.], in *America Singing: Nineteenth-Century Song Sheets Collection,* Library of Congress.

Hare, John S. (1940). "Military Punishments in the War of 1812." *The Journal of the American Military History Institute,* 4(4) (Winter), 225-239.

Harris, Thaddeus Mason (1797). *A Discourse, Delivered at Bridgewater November 3, 1797: At the Request of the Members of Fellowship Lodge.* Boston: Printed by Samuel Hall.

"Harry Bluff" [song sheet]. [New York: H. De Marsan, n.d.], in *America Singing: Nineteenth-Century Song Sheets Collection,* Library of Congress.

Hening, William Waller (1795). *The New Virginia Justice: Comprising the Office and Authority of Justice of the Peace, in the Commonwealth of Virginia.* Richmond: Printed by T. Nicolson.

"Historical United States Census Data Browser," made available on the Internet at fisher.lib.virginia.edu/collections/stats/histcensus by the Inter-University Consortium for Political and Social Research, Ann Arbor, MI.

Hoganson, Kristin (1993). "Garrisonian Abolitionists and the Rhetoric of Gender, 1850-1860." *American Quarterly,* 45(4) (December), 558-595.

Hollick, Frederick (1852). A *Popular Treatise on Venereal Diseases in All Their Forms.* New York: T.W. Strong.

Holmes, Jack D. L. (1983). "Do It! Don't Do It!: Spanish Laws on Sex and Marriage." In *Louisiana's Legal Heritage* (pp. 19-42), edited by Edward F. Haas. Pensacola, FL: Published for the Louisiana State Museum by the Perdido Bay Press.

Hooker, Richard J. (1954). "The American Revolution Seen Through a Wine Glass." *William and Mary Quarterly,* Third Series, 11(1) (January), 52-77.

Ingersoll, Thomas N. (1999). *Mammon and Manon in Early New Orleans: The First Slave Society in the Deep South, 1718-1819.* Knoxville: University of Tennessee Press.

Jabour, Anya (1998). "Masculinity and Adolescence in Antebellum America: Robert Wirt at West Point, 1820-1821." *Journal of Family History,* 23(4) (October), 393-416.

Jabour, Anya (2000). "Male Friendship and Masculinity in the Early National South: William Wirt and His Friends." *Journal of the Early Republic,* 20 (Spring), 83-111.

Jackman, S. W. (1961). "A Young Englishman Reports on the New Nation: Edward Thornton to James Bland Burges, 1791-1793." *William and Mary Quarterly,* Third Series, 18(1) (January), 85-121.

Jacobs, Harriet A. (2000). *Incidents in the Life of a Slave Girl, Written by Herself.* Cambridge, MA: Harvard University Press.

Johnson, Loretta T. (1990). "Charivari/Shivaree: A European Folk Ritual on the American Plains." *Journal of Interdisciplinary History,* 20(3) (Winter), 371-387.

"The Jolly Young Waterman" [song sheet]. [New York: H. De Marsan, 1860], in *America Singing: Nineteenth-Century Song Sheets Collection,* Library of Congress.

Jordon, Winthrop D. (1968). *White Over Black: American Attitudes Toward the Negro, 1550-1812.* New York: Norton.

Journals of the Lewis & Clark Expedition (1983-2001). Gary E. Moulton, editor. Lincoln: University of Nebraska Press.

Kann, Mark E. (1991). *On the Man Question: Gender and Civic Virtue in America.* Philadelphia: Temple University Press.

Kanter, Rosabeth Moss (1968). "Commitment and Social Organization: A Study of Commitment Mechanisms in Utopian Communities." *American Sociological Review,* 33(4) (August), 499-517.

Karlen, Arno (1971). *Sexuality and Homosexuality: A New View.* New York: Norton.

Katz, Jonathan (Ed.) (1976). *Gay American History: Lesbian and Gay Men in the U.S.A., a Documentary.* New York: Thomas Y. Crowell.

Katz, Jonathan Ned (2001). *Love Stories: Sex Between Men Before Stonewall.* Chicago: University of Chicago Press.

Kennedy, John P. (1854). *Memoirs of the Life of William Wirt, Attorney-General of the United States.* Philadelphia: Blanchard and Lea.

Kern, Louis J. (1981). *An Ordered Love: Sex Roles and Sexuality in Victorian Utopias, the Shakers, the Mormons, and the Oneida Community.* Chapel Hill: University of North Carolina Press.

The Key (1798). (Fredericktown, MD), 1(14) (April 14). Printed by John D. Cary.

Kinsey, Alfred, Wardell B. Pomeroy, and Clyde E. Martin (1948). *Sexual Behavior in the Human Male.* Philadelphia: W.B. Saunders.

Klepp, Susan E. (1998). "Revolutionary Bodies: Women and the Fertility Transition in the Mid-Atlantic Region, 1760-1820." *The Journal of American History,* 85(3) (December), 910-945.

Koch, Cynthia M. (1991). The Virtuous Curriculum: Schoolbooks and American Culture, 1785-1830, doctoral dissertation, University of Pennsylvania.

Krockow, Christian, Graf von (1996). *Die Preußischen Brüder: Prinz Heinrich und Friedrich der Große: ein Doppelportrait.* Stuttgart: Deutsche Verlags-Anstalt.

Kverndal, Roald (1986). *Seamen's Missions: Their Origin and Early Growth, a Contribution to the History of the Church Maritime.* Pasadena, CA: William Carey Library.

Langley, Harold D. (1967). *Social Reform in the United States Navy, 1798-1862.* Urbana: University of Illinois Press.

Lavery, Brian (Ed.) (1998). *Shipboard Life and Organisation, 1731-1815.* Aldershot: Ashgate.

"Laws of Virginia, October 1792" (1835). In *The Statutes at Large of Virginia* (pp. [3]-202), [compiled] by Samuel Shepherd. Richmond: Samuel Shepherd.

Le Couteur, John (1993). *Merry Hearts Make Light Days: The War of 1812 Journal of Lieutenant John Le Couteur, 104th Foot,* edited by Donald E. Graves. Ottawa: Carleton University Press.

Lemay, J. A. Leo (1976). "The American Origins of 'Yankee Doodle.'" *William and Mary Quarterly,* Third Series, 33(3) (July), 435-464.

Lester, Malcolm (1978). *Anthony Merry Redivivus: A Reappraisal of the British Minister to the United States, 1803-6.* Charlottesville: University Press of Virginia.

Letters of the Lewis and Clark Expedition: With Related Documents, 1783-1854 (1978). 2nd ed., edited by Donald Jackson. Urbana: University of Illinois Press.

Litwack, Leon (1979). *Been in the Storm So Long: The Aftermath of Slavery.* New York: Knopf.

Livingston, Edward (1833). *A System of Penal Law, for the State of Louisiana.* Philadelphia: James Kay, Jun. & Brother.

Lockridge, Kenneth A. (1992). *On the Sources of Patriarchal Rage: The Commonplace Books of William Byrd and Thomas Jefferson and the Gendering of Power in the Eighteenth Century.* New York: New York University Press.

Lockridge, Kenneth A. (1997). "Colonial Self-Fashioning: Paradoxes and Pathologies in the Construction of Genteel Identity in Eighteenth-Century America." In *Through a Glass Darkly: Reflections on Personal Identity in Early America* (pp. 274-339), edited by Ronald Hoffman, Mechal Sobel, and Fredrika J. Teute. Chapel Hill: University of North Carolina Press.

Lott, Eric (1991). "'The Seeming Counterfeit': Racial Politics and Early Blackface Minstrelsy." *American Quarterly,* 43(2) (June), 223-254.

Lott, Eric (1992). "Love and Theft: The Racial Unconscious of Blackface Minstrelsy." *Representations,* 39(Summer), 23-50.

Lott, Eric (1993). *Love and Theft: Blackfaced Minstrelsy and the American Working Class.* New York: Oxford University Press.

Lynd, Staughton (1962). *Anti-Federalism in Dutchess County, New York: A Study of Democracy and Class Conflict in the Revolutionary Era.* Chicago: Loyola University Press.

Lyons, Clare A. (1996). Sex Among the "Rabble": Gender Transitions in the Age of Revolution, Philadelphia, 1750-1830, doctoral dissertation, Yale University.

Lyons, Clare A. (2003). "Mapping an Atlantic Sexual Culture: Homoeroticism in Eighteenth-Century Philadelphia." *William and Mary Quarterly,* 60(1) (January), 119-154.

MacDonald, Robert H. (1967). "The Frightful Consequences of Onanism: Notes on the History of a Delusion."*Journal of the History of Ideas,* 28(3) (July-September), 423-431.

Macpherson, James (1805). *The Poems of Ossian, &c.* Edinburgh: James Ballantyne.

Mallory, Daniel (1842). *Short Stories and Reminiscences of the Last Fifty Years.* New York: D. Mallory; Philadelphia: Carey & Hart.

Malone, Dumas (1970). *Jefferson the President, First Term, 1801-1805.* Boston: Little, Brown.

Marten, John (1708). *A Treatise of All the Degrees and Symptoms of the Venereal Disease, in Both Sexes.* 6th ed., corrected and enlarged. London: Printed by and sold by S. Crouch, etc.

Massey, Gregory D. (2000). *John Laurens and the American Revolution.* Columbia: University of South Carolina Press.

Masterson, William H. (1985). *Tories and Democrats: British Diplomats in Pre-Jacksonian America.* College Station: Texas A & M University Press.

May, Geoffrey (1931). *Social Control of Sex Expression.* New York: William Morrow.

McCalman, Iain (1984). "Unrespectable Radicalism: Infidels and Pornography in Early Nineteenth-Century London." *Past and Present*, 104(August), 74-110.

McLaughlin, Jack (1993). "Jefferson, Poe, and Ossian." *Eighteenth-Century Studies*, 26(4) (Summer), 627-634.

Melville, Herman (1986). *Redburn: His First Voyage, Being the Sailor-Boy Confessions and Reminiscences of the Son-of-a-Gentleman, in the Merchant Service.* London: Penguin Books.

Melville, Herman (1990). *White-Jacket, or the World in a Man-of-War.* Oxford: Oxford University Press.

Menk, Patricia Holbert (1949). "D. M. Erskine: Letters from America, 1798-1799." *William and Mary Quarterly*, Third Series, 6(2) (April), 251-284.

Meranze, Michael (1996). *Laboratories of Virtue: Punishment, Revolution, and Authority in Philadelphia, 1760-1835.* Chapel Hill: University of North Carolina Press.

Merrick, Jeffrey (1997). "Sodomitical Inclinations in Early Eighteenth-Century Paris." *Eighteenth-Century Studies*, 30(3), 289-295.

Merrick, Jeffrey (1999). "Sodomitical Scandals and Subcultures in the 1720s." *Men and Masculinities*, 1(4) (April), 365-384.

Middlekauff, Robert (1980). "Why Men Fought in the American Revolution." *The Huntington Library Quarterly*, 43(2) (Spring), 135-148.

Mirabeau, Honoré-Gabriel de Riquetti, comte de (1895). *The Secret History of the Court of Berlin: or The Character of the King of Prussia, His Ministers, Mistresses, Generals, Courtiers, Favourites, and the Royal Family of Prussia.* London: H. S. Nichols.

Mittelberger, Gottlieb (1898). *Gottlieb Mittelberger's Journey to Pennsylvania in the Year 1750*, translated by Carl Theo Eben. Philadelphia: John Joseph McVey.

Moore, Dafydd (2000). "Heroic Incoherence in James Macpherson's The Poems of Ossian." *Eighteenth-Century Studies*, 34(1), 43-59.

Morris, Polly (1989). "Sodomy and Male Honor: The Case of Somerset, 1740-1850." In *The Pursuit of Sodomy: Male Homosexuality in Renaissance and Enlightenment Europe* (pp. 383-406), edited by Kent Gerard and Gert Hekma. Binghamton, NY: Harrington Park Press.

Napier, James (1953). "Some Book Sales in Dumfries, Virginia, 1794-1796." *William and Mary Quarterly*, Third Series, 10(3) (July), 441-445.

Neagles, James C. (Ed.) (1986). *Summer Soldiers: A Survey & Index of Revolutionary War Courts-Martial.* Salt Lake City: Ancestry Incorporated.

Nealon, Christopher (2001). *Foundlings: Lesbian and Gay Historical Emotion Before Stonewall.* Durham, NC: Duke University Press.

Newfield, Christopher (1996). *The Emerson Effect: Individualism and Submission in America.* Chicago: University of Chicago Press.

Norton, Mary Beth (1997). *Founding Mothers & Fathers: Gendered Power and the Forming of American Society.* New York: Vintage Books.

Norton, Rictor (1992). *Mother Clap's Molly House: The Gay Subculture in England 1700-1830.* London: GMP Publishers.

Novak, Maximillian E. and Anne Mellor (Eds.) (2000). *Passionate Encounters in a Time of Sensibility.* Newark: University of Delaware Press.

Noyes, John Humphrey (1847). *The Berean: A Manual for the Help of Those Who Seek the Faith of the Primitive Church.* Putney, VT: Published at the Office of the Spiritual Magazine.

Noyes, John Humphrey (1849). *Confessions of John H. Noyes, Part I, Confession of Religious Experience, Including a History of Modern Perfectionism.* Oneida Reserve: Leonard & Company Printers.

Noyes, John Humphrey (1997). *Home-talks.* Oneida: Published by the Community, 1875.

Ogbom, Miles (1997). "Locating the Macaroni: Luxury, Sexuality and Vision in Vauxhall Gardens." *Textual Practice,* 11(3) (1997), 445-461.

The Old Bachelor (1814). [by William Wirt et al.]. Richmond, VA: Printed at the Enquirer Press, for Thomas Ritchie and Fielding Lucas.

Olin, Spencer C., Jr. (1980). "The Oneida Community and the Instability of Charismatic Authority." *The Journal of American History,* 67(2) (September), 285-300.

Onania, or, The Heinous Sin of Self-Pollution: And All Its Frightful Consequences, in Both Sexes, Consider'd (1730). London: J. Isted.

Palmer, John McAuley (1937). *General von Steuben.* New Haven, CT: Yale University Press.

Parr, Marilyn Kay (1987). Augustus John Foster and the "Washington Wilderness": Personal Letters of a British Diplomat, doctoral dissertation, George Washington University.

Pascalis, Felix (1811?). *Observations and Practical Remarks on the Nature, Progress and Operation of the Venereal Disease.* [New York?].

Pauw, Corneille de (1770). *Recherches Philosophiques sur les Americains, ou Memoires Interessants Pour Servir A l'Histoire de l'Espece Humaine.* London.

Phillips, Kim Tousley (1989). *William Duane, Radical Journalist in the Age of Jefferson.* New York: Garland Publishing.

Porter, Roy (1990). "The Exotic As Erotic: Captain Cook at Tahiti." In *Exoticism in the Enlightenment* (pp. 117-144), edited by G.S. Rousseau and Roy Porter. Manchester: Manchester University Press.

Quinn, D. Michael (1996). *Same-Sex Dynamics Among Nineteenth-Century Americans: A Mormon Example.* Urbana: University of Illinois Press.

Randolph, John (1988). *Collected Letters of John Randolph of Roanoke to Dr. John Brockenbrough, 1812-1833,* edited by Kenneth Shorey. New Brunswick, NJ: Transaction Books.

Rankin, Hugh F. (1973). *Francis Marion: The Swamp Fox.* New York: Crowell.

Religious Experience of John Humphrey Noyes, Founder of the Oneida Community (1923). Compiled and edited by George Wallingford Noyes. New York: Macmillan.

Rey, Michel (1985). "Parisian Homosexuals Create a Lifestyle, 1700-1750: The Police Archives." In *Unauthorized Sexual Behavior During the Enlightenment*, edited by Robert P. Maccubbin, a special issue of *Eighteenth Century Life*, n.s., 9(3) (May), 179-191.

Richter, Simon (1996). "The Ins and Outs of Intimacy: Gender, Epistolary Culture, and the Public Sphere." *The German Quarterly*, 69(2) (Spring), 111-124.

Richter, Simon (1996). "Winckelmann's Progeny: Homosocial Networking in the Eighteenth Century." In *Outing Goethe & His Age* (pp. 33-46), edited by Alice A. Kuzniar. Stanford, CA: Stanford University Press.

Ridley, Jasper (2000). *The Freemasons*. London: Robinson.

Robertson, William (1803). *The History of America*. London: Printed by A. Strahan.

Rockwell, Charles (1842). *Sketches of Foreign Travel and Life at Sea: Including a Cruise on Board a Man-of-War*. Boston: Tappan and Dennet.

Rorabaugh, W.J. (1979). *The Alcoholic Republic: An American Tradition*. New York: Oxford University Press.

Roscoe, Will (1991). *The Zuni Man-Woman*. Albuquerque: University of New Mexico Press.

Rosenberg, Charles E. (1973). "Sexuality, Class and Role in 19th-Century America." *American Quarterly*, 25(2) (May), 131-153.

Rosswurm, Stephen J. (1975). Arms, Culture and Class: The Philadelphia Militia and the "Lower Orders" in the American Revolution, doctoral dissertation, University of Pennsylvania.

Rotundo, E. Anthony (1989). "Romantic Friendship: Male Intimacy and Middle Class Youth in the Northern United States, 1800-1900." *Journal of Social History*, 23 (Fall), 1-25.

Rousseau, G.S. and Roy Porter (Eds.) (1990). *Exoticism in the Enlightenment*. Manchester: Manchester University Press.

Rowe, G.S. and Billy G. Smith (1995). "Prisoners: The Prisoners for Trial Docket and the Vagrancy Docket." In *Life in Early Philadelphia: Documents from the Revolutionary and Early National Periods* (pp. [57]-86), edited by Billy G. Smith. University Park: Pennsylvania State University Press.

Rubini, Dennis (1989). "Sexuality and Augustan England: Sodomy, Politics, Elite Circles and Society." In *The Pursuit of Sodomy: Male Homosexuality in Renaissance and Enlightenment Europe* (pp. 349-381), edited by Kent Gerard and Gert Hekma. Binghamton, NY: Harrington Park Press.

Rudé, George F.E. (1981). *The Crowd in History: A Study of Popular Disturbances in France and England, 1730-1848*. London: Lawrence and Wishart.

Rush, Benjamin (1812). *Medical Inquiries and Observations Upon the Diseases of the Mind*. Philadelphia: Kimber & Richardson.

Said, Edward W. (1978). *Orientalism*. New York: Pantheon Books.

Sasson, Diane (1983). *The Shaker Spiritual Narrative*. Knoxville: University of Tennessee Press.

Saxton, Alexander (1975). "Blackface Minstrelsy and Jacksonian Ideology." *American Quarterly,* 27(1) (March), 3-28.

Schachner, Nathan (1937). *Aaron Burr: A Biography.* New York: Frederick A. Stokes.

Sedgwick, Eve Kosofsky (1985). *Between Men: English Literature and Male Homosocial Desire.* New York: Columbia University Press.

Shaw, Peter (1981). *American Patriots and the Rituals of the Revolution.* Cambridge, MA: Harvard University Press.

Shoemaker, Nancy (1999). "An Alliance Between Men: Gender Metaphors in Eighteenth-Century American Indian Diplomacy East of the Mississippi." *Ethnohistory,* 46(2) (Spring), 239-263.

Shoemaker, Robert B. (1987). "The London 'Mob' in the Early Eighteenth Century." *Journal of British Studies,* 26(3) (July), 273-304.

A Short Introduction to the Latin Tongue, 1709 (1971). Reprint. Menston, England: The Scolar Press.

Simers, William Hayne (1805). *Medical Advice.* New York: [s.n.].

Smart, George K. (1938). "Private Libraries in Colonial Virginia." *American Literature,* 10(1) (March), 24-52.

Smelser, Marshall (1968). *The Democratic Republic 1801-1815.* New York: Harper & Row.

Smith, Eugene (1902). "Edward Livingston, and the Louisiana Codes." *Columbia Law Review,* 2(1), 24-36.

Smith, Margaret Bayard (1906). *Forty Years of Washington Society.* London: Fisher Unwin.

Smith-Rosenberg, Carroll (1982). "Davey Crockett As Trickster: Pornography, Liminality and Symbolic Inversion in Victorian America." *Journal of Contemporary History,* 17(2) (April), 325-350.

Smollett, Tobias (1979). *The Adventures of Roderick Random.* Oxford: Oxford University Press.

Sprogle, Henry (1887). *The Philadelphia Police, Past and Present.* Philadelphia: [s.n.].

Stamp, Leslie C. Patrick (1993). "The Prison Sentence Docket for 1795: Inmates at the Nation's First State Penitentiary." *Pennsylvania History,* 60.

Steakley, James D. (1989). "Sodomy in Enlightenment Prussia: From Execution to Suicide." In *The Pursuit of Sodomy: Male Homosexuality in Renaissance and Enlightenment Europe* (pp. 163-175), edited by Kent Gerard and Gert Hekma. Binghamton, NY: Harrington Park Press.

Stein, Stephen J. (1992). *The Shaker Experience in America: A History of the United Society of Believers.* New Haven, CT: Yale University Press.

Steinberg, Allen (1989). *The Transformation of Criminal Justice, Philadelphia, 1800-1880.* Chapel Hill: University of North Carolina Press.

Stephanson, Raymond (1997). "'Epicoene Friendship': Understanding Male Friendship in the Early Eighteenth Century, with Some Speculations About Pope." *The Eighteenth Century,* 38(2), 151-170.

Stevenson, Cosmo Gordon (1803). *Observations on the Disease of Gonorrhœa.* Philadelphia: Printed for the Author by A. and G. Way.

Stokes, William Ewart (1955). Randolph of Roanoke: A Virginia Portrait, the Early Career of John Randolph of Roanoke, 1773-1805, doctoral dissertation, University of Virginia.

Stowe, Harriet Beecher (1962). *Uncle Tom's Cabin: Or, Life Among the Lowly.* Cambridge, MA: Belknap Press of Harvard University Press.

Strachey, William (1612). *For the Colony in Virginea Britannia, Lavves Diuine, Morall, and Martiall, &c.* London: for Walter Burre.

Swediaur, Frantz (1815). *A Complete Treatise on the Symptoms, Effects, Nature and Treatment of Syphilis.* Philadelphia: Thomas Dobson, William Fry.

Talley, Colin L. (1996). "Gender and Male Same-Sex Erotic Behavior in British North America in the Seventeenth Century." *Journal of the History of Sexuality,* 6(3), 385-408.

Thompson, Peter (1989). A Social History of Philadelphia's Taverns, 1683-1800, doctoral dissertation, University of Pennsylvania.

Toll, Robert C. (1974). *Blacking Up: The Minstrel Show in Nineteenth-Century America.* New York: Oxford University Press.

Tongue, James (1801). *An Inaugural Dissertation Upon the Three Following Subjects: An Attempt to Prove, That the Lues Venerea Was Not Introduced into Europe from America. . . .* Philadelphia: Printed by the Author.

A Treatise on the Gonorrhoea (1787). By a Surgeon of Norfolk, Virginia. Norfolk: Printed by John M'Lean.

Trexler, Richard C. (1995). *Sex and Conquest: Gendered Violence, Political Order, and the European Conquest of the Americas.* Ithaca, NY: Cornell University Press.

Trumbach, Randolph (1991). "Sex, Gender, and Sexual Identity in Modern Culture: Male Sodomy and Female Prostitution in Enlightenment London." *Journal of the History of Sexuality,* 2(2), 186-203.

Turner, Frederick Jackson (1894). *The Significance of the Frontier in American History.* Madison: State Historical Society of Wisconsin.

Turner, James Grantham (2002). *Libertines and Radicals in Early Modern London: Sexuality, Politics and Literary Culture, 1630-1685.* Cambridge: Cambridge University Press.

Valle, James E. (1996). *Rocks & Shoals: Naval Discipline in the Age of Fighting Sail.* Annapolis, MD: Naval Institute Press.

Virginia. *Statutes at Large: Being a Collection of All the First Session of the Legislature, in the Year 1619.* (1823). New York: Bartow.

von Steuben, Frederick Wilhelm (1985). *Baron von Steuben's Revolutionary War Drill Manual: A Facsimile Reprint of the 1794 Edition.* New York: Dover Publications.

Waldstreicher, David (1995). "Rites of Rebellion, Rites of Assent: Celebrations, Print Culture, and the Origins of American Nationalism." *The Journal of American History,* 82(1) (June), 37-61.

Warner, Sam Bass Jr. (1987). *The Private City: Philadelphia in Three Periods of Its Growth.* Philadelphia: University of Pennsylvania Press.

Warnicke, Retha M. (1987). "Sexual Heresy at the Court of Henry VIII." *The Historical Journal,* 30(2) (June), 247-268.

Watson, John Fanning (1857). *Annals of Philadelphia and Pennsylvania in the Olden Time.* Philadelphia: E. Thomas.

White, Shane (1988). "'We Dwell in Safety and Pursue Our Honest Callings': Free Blacks in New York City, 1783-1810." *The Journal of American History,* 75(2) (September), 445-470.

Whitman, Walt (1964). "The Old Bowery, a Reminiscence of New York Plays and Acting Fifty Years Ago." *Prose Works 1892* (vol. 2, pp. 591-597), edited by Floyd Stovall. New York: New York University Press.

Wilcox, Kirstin (1999). "The Body into Print: Marketing Phillis Wheatley." *American Literature,* 71(1) (March), 1-29.

Wilentz, Sean (1986). *Chants Democratic: New York City & the Rise of the American Working Class, 1788-1850.* New York: Oxford University Press.

Williams, Samuel (1794). *The Natural and Civil History of Vermont.* Walpole, NH: Printed by Isaiah Thomas and David Carlisle.

Williams, Walter L. (1986). *The Spirit and the Flesh: Sexual Diversity in American Indian Culture.* Boston: Beacon Press.

Winthrop, Theodore (1862). *John Brent.* Boston: Ticknor and Fields.

Wood, William M. (1853). "Practical Reflections Upon the Grog Ration." In *Shoulder to the Wheel of Progress* (pp. 135-162). Buffalo: Derby, Orton and Mulligan.

Woodruff, Wilford (1983). *Wilford Woodruff's Journal, 1833-1898: A Typescript,* edited by Scott G. Kenney. Midvale, UT: Signature Books.

The Words of Joseph Smith: The Contemporary Accounts of the Nauvoo Discourses of the Prophet Joseph, compiled and edited by Andrew F. Ehat and Lyndon W. Cook. Provo, UT: Religious Studies Center, Brigham Young University.

Young, Alfred F. (1981). "George Robert Twelves Hewes (1742-1840): A Boston Shoemaker and the Memory of the American Revolution." *William and Mary Quarterly,* Third Series, 38(4) (October), pp. 561-623.

Young, Alfred F. (1999). *The Shoemaker and the Tea Party: Memory and the American Revolution.* Boston: Beacon Press.

Index

Dutton, Chauncey, 234
Dyer, a seaman, 80

Ecclesiastical courts, 40
Edes, Benjamin, 245
Edinburgh, Scotland, 125
Edward I, King of England, 77
Edward III, King of England, 40
Edwards, Benjamin, 20
Elizabeth I, Queen of England, 40, 258
Engle, Gary D., 151
Enslin, Frederick Gotthold, 71-72
Entrapment. *See* Police entrapment
Erotic employment, definition of,
  xvi-xvii
Erskine, Andrew, 121
Erskine, David Montagu, 167, 263
Evan, Frederick W., 223, 226

Fairlie, James, 102, 106, 110, 116, 117
Falck, Nikolai, 135
Fell, Hannah, 205
Fiedler, Leslie A., 175
Filmer, Robert, 9, 11
Fischer, Kirsten, 150
Fish, Nicolas, 103
Fleta, 39-40, 77
Flint, a seaman, 80
Flogging, 61-71, 82
Florida, 8
Folk songs, 87
Fort Bellefontaine, 58-59
Fort Frederick (Maine), 102
Fort Independence, 73
Fort Knox, 62
Fort Niagara, 214-215
Foster, Augustus John
  attitude toward American men,
    171-172
  attitude toward American women,
    170-171
  attitude toward blacks, 172-173
  as British minister, 168
  quote from commonplace book, 1,
    268

Foster, Augustus John *(continued)*
  relationship with Wa Pawni Ha,
    175-182
  as secretary to Anthony Merry, 165,
    166, 167
  on sharing beds with strangers, 261,
    263
Foster, Elizabeth, 168-170
Foster, John Thomas, 168-169
Foucault, Michel, *xv,* 63
Fox, Charles James, 181
Franklin, Benjamin, 96-99, 106, 215,
    221, 249
Fraternal Order of Red Men, 216
Frederick the Great, King of Prussia,
    31-32, 94-95, 96, 98
Frederick William, King of Prussia, 31
Frederick William II, King of Prussia,
    32, 39
Freemasons. *See* Masonic Order
Friedel, Johann, 30-31
Friendship groups, 16-17, 20

Gallatin, Albert, 1, 268
Garland, Hugh, 186-187
Gates, Benjamin, 228
Gay, etymology of the word, 55-56
Gay bars. *See* Clubs and taverns
Gender ratios, 10, 11
Georgiana, Duchess of Devonshire,
    168-170, 182
Geregano, a seaman, 78
Gilmer, Francis Walker, 18, 20
Gist, Mordecai, 72
Glanville, Ranulf de, 77
Godbeer, Richard, 2-3
Goethe, Johann Wolfgang von, 123
Goldsmith, Netta Murray, 40
Green, Joseph, 219
Greene, Nathaniel, 106
Griffin, a midshipman, 81
Guthrie, William, 26
Guy Fawkes Day, 258